Jon Trace is the pseudonym for the Chief Creative Officer of one of the world's largest global television production companies. Trace is also an internationally published thriller writer, an award-winning documentary maker, and creator of multimedia interactive games.

Also by Jon Trace

The Venice Conspiracy

THE ROME PROPHECY

Jon Trace

sphere

SPHERE

First published in Great Britain as a paperback original in 2011 by Sphere
Reprinted 2011

A CIP catalogue record for this book
is available from the British Library.

ISBN 978-0-7515-4301-8

Typeset in Bembo by M Rules
Printed and bound in Great Britain by
Clays Ltd, St Ives plc

Sphere
An imprint of
Little, Brown Book Group
100 Victoria Embankment
London EC4Y 0DY

An Hachette UK Company
www.hachette.co.uk

www.littlebrown.co.uk

To my eldest son, Damian – *Per aspera ad astra!*

PROLOGUE

The Ancient Diary of Cassandra

Italy

Few people know the moment they will die.

Perhaps, for such privileged information, I should be grateful.

I am Cassandra, a proud and noble descendant of the house of Savyna, and I am not afraid to die.

I would rather die than tell them what I am involved in, what I am covering up, what secret I am prepared to take to my grave.

And that, I suppose, is what enrages this ragged mob.

You can see the blood lust in their wild eyes and hear it in their crazed baying. You can even smell it in their animal excitement.

May the gods of the inferno damn them all.

The people of Cosmedin are out in force today.

Out for me.

They line their piss-soaked streets and drip like grease from the windows of their shabby tenements, screaming and spitting as I am paraded before them.

What is my crime?

Not what I am accused of. That is the irony. They are to test

1

me — and no doubt punish me — for sins of much lesser import than the secret I shelter within my bosom.

Graffiti writers suggest that I lie down with one other than my husband. The mimes show me with a nimble youth, cuckolding that fat and cruel senator whom my father made me marry.

Oh that it were the case! I should gladly plead to such an indiscretion, for no woman of Rome would condemn me. My husband is a man of high office and low morals. He is three times my age and half my equal.

I suppose it was my coldness towards him that first made him suspicious. To idiots like Lucius, a wife who will not give herself to his bestial whims and who demands time alone is bound to be adulterous.

Let him be deluded.

I would rather suffer endless agony than disclose to him the existence of the Tenth Book and those I call sisters.

And so the ignorant crowds of Cosmedin pelt me with old bread and rotten vegetables. Most miss the rickety chariot in which I am jolted to my death. Some find their mark, and though they sting and bruise, I will not cry.

I hold my head with chin tipped to Zeus and will not let them see the fear welling inside me.

I will not bow in shame as they want me to.

Not now.

Not even later, at the climax of this terrible ceremony.

I remind myself again — I am Cassandra. A noblewoman.

Strangers' hands now pull at my skirts. Hands not fit to wipe sweat from the brows of thieves and lepers. They tear at my garments, hoping nakedness will complete my humiliation. Fingers pull jewellery from around my neck. Only now do soldiers beat them away with shields. The thief looks at the strange stone he's plundered, a dull black triangle on a plaited cord, and is dumbstruck by disappointment.

Fool.

He'll never know what it's worth.

The chariot rolls on, rocked by the crowd. Like a ship tossed on a sea of jeers.

On the horizon I see it.

La Bocca della Verità – the Mouth of Truth.

One of the justices leads me to it, turns me to the mob. 'Cassandra, wife of the noble Lucius Cato. You are accused of infidelity, of tarnishing the good name of your husband, a senator of the great republic of Rome. The time has come to break your foolish silence, to name the man with whom you betrayed your husband and to atone for your sins. What say you?'

I make my face like clay.

If I told them the truth, they would let me go. Their plebeian shouts would turn to poison in their mouths.

But I shall not.

The truth must be kept secret, even if it means suffering for an indiscretion I did not commit.

The Justice stares through me. His eyes are as cold as the winter snows, his words as hot as the fires of Hades. 'Then by the power invested in me, I today action the order to verify your honour and your loyalty to your husband.'

My arm is taken by a soldier.

I see his dark hairy fingers on my pale skin, dirt caked beneath thin slivers of bitten fingernails.

There is total silence now.

Even the fountain holds its water.

He pushes my right hand through the savage mouth of the giant disc.

I feel nothing.

Now – slowly – an amazing warmth creeps through me. A soldier appears from behind the Bocca and lifts a basket aloft.

The crowd roars.

My world goes dizzy. My legs buckle. As I fall, I see only the basket and in it my severed hand.

My secret is safe.

PART ONE

PART ONE

1

Rome

The Carabinieri's newest captain slips out of her crisply pressed uniform and into the shower in her cramped low-rent apartment.

The *Vanity Fair* photo shoot went well –'warm but not too hot' was how the male photographer mischievously described the shots. One in her captain's uniform. One on the rifle range, shooting in a flak jacket, and her favourite, one in a short sparkling silver cocktail dress that fitted so well they let her keep it.

The force press office is happy, the magazine is happy and even Valentina Morassi is happy.

The perfect end to a perfect first week in her new job.

The twenty-nine-year-old tilts her newly promoted head at the steaming jet. Her long dark hair feels like wire wool as she shampoos away the spray they insisted on using, 'to hold its shape and give it depth'. She also hates the make-up they made her wear. They trowelled it on. Though admittedly, in the shots it looked good.

She looked good.

It makes her smile to think that. Until recently it was hard for Valentina to see anything positive about herself or her life. The death of her cousin Antonio in Venice all but broke her.

They both came from a big extended family, the kind that always holidayed together and shared weekly Sunday lunches. The type of family that was together so much you could barely work out which kid belonged to which parent. They went to the same schools. Attended the same parties. Even opted for the same profession. Antonio was a lieutenant, working undercover on a drugs job when he was killed.

Valentina couldn't believe it.

She tried to carry on working. Managed to see out the murder case she was on, and then her life collapsed. She fell into a huge depression, and had she not passed her exams and moved to Rome, she's sure she'd still be trying to wriggle free from the teeth of the proverbial black dog.

Valentina turns off the shower, steps out on to a frayed mat, snuggles into a thick white towelling robe and shakes her hair like a sheepdog. Her mother used to scold her for it. Antonio used to laugh like a drain when she did it after they'd been swimming.

She still thinks of him.

Often.

But it doesn't hurt as much any more.

She towels her hair dry and sits on the edge of a saggy bed. The walls of the boxy room are a faded white, the filthy window only a little larger than a convict gets. This is not a place where her soul will grow, but it will do for now. At the end of the month she will search for somewhere more colourful – more *her*. An old Disney clock by the side of the small single bed clunks. It's pillar-box red, has black Mickey Mouse ears and has woken her since she was four.

Mickey's hands tell her it's exactly eleven p.m.

Her thoughts turn to tomorrow and the man with whom she'll be having dinner.

An unusual man.

Most unusual.

She met him – and last saw him – in the strangest and most dangerous of circumstances. Had things been different – and had another woman not been part of his life – there might well have been something romantic between them. Despite all of these ifs and buts, he's still probably the one guy she trusts more than any other.

Valentina's cell phone rings and almost gives her a heart attack.

The number on the display is that of her new boss, Major Armando Caesario. She expertly pitches her '*Pronto*' somewhere between friendly and coolly professional.

'Sorry to disturb you so late on a Friday night,' he says, not sounding sorry at all. 'Control has just had a case called in that I'd like you to supervise.' He pauses, covers the mouthpiece and says something as an aside. 'It's a potential homicide, with . . . how shall we put it . . . an *unusual* twist. Lieutenant Assante will *give you a hand*; he's already at the barracks.'

Valentina thinks she hears muffled laughter in the background. She doesn't yet know her new boss well enough to be sure that someone isn't imitating him and playing a prank on her. 'Sir, forgive me, but is this some kind of joke?'

Caesario clears his throat. 'No, no, not at all. Please forgive *us*. I'm here with the colonel and he has something of a dark sense of humour. If you call Assante, he'll give you the full details and then you'll understand. Good night.'

Valentina thinks the call's genuine. She could all but smell the cigar smoke in the officers' club as they swilled brandies in big glasses. She was hoping for an early night. Maybe a glass of red wine before a good long sleep.

She knows she's not going to get either. She calls Homicide and holds the receiver between ear and shoulder while pulling her uniform back on. As soon as the details come out, she understands the black humour, and why the case has been batted her way.

The new girl is being taught a lesson.

She's being given a heads-up by those who think her promotion is purely political, a token gesture of equality.

She's heard it all before.

Morassi *must* have slept her way to the top. Screwed the examiner in charge of promotions. Blown the boss to get the easy cases. And those are just the things female officers say. Those of course who haven't made the rank she has. Granted, twenty-nine is unspeakably young for anyone to make captain, but she deserves it. Her last case had made her, and the man she's going to have dinner with tomorrow, the talk of Italy.

Valentina shuts the front door and heads for her three-year-old white Fiat Punto. It doesn't go nearly as fast as she'd like, but in the Eternal City, where parking is an eternal problem, the tiny Fiat is king.

By the time she's in fourth and has finished cursing its sluggishness, her mind is back on the new case she's just been given.

It's certainly a strange one.

A cleaner at the Chiesa Santa Maria in Cosmedin has discovered a highly unwelcome gift in the portico. The severed hand of a woman.

2

Paris

Tom Shaman is staring at the clear wintry night sky, playing join the dots. He wonders whether he's spotted the Great

Bear or the Little Bear. From what little he can remember of childhood astronomy, on a night as clear as this you should be able to see more than two thousand stars. Given his unique viewpoint, it might just be possible.

Tom is at the top of the Eiffel Tower.

He's on a wind-blown workers' platform, way above the Michelin-starred Jules Verne restaurant. The man who brought him here is Jean-Paul Marty, his best friend in France and the head of one of the many construction companies employed to do near-constant maintenance on the giant structure. Tom and JP have completely different lives but share the same basement gym and passion for boxing. They've even sparred together. A mistake the Frenchman won't make again. The thirty-three-year-old American is as big as an oak and throws a punch that could derail a freight train.

JP puts his hands on the cold steel of the workers' cradle and stares proudly out over the city of his birth. 'I cannot believe that you spend a year in Paris and have never seen the magic of the City of Light from the Tower.'

'C'est la vie.' Tom sits on the rough boards and dangles his legs over the edge. He enjoys the childish thrill of knowing there's more than three hundred metres of air between him and the ground. 'I guess that's what happens when you spend half your time working as a grunt at Eurodisney and a dishwasher at Robuchon.'

JP laughs. 'The restaurant I know about, but you were one of Mickey's mouses? This you keep a secret.'

'No, not at all. I was proud to be a mouse. It was how I learned my Mickey Mouse French. It was how I kept alive for the first six months.' He ticks points off on his fingers. 'First a garbage guy, sweeping Main Street, morning, noon and night. Then acting. I was Disney's best-ever Goofy and I didn't have to speak, so that was kind of perfect too. Then

11

I worked both Planet Hollywood and the Rainforest Café as a kitchen porter.'

'All of France is grateful for your cultured contribution to our society; we will miss you so much. And Robuchon?'

'When I was moused-out, I blagged a cleaning job at L'Atelier de Joel Robuchon and lived on the best leftovers in the world. Not much got tossed, I can tell you.' Tom looks up at the final shining zenith of the tower. 'Thanks for fixing this; it's a good way to go out.'

JP runs a finger down the steelwork. 'You are welcome, *mon ami*. It is my pleasure to show you around, but don't tell anyone.'

'I won't.'

The Frenchman turns his back to the wind and tries to light a cigarette. 'I'd get you to swear to that on the Bible, but I'm not sure such an oath counts if it comes from an ex-priest.'

'It counts.' Tom points off into the darkness and the wind flaps the sleeve of his black cotton jacket. 'What's that?'

His friend glances, unlit cigarette still in mouth. 'The Champ de Mars. You know the Champ de Mars?'

'The big park where they do the military stuff?'

JP laughs and abandons his tobacco for a moment. 'Aah, *oui*, the military stuff. Tom, the Field of Mars is the largest open space in Paris and perhaps the most respected. It is almost sacred. Much food has been eaten on this land and much blood drunk by its earth. During the Revolution, the Fête de la Fédération was held there, and two years after the storming of the Bastille, many people were massacred.'

Tom senses his friend's passion. 'I'm sorry.'

JP finally succeeds in lighting his cigarette. He takes a couple of deep draws and holds it out for Tom to see. 'War and military stuff, as you call it, are engrained in our nation.

Like my father – and his father – I smoke Gauloises. We do it because it is patriotic. Marketers will tell you Gauloises are forever linked with the French infantrymen – the *poilu*. Even the brand slogan is "Freedom Forever".'

'Good slogan, bad place to put it.'

'*Oui.*' He blows grey smoke into the night sky. 'My mother says if the cigarettes do not kill you then the slogan will.'

Tom smiles and looks out over the twinkling lights of the city below. His thoughts drift to his flight tomorrow, his meeting with Valentina and the circumstances that first brought them together. Painful memories surface of how he left his job as a priest in Los Angeles. A very public end to his vocation. His name plastered across every newspaper and news channel in the country. Every person in his parish pointing him out on the sidewalk. Venice seemed the perfect place to run to. A picture postcard of a city to hide in. Somewhere time seemed to have stood still.

Only it hadn't.

Journalists and news crews turned out to be every bit as cruel there as they had been in America. Tom's dark secret didn't stay secret for very long. He'd misjudged Valentina at first and she'd probably done the same with him. Only over the course of the case that they worked together did they find common respect and affection, and by then Tom wrongly thought his future lay with someone else. It all seems so long ago now. Like another lifetime.

JP lowers himself on to the boards alongside his friend and catches his eye. 'You seem so very far away. Somewhere wonderful?'

'Just thinking of the past. Moments like this make you reminisce.'

'Aah, that is not good. Not tonight. Tonight is about *making* memories, not recalling them. When you are old and your bones will not let you climb the Eiffel Tower, then you have time to remember.'

Tom gets to his feet. 'You have a point.' He peers out over the safety barrier and waves into the distance. 'Goodbye, Paris.'

'Aah, *non*.' Jean-Paul throws his arms wide. 'We do not say goodbye, you know this; we say *au revoir*, it is less permanent.'

Tom turns his back on the city and faces his friend. 'I know, but I really think this may be more of a goodbye than an *au revoir*. I don't think I'm going to be coming back from Rome.'

'You have the wanderlust again?'

He nods. 'A little.'

'Or is it more a womanlust than wanderlust?' JP studies Tom's eyes, 'Are you planning to make a home in her bed?'

He laughs. 'I'm planning no such thing.'

'But it is possible, yes?'

'Jean-Paul, as a Frenchman, you know that when it comes to matters of the heart, *anything* is possible, but— '

'*So*,' he jumps in again, 'maybe you do have a little plan, yes?'

'Maybe I have a little plan, *no*. Listen, Valentina and I go back a long way. We met in Venice soon after I left the priesthood in Los Angeles. She was a lieutenant in the Carabinieri and—'

'And she was the first love of your life. The first one to introduce you to the magical intimacy of womanhood?'

Tom frowns. 'No! No, she was not. And no, we were not intimate in any way. Valentina was—'

'But you would *like* to have been.' He leans close to his friend's face, a sparkle in his eyes, 'This Valentina, I sense she is a Roman beauty who has stolen your heart, and now, like a brave Gaul, you will swim oceans and climb mountains to be with her again.'

'What a *hopeless* Casanova you are.' Tom shakes his head in amusement. 'Are you in the least bit interested in the true version, or do you just want to make up your own romantic fantasy?'

'*Oui*. I am very interested. Though I am not sure the truth will be as satisfying as the fantasy.'

'I'm sure it won't be. Valentina is a friend. A *good* friend. We've kept in touch – phone calls, email, that kind of thing. She's just been promoted in the Carabinieri, so I'm going over to celebrate with her.'

'I understand.' JP fights back a grin. 'An Italian woman invites you to stay with her and *celebrate*. This is as good as a proposal of marriage.'

'Only if you're a crazy Frenchman.'

'To that I plead guilty.' He flicks the last of his cigarette into the black abyss and watches it fall like a firefly. 'You didn't say how you met her.'

'You didn't ask.'

'Come, it is a long way down, you can tell me as we go.' JP leads the way to the lift. 'A woman in uniform! Just the thought of it is exquisite.'

Tom hits the call button and hears great winding engines clunk and whirr below them. 'She locked me in one of her cells and interviewed me in connection with a murder.'

He frowns. 'A murder? I cannot see anyone imagining you to be a murderer. Though you fight well enough – for an American.'

'She had good cause, Jean-Paul. I'd just told her how I'd killed two men in LA. And she had every reason to think I'd killed again.'

I lie in the dirt of the square.

The last of my blood drips slowly like warm red butter oozing from my butchered wrist.

My life is ebbing away.

Perhaps I will even die before the sun reappears from the grey, melancholic clouds above me.

I hope not.

I pray to see the great god's face one final time before I pass.

Voices swirl above me.

They are not those of the soldiers – they are all gone now and are no doubt drawing rewards for their public chore. Some will already be bedding whores in the Aventine while telling stories of my demise.

No matter.

My dignity is preserved for eternity. I have a place in history.

One day, when my secret is out, I will be respected and honoured for both my silence and my sacrifice.

Without the guards, I am at the mercy of the mob, and they have no compassion. I see the plebs staring down their noses at me. Some scoff and spit in my face. Others loot the last of my jewellery and cloth. The hands of crude boys explore my cooling flesh.

I feel nothing.

Certainly no pain.

The agony engendered by the sword is thankfully too great for my mind to interpret. I do not scream. Nor do I cry or whimper. I cloak my suffering in a blanket of noble silence.

In the haze of faces above me there are none I recognise. No sign of my brutish husband. No tears from my shamed parents. Not even a last farewell from my friends.

But I am not alone.

My sisters are gathering. They are reaching out from the afterlife and wrapping their arms around me. I am ready to join them and to rejoice.

I am ready to be reborn in the spirit of another sister.

Ready to live beyond the grave.

4

Rome

The Fiat splutters its way south-west down Viale della Piramide Cestia, then right on to Via Marmorata, running parallel to Circus Maximus.

Cars are strewn at angles across the middle of the road near the Piazza dell'Emporio. An argument is heating up. Irate drivers are fencing with fingers around a steaming bonnet and busted trunk.

Once Valentina squeezes through the bottleneck and the cacophony of blaring car horns, it's plain sailing along the banks of the Tiber, down the Lungotevere Aventino and Via Ponte Rotto.

She checks her street map as she turns right on to the Piazza della Bocca della Verità and promises herself that tomorrow she'll find time to buy a sat nav.

She knows she's arrived when the famous Romanesque bell tower of the *chiesa* comes into view.

Valentina slides the Punto into an envelope-sized space opposite the church and parallel to a spectacular fountain that on another occasion she'd love to linger around. She locks up and walks across to a young officer guarding the taped-off scene. He watches her every step and gives her shapely form an approving smile.

Before the young soldier can embarrass either of them, she flashes her Carabinieri ID. 'Captain Morassi. I'm looking for Lieutenant Assante.'

The tape-minder loses his flirtatious smile. 'The lieutenant's inside.' He nods courteously.

'*Grazie.*' Valentina ducks the fluttering ribbon and before entering through a side door takes a quick look around. The main street is open and wide – maybe taking six lanes of traffic during rush hour – and there are parking places nearby for tourist coaches. Even given the lateness of the hour, it's likely that whatever has happened here was seen by someone.

'*Buonasera,* Capitano.' The voice floats out of the cool, waxy darkness of the church interior, long before Valentina sees its owner. Federico Assante looks like a ghost in the pale light. He is in his early thirties, of average height, with thinning black hair cut too short to help his full-moon face.

'*Buonasera.*' Valentina shakes his hand. 'So, what exactly went on here?'

'A good question. Let me show you.' He walks her part way through the side of the church. 'Do you know anything about this *chiesa*?'

'Nothing at all.' She glances around: beautifully painted ceilings, high stained-glass windows that probably make sunlight look as though it has come from heaven, intricate marble flooring and two spectacular staircases leading to prayer lecterns. But everything is past its prime. 'It looks as old as Rome itself.'

'It almost is. Sixth century. In her day this girl was a stunner – hence the name, Cosmedin; it comes from the Greek *kosmidon*, meaning beauty.'

'Impressive. But why do I need to know this now?'

'You'll see when we get to the portico.' He guides her past a dark side altar and into a thin corridor paved in what looks like engraved tombs. 'There's a huge old drain cover in there, stood up by the far wall; it's known as the Bocca della Verità, the Mouth of Truth.'

'Why's it called that?' There's puzzlement in her voice, 'Who would even think of giving a drain cover a name?'

'The sewers in Rome are pre-Christian. Originally they were used for everything, and I mean everything. They even used to dump bodies down there.'

'Ugh!'

Federico struggles to find the handle to the door that will actually let them into the portico. 'There was also probably a demon from the underworld associated with it all, because the thing has a formidable face engraved on it and a wide slit for a mouth. It's spent most of its life stood up on a plinth as part of a ritual whereby you put your hand into the mouth and if you told a lie it got cut off by the gods.'

Valentina puts the pieces together. 'So we have a severed hand being found in the most famous place in the world for severed hands.'

'That's about it.'

'And has this ever happened before?'

'Not for a few centuries.' He finally opens the interior door leading into the portico. 'Be careful here, there's no light. The photo team came but their equipment fused. They'll be back shortly.'

'No spare kit?'

'No spare kit. Cutbacks. Recession. You know how it goes.' He shines his Maglite along the dark pillars and walls. At the far end the beam picks out a drain cover as big as a man.

'That's the Mouth of Truth?' It's so much larger than she'd expected.

'*Si*. The hand was found actually in the mouth.' He plays the beam around the lopsided slit a third of the way up the heavy slab. Blood has dribbled like Burgundy from the corner of the marble lips.

'Was it done here?'

Federico points the light on to the portico floor. A puddle of red answers her question.

Valentina studies the dark mess. 'Looks like it was severed from the left of the victim.' She remembers something that Tom Shaman – the man she's meeting tomorrow – once told her. *Sinister* is Latin for left – traditionally the side of evil.

'Why are you so sure?' asks Federico.

'Lend me your torch, please.' He hands it over, and she scorches the beam down the long wall running to the right of them. 'It would be difficult for someone to stand that side of the victim because of this wall. In this light – or *lack* of it – it's hard to see the blood spatter, but what little I can make out flows left to right, not right to left, so we're looking at the blade cutting from the victim's left, with her kneeling. That would indicate at least two offenders. One to make her kneel and hold her there, one to deliver the precise blow.' She looks across to him, 'Where's the hand now?'

'*Patalogica*. It's in the mortuary in deep freeze.' Federico's cell phone rings, '*Scusi*.'

He steps away to take the call. Valentina notices a sign for tourists that says: 'Only one photograph per person please.' She guesses the crime-scene photographers will have had a laugh at that. No doubt taken their own pictures, too. She walks closer to the blood, but not so close that she'll contaminate the scene.

There's no visible sign of a struggle.

She turns sideways on.

The portico is draped with crime-scene plastic sheeting to

20

keep out prying eyes, but normally it would be very visible from the open road through iron railings.

Surely someone would have seen something?

Heard something?

The victim must have screamed. Unless she'd been drugged or gagged – then she could more easily be manoeuvred into position.

Why?

Why would someone want to do this?

The questions are still stacking up as Federico reappears. 'Mystery over.' There's a real bounce in his voice, a tone of relief. 'Seems some crazy woman has been picked up wandering the streets. She's covered in blood and – you won't believe this – she's carrying some kind of old sword.'

If the light had been better, he'd have seen that the look of disbelief on Valentina's face is nothing to do with the weapon.

She had the attacker down as male.

And the victim is still missing.

'I think your mystery is far from being over, Lieutenant,' says Valentina. 'In fact, I'd say it's only just beginning.'

5

My eyes are closing now.

Shutting for the final time.

Through the milky veil of death I see Arria, my body servant.

Sweet Arria, do not look so sad.

She calls me Domina, then gathers her robes and kneels beside me in the dirt.

The last of the crowd moves away.

Even they know that they must scavenge no more.

The time has come.

I am cold.

Colder than I have ever been. Arria is so alive she seems to burn like a fire next to me. She has brought blankets to wrap around my cooling husk.

No doubt she also has my shroud.

I have not the strength to move a muscle.

Oh, that I could smile to show her my gratitude. But I cannot.

I feel her warm hands press the cloth around me, as she tucks me tight like she once did when I was an infant in a manger.

Her old and bony fingers hold my one remaining hand.

Dearest Arria, I thank you.

In my palm I feel a coin. Enough to pay Charon the Ferryman. Enough to take me across the Styx to the gates of the underworld and stand before great Pluto.

I am being lifted up and carried. I cannot see who bears me. Nor do I wish to.

My eyes are closed fast now.

The lids that once upon the sight of a lover fluttered faster than the wings of a butterfly are now too heavy to move.

I am done.

The unseen hands drop me.

I thud and bounce on the rough wood in the back of a dusty cart.

I feel the heat of the sun surfacing from behind the clouds. Great Apollo, I praise you. Wondrous Pluto, I seek your kindness.

Through the muffled tunnel between life and death I hear the cart wheels trundle towards oblivion.

Someone lifts my head.

It is Arria. I recognise her smell. Her face is close to mine. She knows that my time is over, and as no relative is here, she performs her final duty.

I feel her hand across my bosom, her fingers seeking out my fading heartbeat. She is bent low. Her lips touch my face.
She is ready.
Ready to catch my last breath in her wise old mouth.

6

Rome

Federico gets a message from Central Comms. A street patrol has taken the female prisoner to a holding cell at the Carabinieri barracks in Viale Romania.

By all reports, their new admission is as jumpy as a box of frogs.

A doctor's already been called to sedate her, but Valentina issues instructions that no medication is to be given until they arrive.

The night is cold, crisp and clear. Halogen lights pick out swirls of dust and insects around the giant grey sign identifying the ugly, squat building as the COMMANDO GENERALE DELL ARMA DEI CARABINIERI. Federico is a local boy and he thinks the whole concrete edifice sits like a boil on the face of Villa Ada, Rome's largest and most beautiful park.

He and Valentina travelled separately from the *chiesa* in Cosmedin, but he's waited patiently for her in reception.

They clear the front desk together and are shown through to the cell block where they're left in the unpleasant company of the overnight custody officer, Paulo Ferrera.

A bad-tempered, heavy-set man in his late forties, Ferrera was just about to end his shift and go home before his late-night

23

'guest' arrived, covered in blood. He talks as he walks, breathing more heavily with each couple of steps. 'We haven't a name for her yet. She had no ID of any kind and she's too drunk, drugged or ignorant to tell us who she is – *è matto.*'

Valentina takes an instant dislike to him.

'We were told she had a weapon – where is it?'

'Forensics have it. It's still being processed.' He unlocks one of several security gates. 'I'll call them for you. They have her clothes as well. I say *clothes*; it was more of a gown than clothes.'

'Gown?' queries Federico.

'Hooded. Like a nun or a monk. A long white garment – well, not so white now, not with all the blood on it.'

'Did you take trace evidence from her body?' asks Valentina.

'We managed to swab her hands, but nothing else. She's just been too violent.'

Valentina winces. 'You need to do it. Especially beneath her nails. She may chew and suck away something that we later find out we really need.'

Ferrera glares at her. 'We've tried. It's not that easy. We've actually had to be more concerned with her not hurting herself.'

Valentina stops walking and shoots him a playful smile. 'Oh come on, Officer. You're a big guy. I'm sure you and some of your men could restrain a mere woman and take evidence without hurting her.' She glances at her watch. 'I know it's turned midnight, but to the best of my knowledge, normal daylight practices like acting professional still apply.'

Ferrera says nothing.

The colour of his face shows he's fuming.

The cell-block veteran is still chewing his lip as they enter the new admissions area. He points towards the room where their prisoner is being held and takes a deep breath to ensure there's no anger in his voice. 'Until the doc arrives, we have two officers with her all the time. When you see her, perhaps you'll be more understanding about our difficulties.' He strides past Valentina and unlocks the penultimate cage. 'Watch out for her kicking and biting.'

Valentina takes in her first impression of the small frightened woman sitting between two giant uniformed Carabinieri men.

She's pretty in an old-fashioned way.

Her hair is swept back and parted in the middle. She has dark eyes and a fine, angular face tapering into a slightly dimpled jaw that Valentina is sure men must find attractive. She's wearing white zip-up one-piece overalls that cover everything except her bony hands, which are stained heavily with blood.

It will be a miracle if the victim is still alive.

'I'm Captain Morassi, Valentina Morassi. Can you tell me who you are?'

The woman says nothing.

Valentina tries again 'We need you to help us.' She takes the woman's wrist. 'Your hands and body are covered in blood. We think someone might be badly injured. Can you tell me what happened to you?'

Nothing. No response. Just a blank gaze.

Valentina edges closer. She bends a little and tries to be more intimate. 'Late last night, were you in Cosmedin, at Chiesa Santa Maria, at the Bocca della Verità?'

Suddenly the prisoner lunges.

The top of her head smashes into Valentina's jaw.

The guards are too slow reacting.

The prisoner starts shouting and punching and kicking.

Valentina reels backwards, holding her bloodied mouth.

One of the officers finally grabs the woman.

The prisoner is hysterical, screaming and lashing out uncontrollably.

Ferrera and Federico bump into each other as they rush into the narrow cell.

Blood pumps from Valentina's mouth. She's bitten her bottom lip and maybe knocked a tooth loose.

The prisoner is now pinned on the floor. One of the guards twists her arms behind her back and clicks on some steel cuffs.

'Now do you see what I mean?' says Ferrera triumphantly. He looks across to Valentina. 'With the captain's permission, perhaps we could now sedate the prisoner and save ourselves a lot more pissing about?'

7

My corpse has been bathed.

My colourless skin sags as it is oiled and perfumed by the skilled hands of the pollinctores.

Bless you, gifted artisans from the temple of Venus Libitina.

Bless all of you who have put your judgement aside and now prepare me to stage a dignified escape from my death.

I see familiar faces around me.

My family and friends are dressed in the dull mourning wools of vestes pullae, *their bodies unwashed, their hair uncombed, their nails uncut and clothes unchanged since I passed.*

Flutes play outside in the darkness where they are waiting for me. The conclamatio *has begun.*

I hear my name being chanted.

Cassandra . . . Cassandra . . . Cassandra . . .

One by one they bend over me to say their final farewell, my extremum vale.

Musicians lead the way as they carry me feet first with my face respectfully covered.

The female praeficae *follow. Their tearful funereal dirge further chills the cool night air.*

Sadly, there will be no stopping in the forum. My redemption in death is not complete and the honour that should befall me as the wife of a senator has been denied because of my unjust shame.

The walk to my resting place is a long one. Way beyond the city walls, as decreed by the code laid down in the Twelve Tables.

The dirge has stopped by the time we reach the ustrina, *the sacred enclosures. Those who have carried me are tired but do their best not to look pained or drawn.*

Much work has been done to observe proper ceremony. My husband has shown me more attention in death than in life.

My altar is high. Four equal sides of strong timber. A fine exit.

In the dead of night, the pyre is lit.

The flames rise endlessly into the night sky and reach beyond the earth.

So does my spirit.

Cassandra is unshackled.

8

Paris

Just after midnight, in a cobbled back street off the Champs-Élysées, Tom Shaman finds himself cradling a bottle of Mexican beer in a dubious club. It's the type that privately promotes gambling and other pursuits that even in Paris aren't legal.

Jean-Paul has been coming here for more than a decade. He leads his friend away from the crowded main bar to the back of the club, where raucous cheers come from behind a long row of black curtains.

'Do you know what savate is?' shouts the Frenchman over the top of the crowd noise and the froth of his own beer.

'Not a clue.'

JP leans closer, 'It is the *boxe française*, the only martial art to originate in Europe. It has been shown in an X-Men film, featured in *Captain America* and even Tintin.' He laughs. 'It is very select – very famous.'

'A kind of kickboxing?'

'Yes, if you like. It is a style of fighting with foot and fist made famous by Napoleon's troops. Now it is something of a back-street sport, with heavy wagers. Do you want to see?'

It's his last night in Paris; Tom is up for almost anything. 'Sure.'

JP digs one hundred euros entrance money out of his jeans pockets and pays a burly, bald-headed man in a black suit to pull back the curtains. They're ushered through a door that leads to what was once a large loading bay. Now it is filled with close to two hundred people, clutching drinks and gathered around a large, one-rope ring.

Tom soaks up the scene. He's not a violent man, never has been, but there's something about boxing that attracts him. It's a personal failing. An indulgence of one of his baser instincts. Some overdeveloped survival gene craving release through physical combat.

On the right-hand side of the room, a small, scruffy man in his late twenties is taking bets, marking odds and writing names in felt tip on a whiteboard easel. A metre away, some better-heeled business types are torn between watching the bout and checking on the shifting odds.

In the ring, a hopeless mismatch is under way.

A Neanderthal the size of a house is kicking lumps out of a kid who must only be in his late teens. Judging by the throwback's face, he's been in some nasty fights in his time. Part of his right ear is missing – probably punched or chewed off in a street brawl. His nose has been broken enough times to leave it crooked, and shiny snakes of scars slither across both his cheeks and forehead. The kid is well muscled and gym fit, but gives away more than a foot in height, fifty pounds in weight and around twenty-five years in experience.

JP points to the fighters. 'Originally, the aim of savate was to kick at the shins and legs, up to waist height. You could strike blows to the head only with the palm of your hand. Now you see many high kicks and maybe even sumo wrestling.'

Tom puts his beer down on a thin shelf on the back wall. 'It's a freak show. That kid would need a stepladder to high-kick the giant there.'

'True. But this is part of the entertainment, no? David and Goliath.'

Tom notices something else. 'Why are they standing strangely?'

'The stance is from fencing. You must remember that at one point this was a very noble art, fought not only here but across Europe, and especially in England too.' Jean-Paul warms to his subject, 'There was one famous French fighter, Michael Casseuse, who made the sport his own. He was very powerful. To frighten his opponents he used to carry a cannon over his shoulders as he entered the ring.'

'A canon? You mean like a bishop or cardinal?'

The Frenchman laughs. 'Fool! A cannon like a *ship's* cannon.'

The kid in the ring takes a terrible kick to the face and drops unconscious. Blood spatters the sawdust floor. There are beery cheers. The business types high-five each other and some lackeys drag the boy to the corner and splash him with water. Neanderthal circles the ring, chin up and arms aloft, parading like he's won a championship belt.

'Shouldn't the big guy fight someone his own weight and size?' Tom's eyes never leave the ring.

'Indeed, and in a proper public bout the beast would be wearing gloves and would only fight people of his own grading. But this is a little wilder, no?' JP points to a line of bare-chested young boys waiting their turn to step into the ring. 'You put a hundred euros down and win five hundred if you can last a single round with the beast over there.'

'And what if you beat him?

'You do not beat him.' JP studies Tom's face with interest. 'You do not even think of beating him.'

'No, seriously, what if you beat him?'

A voice from behind them answers. 'Then *I* give you ten thousand euros.'

They both turn to find a tall, thin black man in his mid thirties smiling at them. He's exquisitely dressed in a charcoal-grey Christian Lacroix suit with a crisp white shirt and pink silk Hermès tie. 'I am Sebastian Civrais. The beast – as your acquaintance calls him – has *never* been beaten.' He looks Tom over, 'Now you, my big American friend, I imagine that you could tempt people to wager high that you had a chance to do so.' He flashes a broad grin, 'So, I tell you what, I'll give you five thousand euros if you can last three rounds with him, ten if you can beat him.'

Loud cheers erupt from the ring.

Another slightly drunk and very foolish teenage boy steps on to the canvas and heads to his slaughter.

Jean-Paul is worried. 'Tom, it is best to watch, not to participate. Ten thousand euros will not buy you a new eye or repair a broken jaw.' He glances towards the ring, 'I do not think the brute can only beat small boys. I imagine if we both fought him we would still end up losing.'

Tom isn't so sure. The big guy is really just a bully. 'Okay,' he tells the promoter, 'I'll fight him. But my friend here holds the money. I've seen too many films where the underdog never gets paid. And I want to fight next. I don't want to see any more kids being hurt by your caveman.'

Civrais looks amused. He doesn't have to go anywhere to get the cash; he opens his jacket, pulls out a wad of purple five-hundred-euro notes and peels off the stake. 'Ten thousand.' He slaps it in Jean-Paul's hand. 'You try to run off with this, *mon ami*, and I'll have people hit you so hard we'll be able to spread you like pâté.'

It doesn't take the beast long to swat his latest challenger like a fly. While the boy is being scraped from the ring, the promoter announces the night's surprise new challenger.

Tom walks over to where the other innocents are lining up. He kicks off his black shoes and grey socks, takes off his casual blue shirt and rolls up the bottom of his faded Levis.

Two ring lackeys lead him beneath the rope and into a corner, where there's a small three-legged stool. They're jabbering to each other about how they'd never set foot in the ring with the monster in the opposite corner.

None of it bothers Tom.

He's staring at the money being raked in, fistfuls of it being stuffed into a big red bucket as the odds are taken. Young Civrais certainly knows how to turn a quick buck.

Sitting on the tiny stool, the one thing Tom does regret is the several beers he's had.

He's nowhere near as sharp as he should be.

He must have been crazy to have talked himself into this.

Someone pulls him upright and whips the stool away.

A bell dings behind him. The noise of the crowd evaporates. It's just Tom and the beast.

Face to face across the canvas.

Neanderthal lets out a roar and smacks his clenched fists together.

A kick slaps into Tom's thigh. It's a good shot, plenty of weight, and delivered deceptively quickly for a big man.

The giant Frenchman looks pleased. He smiles and shows off two lines of broken teeth. Massive shelves stacked with ivory trophies.

He thunders forward and swings a haymaker of a punch at Tom.

It misses.

He swings again.

Tom sidesteps it.

The crowd shouts encouragement and it seems to fuel the beast's anger. He snaps another kick against Tom's thigh. The leg muscle starts to deaden. The big guy's not as dumb as he looks. Another kick like that and Tom knows he won't be able to stand, let alone trade blows.

The beast is thinking the same thing. Another grin and he goes for it. Harder and more vicious this time, a brutal kick aimed at bringing the action to a quick close.

But it doesn't connect.

Tom steps inside it. He slams the palm of his hand under the big guy's heel and lunges forward.

The giant doesn't topple, but he wobbles precariously.

Tom drops to the floor and delivers a sweep kick to the back of his standing leg.

Now he goes down.

The whole ring shakes. The crowd goes crazy.

Tom bounces on his toes, fists up, ready to fight when the beast finally gets back on his feet.

But that's not going to happen quickly.

The bell rings for the end of the first round.

Tom walks back to his corner feeling pleased. He got hit twice but at least he didn't end up on his back like the other mugs.

Shame the bell went; he was getting the measure of the brute.

The satisfaction is short-lived.

Tom never makes it to the stool.

A punch like a wrecking ball cracks into the back of his head.

Tom stumbles sideways.

A kick slaps into his kidneys and drops him to his knees.

The crowd explodes.

Instinctively, Tom drops totally flat and rolls away.

The beast aims a rugby-style drop-kick at his head, but only connects with his shoulder.

Whatever rules there were have now vanished.

Tom stops rolling. Most fighting is done with your brain, not your hands and feet. He thinks about what the beast will do next.

He's either going to kick at his ribs or, more likely, stamp on his face.

He goes for the stamp.

Tom guessed right. He shifts his head and grabs the out-stretched ankle. He hooks his forearm around the back of the knee and pulls like he's heaving the root of a giant tree from a swamp.

The beast goes down.

Tom rolls to the centre of the ring and gets to his feet.

The beast gets up quickly and produces a flurry of high kicks and low punches.

Tom takes one in the mouth and feels his lip split.

But it's worth it.

He ducks inside and delivers a sledgehammer blow to the stomach and a perfect uppercut to the jaw.

The Frenchman stands flat-footed. The crowd holds its breath.

Tom feigns a right-hander and then delivers a left-handed punch to the side of the head that would topple a factory chimney.

The beast's eyes go glassy.

His knees shake.

Finally, his legs crumple and he falls.

A rush of primitive energy goes through Tom. He stares at his opponent and prays the guy won't get up.

For his own good, please Lord don't let him get up.

Suddenly the ring is full of people.

Shouting. Cheering. Slapping Tom's arms.

Even embracing him. The beast is down and staying down.

Maybe he's not so stupid after all.

9

They gather my bones and ashes.

Loyal fingers seek out every part of me – what I was, what I am, what I shall be.

They search for the stone. The sacred triangle stolen from around my neck by the thief at the Bocca.

It is gone.

When they discover what has happened, they will find him. Find him and recover the precious scalene.

Then they will kill him.

They poke among the embers of a pyre that was soaked in cups of oil and bouquets of perfume.

My husband is not among the grubbers.

He is no doubt in our matrimonial bed, slaking his thirst for wine and boys.

Arria is here, of course. Sweetest Arria. She will be among the first to remember me at Parentalia. Was not Dies Parentales made for women with faces as sad as Arria's?

The urn they have fashioned for me is a cheap one. From its lack of elegance I know already that they will not carry me to my husband's tomb.

I am pleased. Lying with him in death would be even more unpleasant than in life.

I shall not wait for him beyond the three canine heads of Cerberus. I pray to Pluto that his wasted flesh sticks in their jaws and is chewed for eternity in Hades.

Before me I see my sisters. The others of the spirit world. Those who have for ever been and will for ever be.

They are the keepers of the secrets.

The prophetesses. The betrayed. The goddesses.

They surround me as the mortals take my burned remains to their dank resting place in the Columbarium. Here among the shelved peasantry is my place in the potted history of poorest Rome. My niche in society.

No ornately engraved plaque marks my spot. No statue or portrait. Nor any message of love.

Just a number.

My sisters and I wonder if beyond the grave they can hear us laughing.

The number is X.

10

Rome

It's Saturday morning, so at least Valentina is spared the indignity of walking into a packed office and explaining why she looks like a victim of domestic violence. She can barely begin to think of all the sexist jokes there would be at her expense. Hopefully, by Monday, some good make-up and judicious head-bending will get her through the day without too much embarrassment.

For now, though, the bathroom mirror is telling a different story.

Although the swelling is going down, her lips still look awful. Bloated and discoloured, as though a Botox injection has gone horribly wrong. The prisoner's head butt has left a very unattractive scab on her lip.

And all this on the day of her big date.

Not that she's thinking of her celebratory get-together with Tom Shaman as a date. She keeps telling herself that they're 'just friends'.

But of course, there's always the possibility that he feels like she does.

She checks the clock on the wall of the small kitchen in her apartment.

Midday.

Four hours before Tom's plane lands and she needs to be at the airport to pick him up. Valentina takes another glance in the mirror.

Maybe some of the swelling will have gone down by then.

She decides to coax an espresso out of her coffee machine and turn her attention back to work.

Earlier that morning she spoke to Federico and learned that there was still no trace of a victim.

Assante had already set up a rudimentary incident room and had ensured that all local hospitals had been called. No one with a missing hand had been treated.

Valentina checks her cell and fixed-line phones and finds that there are no missed calls.

She rings the local station and asks to speak to the custody suite.

They tell her that the woman prisoner slept most of the night. No doubt knocked out by sedatives. She refused breakfast. A doctor saw her mid-morning, and within the next hour she's due to be moved to a secure room at the Policlinico Umberto for a full psychiatric assessment.

It takes another twenty minutes of calls and an extra espresso to find out that the medical examiner working the case is a woman, Professoressa Filomena Schiavone, and she happens to be in the morgue at the Policlinico working another case. With a little luck – and a quick dash to the hospital – Valentina will catch her.

The short drive to the Quartiere San Lorenzo is pleasant enough. It's late October and the leaves are falling; rugs of reds and oranges have been thrown down by giant maples and sycamores filtering the day's golden sunlight.

Policlinico Umberto 1, to give it its full name, is the largest public hospital in Italy and one of the largest in the world. Named after the Italian king who ruled from the late 1870s, it's academically and physically intertwined with the famed Università La Sapienza, and as a result is so large it's really a city within a city.

After a few false turns, Valentina finds signs to the morgue near to the unit for tropical diseases over at the Viale Regina Elena entrance. It's almost opposite the gates where she came in.

She parks and walks past several patients in gowns smoking in the doorways to distant wards.

She enters the mortuary block and freshens up in a staff washroom before walking the final few metres to the *professoressa*'s office area.

A cluttered desk is attended by a bespectacled but pretty young woman who Valentina suspects is a student from Sapienza. She dutifully calls through to the medical examiner and then relays to Valentina a message that the ME is just finishing and will give her twenty minutes of her time if she meets her down in the scrub area.

Almost an hour passes before the doctor has finished 'finishing'.

Filomena Schiavone is a small woman in her early sixties with tight curls of white hair, piercing blue eyes and an impatient look on her grandmotherly face. 'Remind me – who are you? Why are you here? The girl minding my phones wasn't very clear.' She strips off her greens and drops them in a laundry bin. 'I have a lunch date in an hour and I don't want to look like a drowned poodle, so be quick.'

'Captain Morassi.' Valentina produces her ID.

'Put it away. I believe you.' The ME glances at her. 'What have you done to your face? You look like a trout.'

Valentina puts her fingers to her lip. 'I got hit by a woman prisoner. She was arrested near Cosmedin in connection with a severed hand that I believe you took possession of.'

The ME laughs. '*Took possession of.* How sweet. You police officers do mangle our language. It was sent to me in a plastic bag, packed with ice. Someone obviously hoped it might be sewn back on to whoever lost it. I examined it, made notes and put it in the fridge.' She opens a long metal locker and gets out a simple but stylish black maxi dress.

'What do you think? Too dull? I have a Grecian-drape affair upstairs, just back from the cleaners.'

'First date or second date?'

'First.'

'Then it looks most appropriate.'

'*Appropriate. Va bene.* I am *in possession* of an *appropriate* dress.' She undresses and steps into it. 'The hand is a woman's right hand, severed at the wrist. All the carpal bones have been cut. Cut very badly. It wasn't a clean dismemberment at all.' She puts the fingers of her left hand against the wrist of her right hand. 'It was hacked off. The first blow came here, near the thumb area. The second was made from higher, above the top of the wrist, parallel to the knuckles. I suspect the arm was turned back and more chops attempted from the first area below the thumb, until finally the hand separated rather raggedly from the wrist. Nasty. Very bloody and nasty.' She pulls out two pairs of shoes from the bottom of the locker 'Stilettos or pumps? What do you think?'

11

The easyJet plane from Paris into Rome Ciampino arrives late. It hits the tarmac just before five p.m., or almost seventeen hundred hours, as Valentina has grown accustomed to calling it.

It takes twenty-five minutes for Tom to clear customs and baggage control, and when he appears she almost doesn't recognise him.

He's dressed in a brown leather jacket, ribbed brown sweater, faded blue jeans and smart brown cowboy boots. His hair is much longer than she remembers, and unless she's mistaken, his chiselled face is shadowed with a hint of designer stubble.

Tom can't see her.

She's hidden in a dense crowd of expectant families and taxi drivers holding signs with the names of businessmen they're picking up.

'Tom! Tom!'

His head turns. Now he spots her.

He swings his suitcase her way and within seconds she throws her arms around him and buries her head against his face. He squeezes her tight and then holds her by the waist like he's admiring a giant bouquet of flowers. 'You look amazing. Wow! I bet you're the hottest *capitano* the Carabinieri have ever seen.'

'*Grazie.*' She strikes a pose for him and smiles. 'And you look good too. But what happened? Someone take a punch at you?'

Tom looks embarrassed. 'A long story.' He points to her mouth. 'I could say the same. Have you been brawling with your new bosses?'

She touches her face self-consciously. '*Sono stupido.* A prisoner hit me with her head.' She slaps a palm on her forehead. 'She just went crazy in her cell. I'll tell you in the car.'

The traffic isn't good and the journey from Ciampino on the south of the city to Valentina's apartment off Via Annia Faustina gives them plenty of time to catch up on things. She tells Tom all about the strange happenings the previous night in Cosmedin, and he tries to explain his bruises and busted lip.

'So you have some money to spend on me,' says Valentina

40

mischievously. 'I think tonight you can pay for dinner. It can be your punishment for behaving like some drunken teenager.'

Tom protests that he was championing the cause of vulnerable French youths against a seasoned bully, but somehow the reasoning doesn't seem as sensible as it did last night.

Valentina squeezes the little Fiat into a gap between a Smart car and an old Ford Fiesta that looks like it's never been washed. She links Tom's arm and leads him through an iron gate in a long brick wall that cordons off her apartment block.

One set of stairs later, she opens the front door to her tiny apartment and instantly wishes she'd made more of an effort to tidy up.

'Nice,' says Tom, 'small but very nice.'

'Liar. It's horrible.' She abandons her jacket and handbag and heads straight to her treasured DeLonghi coffee machine. 'Are all ex-priests bad liars?'

'It's possible,' he concedes, standing by her settee, not sure what to do with his suitcase.

She switches on the machine and smiles at him. 'Now we're inside, I have something to ask you.'

'What's that?'

'You need to come over here to answer it.'

Tom drops his jacket over the case and steps into the kitchen area. She puts a finger gently to his damaged lip, almost as though she's inspecting it. 'Is your mouth too sore to kiss me a proper hello?'

'A *proper* hello?'

She doesn't let him prevaricate any longer. She tilts her head and gently kisses him. The unharmed corner of her lips touches the unharmed corner of his. A kiss as light as the fluttering wings of a butterfly.

Neither of them close their eyes. It's like they're watching each other unwrap long-awaited presents.

Tom's hands find her waist.

She lets the tip of her tongue run sensually along the length of his dry lip.

The contact is minimal but electrifying.

They press together, so close they can feel nothing but the warmth of each other.

Somewhere in the room her phone rings.

Valentina tries to ignore it.

Tom slowly kisses the side of her neck.

She goes weak at the knees.

The phone trips to the answering function. 'This is Lieutenant Assante – Federico. I tried your cell phone and left a message. Forgive me calling your home, but we have an incident at the hospital with the woman we arrested. I really need to talk to you urgently. If you can't reach me, it may be because I'm already leaving for the pysch unit and I don't have hands-free in my car. *Ciao*.'

12

I am blessed by Her now.

Blessed by Mother.

In death She became life so that in ashes I may become spirit.

The spirit of Mother and those of my sisters are with me.

Henceforth they will always be with me and I with them.

This is how it is meant to be – how it was written – how it will always be. We are followers of the Great Books and writers of the future. Their word is our truth and our words are the truth of their tomorrows.

My sisters lead me through the darkness to Her house, to the great temple that lies at the magical confluence of three pathways in a womb-shaped clearing.

It is gated above ground and guarded below by the Galli.

I can hear drumming, dancing and chanting as we enter.

The Korybantes pound spears against shields and stir the air with their nimble steps.

A deep thumping beat flows through the bodies of all those gathered. We are touched by the unseen.

Mother has become the rhythm.

Mother the heartbeat.

She becomes the air and penetrates our skin.

She flows through our blood and our organs and makes us quiver with Her power.

My heart trembles as Her sound presses into me.

Mother is invisible, like the start of the rain.

Mother is all powerful, like the pull of the ocean.

Mother cleanses and renews us throughout our life and our death.

The sisters of the mortal world look frightened.

They should not.

Mother will care for them. Mother will transform them.

Feet apart, they stand in innocence and clumsily begin their incantations. Uncertain hands touch genitals, wombs, hearts and foreheads.

Hesitant fingers stretch to the sky and reach out to Her.

Soon She will reach out to them.

We will eat from the drum.

We will drink from the cymbal.

We will be immortal.

This is how it is written.

This is how it will be.

13

Valentina rings Federico back but only gets his voicemail.

She's left with no choice but to head off to the hospital.

Her long-dreamt-of moment of intimacy has been ruined, and a part of her fears it may never happen again.

Work certainly has a way of screwing with your personal life.

She hangs up and turns back to Tom. 'Sorry.'

His lip is smeared shiny red, and from the salty taste on her own lips she realises it's blood. Her blood. The realisation is strangely exciting.

'What's wrong?' He stands in a no-man's land between before she kissed him and what happens next.

'I have to go. Emergency at work. All that clichéd stuff.'

He smiles. 'I understand. I guess clichés are clichés because they get said so often.'

Small talk. The moment's certainly gone. She gathers her stuff and heads for the door, sensing a trace of awkwardness in the air.

She's still cursing Federico as she fires up her Fiat and drives to the Policlinico.

It's an awful place to navigate around. Most of the multi-storeyed buildings seem to be salmon-coloured with green shutters. Hilly roads open up into smart areas of lawn, and some giant palms and occasional flagpoles make the place look almost like a holiday hotel that's seen better days.

Inside, a maze of depressingly dark corridors lead her to the psychiatric unit, where she finds Federico the Interrupter sitting in the reception area looking over notes in a pocket book.

'*Buonasera*,' grunts Valentina. 'I hope this is every bit as urgent as you said.'

The Lieutenant looks up and is startled to see his boss in a fetching floral dress, wearing make-up and with her hair down. '*Buonasera*. I see I ruined something. *Scusi*. I'm afraid it *is* important. Our prisoner has told us her name.'

Valentina's not impressed. '*Oh, bene.*'

'She even wrote it in my notebook for me.' He swivels it around so she can see.

'Cassandra? What is this?' She scowls at him, 'She writes down *I am Cassandra* and you call me out on a Saturday night to get *only* a Christian name. You could have told me that on the phone, Federico.'

'I could. But that's not the point.' He flicks through several other pages. 'Take a look at all this. She damn near filled my book with her writing. Read it and then see if you still want to kick my balls for dragging you out here.' He thrusts the notebook at her.

Valentina takes it and peers at the old-fashioned handwriting: *I am Cassandra, a proud and noble descendant of the house of Savyna, and I am not afraid to die.*

The woman's handwriting is creepy. It's been done with such pressure on the pen it looks intense, violent, almost as if it's been carved into the paper.

The people of Cosmedin have come out in force today. Out for me. They line their piss-soaked streets and drip like grease from the windows of their shabby tenements, screaming and spitting at me as I am paraded before them.

Valentina can't help but speed-read the rest. Key lines jump out at her: *I will take my secret to the grave . . . the secret I shelter within my bosom . . . this terrible ceremony . . . La Bocca della Verità . . . I see only the basket and in it my severed hand . . . My secret is safe.*

'She wrote this in front of you?'

Federico nods.

'And did this obviously deluded woman explain any of it?'

He shakes his head. 'She still hasn't spoken. Hasn't said a word.' He takes the notes back, turns a page and points out another section. 'Read this.'

Valentina takes it from him.

The thief looks at the strange stone he's plundered, a dull black triangle on a plaited cord, and is dumbstruck by disappointment. Fool. He'll never know what it's worth.

She wrinkles her nose. 'I don't understand. Is all this hand-severing about some petty theft?'

'No,' Federico hands over a plastic bag, 'It's about this.'

Valentina's eyes widen.

Inside is a triangular black stone on a necklace made from rope. 'Bizarre. This is the necklace from the woman's story. Fact and fiction are all messed up together.' She glances around. 'They've certainly got her in the right place.' She hands back the evidence bag. 'Where did you get it? Wasn't she searched at the police station?'

He folds it up and replaces it in his pocket. 'She was, but they didn't find it.'

'What? Those idiots missed something around her neck?'

'Not quite. The prisoner had stuffed it . . .' He puts his hand between his legs. 'The nursing staff found it.'

'How strange that she wanted to hide it. The thing doesn't look worth much. Is it hollow?'

'No.'

'Nothing concealed inside it?'

'Not that I could tell. I'll send it to Forensics when we're done here. Now do you understand why I called you?'

'*Si.*' She realises she's been short with him. 'I'm sorry. This case has sort of ruined my weekend, both last night and tonight.'

'Big plans?' He tilts his eyes up and down her dress.

Valentina shoots him a look that says it's none of his business. She's still holding his notebook. She taps it against her other hand. 'What do you think of her writing? Is it some way of justifying that she's chopped someone's hand off? Groundwork for an insanity plea?'

'Perhaps. Maybe it's more than a hand she's chopped off.'

Valentina takes his point. 'There's still no sign of a victim, so we could be looking at full dismemberment.'

'Could be. It's certainly not unreasonable to think we're going to find other body parts spread across the city.'

'You're right.' She hands back the notebook. 'Can you get some copies of that made?'

'Done already.' He reaches over to a hard chair on his left and picks up a stack of stapled photocopies. 'The nurses' office has a printer. A young sister in there pressed all the buttons for me.' He gives her a playful smile.

'I bet she did.' Valentina takes a copy. 'Let's go and ask our mystery girl about all this nonsense.'

'I really don't think so,' says a woman approaching them. 'I'm Louisa Verdetti, the unit director, and I'm afraid you're not going to see this patient until I've finished my diagnosis.' Verdetti is in her late thirties, with short dark hair, and looks as though she was born to wear a white doctor's coat and dangle expensive black glasses from the tip of her nose. She nods contemptuously towards Federico. 'Your colleague shouldn't even have been in the room with her, let alone tried to ask questions. She's clearly in a very disturbed state of mind and—'

Valentina can't help but interrupt. 'Doctor, whatever state of mind your patient is in, it's nothing compared to that of the woman whose hand she chopped off.'

Verdetti glares at her. 'I don't want to be unhelpful.'

'Then don't be.' Valentina waves the photocopies in her face. 'Does this stuff she's written mean anything to you?'

The doctor softens, 'Come into my office.' She motions to a corridor off to their left.

Valentina follows her and Federico tags behind.

The room is dark. There is a desk opposite the doorway stacked with papers and lit only by a silver Anglepoise lamp. The psychiatrist gestures towards a far corner, where two grey cotton sofas flank a cheap glass table marked with rings from old coffee cups.

They settle, and Louisa Verdetti pulls a quizzical face. She's wondering how much to tell the Carabinieri and how much they'll understand. 'Let me start with the writings. They are highly unusual.'

Valentina feigns astonishment. 'You need a doctor's degree to have noticed that?'

'Please!' Verdetti's face begs more patience.

'I'm sorry. Go on.'

'Unusual because they are indicative of a rare condition, one that not many psychiatrists in the world, let alone in Italy, have treated.' She can see she now has their complete attention. 'The patient has DID, dissociative identity disorder.'

'What's that?' asks Federico.

'It's what used to be called multiple personality disorder.'

He's still not sure he gets it. 'You mean she thinks she's two people? Whoever she *really* is and this woman Cassandra from Cosmedin.'

Verdetti thinks about disagreeing – about explaining the true depth and danger of the disorder – but decides the detail can wait for another time. 'Sort of. It's sufficient to say that at the time she wrote the text that you have, she truly believed that she was Cassandra of Cosmedin and was being taken to the Bocca della Verità to have her hand cut off.

Incidentally, the Bocca would not have been in Cosmedin during the Roman period that she's describing – as is common in most fantasies, timelines and other facts become distorted.'

'Let's focus on reality, then,' suggests Valentina. 'She concealed something vaginally. A necklace of some kind. Have you seen it?'

'*Si*. I asked my staff to hand it to your colleague.'

'I have it.' Federico holds up the bag.

Valentina turns to Verdetti. 'Do you know why it was so important to her? Why she felt she had to hide it?'

'No. It's probably personal and not of any real value or importance. DID sufferers sometimes attach enormous significance to certain objects, just like babies do to favourite teddy bears or blankets.'

'But she wrote about it,' says Valentina, 'in some weird Roman story.'

The doctor gives them a comforting smile. 'Again, I don't see anything unusual. The young woman we're treating is *very* disturbed. She needs close attention and understanding. Did you notice her wrists, her arms?'

Federico shakes his head.

'Drug tracks?' asks Valentina.

'No,' says Verdetti. 'Something even harder to treat. Her arms are laced with scars from self-harming; her psychological state is very disturbed.'

Valentina has seen self-harming before. Way back when she was a recruit, she arrested a teenage girl for shoplifting whose forearms were slashed to ribbons. 'She cuts herself when she's stressed because it gives her some strange sense of relief?'

'That's right. It's symptomatic of deep-lying trauma or abuse, and by the look of it she's been doing this for years.'

'I'm sorry; I hope you can help her.'

'We can, given time. Come back tomorrow. Give us twenty-four hours to continue our assessments and diagnosis. Let us make her feel safe and comfortable, and then I'll consider giving you access, under supervision, to interview her.'

Valentina nods. She knows she doesn't really have a choice. It's clear that no amount of pressure is going to change Verdetti's mind. 'We'll be back in the morning. *Grazie.*'

'*Prego.*' The doctor rises to shake hands.

'One thing before we go,' adds Valentina. 'Patients with . . . er . . .' She struggles for the clinical name she's just been told.

'Dissociative identity disorder.'

'*Grazie.* Patients with dissociative identity disorder, are they capable of murder?'

Verdetti's face hardens again. 'Undoubtedly. They're capable of almost anything.'

14

On the drive back to Via Annia Faustina, Valentina sticks an earpiece into her iPhone and calls her boss.

He's at home and answers as though he's shouting out a swear word. 'Caesario.'

'Major, it's Captain Morassi. I thought you might appreciate an update on the case you sent me out on.'

He lets out a tired sigh. 'Capitano, you've arrested a woman in her late twenties who calls herself Cassandra, and she's so crazy she's already locked up in a psych ward. Lieutenant Assante says Forensics are working on some bloodstained clothes and a weapon, but there's still no sign of a victim. Do you have anything to tell me that I don't already know?'

Valentina is shocked that Federico has gone behind her back and spoken directly to the major. 'We're hoping to interview the suspect in the morning.'

'So I understand. Anything else?'

Valentina now makes no effort to hide her annoyance. 'Yes, sir, did you ask Assante to report directly to you? I certainly didn't.'

There's a brief pause. 'For the sake of keeping this conversation short, let's say I did. Now good evening to you, I have a far more important disagreement to finish with my wife.'

Valentina's left listening to dial tone. She punches the steering wheel with the palm of her hand and drives off at a speed she knows she shouldn't.

It's eight p.m. by the time she re-enters her apartment.

It's dark and lit by candles in the kitchen.

She smells fresh flowers long before she sees the spray of pink and cream roses in a water jug on the worktop.

'My goodness, you've been busy.'

'You'd better believe it.' Tom is in the narrow kitchen, his back to her. 'Give me a sec to uncork this wine, then I'll tell you all about the spectacular piece of fish I'm cooking for you.'

She flinches. 'I booked a table. I told you we were going out.'

He turns around and smiles. 'Cancel it. Fish is my speciality. You won't find better food or service anywhere in Rome.'

She can't hide her disappointment. 'It was tough to get a table. *Very* tough.'

He feels too awkward to say anything.

She scratches at the back of her neck. 'Why is it men always believe they have the right to do whatever they want, regardless of whether it's the opposite of what women want?'

Tom's taken aback. 'I'm sorry. I'd foolishly hoped the candles, flowers and wine might have rekindled some of that friendliness you expressed earlier.'

Valentina sits on the arm of the sofa, buries her head in her hand and swears softly. '*Porca vacca!*'

He moves towards her. 'Those are bad words, aren't they?'

She manages a muffled laugh. 'Not the worst I know, but yes, they're bad.'

He puts a hand on her shoulder. 'I only just warmed things a little, because I didn't know when you'd be in. I can easily turn it all off and we can go out.'

She looks at him. 'No. I'm sorry. What a cow. I've had a difficult day with my boss and I just snapped.' She glances around. 'It's really very nice that you went out, bought everything and did all this.' She smiles. 'Quite romantic.'

He smiles back. 'I can be. Given the chance.'

'Is that so?'

'Certainly is.'

They trade looks, eyes sparkling with excitement. 'Do I have time to change for dinner?'

'Sure. Plenty.'

She heads to the bedroom.

Tom calls after her. 'You want some help?'

She doesn't answer.

He sits for a minute on the same sofa arm where Valentina has just perched and wonders if he's doing the right thing. His body is tingling with the thrill of flirtation and the anticipation of what could be. At the same time a part of him wants to run.

Valentina reappears.

She's wearing a cream silk robe.

Her dark hair falls lavishly against the porcelain whiteness of her neck. 'Did you finally get that cork out? Or do you need a woman's help?'

Tom gets up and heads to the abandoned bottle, his heart flipping like a pancake. He has to calm himself in order to safely use the corkscrew.

Valentina picks up a big-bowled wine glass by its stem and tilts it towards him. 'Your lip still hurt?'

He pours a drizzle of golden Meursault into her glass. 'No. Yours?' Their eyes lock again.

'Not at all.' She moves the glass away, leans slowly forward and kisses him tenderly but fully on his bruised mouth.

Tom just about manages to put the bottle down safely.

Somehow Valentina finds a kitchen worktop to rest her glass on.

His hands undo her robe and slip inside the warm silk. Her skin is smooth and she smells of coconut.

He kisses her again and glides his fingers up to her shoulder blades, massaging them as she curls into him.

Valentina moves her hands from the back of his neck to the front of his shirt. Some buttons she manages to undo, others just snap off as she pulls the cloth open and tugs it down his thick arms.

They're both almost breathless, mouths bleeding from the intense contact, bodies flushed with excitement.

Valentina smoothes her palms across his hard chest and feels his nipples stiffen. He's much taller than she is. She pulls him down to her height, then all the way to the dirty kitchen floor.

Tom's fingers find her legs and thighs. He plants rows of soft kisses across the silken pastures of her stomach and breasts.

She lets out a warm sigh of expectancy.

He slides his fingers around the arch of her back and slips off her small red La Perla briefs.

Valentina stretches like a cat as kisses trickle across her hips, then along her bikini line, and finally gather between her legs.

His hands cup her buttocks and his tongue snakes deep inside her.

She clings to him. Digs her nails into his vast back and holds on like she's going to fall off a cliff.

And in a way she does. A vast tumble into oblivion, her head spinning and her heart pounding while a river of pent-up emotion breaks wonderfully free.

15

The guard outside the hospital room is the first to notice that the prisoner is out of bed and moving around.

He can see her through a slit of unfrosted glass, shuffling close to the wall.

The young man is about to call the nursing station when the night sister appears. 'She's out of bed,' he announces in a worried tone.

'I know.' Sister Elizabetta Erio is a slightly overweight forty-year-old. 'She pulled the emergency cord. Let's see how she is.'

They enter the room together and find the prisoner-cum-patient sitting on the floor in the corner adjacent to the bed. Her hands are wrapped tightly around her drawn-up knees. She looks like a small, terrified child.

'Come on, young lady,' says Sister firmly. 'You shouldn't be down there. Let's get you back into bed and make you comfortable.'

The guard bends down to help her, but this makes the

woman cower even more. He guesses she's afraid of the uni-form and the white-holstered gun on his belt.

Elizabetta steps forward, takes her by the elbow and helps her to her feet in a no-nonsense way. 'You're going to freeze down there. Now let's get you tucked up again.'

The prisoner allows herself to be moved back to the high metal bed. Her eyes never leave the guard.

Sister Erio quickly adjusts the patient's faded hospital nightgown and covers her up. She's read the woman's case notes and knows she needs to stay alert. While the patient looks as meek as a mouse, and hasn't spoken since admission, the huge bruise on her forehead is a reminder that there's a constant chance of sudden and unexpected violence. 'Does your head hurt, honey? That's quite a bump you've got there.'

The woman scowls and tentatively puts her fingers to the patch of purple and black skin.

'I'll get you some painkillers. Would you like me to bring you a drink as well? Some nice cool water?' She looks for a confirmatory nod.

'*Si. Grazie.*'

Elizabetta's shocked. She stares disbelieving at the pris-oner's lips. 'Okay. It's good that you're talking. Give me a minute, I'll go and get some for you.'

On the way out, she pulls the guard aside. 'Watch her. Watch her closely. I'll be back in no time.'

Elizabetta phones the night doctor and grabs 400 mg of ibuprofen. She takes a plastic cup from the cooler in the corri-dor, fills it with chilled water and is back in the room within a minute.

The patient pops the tablets and drains all the water. '*Grazie.*'

'*Prego.*' Elizabetta sits on the edge of the bed. 'I'm going to take your pulse and your blood pressure. Is that all right?'

The woman nods nervously. 'Where am I? Why am I here?'

'You really don't know?'

The fear in her eyes says she doesn't. 'I have no idea.' She bites at an already well-chewed thumbnail and looks around. 'Was I hurt? Was I in some kind of accident?'

Elizabetta glances towards the guard. 'The Carabinieri brought you here. They'll probably want to talk to you, tell you about everything.' She gives her a kindly smile. 'Don't worry about things; we're going to look after you. Can you tell me what your name is?'

'Suzanna.'

Elizabetta looks pleased.

'*Va bene.*' She reaches for the clipboard at the end of the bed and writes on some notes. 'And your last name, Suzanna, what's your last name?'

'Grecoraci. Suzanna Grecoraci.'

'Excellent. That's a good start.'

The patient looks puzzled. 'You didn't know who I was?'

'No. No, we didn't.'

Suzanna dips her head; when she raises it again, she looks ashamed. 'Was someone else here?'

'What do you mean?'

'Sometimes the others come. They come and take my body without me knowing. Then they do things that I don't know about. Bad things.'

16

It's a long time before Valentina and Tom make it to her bedroom, and even longer before they return to the kitchen for a much-delayed dinner.

Valentina throws on a black jogging suit, not at all what she'd imagined she'd wear for their date, but it seems suitable when she clambers out of her wrecked bed.

They work side by side in the kitchen, cooking, chatting, sharing wine as though they've been a couple for years rather than minutes. She gets old white plates out of a top cupboard beside the cooker where he's working. 'You've changed a lot since we first met.'

The comment amuses him, 'How so?'

'More confident. More worldly.' She puts down the plates and sits up on the work counter so she can see his face while he cooks. 'Was that what living with Tina did for you?'

Tom feels uncomfortable for the first time. 'I suppose.'

'You don't want to talk about her?'

'Not really.' He drops chopped onions into the heavy heated skillet to make a base for a sauce and begins to crush a garlic clove while musing on how much more he's prepared to tell her. 'It's just over a year since we split up. I guess it was inevitable. You remember Tina, she was a professional woman determined to build a career and have a settled life. Me, I was an ex-priest determined to drift a bit and certainly not keen to have any responsibility after what happened in LA and Venice.'

Valentina remembers how she and Tom first met, how she was shocked at discovering that he'd accidentally killed two street thugs in LA who were attacking a woman near his old church. She remembers too the case in Venice she got him involved in and how they both nearly died solving it. She picks up her glass of wine and wonders whether it was the fact that they'd nearly died together that led to this moment when they slept together. She watches him chopping tomatoes while browning onions and somehow the picture of domesticity prompts her to ask a question she never thought she'd ask. 'You loved Tina, didn't you?'

He doesn't look up from the sizzling onions. 'Yes. I think so.'

'You *think* so?'

'I tried to. I wanted to.' He slides the tomatoes into the pan, stirs with a wooden spatula and adds spices. 'We both tried to, we both wanted to. You have to remember that Tina was my first relationship since leaving the priesthood. The first person I'd ever . . . you know. Certainly the only woman I've ever lived with.'

Valentina is surprised. 'She was?'

'Yes, she was.' He smiles at her. 'Despite what you read in the papers, most of the Catholic clergy don't have active sex lives.'

She laughs. 'Didn't you – you know – have sex *before* you went into the priesthood?'

He seasons two substantial tuna steaks, adds them to the skillet and covers them in the rich tomato sauce. 'I feel like you're interviewing me again. Any second now your old boss Vito is going to walk in, and the two of you are going to give me the third degree all over again. Only this time it won't be about a body in a canal; it'll be about my sex life as a teenager.'

She leans towards him, not confrontationally, just enough to catch his eye and make sure he understands she's playing with him, merely digging around a little to get to know him better. 'If I *were* interviewing you, I'd be suspicious, Tom Shaman, because you just avoided answering my question.'

'And I, Captain Morassi, would be asking for my lawyer and saying no comment. But as you seem determined to have a straight answer, no, I didn't have a full sexual relationship with anyone before I became a priest.'

'Aah, a President Clinton answer.' She fakes a deep American voice, '*I did not have a full sexual relationship with that woman.'* She leans on his shoulder. 'But maybe there was a bit of fooling around, yes?'

He can't believe she's doing this to him. 'Maybe. Now, can we change the subject? Or else I'm going to burn your food.'

'Okay.' Valentina knows she'll have other opportunities to open him up. She swings herself down from the worktop and wanders across the apartment.

Tom tries to concentrate on the cooking. The whole process is a wonderfully therapeutic ceremony and one he fell in love with while in France.

A few minutes later Valentina calls to him, 'Would you look at something for me? Give me a second opinion.'

'Just a minute.' He removes the skillet from the heat and slides the tuna on to pre-warmed plates. *'Fantastico!* Wait until you taste this.'

Valentina picks papers up from the sofa. 'The woman we arrested, the one I told you about, she wrote down some strange things. I've got photocopies here.'

He carries the plates waiter-style, one across his wrist, the other on his palm, gripped by the tip of his fingers. 'You want more wine?'

'Not yet. Thanks.' She taps the sofa. 'Sit next to me. I'm sorry there's no dining table. Not yet. Probably not ever in here, it's too small.'

He hands over her plate and a knife and fork, *'Buon appetito.* I hope you like it.'

'Looks good.' She grins a little. 'I'm sure it's worth staying in for. Have a look at these while you eat.'

He takes the photocopied papers, smoothes them out on the arm of the sofa and tastes his food.

The tuna is cooked too little and the accompanying green beans boiled too much. So much for trying to make an impression.

He works slowly through the papers, wondering if he should offer to re-cook her fish. A glance across the room shows it's not necessary. She's almost finished.

He taps the paper as he reaches the end. 'This is fascinating. What's your prisoner like? Intelligence? Age? Looks?'

Valentina thinks for a second. 'She's late twenties. White. Italian – I think. Not very tall. Not very fat. Not very strong. In fact, not very anything. She's mousey. Hasn't spoken. The only communication has been through those written words, so I can't really say how intelligent she is.' Then she remembers something. 'I did notice that her nails were all broken. Her hands looked rough – that is, once we cleaned the blood off them. So I'd guess she's a manual worker rather than a brainier office type.'

'Don't write manual workers off as unintelligent.' He wags a fork at her. 'I washed dishes in every other kitchen in Paris; that doesn't make me stupid.'

'Never said it did. Why do you ask about her intelligence?'

Tom waggles the photocopy. 'No spelling mistakes. Good grammar. She has an old-fashioned, formal and educated style of writing.'

The comment amuses Valentina.

'She should have. She says she's a noblewoman, of noble birth.'

'The scene she wrote of is ancient Rome, certainly pre-Christ, and given the respectful references to the Senate, maybe even pre-Julius Caesar.'

Valentina's impressed. 'My, you *are* a smart old kitchen porter, aren't you?'

'Less of the old!' He forks another bite of tuna, loads it with sauce and looks again at the paper. 'The writer's descriptions contain religious and ritualistic references; the whole thing is intriguingly riddled with allusions to secrets and truths. Do you know what the name Cassandra means?'

'Nope. Can't say I do.' Valentina mops up the last of the sauce with a final forkful of fish. 'I can't believe I ate all this. You made me so hungry.'

'Doom,' says Tom, 'Cassandra was a prophet of doom.'

17

Mother picks me out.

She takes me to one side, away from the others, and talks only to me.

I am special.

She tells me so.

I am Her favourite and I am to be called Melissa. I will be one of Her Melissae – Her little bees.

She speaks to me about Lagash, Anatolia, Phrygia, Crete and Malta. She talks of Hellenic and Roman civilisations, of the kings and emperors She's known.

Of rulers who've worshipped Her.

Of fools who have ignored Her.

Of Her love for Attis, and how She killed him and then raised him from the dead.

'Death and Life,' She whispers in my ear, then speaks for a long time of creation and destruction and Her glorious part in it all.

The part I will play in the future.

Mother holds me to Her bosom and strokes my hair while teaching me how to change sea to sand and sand to grass. She tells me how together we will turn the grass to stone and the stone to marble and the marble to towers of glass and steel that will stretch beyond the sun.

There is nothing Mother cannot achieve. Nothing she cannot create.

Around us there are women of every race, every colour and every age. Mother could have picked any one of them, but She has chosen me.

I am special.

She tells me so.

Outside of the warm womb that is our temple, a pale moon rises and paints its whiteness on the naked flesh of my gathering sisters. The first sparks of a fire crackle close by. A large, flat stone is brought in, laden with bread and wine.

The Galli come.

They beat their drums, fine instruments made from skins of fish and goat, let loose a primal rhythm.

Mother catches it and shares it with us. She seals the rhythm inside us. It becomes our pulse. It flows through our genitals and rests in our wombs.

Mother tells me to close my eyes.

She tells me that She loves me. Loves me from the cool brow of Her stone-figured image on the heights of Mount Sipylus to the bloodstained soil of Rome where She now lies down with me.

I am not to be frightened of what She will do to me.

I am special.

She tells me so.

18

Sunday morning gathers around Valentina Morassi like a cool mountain mist.

She opens her eyes slowly and sees untidy puddles of pale daylight shimmering on the wooden bedroom floor.

Leakage from the real world.

An unwelcome clue that her night's rest is over.

Not that she got much rest.

Valentina's normally an eight-hours-a-night person. She squints at her Mickey clock and realises she's had less than six.

Her own fault.

Hers and Tom's.

The thought makes her smile. She's happy to lose a lot more sleep if the man next to her is the reason why.

She has a plan for the day, and it's a simple one.

Sleepy lovemaking. Breakfast in bed. Less sleepy lovemaking. Shower – dress – reluctantly think about work.

It's all a nice change from her normal pattern of putting work first.

Great sex turns everything upside down.

Fill your body with pesky orgasms and suddenly your all-important life-defining job can go hang itself.

Valentina slides close to Tom and drifts her hand down his impressive rack of abdominal muscles.

He stirs a little.

Still asleep.

But not for long.

Before Valentina rouses him, she thinks about yesterday, about how nervous she was meeting him at the airport. About whether he would feel the same way about her as she did about him. Whether any sexual advance would jeopardise their friendship.

Then there was their first kiss.

It seems unfair that romance can live or die in only a few seconds or just a few words. Had she not been bold enough to ask that he kiss her 'a proper hello', then maybe nothing would have happened between them.

How many great loves have never happened because someone lacked the courage to make the first move?

She tries to clear her mind and return to the matter in hand.

Her right hand, to be precise.

Tom lets out a sigh that comes from so far inside of him it's like the distant growl of an animal in a far-off jungle.

Her fingers bring the beast closer.

As he stretches and hardens, she kisses his back and presses her soft flesh against him.

He rolls over and looks at her. Eyes still sleepy, the colour of beaten pewter, but alive enough to show his pleasure at being with her.

Valentina doesn't even let him say good morning. She presses her lips gently against his. She wants to capture the precious intimacy growing between them. Make sure it never escapes.

Her romantic thoughts and plans for the day come to an abrupt end.

The phone rings.

It's bad news.

She knows it is.

Bad news has a way of preceding itself. Like the stench of rotting fish – you're aware of it before you even see it. Similarly, the one thing you can't do is ignore it.

'Sorry,' she says, in a breathy voice as soft as kitten fur.

Tom manages a moan of understanding.

The call is from Federico Assante. He gets straight to the point. 'I've been rung by the hospital – it seems our prisoner had a good night. So good that she gave the staff a real name and apparently is willing to be interviewed.'

Valentina is surprised. 'Who is she?'

He glances at his notes. 'Suzanna someone. Hang on, I wrote it down. Now where is it? Grecoraci – Suzanna

64

Grecoraci. Apparently, before we get to see her, the bossy doctor we met yesterday, Verdetti, wants to talk to us, and she's only going to be at the unit for another hour.'

Valentina glances at the only thing she's wearing, her watch; it's not even nine a.m. Her tone gives away a distinct lack of enthusiasm. 'I guess I can be there in twenty minutes. Does that work for you?'

Federico says it does and they agree to meet in reception.

She thinks about mentioning that she knows he called Major Caesario, but decides to save it until they're face to face.

When she's finished, Tom is sitting up in bed, bare-chested, hair tousled and eyes full of expectancy. 'I'm *so* sorry,' she says, 'I have to go straight away. I'll be back as soon as possible, promise.' She wants to kiss him, a kiss just to apologise, to show he's not second choice to work. But she daren't.

One kiss won't be enough.

One kiss will result in making her at least an hour late.

She dresses quickly. Smart black Armani jeans and a warm grey sweater. She's still explaining her rushed exit as her head pops through the floppy cowl neck. 'The woman in charge of the psych unit is difficult; I don't want her to change her mind. I'm *really* sorry.'

'Stop apologising. It's not a problem.' Tom is almost as fascinated watching her dress as he was watching her *un*dress. 'Do you think your colleagues have a camera on us?'

'What?'

He peers up as though he's searching for a lens hidden in the ceiling. 'Only it seems that any time there's a hint of romance between us, someone from the Carabinieri always rings.'

She laughs. 'Don't say that. We're safe, I promise.'

'If you like, I can grab the metro and meet you somewhere,

when you know what time you're finishing, and where you're going to be.'

'Could be an idea. I'll call you. There's food in the kitchen, but of course you know that from your shopping.'

'Thanks. Have you got a computer, a laptop I can use?'

'There's a little Sony in a case in the lounge.'

'Password?'

'Electra.'

'Elector?'

She chuckles. 'No, Elec*tra*, as in the big Electra Glide that I'm going to one day treat myself to.' Fully clothed, she now risks kissing him.

But only lightly.

Well, it starts lightly.

It's meant to be just a peck, but it turns out to be more passionate. She pulls away and lets out an almost painful sigh.

Her thoughts about Tom – and that brief kiss – have a tingling and hypnotic effect that last throughout the drive from her home to the Policlinico.

Valentina only clears her head when she is inside the disinfectant-smelling hospital and approaching the psychiatric ward.

Federico is obediently waiting in reception, engrossed in a well-thumbed gossip magazine.

'*Buongiorno,*' he says amiably, dropping the mag and standing, 'Verdetti's waiting for us.'

She skips the pleasantries as they walk to the doctor's office. 'Tell me, Federico, did you call Caesario, or did he call you?'

He lets out a dismissive *humph*. 'He *is* my boss – he asked that he be kept in touch, so I did as he asked.'

A good answer, but she's not letting him off that lightly. 'No. He's *not* your boss. *I* am. I'm your immediate boss and you report directly to me.' She waits for a reaction. He should look a little ashamed, a little afraid because he's being dressed down for undermining a senior officer, but he doesn't. He should be eager to apologise, say he's sorry and promise not to do it again, but he clearly isn't going to.

They stop outside Verdetti's office and Valentina lets off more steam again. 'Lieutenant, we have ranks and reporting procedures for good reasons, so make sure they are respected and followed in future. If Major Caesario needs informing of something, then *I'll* do it. You report only to me, unless instructed otherwise. Do we understand each other?'

He shrugs and makes to open the door.

Valentina grabs his wrist and stops him. 'I asked you a question. Do you understand the order I just gave you?'

He looks at her tight grip on his arm and reacts for the first time. A flush of colour to his face. A twitch of his Adam's apple as he swallows and tries to stay calm. 'I understand.'

'*Va bene.*' She lets go of his wrist and allows him to open the door.

19

We are below ground.

In the womb of the earth.

Mother's womb.

When I am frightened down here, Mother comforts me. When I am filled with panic, She brings me special peace. It enters my lungs and calms me. Makes me see things differently.

And when She punishes me, I understand that it is for my own good.

I know that the pain I suffer is necessary.

Necessary to ensure so I keep the secret.

But I wish it would stop.

When I am fasting, the hunger gnaws inside my gut like a rat in the carcass of a cow, but that pain is nothing to the fires of humiliation that burn in my soul.

Mother says She will cure me. She will rid me of my anguish.

Whatever the price.

Whatever the pain and humiliation.

She says I should remember that it hurts Her more than it hurts me.

I will never forget.

She says that if I did better, if I earned Her trust, then She wouldn't have to do these things to me. Wouldn't need to teach me Her lessons.

I tell Her I am trying.

I am trying very hard to learn.

But then She laughs at me.

Not a nice laugh.

Not the laugh a mother should share with a daughter.

She stares into my eyes and tells me She has Her doubts.

Says She wonders if I am worth it.

Worth all the effort that She puts in.

I am frightened.

She puts Her face close to mine and She tells me that She knows what I'm doing.

Knows that I am letting 'the others' in.

She laughs again.

The not-very-nice laugh.

I try to look away, but She grabs my face and forces me to look at Her. She says that She knows about them and will find them and punish them as well.

She will trap them and make them all one.

Make them all Hers.
I tell Mother there are no others.
But She knows.
Mother beats me again.
She sticks cloth in my mouth so I can't scream. So 'the others'
can't hear me.
Then She teaches me Her lessons.
And when She's done, She leaves me.
Alone.
In the dark.
Underground.
In the safety of Her womb.

20

Tom showers and shaves. He pulls on black Levis and a black shirt.

A passing glance in the mirror appals him.

Bar a dab of white on the collar, he looks like a priest.

He changes the shirt for a green one made from thick Egyptian cotton. One warm enough never to need a jumper over the top.

He pulls out his cell phone and sends a text message to the only old friend he has in Rome, Alfredo Giordano. Being Sunday, he knows exactly where Alfie is, and it's not the kind of place where you can have a phone ringing.

He's at church.

Saying Mass.

While he waits for Alfie to reply, Tom makes espresso as

thick as treacle and fires up Valentina's Vaio. There's mail stacked high in his AOL account, but that's not what he's looking for.

He finds several Google entries for 'Cassandra Prophet of Doom' and is pleased his basic grasp of Greek mythology hasn't completely deserted him. Cassandra, also known as Alexandra, was the daughter of King Priam and Queen Hecuba of Troy. She was so beautiful that Apollo granted her the gift of prophecy.

Tom vaguely remembers that Sassy Cassy spent a night at Apollo's temple, and when she fell asleep, magical snakes licked her ears so clean she was able to hear the future.

Neat trick.

If only you could order a couple of snakes like that from iwantoneofthose.com.

After a little searching, he tracks down Cassandra's family tree. Her father Priam was the son of Laomedon and grandson of Ilus and ruled during the Trojan War. Tom becomes lost and bored as he traces the generations back through Trus, Erichthonius and Dardanus, but he feels compelled to complete the task.

He makes another espresso and is pleased when he recalls that Dardanus was the son of Zeus and Electra.

No Harleys back in those days!

The temporary amusement disappears when he reads that the wife of Dardanus was Batea, the daughter of a king called Teucer.

Teucer.

He sits back from the computer.

Until a few years ago, the name Teucer had never meant anything to him.

But then there was Venice.

In Venice, he became more than familiar with it.

Teucer was the name at the centre of a case that stretched

back six hundred years before Christ. A case that almost killed him and Valentina.

He comforts himself with hard logic. These are different Teucers.

Very different.

One was from Greece and ruled Troy. The other was from Etruria and was part of a dark satanic legend.

But he can't help but add up the coincidences.

A crazed woman believing she is Cassandra, who is a dark descendant of Teucer, turns up covered in blood after a ritual dismemberment at a legendary site of truth and justice. On its own it's disturbing.

That it should happen at exactly the time that Tom is visiting Valentina is more troubling. It's almost as though fate – or God – has decreed that he has to be here.

That this is the place where he is needed.

He puts his hand to his lip.

It's bleeding again.

Outside the window he hears church bells ringing. The sound of Mass beginning makes him check his phone to see if there's a message from Alfie.

There is.

Tom reads it and can barely believe his eyes.

21

Louisa Verdetti looks up from the paperwork on her desk and over the top of her black-framed spectacles. 'Please, sit down.'

Valentina and Federico pull up chairs.

The director updates them. 'The lady you brought in seems stable and calm this morning. Certainly well enough for you to interview, though we haven't yet had time to do the full range of diagnostic checks that we'd like.'

Federico flips open his notebook. 'Suzanna Grecoraci. Has she said where she's from? How old she is?'

Verdetti smiles. 'She has. She's from Corviale, she's twenty-seven years old and has two children. They're called Carina and Carlo. The girl's five and the boy three.'

'Poor kids.' The lieutenant starts to write down their details and wonders how they're going to react when they find out their mother is as nutty as a fruitcake and is going to be locked up for a long time.

'Save your ink,' interrupts Verdetti. 'That's *not* who she is. And her children don't exist.'

'I don't understand.' Valentina looks perplexed.

'We checked our computer network systems for her medical records. No one by that name is on the local register. Nor are either of her children.'

Federico has formed such a strong image of the children that he can't now clear them from his mind. 'Maybe the family only just moved to Rome? You know how bad this city is at keeping records.'

'No,' insists Verdetti. 'We found several Suzanna Grecoracis in the area. None of them is the right age, marital or parental status to be her.'

Valentina spreads her hands in a gesture of bewilderment. 'I still don't get it. Why would she lie about this? We've arrested her and she's going to jail.'

'Probably not.' Verdetti lets the shock of her response sink in and then explains. 'Suzanna is another alter – another personality that steps forward in the host body to take control.'

Valentina shakes her head. 'So we have Cassandra and Suzanna. Two alters? Two personalities other than that of the real person?'

'That's right. We call the real person the host. The host may be taken over by multiple personalities.'

'How many is multiple?' asks Federico.

Louisa tries to keep it simple. 'That all depends. Usually, the number of alters is determined by the levels of trauma in the host's life. The more trauma, the greater the multiple of personalities.'

The two police officers exchange looks. They know that what Verdetti has just said is the kind of expert testimony that would ensure their prisoner would never face criminal charges.

The clinician interrupts their ponderings. 'As I said, you can see her, but I must insist on being in the room as well.'

Valentina nods. '*Capiamo.*'

'*Va bene.*' Verdetti pushes back her chair and leads the way.

Valentina is revising her opinion of the director. Sure, she's stern. Maybe a bit of a control freak as well. But she's impressively professional and must have the patience of a saint to deal with people as disturbed as Suzanna, or whoever she really is. *And* – on top of all that – she's wearing a pair of black Gucci sneakers that Valentina would kill for.

The doctor opens the door.

Suzanna is sitting in a chair by her bed.

She doesn't look in the least bit intimidated by the sight of the Carabinieri officers.

Verdetti makes the introductions. 'Suzanna, these police officers would like to ask you some questions. Are you okay with that?'

'Of course.' She sits up straight and smiles. Valentina and Federico pull over some hard-backed visitors' chairs.

Federico cautiously starts the ball rolling. 'You say you're Suzanna Grecoraci from Corviale. You are married and have two children – is that right?'

Her face lights up. 'It is. I have two *beautiful* children. God has been very kind to me; they're my angels.'

'I'm sure they are. Where exactly are they now?' asks Valentina.

'With their father, Romano. He's travelling the world with them.' She looks a little sad. 'They're in Australia at the moment.'

'Australia.' Valentina repeats the word for no reason other than the fact that she can't yet get a grasp on what's unfolding.

'Yes, I know that's a very long way away.' Suzanna laughs nervously. 'Romano's parents are down there. They're very old and not in good health, so he wanted them to see their grandchildren – you know, one last time.'

Valentina tries to sound sympathetic. 'Why didn't you go with them?'

'Oh, that's a long story.' She looks embarrassed. 'I have a fear of flying. I've never been in an aeroplane. Don't think I ever will.'

Valentina nods understandingly. 'Do you recognise me, Suzanna? Do you remember where and when we met before?'

It's clear from her face that she doesn't. 'No, no, I'm afraid I don't. I hadn't thought we'd met until now.' She glances towards the doctor. 'No one has given me your names, so I'm afraid you're both strangers to me.'

Valentina keeps her tone non-judgemental. 'I visited you in a police cell in Viale Romania and you attacked me.'

Suzanna looks shocked. 'Oh no. That's not possible. I'd

never attack anyone. I've never hurt anyone or anything in my whole life.'

Verdetti tries to help everyone out. 'If it wasn't you, Suzanna, then who could it have been?'

'One of the others, you mean?'

'Yes.'

'Oh, I see.' She thinks for a while. 'Well, if it *was* one of the others, it was most likely Claudia.'

'Not Cassandra?' queries Valentina. 'Cassandra seems to be mixed up in a lot of bad things. Could it have been her?'

Suzanna stays quiet.

Federico sees an opportunity to push further. 'Unless of course there is no Cassandra, and you're lying about all this.' He leans forward on the edge of his chair. 'Are you lying, Suzanna? Are you making all this up?'

Valentina tries to cut him off. 'Federico . . .'

He scents blood and won't stop. 'You don't have any husband, or children. You're just inventing all this rubbish about "others" because you've seriously hurt someone and now you're trying to act crazy to avoid the consequences of your actions. Aren't you?'

Suzanna grows tense.

The lieutenant presses his point. 'Best tell us the truth now, before you make things worse.'

Valentina studies the prisoner. She no longer looks nervous. She seems angry.

Angry in a peculiarly restrained way. Like a politician or a headmistress when they're under pressure.

'I think you should go now,' says Verdetti, sensing a mood change. 'This may have been a bad idea. It's too soon for her to face this kind of thing.'

Valentina ignores her. Her eyes are still locked on the prisoner and the extraordinary look on her face. If she turns violent again, she'll be ready this time.

The patient stands and starts to pace the room, mumbling to herself.

She turns and glares at them.

Her face is filled with rage.

Her whole body shape has transformed into someone more powerful and more confident.

'*Juno inferna!* How *dare* you common plebs question my veracity? How in the name of Zeus dare you?' She shoots Federico a contemptuous look. 'Sweet Veritas should geld you for your impudence.' She strides to within a foot of Valentina. 'And you, *girl* – you are but a trollop with a mouth made loose by pleasuring too much cock. Now get out! Get out of my sight before I have you tied to the wheel of a chariot and whipped.'

Valentina gives Louisa a shocked look. 'Is this Cassandra? The Cassandra in the note she wrote?'

The doctor looks worried. 'Perhaps. Will you and your colleague please wait outside?'

'Yes! Yes, I am Cassandra.' She strides defiantly towards them. 'And Cassandra is too proud to have whores like you speaking about her in whispers.'

The clinician opens the door and again urges the officers out. 'I have to insist that you go.'

Federico turns to Valentina for guidance and she gives him an assenting nod.

They slip outside and close the door.

Valentina hears one final outburst from inside the room.

'I know what you want. Oh yes, I know *exactly* what you and the snuffling pigs in that septic Senate want. I will never tell you. I would rather take my secret to the grave than tell you. You want the book, don't you? You want to get your hands on it and ruin everything. Well, it will never happen. Never!'

22

The new one tries to hide her fear, but I see it.

We all see it.

It is glazed in the whiteness of her eyes as they lower her into the pit. Pass her into the womb of the earth.

She is naked and pink. Curled and cowed like a foetus.

Her soft, virgin skin is like a dropped silk handkerchief in the centuries-old soil. She sits on a cushion of earth, encrusted with the dried blood of many sacrifices.

Soon there will be more.

Above her, the drumming begins.

It starts like the peck of a bird, becomes the thump of a hoof, and grows into the stampede of cattle.

Taurobolium *has begun.*

The new one peeks through her fingers into the blackness above her and sees the first flickers of our lights.

I feel for her.

I envy her.

I love her and hate her.

We are lighting candles around the edge of the triangular pit.

Her eyes catch mine and I fail to see what is so special about her. They say she is 'the one'.

The favoured one.

But I see nothing that will stop me usurping her.

Nothing that will prevent me from taking my rightful place in line.

The Korybantes dance their way to the front, naked but for their shields, swords and helmets.

The sound of metal on metal makes a sinister percussion.

The steel is there to slice.

To cut.

To kill.

There is an orgiastic surge in the music.

The Galli begin their chanting.

We gather closer and bond tightly with our sisters from Babylonia, Syria, Asia Minor, Etruria and Anatolia.

The nine Korybantes are joined with the three magical Dactyls.

We are all one.

The music, drumming and chanting reaches its climax.

The goddess is here!

Our Mother has arrived.

She holds aloft the hands that eight thousand years ago dug into the earth of Çatal Hüyük, the hands that spread the soil of time while She gave birth flanked by leopards.

We all scream.

Scream so loud our spirits almost fly from our throats.

Somewhere down in the blackness, the special one gathers the fine clothes we have sewn for her and dresses herself.

She moves to the centre of the pit.

The limbs of eunuchs strain on thick ropes and the rafters creak.

Above us, a bull that has trod pastures for six summers bucks in its harness.

Then it thrashes no more.

The blades open up its sacred rivers of blood and they pour down on the libation boards across the pit.

My sister showers in the animal's life force.

She dances joyously as the blood from the Bull of Heaven purifies her.

Now she is born again — for eternity.

Unless I can stop her.

23

Father Giordano is covering for a friend and working a double shift.

That said, he's doing it at a place where priests don't mind putting in unspecified amounts of unpaid overtime.

St Peter's.

Or, to give the greatest building of its age its full name, the Basilica Papale di San Pietro Vaticano.

Tom has scurried across the city to be there for Alfie's final appearance of the day, and already all the effort is worthwhile.

The basilica is breathtaking.

Tom can't think of any other way to describe it. The beauty of the vast seventeenth-century façade built of pale travertine stone, with its giant Corinthian columns, makes him dizzy.

Then there's the inside.

The spectacularly arched entrance with its heavenly stained glass just about holds Tom's eyes before they fix on Michelangelo's central dome, still the tallest in the world at more than a hundred and thirty-six metres. Then there's the basilica's wonderful nave, narthex, portals and bays to feast on, before his favourite visual treat, the main altar, with Bernini's astonishing bronze *baldacchino*, a pavilion-like structure that stands almost a hundred feet high and looks even taller.

St Peter's is visual gluttony. No sense is left unstuffed. No emotion left sober.

Mass is said at altars great and small throughout the cavernous building, so Tom has to search a while before he finds his friend in the relatively modest Chapel of the Blessed Sacrament.

Modest is the wrong word.

The gilded bronze Bernini tabernacle alone is worth more than the entire church that Tom last officiated in.

He kneels with the rest of the congregation and can't help but feel proud of his tall ginger-haired friend as he works his way gracefully and passionately through the service.

For Tom, the Mass is over all too quickly.

He settles back in a pew and enjoys the peace while he waits for Alfie to change and reappear. Few places in the world have the intense silence of a church, and he still finds it the most effective place to examine his own thoughts.

And right now there are lots of them.

Was it smart to rush into a relationship with Valentina?

What does she expect from it?

Where does *he* hope it will go?

How is it most likely to end?

So many thoughts. All backed up and jostling for attention like closing-time drinkers in a city-centre bar.

Looking back, he can see that they grew close after the death of her cousin Antonio. But maybe there was always a spark between them. Some genetic trigger that attracts people and compels them to be together was pulled.

But he thinks there's more than that.

More than just the physical.

He admires her strength and ambition, respects her individuality and her determination to make a go of things on her own. He loves her sense of humour and her desire to do good.

Yes, Tom concludes, it *was* smart to throw himself into a relationship with her. Chances of happiness don't exactly queue up outside your door and knock noisily for an appointment. Especially if you're an ex-priest with no job, no home and no savings.

He looks up from the old dark wood of the pews and sees Alfie, his face beaming as brightly as the winter sunshine filtering through Michelangelo's dome. The service is over.

'Well, if it isn't the planet's most troublesome ex-priest.' He opens his arms.

Tom embraces him warmly and puts a hand gently to his face. 'You looked magnificent up there, my friend. I'm so proud of you. How did you end up saying Mass in here?'

Alfie puts an arm around Tom and guides him towards the door. 'A long story, best told over hot coffee and Italy's finest pastries.'

'Sounds heavenly.'

'Sufficient to say it was God's will. That and the fact that innumerable first choices went down with a severe dose of the shits after a very poor communal meal.'

24

The hospital cafeteria is sickeningly warm and smells queasily of hot fat and bleach.

Over barely warm coffee and day-old croissants, Valentina and Federico try to make sense of what's just happened.

Not that there's much to make sense of.

The woman prisoner is bark-at-the-moon mad. And from

the quick check Federico does with HQ, there's still no sign of a victim.

When the dregs of a poor espresso have been drained, Lieutenant Assante heads off with instructions to write up his notes, mail them to Valentina and not mention the case to anyone else until she tells him to. He resents the tightness of her leash, but with any luck he'll be off it and back with his wife and family by lunchtime.

Valentina's about to call Tom when she's struck by an urge to return to the ward. If nothing else, she'd like to learn more from Louisa Verdetti about the patient's latest outburst, providing of course the director hasn't already left.

She has.

Her office is empty. Lights out. Blinds down. Door locked.

It looks like most of the nursing staff have gone too. No doubt the skeleton Sunday crew has been stretched to invisibility doing routine jobs.

Valentina takes advantage of the slack supervision. She flashes her ID at the guard in the corridor and within a minute is once again face to face with Suzanna.

'Hi. How you doing?' She closes the door gently behind her.

The young woman is sitting up in bed, hunched over a wooden roller tray, the type patients are served meals on.

She glances towards the captain but doesn't say anything.

Valentina makes small talk as she heads her way. 'You look as though you're busy. Are they making you work for your stay?'

A tiny voice comes back. The voice of a sad child. 'Mommy says I have to do my homework. She says if I don't get it done I'm not going to be allowed to go with Daddy when he comes for me. Do you know what time it is?'

Valentina stays calm. 'Plenty of time, honey. You've got plenty of time. What's your name?'

She doesn't look up from her writing. 'Suzanna.'

82

Valentina is relieved. 'That's right. Suzanna Grecoraci, I remember now.'

'No, silly. That's not my name. I'm Suzanna Fratelli. *I'm* only eight. Suzanna Grecoraci is the name of that old lady, the one who is friends with the others.' She looks up and gives Valentina a childish giggle. 'You must be *really* silly to mix us up.' She adds a critical stare to her facial repertoire. 'Have you been drinking? My daddy mixes things up when he's been drinking.'

Valentina moves closer to her. 'No, I haven't. Do other people mix you up?'

'Sometimes.' She looks down and works some more on the paper in front of her. 'The others call me Little Suzie; that way when I leave notes and things they don't get us confused.'

'The others? What others are they?'

'You know. *The others,* the ones who live in here with us.'

Valentina's out of her depth and she knows it. 'How many, Suzie? How many others are there?'

Suzie stops her work and counts them off on her fingers. 'More than that!' She holds up two outstretched hands, fingers spread wide. '*Lots* more.'

'Really?' Valentina works her way around so she can see over Suzie's shoulder. 'That's really good. What is it?'

Suzie moves her hands to reveal a large crayoned drawing. 'Romans. Do you like Romans?'

'Some of them.' Valentina leans closer. The crayoning is good. She can easily identify Roman soldiers, a crowd, senators in togas and – she has to look twice – a woman with her hand in the mouth of a giant white disc.

The Bocca della Verità.

'That's blood!' says Suzie, jabbing excitedly at a smear of red. 'It's from Cassandra.'

The background of the drawing is filled with strange

shapes: a sun, maybe a moon, and some badly drawn stars, so bad they're more triangular and lopsided than star-shaped.

'Cassandra is having her hand cut off,' explains Suzie, almost as though she were recalling a favourite fairy tale. 'It's because she won't tell them about the secret.'

'Oooh, it looks nasty.' Valentina rubs her own wrist. 'What secret is that?'

Suzie frowns. 'I don't know. It's Cassandra's secret and she never tells. No matter what.'

There are sounds outside the door. A trolley being wheeled into an adjacent room. A woman's voice talking loudly.

Suzie looks scared. 'You should go now.' She glances nervously towards the door. 'If you don't go, Momma will find you – *then* you'll be sorry.'

Valentina gives her a reassuring smile. 'I'm a police-woman, Suzie; nothing bad is going to happen while I'm here. I promise you.'

Fear takes Suzie's voice up another ten decibels. 'Please go! I don't want you in here. If you don't go, Momma will take it out on me and she won't let Daddy come.'

The trolley is on the move again. They can hear its wheels squeaking. The door to the room next to them is opening. Valentina is desperate to ask more about Cassandra – about the secret – but she can see it would be pointless.

The poor girl is petrified.

She'll come back and do it when she's had time to gather her thoughts and think the whole crazy thing through a little more.

She gives Suzie a smile and moves away to open the door. 'Don't worry, no one will hurt you. I'll come back tomorrow and make sure you're all right.'

Suzie doesn't reply.

She's already pulled the bed sheet above her head and curled herself into a tight ball.

25

There is whispering in the womb.

Hushed voices.

Confidential tones.

But I hear them.

I lie curled up, pretending to be asleep, but I hear all their secrets and their laughter.

Mother and the special one — the favoured one — are together.

They are out of sight, hidden in the darkness, but their sentences fly like birds and nest in my ears.

It is easy for me to picture them there.

Easy but painful.

They sit side by side and Mother has her arm fondly around her. She strokes my sister's hair and tells her how beautiful she is.

The most beautiful of all of us.

She tells her how clever she is.

By far the cleverest among us.

And She tells her how like Her she is.

And how She likes her the most.

The others want me to run away.

Escape.

They say they know how and can set me free.

They tell me they have done it before — in Phrygia, in Crete, in Anatolia, in Etruria, Hellas and Rome.

They can do it again.

But I know Mother will stop them. She will stop them and She will stop me.

And deep inside I feel that I don't want to escape.

I want to belong.

I want to be the one to sit beneath Mother's outstretched arm and be cherished and confided in.

I strain to listen.

I wait patiently for the word birds to nest again in my ears.

They are coming now, their beaks heavy with secrets carried from centuries long ago.

They drop them gently and I pick through them.

Precious stories about the kings of Rome, the Seven Hills of the Eternal City, the Prophecies.

And more.

The Tenth Book.

The secrets of the Tenth Book.

These are the scraps I am left as the voices fade in the darkness of the womb.

Now there is only silence, darkness and one thing else.

The silent screaming of my mind.

PART TWO

26

Monday morning isn't Louisa Verdetti's favourite time of the week. Especially, if she's already worked Saturday and Sunday.

To make matters worse, the first part of her least favourite day is being spent with the man who tops her list of least favourite people.

Hospital administrator Sylvio Valducci is mid-fifties. He has white hair and is one of those bosses who one minute manages from a distance of six miles and the next from six inches. He's the kind that conveniently ignores you when you're in the middle of a crisis but is all over you about the cost of paper clips when it's annual budget time. He and Louisa only have one thing in common – a mutual loathing of each other.

Valducci doesn't knock on her office door or even manage a good morning as he bursts in. 'I'm told you have something of a cause célèbre.' He tosses a manila file on her desk and enjoys watching it slide. 'I'd very much like to hear about it. In person. From you. I prefer it that way – it's much better than getting it second-hand from the animals who gather around the water cooler.'

Louisa takes off her glasses. She slowly spins her desk chair and vows not to lose her temper. 'I'm not sure I would call it a cause célèbre, but the patient is certainly interesting.' She opens the file he dropped and sees inside a copy of medical notes she's made. 'As it says in here: our admission is an Italian woman, identity so far unknown, mid to late twenties, well nourished.'

'This I know.' He pats his mouth to stifle a fake yawn and settles into a seat opposite her.

'And as you are also apparently aware, she's exhibiting as DID. Dissociative identity—'

'I know what DID is,' he snaps. 'Or to be more specific, what it *isn't*.' He shows his teeth, in what he mistakenly believes is an enigmatic smile. 'Better doctors than you have made fools of themselves with this little acronym.' He melodramatically puts his hand to his forehead. 'And my, isn't it strange that patients with DID are so often involved in criminal activity? Crimes they conveniently blame on one of their many other personalities. Stranger still if you ask me that none of those other personalities turn up at the police station and confess, or rat on the offending alter, as you so ridiculously call them.'

Louisa tries to ignore his goading. 'Our patient is presenting classic symptoms. She's writing and drawing in different personalities. Speaking in multiple voices and tones, as though she were different people of different ages. Her mood swings are extreme – from timid to violent.'

He waves a hand dismissively. 'Fakery! This is all rubbish and you know it. Have you run diagnostic tests for borderline personality disorder?'

'Of course we've run tests – and we're running more. You don't need to tell me how to do my job. We've taken more blood and urine samples than an Olympic doping committee, and before you ask, no, there is no chance of amphetamine-induced psychoses, if that's what you're fishing for.'

He's amused by her anger.

Pleased that he has roused it so fully.

'There's nothing wrong with fishing, Louisa. When you have but a small crack in the ice of the mind, fishing is the best thing you can do.'

She is bursting to tell him not to be so stupid and so pompous.

He stands and folds his arms autocratically. 'And while we're angling away, we should make sure we also run endocrine function tests to rule out hyperadrenalism, pernicious anaemia and thyroid disorders.' He takes her silence as a sign of his intellectual victory. 'Given the delusionary symptoms, don't dismiss the possibility of schizophrenia. It's tricky to diagnose—'

Louisa's out of her chair before he can finish. '*Schizophrenia?* She's no more schizophrenic than you or I. With all respect, can I remind you that I am a qualified neuropsychiatrist? At least credit me with *some* expert judgement.'

Snapping point. He just loves it when he gets people here. 'Not in this country.' He wags a finger at her, 'Your qualification is an American one, and as you know, we don't follow the outdated bible of the *Diagnostic and Statistical Manual of Mental Disorders* quite as slavishly as your American mentors do.'

Louisa shakes her head at him. Boss or no boss, he's a sentence away from getting a slapped face. She worked damned hard to get qualified, and even in Rome, ten years at Johns Hopkins should stand for something.

The administrator picks his file up off her desk. 'Blood tests, urine tests, tox tests: I want more doing – and all of them completed – before you even mention DID again. Do I make myself clear?'

If looks could kill, he'd be no more than a plasma stain up Louisa's office wall. 'Perfectly.'

'These beds are expensive. If she's fit, I want her out on the street and off my budget as quick as possible. Let the police work out what to do with her.'

Before Louisa can explode, her door bangs shut and he's gone.

<h1 style="text-align:center">27</h1>

Valentina Morassi's start to the day isn't going much better than Louisa's.

She planned to take this week off as holiday, but the incident in Cosmedin has scuppered any hopes of spending much time with Tom.

She forces herself to leave him naked in bed, sleeping off the wonderfully numbing effects of another night of excessive sex and the great bottle of Barolo they shared after getting home from a local restaurant.

Dozens of doubts and hundreds of hopes jangle like wind chimes in her mind as she drives from the apartment to the office.

Federico is already at his desk, and he looks even worse than she feels. Wife problems, he calls it, solved by half a bottle of brandy and a night on the couch. It's not something Valentina wants to discuss.

Love is meant to bloom, not wither and die.

He gets his act together after several long slugs of tar-black espresso and a sneaky cigarette in a toilet cubicle. 'I'm going to the labs to see what they've done with that bloodstained robe we got from the crazy woman. You want to come?'

Valentina certainly does.

It's not long before Federico soon regrets asking her. All the way to the offices of the Raggruppamento Carabinieri per la Investigazioni Scientifiche, she pushes him for progress reports on every aspect of the inquiry.

'Please stop busting my balls,' he pleads as they're ushered through reception and climb some stairs. 'It all takes time. You need to learn that in Rome things move at a certain pace.'

'Snail's pace – and it's not fast enough,' says Valentina. 'I want to bury this case quickly. I've got a feeling that if it hangs around, it's going to cause us all kinds of problems.'

Federico doesn't fight her.

He leads the way down corridors with walls as brown as tobacco. They finally reach a door to a small office filled by a very fat middle-aged man in a white coat. He's sitting on a swivel chair that's way too small for him. Valentina notices that he has a telephone tucked between his left shoulder and ear and a dried waterfall of croissant crumbs down the front of the black T-shirt he's ill-advisedly wearing beneath his lab coat.

Federico does the introductions with a wave of his hand. 'Professore Enrico Ferrari, this is my boss, Capitano Valentina Morassi.'

'*Buongiorno*. I am charmed to meet you, Capitano.' He looks at his friend. 'And I must confess, I am somewhat surprised. I have never known Federico to venture out this early in the day.'

Valentina shakes his hand and resists obvious remarks about him not looking like any Ferrari she's ever seen. 'I believe you have the clothing and weapon recovered from the case in Cosmedin?'

'I have.' He struggles off his chair and brushes some of the crumbs from his chest. 'The sword is actually in this locked cabinet over here. We are going to take some more photographs of it this morning. An amazing object.'

He opens the top drawer of a three-box cabinet and lifts out a heavy chunk of metal wrapped in brown paper. 'It's been fingerprinted already and there are several latents on it, but we don't have any direct matches as yet.' He places it on his desk and moves papers, a stapler and laptop to one side so he can unwrap it. 'It's very old.'

'Bravo!' mocks Federico. 'All your training and *very old* is the best you can come up with?'

'Okay. Then it's very, *very* old.' Ferrari smiles at his friend. 'I know you want facts, but until we've X-rayed and carbontested it, I'm not even going to guess at a date. What I will say is this is *not* a replica. It is an ancient Roman weapon forged several centuries ago.'

Valentina struggles to picture Suzanna with it. A frail Italian woman in the twenty-first century wielding a heavy Roman sword in a church is an insane image. Almost as crazy as the thought of how it could have come into her possession. Family heirloom? Stolen from her husband, boyfriend or lover? 'And this thing could actually cut a hand off?'

'I believe it could.' Ferrari lifts it so the blade is close to Valentina's eyeline. 'I haven't chopped anything with it, but the metal has probably been tempered. That would make it sharper, stronger, even deadlier, but ironically a little more brittle. Against a heavier weapon it might shatter, but it would slice through flesh like a hot knife through butter and, with several hacks, would go through bone.'

Despite Suzanna's mental problems, Valentina really can't envisage her cutting off another woman's hand.

Maybe Tom's right.

Perhaps there's more to this than she first imagined.

Ferrari dispassionately continues his run-down. 'The clothing is in the evidence store at the end of the corridor. Let me call through to my assistant and she'll have someone find it for us.' He opens a door and jabbers a message to his secretary.

'Rome is full of artefacts,' says Federico to Valentina, 'but one as well preserved as this is extremely rare. It must have been stolen from somewhere, a museum or private collector. It should be easy for us to trace.'

Ferrari returns to the desk, wraps up the weapon and carefully replaces it under lock and key in his cabinet. 'Shall we go to the store?'

'Please,' says Valentina.

The scientist can't help but stare at her.

'I'm sorry. Forgive me gawking at you. I was just thinking that you're remarkably young – and pretty – for a female captain.'

Federico barks out an embarrassed cough.

Valentina treats Ferrari to a well-practised look of indifference.

Ferrari tries vainly to dig himself out of his hole. 'They're unusual – female captains; in fact, the only other one I've met must be twice your age, and come to think of it, I actually suspect she's a he.' He laughs nervously and turns to Federico. 'What do you think, is Giovanna Ponti a man or a woman?'

'Neither,' interrupts Valentina coldly. 'She's a senior Carabinieri officer and you'd do well to afford her the respect she deserves.'

'Quite.' Ferrari frowns at his faux pas, then moves slowly ahead of them. 'I didn't mean to be sexist, Capitano. Federico will tell you, I have a sad knack of saying the wrong things when it comes to ladies. I'm sorry if I upset you.'

They make the rest of the short walk in silence and enter a cool storage room full of freezers, shelves, drawers and wall cupboards.

'We're still compiling the DNA profiles,' explains the scientist, grateful to change the subject and get back on a professional footing, 'but I can already tell you something interesting about the blood samples taken from the dismembered hand, the weapon you recovered and the clothing that your prisoner was wearing.'

Valentina's patience is short. 'And that is?'

'They don't match.'

He watches their faces as they struggle to absorb the significance.

'*None* of them?' queries Federico.

'None of them,' he confirms. 'The blood from the victim's hand is different to that found on the weapon – and from the blood on the clothes of the woman you arrested.'

Valentina feels like she's doing Sudoku.

A young female lab assistant arrives on cue, holding a hooded white gown covered in a transparent evidence sheet.

Ferrari takes it from her and turns it round so they can see the stains and spatters on the front. 'Just so you're really clear, the blood on this garment is *not* from the severed hand and *not* from your suspect.' He pauses, then explains: 'The blood on this gown is AB. The blood on the sword taken from your prisoner is Rhesus positive and the blood on the severed hand is Rhesus negative.' He gives them something to grab on to. 'Rhesus neg is present in only about fifteen per cent of the population.'

Valentina lets out a long sigh and realises she's been holding her breath. 'That at least is helpful. We have a victim with unusual blood. If she got a transfusion, we should be able to trace it.'

'Let's hope she did,' says Federico ruefully.

Valentina picks up the transparent bag. 'If this blood isn't from the victim with the severed hand, and it isn't from our prisoner, then who the hell *is* it from?'

No one answers.

They don't have to.

They all know that it's only a matter of time before another victim turns up.

At least one more.

28

Mother tells us Her story.

The one about how the old King could have had all nine books.

If only he hadn't been such a fool.

If only he had realised that what Mother was offering him was the greatest prize on earth.

Nine books that would have secured the safety and success of Rome until the end of time.

Nine volumes that would have protected his throne, his people and himself.

But the old fool laughed in Her face.

He held his fat belly like it had been freshly filled from royal feasting and he roared like a drunkard in the Aventine.

Mother says She'd never been so humiliated.

All She'd asked for was a small share of the riches She'd helped create.

A meagre portion of the prosperity Her prophecies had produced.

But he waved Her away like he would a kitchen skivvy.

My sisters and I can feel Mother's pain. Even now it hovers in Her spirit as she tells us how She refused to go. How She stared the King down and set aflame the first three volumes of Her treasured work.

He showed not a hint of concern.

Indeed, he even smiled as the fire's flame-red lips greedily chewed their way in blackening bites through Her sacred works.

Poor Mother.

She says some madness must have visited the monarch, for he laughed uncontrollably and even warmed his hands in the heat of the hearth as the pages turned to ash.

And so Mother left.

In Her absence, the winds of pestilence and the rains of plague began to gather in the Roman skies. From the dark holes of the underworld, the goddess Proserpina and her minions slowly turned their heads with great expectancy towards the Eternal City.

The King's augurs could see the dark clouds of calamity gathering and they urged Mother to return.

But still She was not welcome.

We ask Her why She subjected herself to such indignation. Mother tells us everyone makes mistakes.

Even kings.

Everyone deserves a second chance.

Even fools.

And so the foolish King was given his second chance to secure the remaining six books at the same price that Mother had originally demanded for all nine.

But the wisdom of Minerva was not with him.

He said the price was too high — far too high for something of such little worth.

Mother told him his foolishness bordered upon blindness.

She decided to show him the light.

She burned three more books.

It seemed to work.

Now, while he watched the flames grow, the gods whispered in his ear. It was as though fleet-footed Mercury had rushed to the King's side with words straight from Jupiter and Juno.

'Stop!' shouted the King.

Mother smiles and we hang on every syllable of Her story.

She tells us that with six of the books gone, the King now begged for the remaining three.

We all cheer!

Mother bids us be quiet.

She explains that although She was now offered all She'd wanted – recognition, power, land and much coin – She was filled with great sadness.

Sadness and a doubt that the King and his descendants would properly use and protect the knowledge they'd been given.

We bow our heads, because we know of Mother's gifts of prophecy and that Her fears would come true.

The last three of the nine books would eventually meet a similar end to the first six.

She smiles at us.

'Worry not, my sweet ones,' She says. 'It is because of these doubts and these fools that you are so treasured, that your innocence is of such import. It is why the Tenth Book was created. And it is because of these reasons and our enemies that its contents and where-abouts must never be known to anyone.'

29

Major Armando Caesario sits attentively behind his old walnut desk in a high-backed leather chair, with his chin resting on his folded hands.

It's quite a story that his new *capitano* is telling him, and he can't wait for her to leave so he can ask Assante if she's gone completely mad.

Female captains are not a good idea.

Never have been. Never will be. High Command, in all its forward-thinking wisdom, seems to believe it's wise to promote more women.

It isn't.

It's a big mistake, and one day they'll realise it.

Until then, long-suffering officers such as Caesario have to suffer the likes of Valentina Morassi and her meandering report about churches, severed hands, hooded gowns and ancient swords.

What rubbish.

He blames himself.

He sent her out to Cosmedin because she'd come from Venice with a reputation for working some big case with juicy headlines about Satanism, and he thought it amusing to send her back to a church again.

Now he wishes he hadn't.

'No,' he says out loud. 'No extra resources. No extra manpower. No extra anything.'

Even Assante looks shocked.

'I'm saying no because you don't even have one victim, let alone two.' Caesario scratches an ear. 'All this might be some crazy joke. Maybe this madwoman got the body part from a hospital and it was a sick prank that went wrong and traumatised her.'

'The blood on what you call the madwoman's gown didn't come from the hand,' stresses Valentina, annoyed at his tone and that he's missed the point of her lengthy explanation. 'It's probably from another victim.'

'I know,' says Caesario angrily. 'None of this makes sense, and I'm not about to waste any more precious hours and money on what so far is a crime without a body.'

Valentina is about to press her case.

Caesario doesn't let her. 'Captain, you've got forty-eight hours to come up with a victim – or victims – or I shut this case down. Now could you leave me, please? I have another matter to discuss with Lieutenant Assante.'

Valentina's out of the room in a flash. She's angry enough to punch a hole through a wall.

Body parts from hospitals?

Is he serious?

Her heart is pounding and she can't bear the thought of waiting at her desk for Assante to reappear with a sexist grin on his face.

She grabs her coat and car keys and heads outside, wondering why on earth she didn't stay in Venice, where she was known and respected.

In less than fifteen minutes, she's zipped in front of a number 30 tram grinding its way down Via Regina Elena, parked the Fiat inside the grounds of the Policlinico Umberto and is opening Louisa Verdetti's office door.

'Oh no, really no.' Louisa gets up from her desk. 'Captain, please, I'm having a morning straight from hell, and—'

'So am I,' interjects Valentina, 'and mine is to do with short-sighted, narrow-minded men who can't see further than their diminutive penises and even smaller brains.'

Louisa starts laughing. She recognises the symptoms. 'Our afflictions appear remarkably similar.' She gestures to a sofa. 'Would you like a coffee? I'm really up to my neck in work, but I have ten minutes for a fellow sufferer.'

'That would be great. Espresso. No sugar. *Grazie.*'

Louisa phones it through and takes a seat on a sofa opposite her surprise guest. 'So, how can I help? Suzanna Grecoraci, I presume.'

'*Si.*' Valentina struggles out of her short wool coat and wishes she'd taken it off before sitting down. 'We still haven't found a victim to connect to the blood found on her, and my boss will shut the inquiry down if I don't come up with something tangible in forty-eight hours.'

'I have a similar gun to my head. My administrator is talking about releasing her. Putting her out on the street so you'd have to look after her.'

Valentina runs her hands through her hair. 'If he does that, we'll just lock her in a hospital ward inside the barracks without any proper treatment. That's assuming I can even find a charge that would stick.'

Louisa lets out a pained breath. 'How do these guys get to such positions? They're not idiots, obviously, but it seems like they're capable of behaving like them.'

'One of life's mysteries.' Valentina ventures to mention a notion she's been considering. 'I remember in psychology at college reading about the Cassandra Complex. Could that be anything to do with Suzanna?'

Louisa looks surprised. 'Interesting notion. Cassandra because of the story she wrote?'

'Yes.'

The doctor remembers, 'The Cassandra Complex was a term coined in the late 1940s by the French philosopher Gaston Bachelard to deal with patients who believed they had the power of premonition.'

'So it fits?'

Louisa flinches. 'Not really. Suzanna's alter called herself Cassandra but she didn't predict anything. In the account, she wrote down that she was publicly punished and humiliated because she was hiding something.'

'A secret. She said she'd rather die than disclose what she was involved in. What if the secret itself was a premonition, a prophecy or warning of some kind?'

Louisa doesn't say anything; she's silently sifting through her dusty back files to recall lessons from long ago.

Finally, something comes back to her. 'There's a Jungian analyst called Schapira who wrote a lot about the Cassandra Complex in relation to very disturbed patients who were disbelieved when they disclosed the true cause of their problems. Let me look it up online.' She moves back to her desk and talks as she types into a medical search engine. 'From what I can remember, all of this metaphorical referencing is linked back to Greek mythology. Hang on, here we are.' She reads silently, then paraphrases the text for Valentina. 'Schapira says that Cassandra women see something dark that isn't apparent to others and can't be corroborated by facts. They envisage negative or unexpected outcomes to situations and disclose so-called truths that apparent authority figures find hard to accept.' She turns to her guest. 'Sounds like she encountered a lot of sexist men as well.' Louisa returns to the monitor and adds, 'In frightened, ego-less conditions, Cassandra women shout out whatever vision they are having, unconsciously hoping that others might understand. But of course they don't. To them, the disconnected words are just melodrama or nonsense.'

Coffee arrives on a plastic hospital tray brought in by a skinny assistant in her late thirties. She's in and out so quickly she could pass as an apparition.

Valentina cradles the warm cup in her hands. 'Is it possible for me to speak to the patient?'

Louisa returns to the sofa and picks up her drink. 'Suzanna, you mean?'

'No. Not Suzanna. Could you help me speak to Cassandra? Get Suzanna to persuade Cassandra to talk directly to me?'

30

There are a hundred good reasons why Louisa Verdetti shouldn't be doing what she's doing.

But she's still doing it.

Going against the norm. Taking risks. Being unorthodox.

They're all things that past mentors and paternal tutors have tried to knock out of her, but none of them have ever succeeded.

She goes with her gut.

It's part of what makes her a great clinician. Theory and reading can only take you so far. Experience can carry you another lap. An unorthodox approach nudges you over the finishing line.

Or gets you sacked.

She shuts the last thought out as she finishes introducing Suzanna to Valentina and makes sure the bedroom door is locked.

Valentina carefully follows the brief she's been given. Go slowly. Be gentle. Back off if the patient is the least bit distressed.

She leans slightly forward as she speaks in a gentle tone. 'Suzanna, I need to talk to Cassandra. Could you please see if she will speak to me?'

The pale young thing sitting in the chair next to the cream metal bed gives her a pained look. 'I can try, but I know Cassandra is in a bad mood. When she's in a bad mood, she doesn't like to see people.'

'Will you try for me? It's really important.' Valentina's now close enough to take Suzanna's hands in hers.

'What are you doing? Don't you dare touch me!'

The voice is no longer Suzanna's. It's stronger. Deeper. Far more confident.

'Impudent girl. Who are you? Do you not have whoring to attend to?' She almost jumps out of her seat and huffs indignantly. 'Where did you come from? Some brothel, no doubt. Dear gods, why have you vexed me with such poxed company?'

Valentina watches the woman pace. She's completely different to the mouse who was there seconds earlier. There's anger in her every step. Tension chiselled across her brow. She juts her jaw challengingly towards Valentina. 'What do you want, girl? Speak up now or be gone.'

Valentina remembers what she's supposed to say. It's going to sound strange, but it's meant to be a bridge, a psychological route into the unknown. 'Cassandra, we have been sent to you.' She nods towards Louisa. 'My friend and I are here because we are believers. We know you have things that you want to tell us. Things that others don't believe.'

Cassandra looks as them curiously. She regards them much as a mother might watch a child taking its first unsteady steps. 'What do you speak of? What things? Pray tell.'

Valentina is well versed in games of interview bluff. 'You know we can't simply speak openly. We must be guarded. Mustn't we?'

'Indeed.' Cassandra settles back into her chair and puts her hands on its arms as though it were a throne. 'What is your dedication to Mater?'

Valentina doesn't know what to say.

'I asked you a question, girl.'

She has to bluff. 'How do I know I can trust you?' She frowns. 'You may be a fraud, you might be lying.'

Anger flares in Cassandra's eyes. 'Lying? You accuse me of lying? Some runaway who smells of the *forica* has the gall to suggest I am a fraud and a liar. Be gone before I have you whipped and thrown back into the latrine.'

Valentina turns around to Louisa. She needs help. There's only so long she can keep shooting in the dark.

The clinician steps in. 'Cassandra, I think it is time for you to be quiet now. Time to give way to Suzanna. Let Suzanna come back and talk to us.'

In the split second that Louisa looks to Valentina to signify that the interview must come to an end, things go horribly wrong.

A bony hand grabs the doctor by the throat and runs with her until her head bangs against the far wall. '*Domina! Dominus! Templum! Libera nos a malo!*' The patient squeezes hard. A vice-like choke hold. '*Domina! Dominus! Templum! Libera nos a malo!*'

Valentina moves quickly. From behind, she loops her left arm around Cassandra's neck and smashes her left forearm downwards to break the grip on Louisa. The doctor falls free.

Valentina sweeps her right knee behind Cassandra's legs to unbalance her. She goes down shouting.

Valentina pins her to the floor, rolls her over and cuffs her hands. '*Suffragio! Le anime nel purgatorio. Suffragio!*'

'Be careful. Don't hurt her.' Louisa is purple in the face but still worried about the patient.

Within a second, Valentina has Cassandra upright and is manoeuvring her backwards on to the bed.

The two women's eyes meet.

She's changed again.

Cassandra has gone.

31

Neither Valentina nor Louisa ever drinks in the middle of the day at work.

Except today.

A bottle of rough red given to the doctor last Christmas is

106

uncorked and half consumed in Louisa's office before either of them can really talk.

'I'm sorry,' says Valentina, back on the sofa where her ill-conceived plan was outlined. 'I feel really bad about her attacking you like that.'

Louisa bolts down the vinegary wine and tops up her glass. 'My fault. I knew better than you that she could have a violent mood swing.' She touches her neck. 'I think I'll have to wear a scarf for a few days, or else there'll be jokes about me dating vampires.'

Valentina laughs. She likes the clinician and wishes she could make amends. 'I owe you one. Any time I can do anything for you, don't hesitate to ask.'

Louisa holds up her hand. 'No need. I know you have a tough job. We can't always help, but when we can, we're usually very willing to do so.'

'*Grazie.*' Valentina wonders whether Cassandra, or Suzanna – or whoever she really is – would have killed Louisa if she hadn't stepped in. She concludes that she probably would. 'Can I ask you to do me a final favour? Nothing risky this time.'

Louisa is wary. 'Perhaps.'

'Cassandra shouted out some words in Latin and Italian. I've made a note of them. If she says anything else, could you write it down and maybe call me?'

'Sure. I can do that.'

Valentina scribbles her private cell phone and home numbers on a business card and hands it over. She notices Louisa's fingers are shaking. 'Can you take the rest of the day off?'

The clinician smiles. 'No. Can you?'

'Maybe.' Valentina glances at her watch. Almost three p.m. She knows she should go back to the office, but she has no intention of doing so. Forty-eight hours. That's all Caesario gave her, and the clock is already ticking faster than she'd like. 'I have to go.' She drags herself from the comfort of her seat. 'Call me if you want. Even if you just feel the need to chat.'

Louisa nods and watches the policewoman leave. She puts her hand to her throat and tries not to cry. She got it wrong. Badly wrong. Maybe Valducci was right. Maybe she is guilty of jumping to conclusions, looking for a rare disorder when there isn't one. Perhaps the woman who had her hands around her throat *is* just a wild psychotic killer after all.

32

Tom's surprised to see her.

Pleasantly surprised.

But then the look on Valentina's face gives away the fact that she's not come home early for recreational purposes.

'Are you all right?' He puts down the book he's reading and gets up from the sofa to go to her.

'Depends on your definition of all right.' Valentina is already at the fridge, pulling out a bottle of water. 'I'll tell you in a minute.' She pours a glass, drinks and tops it up before putting the bottle back in the fridge. 'If I don't drink water as soon as I come in, then I eat like a horse.' She slips out of her coat and goes to hang it up.

Tom can see she's tense. Strung tighter than a new guitar. He lets her pace for a second and then opens his arms. 'Hey, come here.'

Valentina folds herself into his embrace. Puts her face against him and silently enjoys the closeness. She's spent so long coping with problems on her own, it's strange to have someone around to share them with. More than strange. A little awkward. She kisses his cheek and slowly pulls away. 'Can we talk for a minute?'

They sit alongside each other on the sofa and she takes his hand.

'I thought I had everything locked down. Processes in place. Situation under control. Truth is, this whole damned thing isn't making sense, and I'm starting to see shadows.'

'Maybe talking through it will help you see some light.'

She pulls her legs up and sits facing him at the end of the sofa. 'I went to the hospital today to see the woman we'd arrested, and she went insane. She was speaking as though she came from centuries ago and shouting weird things. Then she went crazy and nearly killed Louisa.'

'Louisa?'

'Verdetti, the woman in charge of the clinic. She had her by her throat and was choking the life out of her.'

'Is she okay?'

'Just about. Very shaken, though.'

'I can imagine.' Tom tries to picture the incident. 'Was the attacker right-handed or left-handed?'

Valentina demonstrates. 'Left-handed.'

'I remember that you said that whoever carried out the dismemberment at the church was left-handed. Is this the same person?'

Valentina lets out a sigh. 'That's one of the confusing things. The blood on our suspect's clothes doesn't match the severed hand found at the church.'

'Weird.'

'Tell me about it.'

'Can you put the suspect at the church?'

'Not yet. There are no CCTV cameras around there. Canvassing of locals has come up blank. Forensics are still going

109

over fingerprints and trace evidence to see if there's anything to prove she was anywhere near the Bocca della Verità.'

Tom shuffles round on the sofa so he's directly facing her. 'What was she saying today? You said she was talking strangely.'

'It was unbelievable. She became this totally different person.' Valentina clicks her fingers. 'Snap! Suddenly she was this Cassandra figure, talking as though she was back in old Roman times.'

'And what did she say?'

She pauses to remember. 'Nothing hugely significant. She behaved like she was a very powerful woman with a big house and lots of money.' She laughs. 'Cheeky bitch called me a whore!'

Tom smiles and rubs a foot that has now trespassed on to his lap. 'If only she knew what a virtuous life you lived.'

She gives him a playful kick. 'I was very fine and celibate until you led me astray.'

He can see mischief in her eyes. 'What else?'

She screws up her face. '*Domina! Dominus! Templum! Libera nos a malo!*'

'Mistress. Master. Temple. Deliver us from evil.'

'She said it a couple of times. Like it was a mantra.'

'Somewhat cryptic.'

'Louisa said that was the case with Cassandra women.'

He frowns at her.

'It's a psychological condition. Some kind of problem where women dissociate and start blurting out words or messages that no one else can understand.'

'And that's your problem. You've *got* to understand, right?'

'Right.'

'Anything else?'

'Yeah. *Suffragio. Le anime nel purgatorio. Suffragio!* I know what it means. Suffrage. The souls in Purgatory.'

'That isn't Latin, it's just Italian.'

She scowls at him. 'I know that.'

Tom becomes thoughtful. Drifts away into a world of internal focus. Tries to clear the white noise and pick out the key words. Mistress. Master. Temple. Suffrage. Souls. Purgatory. He feels like he's grasping at straws. 'The Latin she did use is stilted. All I can think of is that maybe it's a reference to some ancient gods who share a temple. Does that mean anything?'

He takes the puzzled look on her face to be a no.

'The last part might be easier. Isn't there a temple or special church dedicated to souls or suffrage?'

She laughs. 'Absolutely. About a thousand of them.'

'No, seriously. I'm sure I recall – from my previous job – somewhere specific, a *chiesa* run by a special mission.'

She unfolds herself and walks across the room. 'My Latin is about as poor as my regular church attendance. All I can remember is *Draco dormiens nunquam titillandus.*'

Tom laughs. 'Never tickle a sleeping dragon?'

'That's it! Straight out of Harry Potter – a Hogwarts motto, I think.' From a shelf she collects a handful of tourist leaflets and guide books. 'These came free with the apartment.' She drops a pile on his lap 'Every place of interest in Rome is covered in there. You search those and I'll look through these.'

She sits back down and makes the mistake of stretching her legs out into his space.

Tom grabs her feet and pulls her flat on to the sofa.

Valentina can't help but let out a girlish shriek.

He leans over the top of her, arms as broad as the pillars of the Pantheon, a smile as wide as the Tiber. 'In a minute. We'll do them in a minute. Okay?'

Valentina's eyes sparkle. She tilts her chin so her mouth is so close to his she can feel his breath on her lips, 'Fine by me. But if we're stopping, it'd better take more than just a minute.'

33

Several hours later, Valentina and Tom are outside the church of the Sacro Cuore del Suffragio on the Lungotevere Prati in the Tiber Meadows, just down from Il Palazzaccio, the giant Palace of Justice.

Neither of them is sure what they're supposed to be looking for.

But both are certain that this is the place they should be looking.

Dusk has turned to total darkness and the moon over the white façade of the *chiesa* makes it look like a fairy-tale fortress fashioned from icicles. It's completely out of context with all the other mundane buildings around it, a twenty-metre-high explosion of innumerable spires, human-sized statues and spectacular stained glass. Tom presumes its visual pureness comes from marble, but as he gets closer, he's surprised to find that the façade has been made from masses of concrete.

No matter, it's still amazing.

The only neo-Gothic church in Rome.

So stunning that in its prime it was christened the Little Dome of Milan.

A small, balding priest in a short-sleeved dog-collared shirt stands in the portico, rubbing thin hairy arms as he watches his two late visitors approach.

He knows what they're here for.

They called ahead to check the church was open.

Valentina gives him her best smile. 'Father Brancati?'

'*Si.*'

She extends her hand. 'Pleased to meet you. I am

Captain Morassi, Valentina Morassi. This is Tom Shaman.'
She thinks of adding that Tom used to be a priest, but
decides not to label him. If he wants, he'll mention it himself.

'*Buonasera.*' Tom gives Brancati a firm handshake. 'Your
church is incredibly beautiful. The frontage is breathtaking.'

'*Grazie.*' Brancati walks them in as he talks. 'The inside
has not the splendour of the outside, but as you apparently
know, it is even more intriguing.'

Tom and Valentina trade glances.

'This is a parochial church served by the Missionaries of
the Sacred Heart, to which I belong. It was built at the turn
of the nineteenth century and consecrated during the First
World War.' He huffs. 'The so-called Great War. I fail to see
why they called it great. No war is great, and that one was
monstrous.'

'Did your family lose people?' Tom blinks as his eyes
adjust to the low yellow candlelight inside the church.

'On both my father's and mother's sides – at the battle of
Caporetto. They died within days of each other, cut down
on the banks of the Isonzo river.'

'I'm sorry.'

'*Grazie.* It is long ago, but in my family it is never forgotten.' He stops and raises his hands to the huge vaulted
ceilings. 'In daylight, the sunlight filtering through the rose
windows is heavenly, especially over the altar. All this was the
dream of a French priest called Victor Jouet.'

They stand for a moment in the cool of the church and
look over the nave, with its three aisles, each ending in an
apse, divided by quatrefoil pillars. Tom has an urge to sit in
one of the pews, a desire to soak up the tranquillity and calm
of the place.

But there isn't time.

Father Brancati is already genuflecting in front of the altar and turning right into an annex.

The most famous church annex in Rome.

A room of miracles.

'So, here you are.' He waves his arms again. 'The Museo delle Anime del Purgatorio – the Museum of Souls in Purgatory.'

It's nothing to look at.

A long glass display case with sliding doors and an ugly hardwood surround dominates one wall. The exhibits are small and are mounted on cheap pegboard. They wouldn't fetch ten euros as a job lot in a car boot sale. They appear to be bits of cloth, books and old papers. Nothing to catch the eye.

Tom studies the objects closely. Just being next to them makes him feel energised. It's as though an electric current is attached to his nerves and is gently pulsing away in wave after wave.

Father Brancati can see he's transfixed. 'You understand what they are? Their significance?'

Tom's eyes don't leave the case. 'I do. They're messages from Purgatory. Pleas from souls trapped there to be cleansed of their sins and allowed redemption.'

Valentina leans close to the glass. She can see scorched hand marks and fingerprints on prayer books.

'It is evidence of another world,' says Brancati, 'proof that when we die, our souls go into Purgatory to be purified and made holy enough to pass into the glory of heaven.' He taps the glass. 'These apparitions reached out. They wanted people to pray for them, to speed their passage into God's glorious company.'

Valentina can't help but ask a police-like question, 'What evidence is there that these relics weren't faked?'

Brancati isn't angered. He's addressed the point a thousand

times. 'All the relics have sworn testimonies by those who witnessed the apparitions. Look closer and you'll see that each exhibit is accompanied by the story of its origin.'

Valentina looks. She's unimpressed. There's nothing there that would stand up in court. But then again, she tells herself, she knows people have faith, and faith can't be detected by Luminol spray or DNA swabs.

Brancati taps the glass. 'In December 1838, Giuseppe Stitz was reading a book of prayers when this mark of a hand appeared on it. He gave testimony that he then heard the voice of his dead brother asking for prayers.'

Valentina has seen enough of the exhibits. 'Thank you, Father. You have been most helpful.'

Tom extends his hand and shakes that of the priest. 'Would it be all right if Captain Morassi and I look around the church and then come back to see you in the sacristy if we have any final questions?'

'I must go in twenty minutes.' He holds up his wrist and a cheap watch. 'Will you be done by then?'

'We will,' Valentina readily promises.

He nods and leaves.

'Well,' she says to Tom, 'what do you make of that?'

'A little more than you do.' Tom glances around. 'But that's not the point. I don't see any real tie to your woman prisoner. Except that she sent us here.'

'*Maybe* sent us here.'

'Maybe,' he concedes, then walks past her into the main body of the church.

The place is in half-light. Searching it seems impossible.

Tom wanders up the left and Valentina the right. It all suddenly seems pointless to her. With most searches you know what you're looking for — a gun, a knife, a murder weapon, bloodstains, footprints, fingerprints, hairs, fibres, a suicide note or even a death-bed confession.

She finds a stack of prayer books.

Pointless.

There are dozens of them.

Each with hundreds of pages and thousands of words.

She looks across the church and pauses. What did she just think of?

Notes, suicide notes, confession notes. She makes her way through the pews to one of two old-fashioned confessionals pushed against the right-hand wall of the church.

Tom sees her from the other side and drifts across.

Valentina slips through a rusty-brown curtain and sits on the bench where the priest normally positions himself. She notices there are two wooden shutters, allowing him to hear confession from either side. She opens them both and smiles at the sight of a tube of peppermints tucked away in the corner of a narrow shelf.

Tom's face appears through the shutter in front of her and makes her jump.

'Madonna!' she says, pleased that nothing worse slipped out.

'Three Hail Marys as penance,' chides Tom. 'You find anything?'

'Nothing.' She pulls a small penlight torch from her pocket and shines it around. 'Just Father Brancati's food stash.'

'I had a McDonald's during confession once. It was coming up to Christmas and I was doing double shifts. You'd be amazed what goes on in those booths.'

He walks around the outside and squeezes in alongside her.

It's a tight fit.

Valentina has to chase off some sudden and inappropriate thoughts that would surely get her a very long spell in Purgatory, if not somewhere worse. 'How long is it since you've been in one of these?' she asks, shining her torch up across the plaster of the ceiling and wall.

'Seeking forgiveness, or giving forgiveness?'

'Either.'

'Three years since I heard confession. Not quite as long since I wiped the slate clean.'

'Is that really what it does?' She plays the beam across the wood inside the confessional.

'With venial sin, yes. In the case of my mortal sins, no.'

For a second, she remembers how they met. The first time he told her of the incident in Los Angeles. The lives he took in a fight in the gang-infested streets of Compton. She's about to say something comforting when she thinks she sees something. 'Move a minute. Just move to one side.'

Tom shuffles round.

Valentina crouches, and her knees crack. She holds the torch like she's throwing a dart and focuses the beam on the wall. Scraped into the plasterwork are the words DOMINA. DOMINUS. TEMPLUM. LIBERA NOS A MALO.

She focuses on the words.

Cassandra's words.

But Tom's eyes are on something beneath the writing.

A geometric shape, hovering beneath the phrase DELIVER US FROM EVIL.

A triangle.

A very special triangle.

34

Father Brancati goes wild when he sees the graffiti.

'*Vandali!*' he shouts. 'They have no respect. They steal. They wreck things. Not even the Church is sacred any more.'

'A little strange,' Tom points out, more quietly, 'to find vandals who write in Latin.'

Until then the priest hasn't noticed. He's so familiar with the old language that he subconsciously translated the text as automatically as reading a prayer book. 'Yes, I suppose it is. Very strange.' He moves to touch the lettering with his fingers, to feel the imprint of whatever rough tool was used to scrape out the plaster.

Valentina grabs his hand. 'Please don't touch it. It's a crime scene and will need to be photographed.'

He looks shocked. 'Crime scene? What? Why?'

She gently leads him out of the confessional. 'As I mentioned when I phoned you, we're investigating a violent incident, and there is a link to your church that we have to look into.' She eases him round and walks him part way down the aisle. 'You've been very kind and helpful, Father. Would you mind waiting in the sacristy until I have finished here?'

Brancati minds very much, but still does as she says.

He's worried about what's going on.

Worried about the publicity, the effect on the mission, what his superiors might say. He heads for the sacristy and goes straight to the bottle of brandy he keeps in the cupboard alongside the altar wine.

He'll find his mints later.

Tom takes a snap of the writing with his camera phone while Valentina makes a call to the station.

She reappears moments later. 'Federico is sending a photographer and CSI; they'll take shots, and dust and spray everything and anything all around here.' She points at the triangle. 'That's identical to the pendant we found on the prisoner. She even wrote about it in a story, said she'd had it stolen from her while she was being persecuted in ancient Rome. Does it mean anything to you?'

Tom is on his knees, peering closely at the symbol. 'Maybe it's a scalene.'

'A what?'

'Scalene. It means that none of the sides are the same length and none of the angles match. It's the only triangular shape where none of the sides or angles are equal.'

'Geometry wasn't my strong subject at school.'

'What was?'

'Boys,' she says cheekily. 'Aside from the boring geometry, does it mean anything?'

Tom stares at it while he thinks. 'Triangles have always had immense symbolic power. The Nazis used a whole range of them to pick out and persecute minority groups in their concentration camps. Red for political dissidents, green for criminals, purple for Jehovah's Witnesses, brown for Gypsies, black for lesbians and pink for homosexuals. I believe the famous six-pointed star was invented because gay Jewish men had to wear a pink triangle overlapping the yellow one that denoted their religion.'

'Triangle overload,' observes Valentina.

Tom isn't put off by her interruption. 'Indeed. Jewish communists had to wear overlapping red and yellow ones. Modern homosexual communities still use pink triangles as a symbol of gay and lesbian liberation.'

Valentina tries to make a connection to her case. 'So, the

119

Latin – *Deliver us from evil* – and the references to suffrage and souls in purgatory: we take all this as some cry from persecuted souls beyond the grave?'

Tom doesn't answer at first. 'Symbols gets hijacked,' he says finally. 'They're often misinterpreted. You'll have to be careful that this particular one doesn't mislead you. For example, within cosmic geometric symbolism, triangles are also used to signify a connection between heaven and earth.'

'Purgatory again?'

'Maybe. Maybe not. Egyptians used a triangle with an eye in it to symbolise the sun god Horus and his all-seeing ability. It became the basis of charms to ward off evil. Then again, if you go back to the Greeks, the triangle was a very positive symbol; it represented the vulva of the Mother Delta. And for the Hebrews it was a symbol of truth.'

'Truth, as in the Bocca della Verità – the Mouth of Truth.' Valentina scratches her hands through her hair. 'There are too many coincidences now. A woman with an ancient sword talking as though she is possessed or living centuries ago; brutal violence in a famous church linked with rituals about the public acclamation of truth; and now symbols and souls in a *chiesa* dedicated to suffrage and Purgatory.'

'And that's not all.' Tom stands up and stretches.

Folding his six feet three inches into a cramped confessional hasn't been a comfortable experience.

'There's the obvious connotation of the triangle. The one we haven't mentioned.'

Valentina looks duly annoyed that she has to ask. 'Which is?'

'The occult one. The one Satanists protect. The pentagram. Five interlocking triangles representing the elements of earth, wind, fire and water, plus a fifth component, the supernatural spirit. It's a symbol that has different powers according to how it's drawn and where the spiritual segment of the triangle is located. Drawn pointing down, it is used in occult rituals to direct specific forces and energies against people. Drawn pointing upwards, it is used for protection.'

'You learn something every day.' Valentina throws her hands open. 'But this leaves us where? How can I make sense out of it all?'

'You can't,' says Tom. 'We know there's only one person who can do that.'

35

Once the photographer and CSI have been briefed, Valentina leaves the evidence-gathering at the church to a junior officer called Paulo Benchabo. A man who smells strongly of garlicky pasta and more than just the first glass of red wine.

She and Tom are about to return home when Louisa Verdetti calls her.

The medic still sounds edgy. 'I'm sorry to trouble you, it's just that I know you're chasing a deadline and I have just had quite a session with Suzanna.'

Valentina traps the phone between her ear and shoulder as she zaps the Fiat open with her key fob. 'Did she tell you what happened at the church, where the blood on her clothes came from?'

'No. No, I'm sorry she didn't.' Louisa sounds stressed. 'Listen, I don't want to raise your hopes; this may be something or nothing. I just thought you should know what happened.'

'Thanks.' Valentina slips into the Punto and quickly opens the door for Tom. 'What exactly did she say to you?'

'It's complicated. She became yet another personality, another alter. More riddles, I'm afraid.'

Valentina holds her head in her spare hand and jams the keys in the ignition slot. This is the last thing she wants. 'Hold on, I'll get a pen and paper.'

'Better you come and see. I videoed it. This new alter manifested while I was doing a routine recording of a diagnostic session.'

Valentina starts the engine. 'I'm on my way. I'll be with you within the half-hour.'

Both she and Tom know that's optimistic. The journey is less than seven kilometres, but traffic is always bad around the Piazza del Popolo and Viale del Muro Torto.

By the time they've battled their way through and parked, it's closer to forty minutes.

Louisa Verdetti is alone in her office, blinds half drawn, desk lamp on. She looks up as Valentina knocks and enters. '*Buonasera.*' Her expression shows she's drained.

'*Buonasera.* Doctor, this is Tom Shaman, he's a friend and has been unofficially helping me.'

'*Buonasera.*' Tom shakes Louisa's hand and smiles warmly. 'I hope you don't mind me being here. I can wait outside if you prefer.'

That's not what Valentina wants. 'Tom is a former priest. He and I worked together in Venice on a serious crime case, and I can vouch for his confidentiality.'

Louisa looks too tired to argue. She waves a hand at the sofa and picks a DVD off her desk. 'Please sit down. Let me play this for you. Would you like a drink?'

'Just water, please,' replies Valentina.

Tom agrees, so Louisa grabs three glasses and a bottle from off the top of a metal filing cabinet and pours the drinks. She slips the DVD into a player beneath a TV mounted on the wall and starts the recording. She studies the time code at the bottom of frame, then skips it on, until the recording starts mid-sentence.

Louisa: '. . . all right to continue, Suzanna?'

Suzanna: 'I'm not Suzanna. Why do you call me Suzanna? Get down on the ground, quick, get down with me. Keep low!'

Louisa: 'I'm sorry, I thought Suzanna was your name. Who are you then?'

Suzanna: 'Claudia. I'm Claudia.'

Louisa: 'Claudia. That's a nice name.'

Claudia: 'Who are you? I didn't see you arrive. You didn't travel with us. Are you some demon sent from the underworld to punish me?'

Louisa: 'No. No, I'm not. Don't be frightened. I'm here to help. You can trust me.'

Claudia: 'Then get down flat like me; lie on your belly, or they'll see you.'

Louisa: 'Like this?'

Claudia: 'Flatter. Right down, like you're a snake.'

Louisa: 'My chin's almost on the floor, Claudia, I can't get—'

Claudia: 'Shush. Quiet! If they hear you they'll take both of us again.'

Louisa: '*Who?* Who will take us?'

Claudia: 'The soldiers over there. The ones lying like lizards on the rocks.'

Louisa: 'I can't see any soldiers, Claudia. Outside the door there's a Carabinieri guard, that's all. He's there to protect you, not hurt you.'

Claudia: 'How can you say that? We are at war with them. They took my sister, my friends. They killed my brother and my father. We are at war with them.'

Louisa: 'I don't understand. What war?'

Claudia: 'The war that never ends between us Sabines and those pig-faced Romans. Our men have either fled, been killed or are still in battle. My brother fought for me, but a brute like that one out there came along and cut him down with his sword.'

Louisa: 'How did you get away, Claudia? Did you run, is that how you escaped?'

Claudia: 'No. At first, the Romans took me. They trussed me up like a lamb for slaughter, then flung me in a cart with the other Sabines. Sweet Curitis, our divine goddess, must have been protecting me. There was a battle some hours back. The soldiers had to leave our cart to fight with troops sent by Mettus. We were on low-lying land by the bend of the river near where an island floats in the great water. We could see Romans on the hills, moving around near their fires, working their lands. While the soldiers fought, another woman and I escaped from the cart. We cut our bonds on sharp rocks by the shore. We were beneath a bridge about to try to make it to the island to hide, when . . .'

Louisa: 'What happened, Claudia?'

Claudia: '. . . a soldier grabbed me. I didn't see him. He came up behind me and put his arm around my throat. I thought I was going to choke to death. I'm sure I would have if it hadn't been for the other woman. She was very brave. Very quick.'

Louisa: 'What did she do?'

Claudia: 'She hit him. She had to. She hit him with a big stone. Hard. Hard on the back of his head. It made a sound like a dropped melon. She kept hitting him and he fell. Then . . . then she picked up his sword and plunged it into his stomach. It was horrible. His blood was everywhere. All over him – all over my face and my clothes. I was terrified.'

Louisa: 'Are you all right?'

Claudia: 'I can still see his eyes. Staring at us. She pulled out the sword and stabbed him again and again to make him be quiet.'

Louisa: 'It's okay. It's all over. We don't need to talk about this any more, Claudia.'

Claudia: 'We hid his body. We hid it beneath a place where they launched boats to the island. Just piled boulders, wet with plants of the river, on top of his corpse and left him. The woman said she hoped that Mars, the soldier's god, would forgive such an inglorious death.'

Louisa: 'This other woman – what was her name?'

Verdetti stops the tape.

She looks towards Tom and Valentina. 'She didn't answer. I asked her several times but it just became incredibly distressing for her.' She points to her desk. 'She was so emotionally exhausted and so frightened she crawled right under my desk and fell asleep. I couldn't move her. It was almost as if she was in a coma.'

Valentina wishes she had time to sympathise.

But knows she doesn't.

She looks down at some notes she's made and tries to ask her questions as gently as possible. 'Louisa, I have to confess my ignorance. I'm not from Rome. Are there significant things in what she said? Things that have special Roman meanings.'

The doctor nods. 'The place Claudia is describing – the spot where she said her friend killed the soldier is on the edge of *Campus Martius,* The Field of Mars. I know exactly the area that she's describing. It's the Ponte Fabricio, what I think is the oldest surviving bridge in Rome – maybe in the world – and a link to Tiber Island. She mentioned seeing Romans on the hillsides across the water – that would be right as well. I think she would be looking towards the Quirinal Hill.'

'What's that?' asks Tom.

'An area of Rome, like the Aventine, but originally it was essentially a shrine to Quirinus, the Sabines' equivalent of Mars.'

Valentina takes a deep breath. She knows she shouldn't ask what she's about to, but she's going to anyway. 'Louisa, this may sound strange, but would you take us there?'

Verdetti frowns. 'Now?'

'I know,' says Valentina, 'It's dark, cold and ridiculously late. But I'm running out of time. Will you? Please.'

36

Tom folds himself into the back of the Punto and they trundle towards the Field of Mars.

It's a near-impossible fit.

Certainly a feat worthy of a Guinness World Record for the biggest ex-priest carried in the smallest ever space.

Tom remembers just a few days ago standing on top of the Eiffel Tower with his friend Jean-Paul, looking down at the Parisian park by the same name.

Coincidence?

He certainly hopes so.

There must be dozens of military parade grounds throughout the world dedicated to the god of war. The only nagging doubt is that while looking out across the great darkness, he felt the overwhelming conviction that he would not be returning to France. Since then, he has increasingly felt that Rome is where his own god wants him to be, the

place where a very specific type of modern battle is abo[ut to]
be fought.

His type.

Louisa coaches Valentina on the route. 'You'll have to
cross the river twice because of our stupid roads. Go west at
the Popolo, south down the Lungotevere, all the way past
the Ospedale Santo Spirito and keep on until I tell you.'

'Frankly, I'm struggling with all this,' says Valentina. 'Not
the roads, the case. I thought I was making sense of the
Cassandra Complex, then *phew*, straight out of the blue,
another alter breezes in and turns everything upside down.'

Louisa smiles. 'I know. I find it difficult too. There is a
pattern, though.'

'There is?'

'Our patient is fixating on special women and events.
Cassandra is the name of a goddess.'

'And Claudia?'

'Almost as special. The Claudii were among the most
powerful and respected clans of ancient times. Just as the
Cassandra alter was caught up in the history of the Bocca
della Verità, Claudia is caught up in the epic chapter depicting the Rape of the Sabines.'

'Not rape as we generally refer to it,' adds Tom from the
back seat.

'No, that's right. It wasn't enforced intercourse. Well, at
least not initially. We're way back in history, probably the
days of Romulus, when Rome was mainly male and there
was a shortage of wives. The incident she was living out was
when Roman soldiers crossed into Sabine, the area we now
call Lazio, Umbria and Abruzzo, and carried off the
women. They brought them back to the Seven Hills to raise
families.'

The thought makes Tom shudder. 'Horrendous.'

'Well, actually, after the kidnapping, the women were

ated very well. Most became dutiful wives and mothers. hey probably wouldn't have returned even if they'd been able to.'

Valentina thinks she understands. 'An early form of Stockholm Syndrome?'

'Something like that.' Louisa points through the windscreen. 'That's Tiber Island, the Insula Inter-Duos-Pontes.' She half turns to Tom. 'It means the island between two bridges. We're on the wrong side of it. Claudia would have been on the eastern side, so you need to take the road to your left.'

Valentina turns the wheel and takes them across the Ponte Garibaldi, a fast modern carriageway that speeds traffic both ways across the Tiber.

For the next half-hour or so they loop back and forth over this causeway and the Ponte Cestio, a bridge that runs to Tiber Island from the south side of the river, leading to the Ponte Fabricio, which in turn connects the island to the eastern bank. During the day it's a walkway teeming with musicians, artists, hustlers and pickpockets.

Now it's deserted.

They park up and walk back and forth along the bridge and both embankments.

Just after midnight, a cruel winter wind begins to swirl off the Tiber and hits their faces like a million skimmed stones.

Tom insists Valentina and Louisa go back to the Fiat to get warm while he does a final search on the walkways running north and south of the old bridge.

They don't argue.

Tom isn't exactly sure what he's looking for.

A sign, he supposes.

Some strange clue, like the one he and Valentina found in the Sacro Cuore del Suffragio.

Anything that links the harsh, cold reality of this winter night to the ramblings of some mentally ill woman he's never met.

He tries to tune out the modern world – the street noise, the cars and the fashionably dressed couples hurrying home arm in arm. He wants to imagine the early days of Rome, the fear of the Sabines during a time when rape and pillage were as common as breakfast and supper. It was a savage age. An era when a pantheon of gods was thought to guide every mundane act and superstition cast its shadow over everyone and everything.

Walking the pavement along the Lungotevere, he realises that if, like Claudia, he was on the run from soldiers, he'd be on much lower ground, on the eastern bank of the river, so that he couldn't be seen from the vast open plains around.

A steep flight of stairs takes him down from road level and opens up on to a wide, potholed gravel path. To his right is Tiber Island. Straight in front of him is an isolated ancient arch in the middle of the Tiber. Behind him, the Ponte Palatino.

He begins to head towards the Fabricio, then on instinct turns and heads south. Close to the edge of the lower walkway, he sees there's a further drop on to a banking of rocks.

In places it's almost sheer, and threatens a comedic slip into the fatally icy water. Gradually it becomes less treacherous, and eases out into a gentler incline that he's able to work his way down.

Being next to the roaring black beast of the Tiber makes him nervous.

The river is astonishingly fast and dangerous.

He can easily envisage its spectral claws grabbing his ankles and sweeping him away to an unseen death.

Tom looks off into the darkness towards the Field of Mars, the place where centuries ago the most formidable army on earth trained for battle.

Lights of apartments flicker now where there were once the camp fires of soldiers.

He gets out the Maglite that Valentina gave him and shines it along the banking.

Soon he reaches the point where the Ponte Fabricio joins the Lungotevere dei Pierleoni. Out in the furious flow of the river there's a giant scrub of land between the bank and Tiber Island. Centuries ago, before it was eroded by the relentless Tiber, it was probably connected to either the bank or the island.

Tom turns away and steps over some rocks.

He shines the torch beam in front of him to make sure he doesn't twist an ankle and take a tumble. The ray catches something pink to his right.

Flesh.

A human face.

His heart jumps.

'*Vaffanculo!*' A male voice shouts at him.

A hand comes up to dark, angry eyes.

Tom can see the man now.

He's sitting on a patch of grass with his back against some rocks. His trousers are around his ankles and a woman is bent attentively over his crotch.

Tom diverts the light and walks on. He wonders whether the closeness to the murderous water adds a fetishistic frisson to the sex act he's just fleetingly witnessed.

He starts to work his way up the banking towards the street.

There's no grass now, just mounds of rocks, gathered as a sort of breakwater for the tide. He crosses them as you would stepping stones in a small stream, moving sideways almost as much as forward.

The bouncing Maglite picks out another couple.

No, not a couple, just a man.

A tramp sleeping off too much booze, or perhaps h sheltering from the wind and the abuse on the street.

Tom plays his light over the hobo.

At first his mind tricks him.

He thinks he can see all of the guy's outline.

But he can't.

He can only see a leg – and part of the man's right side and arm.

The rest of him is buried.

He's dead.

Tom puts the torch down.

It rolls off a rock and blackness hides everything.

He feels around for the Maglite.

Re-positions it.

The beam illuminates the corpse.

He steps closer to the body.

Carefully he pulls away several boulders and stacks them so they don't roll down into the river and lose any evidence that might be attached to them.

He still can't see the entire corpse, but he sure can smell it.

His own body momentarily blocks the light and his hands touch something.

Something soft and broken.

The skull has been caved in.

He fingers a crawling moist mass inside the shattered cavity and jerks his hand away.

Something is still slithering over his fingers.

Maggots and crustaceans that have been feeding on the brain.

He furiously rubs his hands on his jacket and feels them turning sticky and dry.

It takes almost a full minute for him to catch his breath and calm down.

He reaches for the torch and plays the light across the exposed cadaver.

bloated. Swollen. Pumped up.

Tom feels his stomach flip. He turns away and vomits.

He spits his mouth clean and tries to suck in fresh air.

He can't help but feel ashamed at his revulsion. His thoughts should be of sympathy and respect for the stranger who died in this barren place.

The ex-priest leans over the body, joins his hands and briefly prays. 'O Lord, let perpetual light shine upon this poor soul and may he rest in peace. Amen.' He crosses himself and looks around.

He knows he should step away now and phone Valentina. He certainly shouldn't touch the corpse or disturb the scene any more than he already has done.

But he can't do that.

The curiosity is too great.

He has to see.

He turns the body over.

Even in the darkness, it's obvious what's happened.

There's a gaping hole in the man's abdomen.

He's been stabbed to death.

37

The next hour is a blur.

Time speeds up to a frightening pace. Tom feels like he's caught in one of those trick photographs, the only static image in the centre of a blur of dashing bodies and streaky car lights.

After Valentina briefly inspects the mutilated body, she

calls Federico. He informs Central Contro. request for a support unit.

A taxi is called to take Louisa Verdetti home.

The entire scene is cleared of civilians and secu.

The automatic machinery of a homicide invest clicks into gear.

An officer is posted to control access and keep a log anyone who comes and goes.

A police doctor arrives to pronounce death.

The duty pathologist turns out.

A crime-scene photographer starts snapping away.

Forensics set up arc lamps and strategic walkways to access the corpse, and ensure the crime scene isn't compromised or contaminated any more than it already has been.

Officers begin working the street, taking statements from nightclub stragglers and local residents, who've already started to gather around the taped-off area.

Tom sits with Valentina in her Fiat.

He's still dazed. 'Is this going to be awkward for you?'

She manages the outline of a smile. 'Very.'

'I'm sorry.' He reaches out a hand and squeezes hers. 'What will you tell your bosses about us and how I came to discover the body?'

She shrugs. 'Everything. Or maybe nothing.' She turns to him. 'I won't lie to them, Tom. I've done nothing to be ashamed of and I'm not going to deny we're having a relationship.'

'I'm sorry.'

'Stop saying that. Without you, we would never have found this body. You've done nothing to be sorry for. Far from it.'

She knows he's right, though. Explaining how a foreign civilian came to be at the centre of a criminal investigation and found a mutilated corpse won't be easy.

...ks through the windscreen and sees Federico. ...his long wool coat is up, Elvis style, and he's ...lloons of cool breath up into a blood-orange ...y.

...gets out of her car and walks over to meet him.

'Buongiorno, Capitano.' He rubs his hands together for ...armth. 'Working with you really isn't conducive to getting any beauty sleep.'

She ignores the small talk and walks towards the body. 'We've got a dead male, pre-mortem injuries to the head and stomach, lots of post-mortem injuries as well, due to the fact that rocks were stacked on him. He's somewhere in his twenties or thirties – given his state, it's hard to tell.'

'Decomposed?'

'Not completely, but I think he's been in and out of the water. I guess the body was left when the tide went out, and of course it got covered later when it came in.'

'That would follow.' Federico starts to duck under the tape. 'How was it discovered?'

Valentina hesitates. 'A man walking by the river found him.'

'Vagrant? Down-and-out? You get a lot of them around here. They shelter from the wind and use the Tiber as a toilet.'

She still holds back. 'No. He's respectable. A foreigner. American.' Impulsively she starts to take the plunge. 'He's sitting in my car.'

'Great.' Federico senses an early trip home. 'You've already interviewed him then, taken a statement?'

'No. And it's best if I don't. You should do it, or have someone do it for you.'

Federico senses her awkwardness. 'Why?'

She stops walking. 'Look, I hope this can stay between us. I know the man. He's staying with me at the moment.'

Valentina looks through the windscreen and sees Federico. The collar of his long wool coat is up, Elvis style, and he's blowing balloons of cool breath up into a blood-orange dawn sky.

She gets out of her car and walks over to meet him.

'*Buongiorno,* Capitano.' He rubs his hands together for warmth. 'Working with you really isn't conducive to getting any beauty sleep.'

She ignores the small talk and walks towards the body. 'We've got a dead male, pre-mortem injuries to the head and stomach, lots of post-mortem injuries as well, due to the fact that rocks were stacked on him. He's somewhere in his twenties or thirties – given his state, it's hard to tell.'

'Decomposed?'

'Not completely, but I think he's been in and out of the water. I guess the body was left when the tide went out, and of course it got covered later when it came in.'

'That would follow.' Federico starts to duck under the tape. 'How was it discovered?'

Valentina hesitates. 'A man walking by the river found him.'

'Vagrant? Down-and-out? You get a lot of them around here. They shelter from the wind and use the Tiber as a toilet.'

She still holds back. 'No. He's respectable. A foreigner. American.' Impulsively she starts to take the plunge. 'He's sitting in my car.'

'Great.' Federico senses an early trip home. 'You've already interviewed him then, taken a statement?'

'No. And it's best if I don't. You should do it, or have someone do it for you.'

Federico senses her awkwardness. 'Why?'

She stops walking. 'Look, I hope this can stay between us. I know the man. He's staying with me at the moment.'

calls Federico. He informs Central Control and actions her request for a support unit.

A taxi is called to take Louisa Verdetti home.

The entire scene is cleared of civilians and secured.

The automatic machinery of a homicide investigation clicks into gear.

An officer is posted to control access and keep a log of anyone who comes and goes.

A police doctor arrives to pronounce death.

The duty pathologist turns out.

A crime-scene photographer starts snapping away.

Forensics set up arc lamps and strategic walkways to access the corpse, and ensure the crime scene isn't compromised or contaminated any more than it already has been.

Officers begin working the street, taking statements from nightclub stragglers and local residents, who've already started to gather around the taped-off area.

Tom sits with Valentina in her Fiat.

He's still dazed. 'Is this going to be awkward for you?'

She manages the outline of a smile. 'Very.'

'I'm sorry.' He reaches out a hand and squeezes hers. 'What will you tell your bosses about us and how I came to discover the body?'

She shrugs. 'Everything. Or maybe nothing.' She turns to him. 'I won't lie to them, Tom. I've done nothing to be ashamed of and I'm not going to deny we're having a relationship.'

'I'm sorry.'

'Stop saying that. Without you, we would never have found this body. You've done nothing to be sorry for. Far from it.'

She knows he's right, though. Explaining how a foreign civilian came to be at the centre of a criminal investigation and found a mutilated corpse won't be easy.

He looks confused. 'Staying with you?'

'Yes. He's a friend. Someone I've known for a long time.'

'Known as in *sexually* known?'

'That's none of your business,' she snaps.

'Well, actually it is.' He points to the body. 'It seems I'm investigating a murder, and it turns out the corpse was found by the lover of the officer in charge.'

Valentina has no real response.

'Can we discuss this later?' She rubs her arms. 'It's cold, I'm tired and I need you to examine the scene and interview a key witness. Okay?'

Federico thinks about pressing for more information, but decides to leave it. She's his boss. Admittedly a very strange one, but nevertheless, still his boss. '*Bene.*' He straddles the wall and crabs down the banking.

It's an area he knows well.

Most people born in the city do. He waits for Valentina to catch him up and sign them through the log point. He points to the nearby bridge. 'This isn't just a crime scene,' he says. 'You're standing at the very birthplace of Rome. This is the focal point of the greatest legend in all our history.'

38

By the time Tom has been interviewed and he and Valentina return to her apartment, it's already gone six a.m.

Going to bed seems pointless.

Valentina showers and changes for work.

Tom cooks scrambled eggs and brews coffee.

An old paint-splattered radio on the windowsill plays Europop into the brown ears of a dead plant.

The winter sun slowly warms up a spot at the breakfast bar where they both wearily settle and eat, hunched opposite each other.

Valentina is famished. 'Mmm, good egg!' she manages between her second and third forkful.

Tom laughs. 'Me or the scrambled?'

'*Scusi?*'

'It's a joke. There's an American – or maybe British – expression, in which you call someone a good egg if they're a really nice person.'

'Sorry. I think I may have left my sense of humour down by the Tiber.' She reaches across and touches his hand, 'Then you too are a good egg.'

'*Grazie.*'

Tom suspects she left more than just humour down there. A cop friend once told him that every murder scene stole a piece of his spirit.

He briefly takes her free hand and squeezes it. 'You okay?'

She smiles at him, 'It's a long time since anyone asked. I'm fine. You?'

He nods. 'Did I hear someone say that the place that poor guy's body was found is the *exact* spot where Romulus and Remus were supposedly found by the she-wolf?'

'That's what Federico said.' She places her fork on her clean plate and gives him a satisfied look. '*Very* good egg.' She grows thoughtful. 'Why? What are you thinking?'

'That island – Isola Tiberina – what was so special about it? I mean, I know the bridge is very old, and there's the legend of Romulus and Remus on the banks, but what about the island itself?'

He rises from his seat, still chewing. 'Mind if I use your laptop?'

'At this time? Shouldn't you be off to bed, try to get some sleep?'

Tom laughs at the idea. 'I'm so wound up, I may never sleep again.'

He flips up the screen of her Vaio, clicks it off standby and Googles Tiber Island.

While he's searching, Valentina clatters away in the small kitchen area, collecting dishes and running a bowl of hot soapy water to leave them in. With any luck, Tom will wash and dry them later.

'Okay. This is interesting, come and see.'

She pads over and can't resist wiping soap bubbles off her hands across the back of his broad neck.

'Hey!'

She rubs them off, kisses the wet patch and drapes her arms over his shoulders.

'It's the only island in the Tiber River,' says Tom, reading from the on-screen text. 'Linked – as we know – by the Fabricio Bridge, which joins it to the Field of Mars, and also by the Ponte Cestio.' He jabs the monitor. 'Now look here, *another* legend.'

'Don't get so excited; there is a legend in every corner of Rome.'

'You may be right. This one concerns one of the last Etruscan kings. He was overthrown and his body dumped in the Tiber, a final act normally reserved only for lowlife sinners. Folklore has it that Tiber Island was created from a mound of silt and driftwood that formed over the body of the tyrant king.'

'Nice.' Valentina can't resist a sick pun. 'At least even after death he had his own form of king-dam.'

Tom might have laughed had he not been reading on. 'Listen. For centuries the island was a dumping ground for the worst of criminals and the contagiously ill. Then when

137

Rome was hit by a plague, some sibyl – which I think is a Latin adaptation of the Greek word *sibylla*, meaning prophetess – recommended that a temple was built there to Asclepius in order to stop the diseases spreading.'

'Who?'

'Asclepius, Greek god of medicine and healing.'

Valentina is impressed. 'You knew that?'

'I did. You remember the other night you said sex was the panacea for all ills?'

She blushes a little.

'Well, Panacea was Asclepius's daughter. While her name is used – and abused – much more in modern life, it was her father who dominated Roman and Greek times. The Rod of Asclepius is still a powerful astrological symbol and is the thirteenth sign of the sidereal Zodiac.'

'What's so special about it?'

'It's a staff entwined with a serpent.'

'Oh God,' she exclaims with high melodrama, 'not more snakes and devils.'

'It's not what you think. Not Satanic. Asclepius was a brilliant physician, so brilliant that he reputedly brought people back from the dead. You'll find his symbol is still used in America by the Medical Association, the Academy of Psychiatry and Law and the US Air Force Medical Corps.' Tom suddenly thinks of more organisations, 'In fact, the British Royal Army Medical Corps also use it, as do the Canadian Medical Association and even the World Health Organisation.'

'Okay, I surrender under the weight of all those mighty medical bodies. But what's your point? What's the significance of the serpent and the staff in relation to our case?'

'I'm not sure I can give you a perfect answer. But consider this: Asclepius left the legacy of a powerful cult that has influenced the most important medical minds in the world. The serpent and the staff are symbolic references to the oxymoronic fact that medicine is built on using drugs that in small doses heal but in big doses kill. In short,' adds Tom, 'in the modern world, doctors play god. They're the ones with the everyday powers of life and death.'

39

Louisa Verdetti arrives at work exhausted.

She hasn't slept.

The first thing she does is head to Valducci's office and tell him everything about her overnight adventure with the Carabinieri.

The administrator says little as she explains about the body and possible links to the patient on their ward. 'I'm sorry. I should have called you and informed you of the police request for me to accompany them.'

'You should. You exposed both yourself and the hospital.' He swivels in his black office chair and looks out of the window as he talks. 'Are they likely to interview you formally?'

She shrugs. 'I don't know. I suppose so.'

He turns to face her. 'It's not an offence to help the police, but I do want to be kept in the picture. Is that too much to ask?'

'Of course not.'

'Okay.'

She starts to raise herself from her seat.

'Before you go, I want to compare notes on our increasingly famous patient.'

'*Scusi?*'

'Diagnostics. You keep telling me she's DID and I keep thinking schizophrenia, so let's try to settle the matter so that when your police friends start asking, we're on the same page.'

What he's saying makes sense, although she'd really rather not do it right now.

Valducci senses her discomfort. 'Louisa, if your diagnosis won't hold water when analysed by a friend and colleague, then what hope have you in the stormy sea of external critique?'

'I'm sorry. It's just that I had such a bad night and I have a migraine.'

'Then a contextual review of the symptoms of both schizophrenia and dissociative identity disorder will clear the fog for you. What diagnostic tools have you used so far?'

She's annoyed that she's being asked. 'DES, DDIS, SDQ-20. We've been through the whole tick list on amnesia, depersonalisation and derealisation before making a final diagnosis.'

'Good, then you're well prepared. I want you to list unique symptoms that are not indicative of schizophrenia. Let's start. Symptom one . . .'

She grinds her brain into first gear. 'Identity confusion. Suzanna consistently has identity problems. These are obviously manifested in the form of her alters.'

'Obviously,' he answers sarcastically. 'Schizophrenics also have a lack of a sense of identity and can't see their role in society. So no uniqueness there. Point unproven. Next.'

'Schneiderian symptoms and delusions. Again these are evidenced in the presentation of multiple personalities and even include bodily changes from alter to alter.'

'Hmm, I'm not so sure they do. Any physical changes could be psychosomatically caused. Besides, schizophrenics are notoriously delusional – our wards are full of people who think they are being chased by aliens or are on the run from the government or the mafia.'

'I suspect some of them might well be.'

Valducci almost laughs. 'Point unproven. Next.'

'Comorbid diagnoses.'

He stares at her. 'You know your patient to be clinically depressed?'

'No. I'm clutching at straws, but I strongly suspect it. It's likely she—'

'Not good enough. Besides, even if full depressive or manic syndrome coexisted with your dissociative syndrome, it still wouldn't be unique. Schizophrenics have more than their share of mood episodes. Point unproven. Next.'

Louisa feels totally stressed. 'Okay. We can do this all day. I throw up a DID symptom and you knock it down by matching it to schizophrenia, but *that* doesn't resolve any-thing. Suzanna doesn't have many of the things schizophrenics have.'

'Such as?'

'Catatonic behaviour.'

'Good.'

'Other psychotic symptoms.'

'Such as?'

'Well – her thinking isn't characterised by incoherence.'

'Good.'

Louisa dries up.

She's out of ideas and her head is pounding. She rubs the back of her neck and hopes to massage a brilliant thought or remark out of her dulled brain.

'More, come on!'

The best she can manage is a confession she really hoped not to make. 'I recorded my last session with her.'

'What?'

'It was mainly for diagnostic purposes, though I hoped it would present a platform to therapy. Let me send it round to you. Please watch it and tell me what you think.'

He looks like a hog that's found a truffle. 'I'd be delighted to!'

She stands and makes for the door. 'I'll be surprised if – once you've watched it – you don't believe she's a genuine DID case.'

He smiles wryly. 'I won't be.'

Louisa reaches the door and turns. 'Thanks for your understanding about last night. I'm grateful. And I really will make sure you're kept in the picture from now on.'

Valducci doesn't reply.

He knows that if he gives her enough rope, she'll hang herself.

And with a little luck, the Carabinieri might just help her do it.

40

Professor Enrico Ferrari sits at his desk in the crime lab, facing his biggest problem of the morning.

It's one of those dilemmas where you have to eliminate something but you're really torn between what to keep and what to lose.

In his case, it's a big decision.

Raspberry doughnuts or chopped fresh fruit.

Despite going into the coffee shop to buy only an espresso, he ended up also buying the fruit tub and the boxed treats.

It wasn't really his fault.

Temptation mugged him close to the checkout. A little voice whispered in his ear that he was a big guy and that he wouldn't function properly on just chopped fruit. It was his duty to make sure he was on the ball.

So he left with the doughnuts as well.

Now it's a case of diet or no diet. He should eat the fruit and show his willpower by tossing away the box of fun.

But that's not going to happen.

He licks sugar from his fingers.

Wow!

The jammy centre explodes in his mouth. Warm and sweet, crunchy and sugary, and then magnificently chewy deep-fried pastry.

Wow! Wow! Wow!

He knows it's a million calories a swallow and he fully realises he'll be internally imprisoned in fatdom for his sins, but for the next three minutes he doesn't care.

There are no tissues close at hand and he's still in search of a box when Valentina arrives unannounced.

She's the only thing he can imagine tasting better than a second doughnut.

God, for her he would even have missed the fruit and made do with only coffee.

'*Buongiorno*,' he says cheerily. He scans for Federico, but there's no sign of him. 'Are you alone?'

She raises an eyebrow. 'Is that okay? My momma said I was allowed out if I was careful crossing the road.'

He spreads his palms apologetically. '*Scusi*. I just expected Federico.'

She doesn't explain why he's not with her. 'A few hours ago a body was found down near Tiber Island. It's at the morgue now, but last night I asked for a rush blood job on the clothing.'

'Aah, the great quest for *ketsueki-gata*.'

Valentina is completely thrown. 'Ket what?'

'*Ketsueki-gata*. The Japanese believe that blood types are indications of personalities. I'm type A. That means I am earnest, creative and sensible, perhaps with the failing of being a little fastidious.'

'Fascinating, but unfortunately not my type. The type I'm interested in was swabbed off a gutted corpse in the early hours of this morning.'

His hopes of flirtation disappear. 'I've only just come in, so I don't know if it's been done yet.' He brushes his sugary hands together as he walks past her into the corridor. 'Follow me. I'll hunt down the paperwork and we'll see.'

Valentina trails him down one grey corridor after another.

'Do you have a name for the victim?' he calls over his shoulder.

'No. It was male. The samples will have come into the labs around four a.m., so hopefully you don't have too many cases of murdered unknown men at exactly the same time.'

'Let's hope not.' He tilts his wrist and sees it's only just gone nine. 'That shift will have gone home. You'll be lucky if the report's been done.'

'I am.'

He stops walking and turns around. 'You are what?'

'Lucky. I'm one of those people. Lucky in love, lucky in life.' She half corrects herself. 'Well, mostly.'

Ferrari believes her. She's made captain, is super-smart, and when it comes to looks, well, he'd crawl naked through broken glass just to lick dirt from the soles of her feet.

'What?' Valentina frowns at him.

'What what?'

She laughs. 'You're staring at me. Freakishly. What's wrong?'

He shakes himself out of his trance. '*Mi dispiace*. I'm just dazed by your beauty.'

144

'Oooh, good line!' she says, her face bright with mischief. She steps tantalisingly close to him and raises a long, slender finger close to his mouth. 'If I didn't already have a man whom I adore, and if you didn't have jam and sugar spread all over your chin like a two-year-old' – she rubs it away with two fingertips – 'then I might just fall for a line like that.'

The open-jawed scientist is horrified. Fat fingers fly frantically to his chin and he rubs so hard his flesh burns. 'Breakfast!' he blurts. '*Scusi*. I was having my breakfast when you came in.' An open door saves him further embarrassment. He lurches into an office that is already alive with the sound of printers and telephones. Several administrators and secretaries look up as he buries his head in a stack of in-trays on top of a cabinet near the entrance.

Valentina patiently watches him rifling the documents, aware that half the office is watching her watching him. Young secretaries are admiring her clothes and how she has a senior scientist scrabbling around like a puppy on a lead.

'Here!' shouts Ferrari, like he's recovered a ball and brought it back to its owner. 'Blood tests from the clothes of an unidentified male victim found in the early hours, and it has your name as the officer in charge.'

'*Grazie.*' She nods over-graciously to the papers in his hand. 'A little more information, perhaps?'

Ferrari is now actually ahead of her. He knows she's looking for a connection between this new body and the tests on the woman and her sword that his labs have been running. He silently scans columns and paragraphs, then looks up. 'Bad news, I'm afraid. The body last night was covered in only one type of blood, O positive. That's currently the most common type in Italy and actually in most of the world.' He wobbles his hand like it was an unbalanced seesaw. 'At some times, and in some countries, A positive is most popular. But not right here and not right now. Either way, I'm afraid the blood on your new victim does not match that of any of the samples we took for you the other day.'

Valentina feels drained. 'Not any of them?'

'No.' His eyes show sympathy. 'Let me recap for you. The new sample is O positive. The blood on the prisoner's gown we tested was AB. The blood on the sword taken from your prisoner is Rhesus positive and the blood on the severed hand is Rhesus negative. You've got quite an impressive spread of blood types there.'

Valentina shakes her head. She's not impressed at all. She feels like she just lost on the lottery. A full set of unlucky statistics.

She came to the lab hoping for answers, and all she's got is more questions.

Lots more questions.

41

La Rambla is a Spanish bar, slung like an abandoned Vespa on the corner of a busy street between Piazza San Pietro and Ospedale Generale Santo Spirito. Alfie Giordano has been coming here and eating bad tapas and big breakfasts since he was first posted to Rome.

He and Tom sit on tall chrome and leather stools in the traffic-dusted window, remembering old times, while the owner, Josep, treats them to *colazioni* large enough to feed most of the city.

'Valentina has this case linked to a church in Cosmedin.'

'The Santa Maria?'

'That's it.'

Alfie knows it well. 'Dedicated to the Virgin Mary. Also known as Santa Maria in Schola Graeca – Our Lady of the Greek Community.' He passes Tom a tiny espresso cup and saucer.

'But it's famous for this giant mouth?'

'Home to the Bocca della Verità.' Alfie grasps his left wrist in his right hand. 'And to thousands of stories about liars and deceivers having their hands cut off.'

'Well, it has another story now. Valentina's case involves a hand being found in the portico near the Bocca.'

Alfie plops a cube of brown sugar into his coffee. 'I haven't read anything about it.'

'Good. I think that's how she wants it. They arrested this woman, Suzanna Grecoraci, but she seems mentally ill.'

'People who cut other people's hands off usually are.'

'Valentina doesn't think she did it. Even though she wrote some strange first-person story about being a noblewoman in ancient times called Cassandra who was having her hand chopped off at the church.'

Alfie stirs his coffee. 'That seems an unbelievable coincidence.'

'I agree.' Tom thinks about it as he stares out into the street. People have their collars up as they walk by. A scarf is flying from the back of a kid's neck like the flag of a ship in a storm.

Alfie sips his espresso and clinks the cup down on its saucer. 'The Santa Maria is also the resting place of the remains of St Valentine.'

'Really? I should have known that.'

'I've seen the skull. Quite impressive. Though not at all romantic, of course.'

'I guess they do a good trade around St Valentine's Day.'

'Absolutely packed.' Alfie gives him a thoughtful look, 'Talking about love, is it serious between you and Valentina?'

Tom almost splutters espresso. 'In what way serious?'

'In the way that one day I might be called upon to give my services.' He makes an elaborate blessing with his hand.

His friend looks horrified. 'You're *very* premature with that one.'

'Ah, *premature*. That's an interesting choice of word. It means not only that you wouldn't rule it out, but also that you don't *want* to rule it out. Interesting. You could therefore interpret the word to mean "hopefully one day".'

'Hey, a guy who gets to say Mass in St Peter's doesn't need to go touting for work. Anyway, I think she's already married. To her work.'

'Such a shame.' Alfie turns down his bottom lip in mock sympathy. 'This bizarre case is keeping her away from you?'

'It's even more bizarre than I've told you.' Tom pours orange juice for them both. 'Murder, ritual dismemberment, a suspect with dissociative identity disorder and more pagan cults, myths and legends than Tolkien ever dreamt of.'

Alfie laughs. 'In Rome, everything's connected to ancient pagan cults, myths and legends. The entire place was built on them. And – come to think of it – it was also built on more than its fair share of murders and mutilations.'

'That's pretty much what Valentina said.'

'Bright girl. You should marry her.' He scrubs the end of a croissant in some Tuscan cherry jam. 'DID is interesting, though. Are you sure it's multiple personalities and not possession?'

'I thought of that. From what I've gleaned, the alter personalities are psychological, not spiritual. They seem to be a defence mechanism to cover childhood trauma rather than individually evil entities.'

'Can you definitely rule out that at least one of the alters isn't demonic?'

Tom doesn't have to think before answering. 'No, I can't do that. I haven't seen all of the alters, so it would be foolish to be so categorical.'

Alfie rips open a croissant filled with vanilla cream. 'What's the murder? The handless victim in Cosmedin?'

'No, that body hasn't turned up yet. This was last night. A man, found down at the Ponte Fabricio.'

Alfie licks cream off his fingertips. 'I've lived long enough in Rome to know that the Fabricio is practically the birthplace of the empire. What's the connection between this and the rest of the case?'

Tom tries to backtrack. 'The woman who Valentina arrested, Suzanna, spoke about a body beneath the bridge during her time as this alter called Claudia. Valentina, me and the woman's shrink drove down there, and I found the corpse at exactly the place she described killing someone hundreds of years ago.'

Alfie's intrigued. 'So maybe this Suzanna killed him in real life and then couldn't deal with the reality of what she'd done and tried to turn it into a fantasy.'

Tom shakes his head. 'The body was cut up and its skull smashed in. I couldn't imagine any woman doing that, let alone Suzanna. She just doesn't seem like a killer to me.'

'Perhaps you've not seen enough killers to know what they look like.'

'I've seen my share. Remember, I did pastoral care in several Californian prisons and worked the Death Watch at San Quentin. I know they don't have "killer" tattooed on their foreheads.' He catches Josep's eye behind the bar and gestures politely towards their cups for more coffee. 'Do you know anything about the Sacro Cuore del Suffragio and the Museum of Souls in Purgatory?'

'A little.' Alfie finishes the last of the creamy croissant. 'I think some of the exhibits are far-fetched. When you go in there, you feel more like you're visiting a circus tent than a sacred room.'

Tom felt the same way. 'Well, the words *Master, Mistress, Temple* and *Deliver us from evil* were found on the wall of a confessional.'

'Seems a good place to leave those kinds of words.'

'But these were in Latin. And they were the same words used by one of the suspect's other alters, the one called Cassandra, who met her fate at the Santa Maria.'

'Cassandra?' Alfie taps his fingers on the tabletop. 'Cassandra was the Greek prophetess of doom.'

'I know. And on top of that, there was a drawing of a triangle in the plaster.'

'Some kind of symbol?'

'Perhaps. Valentina said the woman she'd arrested had a triangular pendant the same.'

'I imagine lots of women have triangular pendants.' Alfie sounds dismissive. As an afterthought, he adds: 'I remember reading a long time ago that triangles used to symbolise fertility.' He draws the shape in the air, 'It was supposed to represent the pubic region and had quasi-religious connections to the womb.'

Tom nods. 'I said the same to Valentina. The Greeks used it to represent the vulva of the Mother Delta.'

'You're just trying to lead me astray by saying vulva, aren't you?'

Tom laughs. 'Vulva, vulva, vulva.'

Alfie crosses his two fingers to form a crucifix. 'Get thee behind me, Satan!'

They both laugh. 'Of course the sight of a triangle makes me instantly think of a pentagram, but I guess that's because of our religious training.'

'*Pentagrammon, pentagrammos,*' says Alfie, showing off his Greek, 'Five-lined, five-sided. You can trace those damned things back to Mesopotamian writings three thousand years before the good Lord first wriggled his toes into a pair of sandals.'

'Pythagoreans called the pentagram Hygieia, after their goddess of health.'

Alfie's not to be outdone, 'Aah, but medieval neo-Pythagoreans – whom you could argue were not Pythagoreans at all – claimed the pentagram represented the five classical elements.' He draws out the points in the air, 'Four of these represent fire, water, wind and earth and the fifth is the supernatural, the spirit.'

Tom's had enough of the intellectual jousting. 'Look, does any of this make sense to you? Can you see the wood for the trees, because I sure as hell can't.'

Alfie fondly rotates the small espresso cup in his hands. 'Not really. Symbols always mean secrets. Secrets often mean cults. Cults usually attract crazies.'

Tom doesn't see where he's going. 'So?'

'You know how coffee drinkers congregate in cafés like this when they want their fix of the really hard stuff, the excellent stuff?'

'Sure.'

'Well, it would follow that cults and those who believe that symbols have everyday powers will also gravitate to their own centres in order to experience rituals of excellence.'

'Temples, you mean?'

'Exactly. And in Rome, that may even include old temples that have been pulled down.'

'Triangular pendant wearers worship at the temple of triangular pendants. I guess I find the place under T in the phone book.'

Alfie laughs. 'T for temple or T for triangle?'

'This is madness.' Tom begins to peel the label off a bottle of water on the table. 'We have to remember that the poor woman at the heart of all this is mentally ill. She has a severe form of multiple personality disorder and doesn't even know her own name or whether she's married or has kids.'

Alfie takes the bottle off him and gives him the look a mother might give a naughty child. 'Maybe your poor woman isn't totally mad. It's possible that she's using her alters to leave clues, to cry out for help. Perhaps she hopes someone like you – or your future wife – will decode them and help her.'

Tom scowls at him. 'I *was* going to ask you to have dinner with us; now I think it's too dangerous to have you around.'

'*Mea culpa.*'

Tom thinks things over. What Alfie is saying makes sense. If Suzanna's caught up in a cult, she'll be terrified of talking about it, maybe even uncertain she should betray it. The historic alter personalities and the strange clues all point to a desperate cry for help. He finally takes a slug of the wonderfully bitter espresso. 'You said temples.'

Alfie nods.

'I guess there are dozens in Rome. Is there anything like a triangular temple?'

'I know Rome well, but not that well.' Alfie slides down from his stool and steps towards the bar. 'Josep, can we use your computer a minute?' He nods to a new Apple iPad kept under the owner's admiring supervision on a counter near the till.

It's Josep's pride and joy.

'*Si*, but Father, you be careful, yes?' He hands it over like he's being forced to pass a newborn child to a drunken rugby player.

Alfie cradles it and smiles. 'I'll treat it like it was your soul.'

Tom's no technophile, but even he can't help but be seduced by the iPad's sleek design. 'That really is cool. I've heard about these but never seen one.'

'Well, now you get to see – and to touch.' Alfie shuffles his stool around so they can both access the tablet as he opens up its Safari browser. He taps in the keywords: Temple. Triangle. Rome.

And wishes he hadn't.

Up come useless links to Temple University in Philadelphia, the Chattanooga Triangle and an obscure inventor called Leonard Temple Thorne.

The next page is more valuable. It references the use of triangles in the history of Rome and Greece.

'Dive in a bit and let's have a look,' suggests Tom.

Alfie clicks open page after page. There are passages detailing the use of the symbol all the way back to the Bronze Age.

They get sidetracked by articles on Euclidean geometry, and then they chase the use of the symbol through palaces and sacred caves in Crete and mountain sanctuaries and tombs in archaic Greece.

'Let's narrow it down,' suggests Alfie, his tone giving away the fact that he can't take much more browsing. 'I'll just type in "Temples in Rome" and see what we get.'

Two million entries – that's what they get.

Tom sits back in amazement.

'Wuuu! Talk about needles and haystacks. I thought you were narrowing things down.'

'Me too.' Alfie clicks open a Wikipedia link. Up pops an alphabetical guide to temples, cult centres and pagan structures across the Eternal City. 'So, what have we got here?' The temple links are displayed according to area and also according to each person or deity they're dedicated to.

'There seem to be seven areas.' Tom runs his finger across the iPad. 'Campus Martius – the Field of Mars – the Capitoline Hill, the Palatine, Forum Boarium, Roman Forum, Imperial Fora and the Fora Venalia.'

'Yikes,' is the best Alfie can manage.

'And then there are these five other categories.' Tom glides his finger over the super-smooth screen. 'The Temples of Cybele, Elagabalium, Marcus Aurelius, Minerva Medica and Virtus.'

'Double yikes.'

Bright sun is now pouring through the window of the bar. The two friends can feel it on their faces. The warmth makes Tom yawn and reminds him of the sleep deficit he's run up. Settlement time is coming up fast. 'I'm wiped out. I'm going to get the bill.' He eases himself off the chair and goes to pay Josep. 'Will you write down the sites for me, Alfie, so I can give them to Valentina?'

'Sure.' Alfie jots them down on a white paper napkin, then follows Tom to the bar, iPad held carefully in both hands. He goes behind the counter and puts it back on charge. Josep's hawk eyes watch his every move.

They say goodbye with much handshaking and back-slapping and slip into the bright, late morning sunlight.

Neither of them notices the man across the road.

The one who's been watching them for the last two hours.

42

The local cops and mortuary staff call her Nonna.

Professoressa Filomena Schiavone *is* actually a grand-mother, so she doesn't at all mind the nickname.

But it hasn't always been like that.

There was a time when the medical examiner worried almost obsessively about growing old.

Turning thirty was a trauma. The first grey hair had come and agonisingly signalled the end of her girlish world.

Forty was horrendous. A time when everyone was getting divorced or realising their marriages would end childless. It was the first time in her life she'd felt remotely uncertain about the future.

Fifty was catastrophic.

It was an age she lied about. A milestone she denied having reached for as long as believably possible. And looking back, that was quite a while.

Despite hitting the big half-century mark, she still had admirers. Even after the death of her husband four days before her fifty-fifth birthday.

But sixty changed everything.

At last, she learned to accept things.

Life was short, and getting shorter by the moment. It was there to be lived to the full.

Compared to the loss of Mario, white hair and the pull of gravity on flesh were nothing. She'd been rocked by his death. Shaken to her core. She'd been a recluse for five years, finding time only for her daughter, two grandsons and of course her work.

But not now.

Now she's out dating again.

Yep, as ridiculous as it sounds, Filomena's 'playing the field', as she calls it. And right now she's walking out with a former lawyer who's seventy next year.

Life is good.

Or at least it seems that way until she bends over the remains of the corpse that her staff have left on her slab.

The floor is splashed with brown river water and the sauce of death is spilling from his lifeless orifices.

All manner of molluscs and crustaceans have taken up lodgings in the gaping wounds she's gazing down on.

The body is that of a reasonably well-nourished male in his early thirties. He is about five feet eight inches tall and would have weighed around eleven stone had his stomach not been opened up and half his organs washed away. She lifts his hands and sees that many of the finger bones have been broken. Perhaps a sign of torture. Possibly the result of rocks or stones being piled upon him post-mortem to conceal the corpse. A cracked rib cage, broken jaw and damaged eye socket are also consistent with the latter. A little later she'll have x-rays done. Looking at the prints of bone fusion is still one of the best ways of ageing a corpse.

Filomena manoeuvres the cadaver on to its side and notes corresponding pressure injuries on his back. It's not the worst case she's ever seen, but it's up there. The scalp shows a number of minor abrasions to the front and side, but in particular to the rear, where a huge piece of bone has been smashed in. Fragments are inside the jagged cavity of the skull, but for the moment it's hard to be sure whether the wound was made by an attacker before death or was the result of rocks being piled on the corpse.

She lays the body flat and examines the stomach wound.

It's even more peculiar.

The man has not just been stabbed; he's been opened in some kind of ritualistic way. It makes her think of hara-kiri, the Japanese suicide ritual, and a lecture she once attended on the samurai tradition of *seppuku* – stomach cutting. Noble practitioners were supposed to plunge the sword into the abdomen and then move the blade left to right in a slicing motion.

She continues with her examination and ignores the smell of the bloated body. It certainly looks like the cut was made from the victim's left. Marks on the lower ribs show the blade was dragged horizontally, then, by the looks of it, pulled downwards at forty-five degrees for about seven inches. She makes notes on a pad and wonders whether a weapon was found alongside the victim. She's not been told of one, and its absence would certainly indicate murder rather than suicide.

A picture forms of the victim being hit from behind and then stabbed in the stomach as he fell to the ground.

She looks again at the wound.

That theory doesn't seem to fit.

The cut marks against the ribs are upwards, as though the victim was still vertical.

Something else isn't right.

Filomena pulls up the flap of abdominal flesh and jumps back.

From inside the stomach cavity, two dark baby mice bolt for freedom.

She screams like a teenager.

Within seconds, an orderly is in the room.

The best the *professoressa* can do is point at the rodents, both of which are now trying to hide beneath the neck of the corpse.

Roberto, a man in his early thirties, traps them with a stainless-steel bowl, and with all the speed of a magician, palms the offending creatures and heads outside.

The other thing he hides professionally is his smile. Nonna's phobia about mice is legendary, and unfortunately the morgue is not without its unwelcome intruders.

After a brief respite, Filomena shouts Roberto back in.

Only when the cadaver has been checked and declared mouse-free does she resume her work.

Setting a time of death is difficult.

The corpse has been exposed to the elements and has probably been covered by the tide of the Tiber. It's also been masked by rocks, affording a little shelter.

She always tells the police: 'time of death is precisely

between when the victim was last seen alive and when the corpse was discovered'.

The lower part of the torso is heavily damaged by rocks, and the knees and shins show extensive injuries.

She diligently marks them on a standard anatomical drawing.

Only now does she realise that the gaping wounds to the man's head and stomach have drawn her attention away from something she would otherwise have instantly found fascinating.

The man has no scrotum and no testicles.

She looks closer. This isn't a recent injury. In fact, it isn't an injury at all.

It's been done very deliberately.

Judging from the scars, there's been a crude operation to castrate him.

The deceased is a modern-day eunuch.

43

The apartment seems strange without Valentina in it.

Empty. Silent. Soulless.

Tom uses the bathroom, strips and falls into bed.

Maybe his life would also be strange without Valentina in it.

Interesting thought.

He remembers what Alfie had said. You could interpret 'interesting' to mean he hoped one day to be with her for the rest of his life.

Maybe that's true.

He puts his sentimentality down to exhaustion and pulls the quilt up tight around his neck. A long, deep sleep will give him perspective. It always does.

He squashes his pillow a few different ways until it seems right, and shuts his eyes.

It feels wonderful to rest. His tired muscles and joints are relieved to be laid out flat and still.

A couple of hours' sleep will do him the world of good.

But he's not going to sleep.

He knows it.

His eyes are shut, but there's no way he's going to sleep.

One of those awful moments is happening. One where the more you try to sleep the more you know it's not going to happen.

Finally, he gets up.

He wanders to the lounge, grabs Valentina's Vaio and brings it back to bed.

A distraction is all he needs.

His brain will stop buzzing and his eyes will grow weary and then he'll nod off.

Fantastic.

He surfs the net for ten minutes. He checks out the *LA Times* sports pages and scrolls through the latest on the Lakers and Dodgers. He even finds out how the Clippers, Kings and Ducks are doing.

Sleep still seems a long way off.

He can't even glimpse it hiding around the corner.

Tom reaches down the bed to recover his trousers. He pulls out the napkin that Alfie wrote on at La Rambla.

He might as well start a virtual search of the temples.

A is for Apollo Sosianus.

The site takes him to pictures of the Field of Mars – just walking distance from where he found the murdered man.

The site shows that nothing remains of the temple except three tall columns. Accompanying text says there was once a cult of Apollo, established outside the *pomerium*, the sacred boundary of Rome ploughed by Romulus.

Tom Googles Apollo and sees nothing he doesn't already know.

The guy was a superhero. As famous in Greece as he was in Rome. Son of Zeus and Leto, brother of Artemis, the god of everything from archery to medicine, music to poetry.

He gets a bad feeling as he looks at a second-century marble of Apollo holding a lyre and a python.

Snakes always give him bad feelings.

But there are no triangles. No rituals or stories of severed hands to link the deity with his modern-day case.

He goes back to the home page.

B is for Bellona.

This is a temple close to that of Apollo and was dedicated to a goddess of war who seemed to have Etruscan origins. Her followers were said to have syncretised their beliefs with those of another sect, that of the Magna Mater. The web page shows a painting of Bellona by Rembrandt, and Tom wonders if he's ever seen a woman look so masculine. Below it is a bronze by Rodin that makes her look a little more feminine.

He flicks back to pictures of the temple.

It's in ruins. Nothing except broken chunks of marble and busted pillars.

Only a single podium still stands as a reminder of the powerful building that was once there.

He closes his eyes for a second and thinks about what C might be for.

He doesn't find out.

Sleep finally comes, right at the wrong moment.

44

A windy morning miraculously morphs into a mild and sunny lunchtime.

It's a long way until spring but is still warm enough for Valentina to take her tray of food to a table on the patio outside the police canteen.

She's more than ready for the break.

The morning has been brutal.

First the bad news from the forensic labs, then the strange report Federico has just phoned in from the mortuary.

A dead eunuch?

What sense does that make?

She takes a tomato salad, two slices of fresh rustic bread, an espresso and a glass of water off her tray.

While she eats with just a fork, she stifles a yawn and scribbles in her notebook.

The body by the Tiber is a major development, but it's also a huge distraction. All the real clues to cracking the case surely lie in the multiple personalities of the woman they are calling Prisoner X, the thin slip of a thing confined to a hospital bed at the Policlinico.

Valentina downs her espresso and quickly sketches out names, ages and the briefest of details presented by the suspect's several personalities.

The small chart makes fascinating reading.

PRISONER
X

Personality 1
'Suzanna
Grecoraci'
(Married – 2
children)

Personality 2
'Suzanna
Fratelli'
(Aged 8 – aka
'Little Suzie')

Personality 3
'Cassandra'
(Noblewoman –
Bocca della
Verità)

Personality 4
'Claudia'
(Sabine woman –
Tiber Island/
dead eunuch)

Suzanna and Little Suzie seem to be the two contemporary personalities, while Claudia and Cassandra – both classic Roman names – are the 'legendary' alters.

Little Suzie alluded to the fact that there were many others.

Are there really *more*? Questions stick like bugs on a windscreen.

Why do two of the personalities use the name Suzanna? Valentina thinks there's a psychological reason – maybe a bridge to her real life. It could be that Suzanna is the name of someone who's been kind to her, supported her through difficult times, or perhaps it's someone she admired.

Valentina has already made sure the Carabinieri's records team has checked out the surname Grecoraci.

They drew blanks.

So too did the hospital's own enquiries.

No one with that name fitting Suzanna's age and physical description has shown up on any official records anywhere across Italy. But to the best of Valentina's knowledge, no one has run a check on Suzanna Fratelli. She makes a note to action the search – and also for Cassandra Fratelli and Claudia Fratelli.

The sky is starting to cloud over and the warmth is disappearing from the patio. She heads back inside and leaves her food tray on a lopsided rack by the canteen door. She takes the stairs rather than the lift and thinks about calling Tom before she enters what she knows will be a dreadful meeting with Caesario.

Predictably, Armando Caesario's office is one of the grandest in the building. Occupying a south-facing corner position with enough floor space to double as a parade ground.

The wooden floor is dark and polished and creaks as she walks over it. To her left is a seating area, marked by a large Indian rug full of deep reds and two chestnut-coloured leather settees. The rest of the room is dominated by a giant mahogany desk straight in front of her. The small man sitting behind it is backlit by a large sash window with a view across the city. Old hardback chairs covered in faded brown leather stand to attention to the front and flanks of the major's desk. This is not a room where anyone is meant to feel at ease.

'Sit!' Caesario mumbles through his chins while he finishes writing.

There's a knock on the door behind Valentina.

'Enter!'

Even before Valentina turns her head, she knows who it is.

Lieutenant Federico Assante walks noisily across the wood. Without speaking, he takes the chair at the end of the desk. The one nearest Caesario.

The major downs his pen. He clasps his hands and looks up at them both. His face bears the expression of a disappointed father who's gathered his wayward children for a scolding. 'Captain Morassi — it's been brought to my attention that you have without authorisation involved a civilian in a major criminal investigation and as a consequence probably compromised our enquiries.'

Valentina gazes blankly at her superior officer. 'I don't believe anything has been compromised, sir. With respect, the civilian's involvement advanced our enquiries rather than compromised them.'

Caesario sighs and leans back in his big leather chair. 'How so?'

Valentina shoots Federico a withering look. 'The man you are referring to is Tom Shaman. He worked with me on the serial murder case in Venice that you know of and he proved invaluable to our units there. If you wish, I'm sure Major Vito Carvalho will vouch for his integrity. My—'

'*Ex*-Major Carvalho,' interjects Caesario, 'and to be honest, I don't wish. Captain, I didn't ask you for a character reference, I asked you to substantiate your claim that this man advanced our enquiries.'

'Sir, Tom discovered the body. He happened to be with me when I visited the Ponte Fabricio with Louisa Verdetti, the clinical director of the Policlinico Umberto.'

'Stop!' Caesario raises his hand like a traffic cop. 'Let me back up here. Lieutenant Assante, were *you* not the first officer I sent to the original crime scene in Cosmedin?'

'Yes, sir. I was, sir.'

'And as a local officer with local knowledge, did I not give you an express command to keep me fully briefed until this matter was cleared up?'

'Yes, sir, you did, sir.'

'Good. I'm glad we're clear about that. So how is it, Lieutenant, that until this morning, you did not tell me anything about the expanded scale of the inquiry and the involvement of civilians and non-Carabinieri medics?'

'I didn't know, sir. Not until afterwards.'

Valentina tries to jump in. 'With respect, Major—'

'Be quiet, Captain. Keeping your mouth shut is the best way you can show me respect. I'll come back to your explanation in a moment.'

Caesario angles his body towards Assante. 'You were

saying, Lieutenant – you didn't know until afterwards . . . finish your excuse.'

'Captain Morassi called me at home and explained that she had visited the clinic. She said she had spoken to both the doctor and the prisoner and consequently visited the area near Tiber Island where the body of a male was found. It was only when I arrived at the scene that I realised there was a relationship between the captain and the civilian who found the body.'

The major again halts the conversation with his traffic cop hand. 'Explain, Captain.'

'Explain what, sir?' She knows exactly what he means. And what's going on. The sexist pig is dressing her down. Humiliating her. Showing her his station house is run by men – men who don't take kindly to women being given positions of senior rank.

Caesario puts his elbows on the desk and then leans forward on pale, chubby forearms. 'Let's start with your relationship with this man, Tom Shaman. Explain it to me.'

Valentina feels Assante's eyes on her. The disloyal son-of-a-bitch is enjoying every second of this. She swallows and stays calm. 'Tom and I have a *sexual* relationship. A recent one. He is currently living with me.'

Caesario can't help but look smug. 'I see. And . . .'

'Is this a disciplinary inquiry, sir?' Valentina puts her hands on the edge of his desk and pointedly leans towards him. 'Because if it is, then I believe I should have been properly notified, and I haven't been.'

The major can barely believe her cheek.

Valentina's not done. 'Major, I must also formally object to the manner in which you have encouraged Lieutenant Assante to report directly to you on an operational matter that you personally called me in on and asked me to take charge of.'

Now it's Caesario's turn to try to control his anger. 'Oh, must you?'

Valentina stands. Her chair scrapes noisily across the wooden floor. 'Sir, to be clear, I wish to put on record the fact that I believe your instructions undermined my position, and I feel I should inform you that I will be writing contemporaneous notes of this meeting and seeking representation.'

'Sit down, Captain!'

Valentina remains standing.

'Sit down – that's an order!'

Valentina sits. She pulls the chair up under her legs and feels herself shake.

'Assante, get out. Leave us alone.'

The lieutenant rises, salutes and leaves without comment.

The door at the far end of the room clicks shut. Caesario stares across his desk and draws a long breath. 'What are you doing?'

Valentina is fiddling nervously with her cell phone.

'I'm sorry, sir. I forgot to mute my phone and there was a call coming in.'

He can't believe the girl. Insolent. Distracted. Unfocused. 'Put it down! For God's sake, woman, how unprofessional can you be?'

Valentina all but drops the BlackBerry on the edge of his desk. 'I'm not unprofessional, sir. Far from it.'

Alone now, with the door shut, his anger boils over. 'Not unprofessional? I'll tell you what you are. You're a joke, Morassi, that's what you are. If the top brass weren't under political pressure to have some skirts wearing senior rank, you'd be out doing traffic duty. Correction, traffic duty is too important a job for women; you'd be filing reports.'

'Sir!'

'Don't be so damned insolent, Captain. When a senior officer is talking, you sit and listen. Do you understand me?'

'Yes, sir.'

'Good.' His voice becomes almost normal. 'Look, I don't know who you impressed or *how* you impressed them, but I didn't want you here and I still don't want you here. Your face is plastered across magazines, my press office is log-jammed with requests to talk to you. You are a liability, Captain.'

'Sir, it was the press office that insisted I did the *Vanity Fair* shoot. I assure you I have no desire to have cameras pointed at me.'

'Enough!' He drums his sausage fingers on the desk and grits his teeth. 'Let's be straight with each other – officer to officer. You and I both know that you have no future here. I need first-class officers, not political pin-up girls. You're in the Carabinieri, not Berlusconi's cabinet.' He lets out another pained sigh. 'Listen to me. I'm going to give you some advice. This is a good point for you to put in a trans-fer request. I'll give you some time off until we get you posted elsewhere and you can spend it at home with your new lover.' He smiles patronisingly at her. 'How does that offer sound?'

Valentina stares down at the big wooden desk. Caesario's fat little fingers start drumming again, just centimetres from the cell phone he berated her for trying to turn off. She picks it up and turns it in her hands. 'I think your offer sounds fine.' She presses the touch screen on the phone and holds it up towards his face. Caesario's voice rolls out from the phone: '*If the top brass weren't under political pressure to have some skirts wearing senior rank, you'd be out doing traffic duty.*'

Valentina hits pause and looks him in the eye. 'I don't think that's the most damning part of the recording, sir, but I'm sure that even that bit is sufficient to end the career of a misogynistic bully like you.' She turns the BlackBerry off and slips it inside her jacket.

Caesario sits back in shock.

He can't believe what she's done.

A *man* would never have done that. A man would have taken his rollicking and done the decent thing. He can't believe she's been so sneaky, so cowardly, so duplicitous.

Valentina's voice is calm and deliberate. '*Officer to officer*, Major, let me be straight with you. I am not about to walk away from my position here, or this case. So – unless you want a copy of this recording to be the centre point not only of your *own* disciplinary inquiry but also of news reports from one end of Italy to the other, from this moment onwards you'll afford me your total trust and support and allow me to do my job.'

Caesario is still speechless.

'I need an answer, Major.'

He nods.

Valentina stands. 'And for the record, the phrase *total trust* includes me exercising my discretion as to whomever I wish to involve in this case.'

He nods again.

'Thank you, Major. Your support and confidence in me is greatly appreciated.' She allows herself a small smile, and makes sure he sees it before she turns and heads for the door.

45

There are close to thirty busy desks in the open-plan office, which houses two serious crime squads. Federico Assante is sitting slap bang in the middle of all the action. He's talking confidentially to colleagues around him, telling them of the impending demise of his captain.

Phones are suddenly hung up and the chatter of the office vaporises. Valentina has emerged from Caesario's office at the end of the corridor.

Dead woman walking.

The only noise that can be heard is her feet on the floor.

From ten metres away her eyes lock in on Assante and she can see he's struggling to even acknowledge that she's there.

She reaches his desk, calmly folds her arms and looks down at him. 'Make sure you put all your files, memory sticks, actions and contacts on my desk within the next hour.'

'*Scusi?*' He swivels in his chair, looking around the room to show his audience his disbelief.

'Stand when you're addressing a senior officer.'

He hesitates.

Valentina leans across him and picks the phone up off his desk. 'You want me to call Caesario and have him *make* you stand?'

They both have the attention of the entire office. A distant phone rings, someone picks it up and immediately disconnects the caller. No one is going to miss *this*.

Assante slowly gets to his feet and stretches like it's something he was going to do anyway.

She waits for him to finish.

'You're off the case.'

Across the room there are gasps.

'Get all your stuff together – logs, records, contacts, electronic files; anything that has relevance to what I'm working.'

'You're joking, right?'

'I only joke with friends, Lieutenant, and you've made it very clear that's not what you are.'

'I don't understand.'

She laughs. 'Oh, but you do. You thought that by under-mining me you'd win favour with Caesario and further your career. You gambled and you lost.' She shrugs like it's of no concern. 'I guess you played dirty because the stakes were high. So in your case, the price you pay is being dumped from this investigation by the female officer you sought to embarrass. Life is rough. Then again, if you were a woman in the Carabinieri, you'd already know that.'

Applause breaks out from behind her. Valentina turns to see several women standing and clapping,

She swivels back to Assante. 'We're done. I'm going out now and will contact you later with the name of the officer I want you to hand over to.'

Valentina walks the rest of the room to the corridor amid a cacophony of wolf whistles and thunderous applause.

46

The video recordings make fascinating viewing.

Hospital administrator Sylvio Valducci still isn't convinced they prove the existence of dissociative identity disorder, but they're certainly jaw-dropping enough to attract some sub-stantial new grants. The bit where the patient seeks shelter under Verdetti's desk is priceless. Pure theatre.

Who knows, they could even be good enough to land some plum keynote speeches at top medical conferences around the globe.

For him, of course, not Verdetti.

The clinician remains a thorn in his side. He quite hoped

she'd make a terrible mess of this case, then he'd have an excuse to discipline her.

But it's not working out like that.

Even the way she acted with the police doesn't warrant an official warning. At best she was being public-minded. At worst she was slow in notifying him of an instant demand of the Carabinieri. She'd have walked any disciplinary hearing on that one.

Such a shame.

He'd certainly have liked to take the wind out of her ambitious young sails and make his own life easier. The last thing any under-pressure administrator wants is a mouthy clinical director who is trying to do more and as a result spend more every damned year.

Valducci puts the recordings back in their covers and stores them on his shelves.

The distance from his office to Verdetti's amounts to a lift ride and a short walk down a couple of corridors. He's making it to flatter her. To throw her off-guard. He learned long ago that it's politically smart to seize an opportunity to be nice to those you like the least. It allows you to manipulate them towards your own ends, especially when they're tired and stressed.

The eyes of a young nurse at the ward station almost pop out when he rounds the corner. In her fluster she stands up and knocks a plastic cup of water over her paperwork.

'Wipe it! Wipe it!' he barks. 'And don't let it get near the damned computer.'

Eva Boscono quickly mops with tissues, while he leans on the top of the reception station and makes no effort to help her.

'I'm sorry, sir.' She tosses the last of the Kleenex into the waste basket beneath the desk and rubs her wet hands together. 'How can I help you?'

'I'm looking for Dr Verdetti. I just walked past her office and it's in darkness.'

'She left about an hour ago, sir.' She glances down at a calendar on the desk top. 'She's at a funeral. I believe she will be back late this afternoon.'

He grimaces. She never mentioned the funeral to him. Not that he doubts she's properly booked the time – though he'll check, of course. 'Never mind. Tell her I came round. Get her to call my secretary and arrange to see me.'

'Yes, sir.'

He starts to walk away and then has an idea. 'The patient in room 116, how is she at the moment?'

Eva scrabbles through a tray of damp paperwork. 'I'll just find her notes for you to see.'

'I don't *want* to see her notes,' he snaps. 'Just tell me how she is. Surely you know enough about those in your care to have an instant overview?'

Eva reddens. 'I'm told she slept well. This morning when I saw her she was subdued but not sedated. She complained of a headache about three hours ago and was given ibuprofen. An hour ago she was fine and was sitting out of bed, reading and drawing.'

'Drawing? Drawing what?'

The question throws her. 'I don't know. She likes to doodle; it seems to calm her.'

'She had a pen?'

'No. She has crayons to draw with, but there's nothing sharp in her room when she's alone. We're careful about self-harming.'

'Good. Take me to see her.'

'Now, sir?'

He looks exasperated. 'When else? You want me to make an appointment and come back at a time that better suits you?'

'No, sir.' She scurries from behind her desk. 'Please follow me.'

The Carabinieri guard outside the door takes their names and then allows them in.

Nurse Boscono closes the door and introduces her boss to Suzanna. 'This is Signor Valducci. He is the administrator, the man in charge of the whole hospital.'

He smiles at Suzanna, and then turns to the nurse. 'You can leave us now. I'd like to be alone with the patient.'

47

Valentina parks up at the morgue and makes a phone call before she heads inside to see Medical Examiner Filomena Schiavone.

It's not Tom she's calling, but another man.

One she thinks of almost as a father.

'Vito?'

'*Si.*'

'Vito, it's Valentina. How are you?'

'I'm good. Very good. And you – how are you?'

'*Bene. Va bene.* But I could do with your advice.'

And so for ten minutes Rome's newest Carabinieri captain tells her old boss about her brush with her sexist new boss and the dismissal of her disloyal lieutenant.

Former Major Vito Carvalho listens wryly. Discrimination and bullying are nothing new to him. He built his early career in the old days of the armed forces. A time when women were taken on to nurse or file or cook, but very little else.

'He's going to come for me, Vito. He'll be hurting now and lying low, but at some point Caesario is going to come for me. What should I do?'

'You're thinking of handing in the recording anyway?'

'It's on my mind. Maybe if I go to the colonel, it'll lay down a marker. I'll say I don't want to press charges, don't want to cause difficulties, but I'll ask for a guarantee that I'm not going to be set up or wrongly accused of anything.'

'Politics is a dirty game, Valentina.'

'I know. But what choice do I have but to play?'

'None. But don't go to the colonel, leave it with me. I have an idea of how to buy you a little protection, but I need to call some old friends first before I guarantee anything.'

'*Grazie*. I'm so sorry to bother you. It's just that I've always respected—'

'Shush, I'm glad to help.' He laughs. 'It feels good to still be needed by my former staff.'

Now it's her turn to lighten up. 'I think I'll always need your counsel, Vito. I'm pretty much what you made me.'

'You mean troublesome and awkward?'

Valentina laughs now. 'I guess so.'

He's more worried about her than he lets on. 'Have a think about what you did to that lieutenant. Slicing and dicing a colleague in front of a crime squad can have a way of backfiring.'

'What do you mean?'

'Well, I'm sure most people fully agree with what you did. I certainly do. But you can be sure there'll be some who don't. His friends, for a start. They'll stick by him. They have to. That means you made a whole new pack of enemies today. Players who know the local turf and the local game a whole lot better than you do.'

Valentina never thought of it like that. 'You mean the cloud that I thought had a silver lining actually turns out to have an even cloudier lining?'

He laughs. 'Maybe not that bad. I just suggest you give it a little more thought, and work out a smart way to make sure the cloud doesn't turn to rain and leave you surprised and soaked to the skin.' Vito's said his piece and knows it's now time to change the subject. 'I saw your parents a couple of nights ago. They looked very well. Said how proud they are of you.'

She smiles. 'I think they'd be proud of me if I was working tables for five euros an hour.'

'Of course they would. That's the privilege of being parents.'

Valentina sees the time on the car dashboard. She's about to be late for the appointment she's made with the ME. 'I have to run, Vito. Thanks again for your advice. I am indebted.'

'Yes, you are. Never forget it. I'll call you when I have an answer on that other matter. *Ciao!*'

'*Ciao!*'

She's still smiling as she locks the car and walks into the hospital.

If only her new boss could be like her old boss.

Then life would be perfect.

48

'So, who are you today?'

Sylvio Valducci smiles at the cleverness of his opening question as he lowers himself on to a hard bedside chair.

The young woman sitting a metre from him says nothing.

If she's faking, he knows he'll be able to tell.

He can always tell.

The little actress might be able to fool Verdetti, but not him. 'I asked you for your name. Who are you?'

The answer comes creeping back in the voice of a frightened child. 'Suzie.'

Valducci leans forward on his elbows. 'Good. Thank you for telling me that. Suzie, my nurses say you've been drawing. Can I see? Would you like to show me what you were drawing?'

'No.' She puts her hands across a sheet of crayoned paper on her lap.

'No?' Valducci smiles and pretends to peek at the picture. 'What is it? I'd really like to see.'

She looks down at her knees. 'I don't want to show you. I don't have to show you if I don't want.'

'Then tell me about it, Suzie. What's in the drawing?'

She thinks for a minute, then gives in to the trade-off. 'Romans.'

'*Bene*. I like Romans. What are they doing in your picture?'

Grudgingly Suzie takes her hands away and lets him see.

Valducci doesn't know what to make of it.

It's a scribble.

Thick red and orange lines rubbed hard on to the paper like a three-year-old would. There's a sort of stick man in black lying down as though he's sleeping, but nothing to suggest he's Roman. Then there's a bad drawing high in one corner of a star that looks more like a crucifix. 'Can you tell me what the picture is about, Suzie?'

She shakes her head and looks down at her knees again.

'Why not? It's lovely; I'd just like to understand it a bit more.'

'It's not lovely, it's horrid.' Nervously she twists her hair around her fingers. 'It's not supposed to be lovely.'

'It's not? Why not?'

Suzie bites her lip and buries her chin further into her chest.

Valducci kneels in front of her and sits back on his heels so he can see her eyes. 'Please don't be frightened of me. I'm not going to hurt you. I just want to help.'

She turns her head to one side to avoid his gaze.

He lets out a sigh. 'Why won't you talk to me, Suzie?'

She finally looks his way. 'Because you're a stranger. Momma told me not to talk to strange men; they might be bad people.'

Valducci tries to reason with her. 'Aah, now I see. Normally Momma would be right. But not this time. This time is different, because you've been brought to my hospital, and all my doctors and nurses are trying to help you. So you see, I'm not a bad man.'

'Momma says you're bad.'

He's not so easily put off. 'No, Suzie, you said your momma had told you not to talk to strangers because they might be bad men, and that's usually right. But as I just explained, you were brought here to me so I could help you, so I'm not bad, am I?'

'Momma says you're bad.'

Something about her tone intrigues him. 'When did Momma tell you that?'

'Now. She told me just now.'

He looks around melodramatically and then back at the patient.

'Is your momma inside this room, Suzie? Only I don't see her.'

Suzie shakes her head and painstakingly avoids any contact with his eyes.

'I thought not.' He lets out a disappointed sigh. 'You shouldn't lie. You know we really can't help you if you lie to us.'

Suzie doesn't look up. 'I didn't lie.'

He looks quizzically at her.

'She's not inside the room. She's inside *me*.'

Valducci doesn't see it coming.

Suzie's right hand flashes.

Two fingers jab hard into his eyes.

He topples backwards on to the floor.

'Do you see me now?' Suzie bellows, standing over him, her alter changed.

Valducci clutches his face. His pupils are burning. A red cloud billows up behind his eyelids.

'Tell me! Tell me, imbecile! Do you see me now?'

49

Tom sleeps for several hours.

He wakes curled up in Valentina's bed, still thinking about a hundred things all at once.

Valentina.

Temples. Goddesses. Cults.

Valentina.

Triangles. Churches. Corpses.

Valentina.

He's in that state of warm fuzziness where he could fall back asleep, or – with considerable willpower – get himself together.

He thinks he should grab a coffee and try to do something with the remainder of the day before she comes home.

But he doesn't.

Sleep wins.

Tom drifts back into even deeper dreams.

He sees the tall black necks of gondolas bobbing like black swans through the mists of Venice. Somehow the thick fog has rolled inland from the lagoon and is filling the alleyways and shops and restaurants. Everyone is choking and drowning in the gathering darkness. He sees himself with Valentina in a café, and the dark fog is creeping dangerously towards them. They're holding hands like Hollywood lovers and running from the relentless sea of smoke.

It's all so strange, and yet so real that he actually feels like he's choking.

Then he realises he is.

He sits bolt upright in bed.

Gasps.

His lungs are filled with smoke.

The apartment is covered in blackness.

Thick, deadly smoke is pouring into the bedroom.

He jumps from the quilt and resists the urge to open the window. If there's a fire outside the room, then the draught will only fan it.

He drops to the floor and looks through the crack beneath the door.

Red and orange flickering lights.

Flames!

The apartment is several floors up. There are no trees close to the window. No fire escape. The only way out is through the lounge and the front door.

Tom's eyes are stinging. His throat is raw. The lack of oxygen is already making him weak as he tugs the quilt off the bed and steps into the small en suite. He quickly soaks the quilt in the shower and wraps several wet towels around his head and hands. His feet are bare and he knows there's no hope of finding his shoes.

He returns to the bedroom and very carefully opens the door to the rest of the apartment.

Palls of dark smoke and fire seem to turn like dragons and swirl towards him.

For a moment he's thrown.

He'd expected the seat of the blaze to be confined to the kitchen, no doubt caused by him forgetting to turn something off on the cooker.

But that's not the case.

The flames have already engulfed the entrance area. A wall of fire stands between him and the safety of the front door.

There's no more time to think.

Wrapped in the quilt, he runs into the heart of the blaze.

The front door is burned to cinders.

He crashes through the charred frame, ripping into a hinge as he stumbles out on to the concrete landing.

The quilt is on fire.

Tom sheds it.

One of the towels wrapped around his hands is burning like a torch. He drops it and steps away.

The fresh, cold air fills his lungs so sharply that it hurts.

People are running past him. Screaming. Carrying children in their arms or on their backs. They're bowling each other over in the crush to get down the narrow stairwell and out into the street.

Tom runs barefoot after them. Glass cracks beneath the soles of his feet.

By the time he reaches the safety of the street, most of the apartment block is ablaze.

Some streets away are the frantic klaxons of approaching fire engines.

Only now does he care about the fact that he's completely naked.

50

It's the first time Valentina has seen the corpse under any decent lighting.

Down by the bridge under a mix of Carabinieri flashlights and forensic arc lamps, it looked more like an alien life form than anything human.

Now – spread out on Filomena Schiavone's autopsy table – the cadaver looks pitifully real and strangely feminine.

What little remains of the dead man has almost no body hair and no eyebrows.

'*Ciao!*' shouts the ME incongruously, as she happily scurries around the far side of the morgue, almost oblivious to the strip of pallid butchered flesh separating her from Valentina. 'You've come on a very busy day.' Nonna sounds energised. 'We've still got two traffic incidents from this morning, an auto-erotic fatality from last night, an overdose and a new domestic murder.' She points to a set of stainless-steel drawers against the wall. 'There's a full report on your case for you over there. I gave a prelim copy to your lieutenant while your officers were taking prints from the body. Now let me run you through the highlights.' She pauses and smiles. 'I used to say *let me run you through the bullet points*, but then we had a couple of Mafia cases and there really were bullet points, so it was a little confusing.' She laughs at her own story.

'I can see it would be,' Valentina agrees.

'Reasonably well-nourished male,' continues Nonna. 'He tapes out at one hundred and seventy-eight centimetres. Would have weighed around seventy-two kilos, so we're talking of a fit young man in his late twenties.' She stops for a moment. 'You know about him being a eunuch?'

'I do,' says Valentina, 'but as I'm a complete stranger to eunuchs, can you explain to me exactly what it means?'

'You're right to ask. Too many officers presume too much. Traditionally eunuchs were not only castrated males; they were men who'd been castrated early enough to be hormonally affected. Despite, or maybe as a result of their increased femininity, they often made very trustworthy and exceptionally fierce guards. Of course they were more commonly used in both Rome and Greece as body servants and even officials.'

Valentina pulls a face as she looks at the corpse. 'Sounds horrendously unnecessary.'

'Indeed. Though I've met a few men I'd like to have done it to. Interestingly, the word doesn't come from the act of castration. It goes back to the Greek word *eunoukhos*, describing the keeper or guard of a bedchamber or harem.'

Valentina nods towards the table. 'Can you tell if our victim was castrated recently?'

'He wasn't. The scars are old. I suspect he was mutilated in his teens.'

'Urgh!'

'It hasn't been done in a hospital. By the looks of it the entire scrotum, including both testicles, has been tied up with a very tight band and then cut off. The skin remnants beneath the ligature then rotted as the flesh above the band healed. It's a highly dangerous procedure and hugely painful. It's amazing he didn't get gangrene.'

'What a life he had.'

'And quite a death, too. Come around this side and I'll show you how your eunuch met his end, no pun intended.'

Valentina negotiates her way to the top of the table.

The victim's head is elevated on a movable white block and the *professoressa* expertly readjusts the corpse to expose the area she wants Valentina to see. 'The skull has a large hole in it – large enough for you to fit your hand in.' Schiavone puts her fingers against the brutal opening and Valentina flinches. 'There is also evidence of minor blows to the head. Fractures can cross the suture lines of the skull but not other fractures, so I'm sure these are separate injuries.'

The ME shifts around the table to show the front of the skull. 'Now things get interesting. This frontal area, including the nasal cavities and eye sockets, is pitted with soil and grit.'

Valentina doesn't entirely see the point. 'Meaning?'

'Your victim was lying face down when someone threw a large boulder on to the back of his head, causing the damage we've just looked at.'

'To kill him? To finish him off?'

'Possibly.'

'You can't tell if he was alive at that time?'

Nonna looks a little uncertain. 'Technically I'd say alive, but very, very close to death. What I mean, though, is that this final act might not have been one of mercy, of putting the man out of his suffering. It may have been a display of anger. Someone still full of rage and needing to vent it.'

'Classic overkill.'

She considers the phrase. 'Perhaps.'

Valentina points to the cadaver. 'So he's lying face down when he's hit with this rock, then more are piled on top of him. That doesn't make sense, because when the body was found, it was face up.'

'*Fermare!* You're jumping to conclusions.'

Valentina holds up her hands. '*Mi dispiace.*'

'It's okay. Most good detectives jump to conclusions.' She puts her gloved fingers to the corpse's face. 'The dust and grit engrained in the skin wasn't from the river area. I've sent samples off for environmental analysis but honestly, I've examined enough bodies from the Tiber to categorise those samples without a microscope. Your man was killed somewhere else, somewhere more urban. It was post-mortem that the body was brought to the river and buried beneath rocks under the bridge.'

Valentina is wondering why. She can imagine someone disposing of the body *in* the river, but not going to all the risk and trouble of getting it there and then burying it *beside* the water.

Possibilities come to mind: maybe the killers were disturbed; maybe one or more of them fled and the one left behind simply couldn't move the corpse any further.

Schiavone removes the head block and adjusts the corpse's shoulders so it is flat again. 'Now the abdominal injuries. At first I thought these were self-inflicted – hara-kiri or some other form of *seppuku* – but after X-rays and closer examination, I'm convinced that's not the case.'

Valentina stares at the wide cavity. 'Don't fatal stab wounds usually look more frenzied? These appear controlled.'

'Good point. I didn't say the injuries weren't ritualistic; I can't be certain. But I am sure that they're not self-inflicted.' The ME walks around so that she's standing opposite and close to Valentina. She holds out her left hand. 'Imagine a very strong and sharp knife, short sword or bayonet in this hand.'

Valentina nods.

'The attacker held the weapon with the blade vertical.' She puts her index finger against Valentina's stomach. 'There are a number of slash marks, but the fatal incision is on the victim's right side.' She presses until she feels bone. 'The blade was driven in here, twice I think, and nicked the last rib.' She draws her finger across to the other side of Valentina's body. 'A deep cut was then made horizontally straight across the thoracic diaphragm to the left side of the victim.' She presses again, this time on the bottom of the other side of Valentina's rib cage, causing her to wheeze a little. 'You exhaled because I'm pressing on your diaphragm. You get a slight blow here and we say you've had the wind knocked out of you. You get knifed here and it's going to be fatal.'

'What exactly is the diaphragm?'

'I'm glad you asked. I like officers who ask. The diaphragm is a sheet of internal muscle that extends all the way across the bottom of the rib cage and separates the thoracic cavity – the area containing your lungs and heart, et cetera – from the abdominal cavity – the area that includes the stomach, liver, kidneys and such like. You still with me?'

Valentina looks down at Schiavone's finger still stuck painfully just beneath her rib cage. 'Thankfully, I am.'

'*Bene.*' Nonna makes a downward slice with her finger. 'This second movement of the blade precipitated a shift in the way the attacker held the weapon. The grip needed to be adjusted to get enough force to cut from the thorax to the pelvic brim.' Once more she presses hard against Valentina. 'En route, this movement sliced through the spleen and part of the duodenum.' She moves a little closer and then draws her finger up at an angle towards Valentina's diaphragm. 'This final movement completed the disembowelment. It came through the outer part of the duodenum and through both the gall bladder and liver. Another ten centimetres and the killer would have carved out a completed triangle.' She removes her finger and looks at the corpse. 'As it was, only a flap of skin held the last of the cut flesh together.'

A triangle?

Valentina wonders if the shape is a coincidence.

She's heard so much about damned triangles, she's now seeing them everywhere. 'Is this kind of cutting significant or

185

famous in any way?'

'What do you mean?'

'Is it a medical procedure? Maybe an old way of doing autopsies?'

Nonna shakes her head. 'No. Not to my knowledge.' She thinks for a second or two. 'I really can't recall any medical procedures that resemble this.'

Valentina looks at the dead man and tries to picture his final moments.

Instinctively the ME follows the detective's train of thought. 'As you just saw from our crude re-enactment, this kind of homicide is very personal. It has to be done at close quarters in order to be so precise. Had I really been attacking you, you would have been going crazy – wriggling, curling up, falling to the ground, fighting for your life – and I would have been hacking at you with the knife and creating wounds elsewhere. There's no forensic evidence to suggest that anything like that happened.'

'So the victim was restrained?'

'Not necessarily.'

Valentina looks confused.

'He was dead. Or at least very close to death. And judging from the marks of the knife against the bone, I think it fair to say that he was on his back when most of the cutting was done.'

Valentina's cell phone rings.

There's a strange number on the display.

Whoever it is, they'll have to wait.

'Have you seen anything like this before, Professoressa?'

Nonna half laughs. 'Of course. Ritually disembowelled eunuchs are turning up all the time here in Rome! Fitting them in around those other plentiful cases of severed hands found in church porticos is a real drain on the unit.'

186

'Stupid question. Sorry! I was just hoping you might have something more to add.'

Nonna starts to move things away for her next case. 'I'm afraid not. I really wish I had some old case notes or a similar experience I could recall to help you, but I don't.'

'*Grazie.* You've helped a lot.' Valentina walks round and picks up the report the ME left on the drawers for her.

'A little advice.'

Valentina stops in the doorway.

Filomena Schiavone points to the body. 'Whoever did this is extraordinarily dangerous, Captain. Be careful – really careful. The only way I ever want to see you back in here is standing up and asking questions.'

51

On her return to base, Valentina checks her missed phone message.

It's from Tom. Made from a hospital pay phone.

There's been an accident, a fire at her apartment, and he's fine but the apartment is not. It's gutted.

So is she. Apparently she's homeless.

But he's safe, that's the main thing.

She'll call the hospital and arrange to pick him up just as soon as she's dealt with a more pressing matter.

Café Luigi is just around the corner from headquarters. Lots of cops go there for an espresso before work or a beer at the end of the day.

Some probably even go for a beer before the start of their shift.

It's here that she's told Lieutenant Federico Assante to meet her.

He's sitting in the corner.

His hands are wrapped around a mug of black tea.

Valentina unbuttons her short dark wool coat, hangs it over the back of the cheap chair and sits down. Assante looks miserable and worried.

Good.

He's every right to feel that way.

She peels off her black leather gloves. 'Twenty minutes from now, I'm due to be with Human Resources, reviewing a list of lieutenants who can be freed up to help me.' She stares sternly into his eyes. 'I don't want to make that appointment. I want to give you a second chance and have you help me solve this case. Is that something you want?'

He looks surprised. 'In the office you said—'

'I know what I said. I don't have short-term memory problems. Now do you want to work this case or not?'

He doesn't have to think for long. 'I want to work it.'

'*Bene*. Then there are conditions.'

He thought there might be.

'You work your sexist ass off. You put in more hours than you've ever done and you don't grumble or complain about anything to anyone. Understand?'

He nods.

'*Perfetto*. Now I'll tell you what you get in return. If you put in a hundred per cent effort and a hundred per cent loyalty, I'll be the first to sing your praises. Credit where credit is due. But if you screw with me – if you go behind my back and start playing politics – then I'll wreck your career so badly you won't be able to get a job shining Caesario's shoes by the time I'm done. Understand?'

'Understood.'

'*Va bene*. Then we're a team again.'

'*Grazie.*' There's an awkward silence, then he adds, 'Just so you know, the major insisted that I report directly to him. It was his idea, not mine.'

'It doesn't matter.' She stares at him again, a steely gaze that shows he's still on thin ice. 'He won't do it again, and neither will you. From now on we're going to be judged by results, not by whether we're male or female or friends with the major or not.'

'*Si.*'

'Now in the interests of our new relationship, how about you get me an espresso?'

He's up from the table and standing at the bar within seconds.

Valentina smiles. Her old boss, Vito Carvalho, was right. Rethinking what to do with Assante was a smart move.

52

Late afternoon, and a sombre Louisa Verdetti finds herself in Sylvio Valducci's office.

He's tired. His eyes are bloodshot and he needs to keep wiping them with a tissue. Louisa doesn't care enough to ask if he's all right. Besides, mentally she's still at the graveside of her former school friend, a mother of three, who two hours ago was lowered into the earth less than six months after being diagnosed with breast cancer.

The big C. The most feared letter in the alphabet.

They caught it late – far too late – and the tumours had spread all over her body.

'Have you seen it yet?'

Louisa looks up. 'I'm sorry. Have I seen what?'

Valducci triumphantly slips the crayoned drawing across his desk. 'Suzanna's latest masterpiece. Or should I say Suzie's.' He looks like the cat that got the cream. 'What do you make of it?'

Louisa frowns at it. 'Where did this come from?'

'I saw the patient when you were out. I just wanted to personally look in on her, and she was in the middle of drawing this.'

'You saw her without consulting me?'

He shrugs. 'It is my right to. I can see any patient I wish.' He looks at her challengingly, then adds, 'It may please you to know that she manifested many of the signs you mentioned, including violence.'

Louisa now understands the injuries to his face.

Valducci taps the paper and repeats his question. 'What do you make of it?'

She looks at it again. 'Anger?' She runs a finger along the hard red and orange crayon ridges. 'She's pressed so hard here, you can see where the crayon's snapped and left thick wax.' She looks up at her boss and realises she strongly resents him interfering in what she regards as her own special case. But it's more than that. Worse than that. She feels as though her privacy has been invaded, as though he's violated her by intruding into the intimacy she was building with her patient. She looks down at the picture again. 'So what did she tell you about this? What is it, a fire of some kind?'

'Interesting, I didn't see it as a fire.' Valducci swivels the paper back. 'No, she said it was Romans.'

'Romans? It's *always* Romans.'

Valducci can see that she's distant. 'Are you all right?'

It's a strange question.

If a friend had asked her, she'd say no.

She'd most likely open up and discuss the hangover of grief she's got from the funeral, but she's not going to mention that to Valducci.

'I'm fine. Just a little down because of the service this afternoon.'

Valducci jabs a finger in the corner of the drawing. 'I just realised something. I thought this black mark here was some kind of star, but now you've suggested that this is a fire, I can more easily imagine it as a cross, a crucifix, perhaps in a Roman church or temple, with the fire all around it.'

Louisa finally shows interest.

It certainly is a fire.

There's definitely a religious symbol in there and something else as well. A human shape. 'Did she say who this figure is? It looks like a man lying down.'

The administrator is feeling inspired. 'Maybe a statue on top of a tomb. Perhaps she was drawing a fire in a church where a famous saint is buried.'

Louisa remembers the prophetic nature of the story about the murder by the bridge over the Tiber. 'Have you called the Carabinieri?'

'No.' He kicks himself. Had he not been bathing his stinging eyes, he probably would have done. He certainly should have done. It may even have enabled him to completely hijack her case. 'I wanted to discuss it with you first,' he lies.

'I'll call Morassi, the captain I was with last night.' She reaches for her handbag and fishes inside for her cell phone.

'I have an idea,' announces Valducci, his face filled with childish enthusiasm.

Louisa hooks out her phone and plunges her hand back into the bag to find Valentina's card. 'What's that?'

'Forget the cops for now. This is strictly clinical. Doctor–patient confidentiality. If it works, it will help both Suzie and your Carabinieri friends.'

53

By pure coincidence, Tom Shaman ends up being treated at the Policlinico, the same hospital where Valentina spent much of the morning with the ME.

Valentina learns of his whereabouts on the phone and tells him she has a few things to take care of before coming to collect him.

Sitting in A&E reception nursing a brown plastic cup of poor coffee, Tom is pleased to have emerged from his ordeal relatively unscathed.

Apart from a gashed shoulder, a cut foot, a little nausea and a raw cough, he's in good shape. And he's dressed again.

Albeit in dead men's clothes.

One of the porters got them for him. They'd tried the charity store, but Tom's height and width was too tall an order. Most Italian males are considerably smaller and narrower than he is. No matter. He is now modelling some grey cotton trousers that are okay in length but were clearly worn by someone who was clinically obese. He's gathered six inches of spare cloth around the top and choked it off with an old plastic belt. The plain pink shirt with frayed collar and cuffs may well have come from the same guy. It's fine across the neck and shoulders but then billows out into a parachute. Brown socks and black plastic boots with elasticated sides complete his less than fashionable ensemble.

Sometime around four p.m., he falls asleep in the dozy warmth of the reception area, and stirs almost an hour later to find Valentina staring down at him.

He's been dreaming about the burning apartment.

Valentina sees the panic in his eyes. 'Hey, are you all right?'

He breathes deeply.

Yes, he's all right.

The place isn't on fire.

He's absolutely fine.

'Sure,' he answers sleepily, then stretches his long legs. 'You like my new clothes?'

She sees the funny side.

She sits on the hard wooden chair beside him, puts her arms around his neck and kisses him. 'They're very you.'

He pulls her tight.

Her skin is cool and smells of the fresh air.

Her kiss is warm and soft and the touch of her hair against his face melts his stress away.

The very public kiss is shorter and more polite than either of them would have liked.

Valentina pulls slowly away and takes a long look at him. 'Okay, who dressed you? I can get them a six stretch in maximum security for this. Or was it a blind guy? I could show mercy to a blind guy.'

'A dead guy, I think.'

She screws up her face. 'Oooh. I wish you hadn't said that. I've spent too much of the day in the mortuary.' She grabs his hand and tries to pull him to his feet. 'Come on, let's get out of here.'

Tom heaves himself up from the chair where he's spent the last three hours. 'Where are we going? Your place is really badly damaged.'

She folds her fingers between his and leads him to the exit. 'I know. Federico has friends in the fire department; they're scooping up whatever is salvageable before the looters move in.'

'Looters?'

'Sure. Romans burned and looted most of the world. You don't think they'll be all over a newly gutted apartment seeing if there's something worth having?'

'I suppose so.'

Tom walks groggily to Valentina's car.

She zaps the door open.

He gets in, rolls down the window and clunks on his seat belt. 'I'm really sorry about your place.'

'You should be,' she teases. 'Do you have any idea what it will cost to replace my wardrobe?'

He shakes his head.

'The shoes alone will be a year's salary. Not to mention my dresses, skirts, tops, bags, jumpers, coats and lingerie.'

'Oh God, I feel so bad. I really don't know what happened.' He rubs his forehead with his thumb and forefinger. 'I'm sure I didn't leave anything on the cooker. I didn't use it after you'd gone. I just made coffee, that's all.'

'It doesn't matter.' She leans over and kisses him. 'You're safe, that's all I care about. The rest is covered by insurance.' She kisses him again. 'But as punishment, you're going to have to come shopping with me. Lots of shopping!'

54

Louisa can't believe she's going along with it.

All of her training tells her this is a bad idea, especially after Suzanna's attack on Valducci.

Then again, it could be exactly the right moment.

She supposes she's being compliant because the initiative

has come from her boss and it's not her neck on the line if it goes wrong, which it very well could. Then again, Valducci could really hit the bullseye, and she'd like to be in on that happening.

And so it is that she finds herself in the back of the hospital administrator's Alfa, accompanying Suzanna on a trip to Cosmedin.

Cognitive therapy.

Returning to a scene of central psychological importance while the patient is in a high emotional state. Risky but potentially promising.

They park just off the square and Suzanna is already acting nervously.

Her face is pressed to the car window and her eyes are glued to the iconic bell tower of the Santa Maria.

Louisa touches her hand. 'We thought it might be a good idea to bring you back here. See if anything surfaces in your memory that can help us to help you.'

The rear door has a child lock on it, which is a good job, otherwise Suzanna would already have been out of the car and probably killed by passing traffic.

'Hang on! Wait a second!' shouts Valducci from the front seat.

He turns off the engine and cranks up the parking brake.

He gets out of the car, walks around to the rear passenger side and opens the door for Suzanna.

He takes her arm to help her out.

Or at least it looks like he's helping.

In fact he has a grip on her wrist that is tighter than a pair of army handcuffs, and he's sure as hell not letting go. Suzanna feels him restraining her and looks into his bloodshot eyes.

'You have to be careful around here. I'll stay close to you and make sure you don't get hurt.'

Suzanna looks pained. Her attention is fixed on the church and she's backing away from it like she's expecting a bomb to go off.

'Is this the building in your drawing?' asks Louisa, noticing the tension. 'I saw the drawing that you did of the fire. Is this the place?'

Suzanna looks confused.

She peers at Louisa as though she's a complete stranger. Someone who's just stopped her in the street. '*Signora*, I don't know what the fuck you're talking about.' She wheels around to Valducci, who still has hold of her wrist. '*Vaffanculo!* Get your filthy hands off me, you pervert.'

The administrator is struck dumb.

Wham!

Suzanna punches him hard in the face.

He's shocked and stinging but still holding on.

'Suzanna!' shouts Louisa.

Suzanna punches Valducci again. This time she adds a shuddering jerk of her left knee to his balls.

The administrator doubles up and loses his grip.

'*Testa di cazzo!*' Suzanna walks casually away, her back to the church.

Louisa freezes.

Should she help Valducci, or run after Suzanna?

No choice.

'Suzanna, wait!'

It takes close to ten seconds for Louisa to get level – and a safe half a metre to one side. 'Why did you do that?'

Suzanna shoots her a look of disbelief. 'Why? The greasy pig was grabbing at me. You didn't see him? He wanted to get me in his car and crawl all over me. No way, sister. That doesn't happen to Anna Fratelli, no way.'

'Anna?'

'What?'

Louisa hadn't got a question; she'd just repeated the name out loud because it was new.

Unfamiliar and yet distantly familiar.

Finally her memory gets off its ass and helps out.

Suzie Fratelli is the name of one of the alters.

This new personality is combining an old surname, that of little Suzie, with a whole new and profoundly aggressive personality, Anna. Anna itself being a root form of Suzanna.

'Do I know you?' She's walking quickly, striding away from the square down a back street that she seems to recognise.

'I'm a doctor from the hospital you were at. I'm Louisa Verdetti.'

'Naah. I ain't been at a hospital. I been working my ass off. Two jobs a day, that's what I been doin'. Louisa, you say? That's a nice name.'

Verdetti goes with the flow. '*Grazie*. Anna's nice too. That a family name?'

'You're joking, right?' Anna veers left down an adjacent alley.

'Why would I be joking?'

'Well, if you're supposed to be my doctor, then you should know my family history – like I don't have any.' She takes another sharp turn into a road facing a large stretch of old parkland.

Louisa is almost breathless trying to keep up.

She turns the corner and feels something slam into her face.

The force of the blow drops her on her back and leaves her seeing stars and spitting blood.

Tears come streaming to her eyes.

By the time she's moved her hands from her face, Anna is gone.

55

Tom and Valentina grab groceries and toiletries from a small *supermercato* near the hospital and prepare to spend the night in a Carabinieri-owned apartment in the north of the city. It's a safe house. One used by the serious crime squad to guard witnesses about to testify in major trials.

The place is cold and smells of cigarettes and alcohol. Valentina pushes open the windows and searches for an air freshener. Tom finds a central heating switch and turns it all the way up. Neither of them yet feels brave enough to look into the bedroom.

The place is sparsely furnished – a well-worn brown velour settee and chair are staked out around an old black box of a TV, while at the other end of the room there's a teak-effect fold-up dining table filled with squashed beer cans, a full ashtray and a set of dog-eared playing cards. 'Strictly a men-only set-up,' pronounces Valentina, as she surveys the evidence. 'I was warned that the cleaners hadn't yet been in, but I didn't think it would be this bad.'

'Beggars can't be choosers,' Tom replies from a small annex off the lounge that passes as a kitchen. 'At least there's a coffee machine.' He holds up a small Gaggia that he's found in a cupboard.

Valentina claps her hands. 'Yay! Get that working and I may just forgive you for burning down my apartment.'

'Will do.'

Valentina opens the fridge and reels back. It smells like she just prised the lid off a coffin. The cooler box holds a mush of long-forgotten vegetables and enough gas to blow up a small country. 'Yuck! I haven't seen inside a fridge this bad since I was at college.'

Tom abandons plugging the Gaggia in and wanders over. 'How about we just stick the groceries in there in their bags and go to bed.' He puts his hands on her hips. 'I just want to curl up beside you and see the end to this day.'

Valentina kisses him lightly. 'You go. It'll take me ten minutes to sort this. A little boiling water and some washing-up liquid will make all the difference.' She kisses him again and heads for the sink, but never gets there.

Her cell phone rings.

Surely there's no way such a bad day could get worse?

Within thirty seconds it has.

She hangs up and relays the news. 'Suzanna has disappeared.' She flaps her arms in impotent protest. 'Verdetti and her administrator took her back to Cosmedin for what they call cognitive recognition therapy and she overpowered them and ran off.' She flaps some more. 'Can you believe it? Like this woman wasn't dangerous. Why did they think we posted a guard outside of her door, just for fun?' She punches Assante's number in her phone and vents some more of her frustration.

Tom busies himself working the Gaggia and emptying the putrid remains of the cooler box.

By the time she's finished her call, he's drummed up a couple of decent cups of coffee and an almost clean fridge.

'You're an angel.' She takes a small espresso cup from him and cradles it in her hands.

He chinks his cup against hers and wishes it were a glass of red. 'You going to have to go out?'

'Maybe not.' She doesn't look convinced. 'Federico is issuing an alert to all our units, plus the Polizia. Louisa and her boss are on their way to the station to be interviewed.'

'Do you want to be there to do it?'

Her face says she does. 'I want to be here to make sure you're all right.'

'Hey, I've learned my lesson. I swear I won't touch anything electrical after you've gone.'

'I didn't mean that.' She puts a hand to his face, 'You just look wiped out.'

'I am. You must be too.'

She nods and takes another hit of the syrupy coffee. 'Nothing that caffeine – or you – can't cure.'

Her cell phone rings again. 'God give me strength!' She snatches it off the counter top. '*Pronto!*'

Tom watches as the sternness washes from her face and is replaced by something more worrying.

Disbelief.

'*Grazie.*' Valentina ends the call and lets the phone dangle from her hand.

'What's wrong?'

She looks at him like he's standing on ice and might fall through at any moment. 'It was Federico's friend in the fire department.'

'And?'

She moves closer. 'You didn't start the fire, Tom. Someone else did.'

He frowns. 'I don't understand.'

'Petrol was poured through the letter box and then set on fire. The investigators could tell from the intensity of the burns on the ceiling and floor where it was started. And it wasn't the kitchen. It wasn't your fault. The seat of the fire was the doorway.'

Valentina sees the shock on his face and hugs him tight.

They stand silently together. Minds racing, both thinking the same thing.

Who did it? Why? And who exactly were they trying to kill?

56

Not even the safe house seems particularly safe any more.

Nowhere does.

Tom and Valentina travel to the police station together.

There's no way he's going to let her go out alone. And there's no way she's going to leave him in on his own.

It's just before midnight and the night has turned chilly. A frosty reminder that winter is a long way from over.

Only by the time they're parking the Fiat at the police station has the little car's heater managed to kick out some warmth.

Through a glazed partition Valentina sees Louisa Verdetti and Sylvio Valducci sitting in the drab Carabinieri reception area looking cold and drawn. They're like those old married couples who stopped talking to each other about half a century ago but still go out and spend speechless meals together. Valentina takes them through to her office and en route introduces Tom – or in Louisa's case, reintroduces him. It's only partway through these civilities that Tom once more becomes aware that he's still dressed in the pink parachute of a shirt and tank-sized grey pants recovered from dead men at the hospital. Fortunately, the grave and urgent task of trying to find their missing prisoner seems to divert attention away from his crimes against fashion.

Tom sits back in the corner of the office and tries not to fall asleep.

He occupies himself with an out-of-date newspaper left on a low table, but for the most part he just listens and watches Valentina interview the two medics.

The body language between Verdetti and Valducci is more than just interesting.

It's quite hostile.

At one point he tries to comfort her and she squirms away so violently it's almost like they're in an abusive relationship.

Half an hour later, Valentina beckons Tom over to her desk. 'Look at this.' Her tone is sombre.

She smoothes out a creased piece of paper, a child's crayon drawing. 'Our prisoner did this – just hours before she escaped.'

At first it appears to be no more than scribbles of oranges and reds; then he sees what Valentina saw.

A sleeping man under the cross of God consumed by fire.

Every nerve in his body prickles.

Did the patient really foresee what would happen?

He looks at Louisa and Valducci, then back at Valentina. She shakes her head. She doesn't want him to mention anything in front of the medics, especially Valducci, whom she knows even Louisa doesn't trust.

Tom carries his heavy thoughts back to his corner.

Maybe he's reading too much into the picture.

It could be anything.

More likely it's meant to be a Roman battle scene, a picture of soldiers burning a village to the ground and crucifying locals or slaves.

As soon as Valducci and Verdetti leave, Federico arrives.

He gives Tom a courteous nod and then falls into a long, intense and hushed conversation with Valentina.

Tom has another go at the now well-thumbed paper, and then struggles to fight back a tsunami of sleep.

Bleary-eyed, he watches them both note-taking, tapping computer keys and making calls.

Suddenly it's all over.

They both grab coats, turn off desk lights and fire *ciaos*

202

across the room – Federico even manages a wave and a forced smile to Tom.

'Home!' says Valentina, clapping her beautifully slim hands in a symbol of triumph. 'Or at least, what for now passes as home.'

Tom gets to his feet and finds he's bone weary, the kind of tired that seeps through to your marrow and makes you groan whenever you sit or rise.

'What do you make of the drawing?' asks Valentina as they take the stairs.

'Maybe nothing. We're both tired, and that makes you see spooks everywhere. Let's talk about it tomorrow, when we've got fresh brains.'

Valentina thinks he's dismissing it too easily, but she can see that right now it's not something he wants to dwell on.

They only need to take one step outside to notice that the temperature's dropped further and their breath quickly frosts in the early-morning air. Thankfully there's still a little heat hanging around in the Fiat. Valentina starts her up, pulls out of the car park and moves the conversation smoothly on. 'Seems our lady has quite a new personality.'

'Let me guess, another legendary Roman.'

'No, not this time.' Valentina corrects herself. 'Well, actually it probably is Roman, just not historic.'

'What do you mean?'

'Anna Fratelli, that's the name of the latest alter. Apparently a real foul-mouthed she-cat. She was in the control of this personality when she escaped from Louisa and her boss.'

Both Tom and Valentina think the same thing at exactly the same time, but he's the first to say it. 'Maybe that's not an alter. Maybe that's her real personality. She sounds tough enough to survive.'

'You think so?'

'Why not? There has to be a default, an original person still existing deep down in there somewhere.'

'Right. Louisa called it a host.'

Tom wipes condensation from the small passenger window and looks out into the cold darkness of the night. 'I had a friend in the LAPD helped me out at the community centre in Compton. A big black guy called Danny Moses.'

'Moses?'

'Yeah. His name always raised a laugh from the gang-bangers down there. They'd call out, "Here comes Moses and the Jesus guy!" They'd slap their sides and hoot like it had never been said before. Anyway, Danny was a dab hand at finding runaways. Creatures of habit, he'd say. They run for home, they run to friends or they run to somewhere they go regularly. We even found several kids who'd stolen stuff from the church actually hiding out in the church community hall.'

Valentina catches his drift. 'So you think what? Anna's gone back to the hospital? Or back to Cosmedin?'

Tom's not sure.

He's almost sorry he came out with the anecdote now. 'I don't know. Tonight is cold enough to freeze hell over, and she was on foot, so she must be holed up somewhere local. Maybe she's not far from wherever she left Louisa and that pervert-looking boss of hers.'

'Valducci? You think he looks like a pervert?'

'God forgive me, I shouldn't be so judgemental. But yes, he looks very pervy – and believe me, I've been around enough Catholic priests to know.'

Valentina laughs and swings the Punto west towards Cosmedin. 'You mind if we quickly visit the place Louisa last saw her? We're only a couple of kilometres away and I'll sleep better if we take a look.'

Tom scratches his head. 'Sure. Though it's not necessary.'

Valentina frowns across to him.

'I've already discovered there are other ways to make sure you sleep *very* soundly.'

57

En route to Cosmedin, Valentina makes a series of calls to the overnight team working Central Control. She keeps Tom busy writing down several addresses that she calls out.

By the time they reach the Piazza della Bocca della Verità, he's recorded five separate locations for variously aged Anna Fratellis, but only one for a twenty-seven-year-old living in Cosmedin.

Valentina turns off the engine and has a pang of guilt.

Despite the lateness of the hour, she calls Federico's cell to tell him where she is and what she's up to. She feels better that it's turned off and coolly leaves a message promising to update him in the morning. There are several reasons why she's relieved he hasn't picked up, not least because she's simply too tired to wait around for him to drive out and join them. He'll be pissed when he gets the message, but so what?

After everything he's done, he's damned lucky she even thought to ring him.

The address is south of the small basilica. It's off a series of back streets behind a thick clump of parkland that surrounds a tiny three-star hotel.

Valentina drives with her lights off and parks up at the end of the street, a good way from the target address.

It's a ground-floor apartment in a four-storey block.

The position of Anna's name on the bell block shows the apartment is on the left-hand side. Valentina cups a hand to Tom's ear and whispers, 'Stay outside, in the side road, and watch those windows.' She points out two frames. 'The frosted one is a bathroom; the other may be the bedroom or lounge. If she bolts again, it will have to be through one of those.'

Tom nods and rubs cold from his arms. His parachute of a shirt is not suitable attire for a sub-zero stake-out.

As she feared, Valentina finds the front door to the apartment block is on a magnetic lock. She buzzes several fourth-floor addresses until someone swears through the intercom and then opens up for her.

She moves quickly inside.

Anna's apartment is just a few metres away to her left.

She knocks hard three times and shouts, 'Carabinieri! Open up!'

She puts her finger on the buzzer to the right of the door and presses long and hard, then bangs again with her fist. '*Rapidamente!*'

She puts her ear to the door.

She can't hear anything.

Nor can she wait any longer. She's made enough noise to wake the whole block, so if someone's in there they've had plenty of chance to get to the door.

She pulls out her Beretta and takes a well-practised running kick at the door.

It splinters below the lock, but holds firm around the mortise.

'*Cazzo!*' It's deadlocked.

She backs up and hits it again.

This time the jamb splits and the door booms back on its hinges.

Valentina put so much effort into the kick, she stumbles to a stop in the middle of a strange dark room.

Instinctively she sweeps the gun in a protective arc and tries to get her bearings.

A door is opening.

Yellow street light starts bleeding in from somewhere off to her left.

A ball of shadow and noise hurtles towards her.

Valentina sidesteps and knocks something over.

A glass lamp crashes behind her.

The shadow ball smashes into her legs, sends her tumbling backwards into a wall.

Her Beretta spills into the darkness.

Arms and hands close like monstrous tentacles around her knees.

She slams her elbow down hard and feels it connect with the bone of a skull.

There's a dull cry from beneath her.

The monster hands shift. But they are not gone. Now her attacker has hold of her feet and starts to pull her across the floor.

Valentina slides in the broken lamp glass. It digs into her back where her blouse has come up and spikes into her scalp like a crown of thorns.

She tries to lurch forward as she's pulled. Grabs at thin air. Swings a wild punch and connects painfully with a wall to the right of her.

One of her legs flops free.

From the blackness comes a hard kick to her kidneys. She whooshes air and pirouettes in pain.

A follow-up kick catches her in the spine and she gets her first rush of panic. Maybe she's going to get badly beaten here. Or worse.

There's a blinding flash.

The light is on.

Tom is standing by the door with his hand on the switch.

He sees Valentina and her attacker bent over her.

It isn't Anna. It's a man.

There's a second of inaction, a moment when everyone is overwhelmed by the first sight of each other.

Tom ends the stand-off.

The room is small, and within two steps he's able to plant a high kick deep into the man's abdomen.

Before he even doubles up, Tom slips behind him and executes a lethal choke hold. The guy is a good six inches smaller. All the big American has to do to fully immobilise him is turn his hip and inch him up along his outstretched leg.

Valentina gets to her feet.

She unholsters her handcuffs and locks them around the man's wrists. She pushes him to his knees and breathes a sigh of relief.

Tom wants to go over to her, take her in his arms and comfort her, but he knows he can't. This is her stage.

She has to be the one in control and he has to back out.

Valentina walks around the front of the kneeling man and gets in his face. 'What's your name?'

He dips his head.

She grabs his chin, reaches for her back pocket and pulls out her ID card. 'I'm Captain Valentina Morassi. Who are you? Why are you here?'

He doesn't answer.

There's something about him that's unnerving.

Now she spots it.

He has almost no facial hair.

In fact he looks almost feminine.

Valentina gets a flashback to the morgue.

The ball-less eunuch found bizarrely butchered beside the Tiber.

Could this be another?

'Get up!'

The man either can't or won't.

'Tom, help me.'

Between them they drag the prisoner to his feet. Valentina starts to unbuckle his black jeans.

Tom is shocked. 'What are you doing?'

Valentina clearly has no concern for his rights. She drags his jeans and underpants down around his ankles, pushes him back on to a sofa and uses her foot to spread his legs. '*Porca vacca!* Another eunuch.' She wheels away from the debagged prisoner and pulls out her radio.

While she calls in the arrest, she pushes open the bedroom door, gun extended.

The place is in darkness.

She can just make out the outlines of a low bed, a small dresser and a wardrobe.

No Anna.

She returns to Tom. 'Can you re-dress this asshole while I clean up? I have glass in my hair and God knows where else.'

'Hey, that's above and beyond what comes within the boyfriend remit.'

She manages a smile and walks away. 'I know. Loop the cuffs under a chair leg and sit on him.'

Tom shoots her a look that says he can handle the small guy without needing to do that.

The bathroom is tiny.

Valentina finds there are only women's things in there. One toothbrush, one tube of paste and some eyebrow tweezers on a glass shelf beneath a cheap white plastic mirrored cabinet. She pulls it open. Inside there's a tube of thrush cream, a box of Tampax, a bottle of headache pills and some AllergEze.

No sign of the cotton wool or cotton buds that she was hoping for.

She closes the door and squints at the mirror. When she puts her hand to her head, she feels several splinters of glass. Carefully she picks them out with her fingers, briefly inspects the sparkling fragments then washes them away. It takes several minutes to be sure her scalp is glass-free.

She takes off her blouse and by twisting in front of the mirror she can see small slivers of smashed glass embedded in her spine. There's also an angry red mark around her lower vertebrae where she's been kicked.

Valentina contorts her fingers and uses the eyebrow tweezers and mirror to pick out the shards. She looks at the nearby shower. It's a temptation. A hot soak is just what she needs, but she knows that's a long way off. Just processing the piece of shit in the other room is going to take ages.

She pulls her blouse back on and now becomes aware of her damaged right hand. She can wriggle all of her fingers, but her knuckles are grazed and swollen. A pity she didn't connect with the son-of-a-bitch's jaw instead of the wall.

Her attacker is flat out on the floor when she re-enters the room. Tom is sitting near him, his foot in the middle of the guy's back.

'All okay?' she asks.

'Fine.' He looks almost bored.

'I'm going to check the rest of the place, all right?'

He nods.

Valentina goes back to the bedroom, fumbles for a switch and eventually finds it. She pushes it down, but the light doesn't come on. She clicks it again.

Nothing.

Something is wrong.

She senses it.

She missed something earlier.

Something important.

58

Before Valentina can enter the bedroom and satisfy her curiosity, the arrest team arrives.

She fills them in on the prisoner.

Maybe a night in the cells will loosen the eunuch's tongue. Come tomorrow she'll have enough energy to find out what the hell he was doing in the apartment rented by their missing woman.

She borrows a flashlight and returns to the bedroom.

The room is spookily cold and smells of damp, like wet and rusty iron.

Under the glare of the torchlight, the darkness gives way to a tobacco-coloured creaminess. Beyond the burn of the beam, all the walls and even the ceiling seem to be lined with some kind of shabby tiles that are hanging loose.

She shines the light up.

There's no central lightshade or bulb, only a dangling flex and raw open socket where the appliance should be.

Valentina moves the beam around.

Dozens of strange shadows crawl over the walls and move in sync with her torch.

She flicks the beam back to the ceiling.

Unbelievable.

Hundreds of identical rosary beads, complete with silver crucifixes, dangle cross down from the plaster ceiling.

'Tom! You need to see this.' She twists the beam to full flood.

He comes to the doorway and stops.

Valentina moves the torch around. 'What do you make of it?'

He has to shield his eyes from the brightness. 'Nothing to be frightened of. Do you mind? You're blinding me with that thing.'

'*Scusi.*' She dips it and in doing so notices that the floor is also strangely covered.

Tom moves to the centre of the room and touches her hand. 'This is a place of sanctuary. It's a refuge for someone who is very frightened.'

'And someone totally damned crazy.' Valentina pans the light beam back and forth across the floor. 'Isn't this the Bible? Isn't the whole floor covered in pages from the Bible?'

Tom bends so he can see. 'Yes, it is. In Latin, too.'

She shines her light upwards and around. 'And the walls and the ceiling; the whole room is covered in Biblical text.'

Tom crosses himself.

Valentina runs her hand over the papered wall. 'It's so creepy.'

'The word of God is creepy?'

'Yes. When it's plastered all over the place like this, it's *immensely* creepy.' Valentina's light picks out brass candlesticks arranged around a small painted statue of a Madonna and Child. 'Not only creepy, but a fire risk. It's a wonder this place didn't go up in flames every time she lit a candle and said a prayer.'

Tom examines the papered walls. Unless he's mistaken, it's not only a Vulgate, a standard Latin Bible, that has been ripped up and stuck there. He recognises some other pages as sections of the Polyglot Bible for the Greek New Testament. He moves along, his hands feeling and tracing the wallpapered text.

He points out several pages of old print. 'These are extracts from the Septuagint, the oldest Greek version of the Jewish Bible.' He slides his hand along, 'Next to it are pages from the classic Hebrew Bible.' He points a long, shadowy finger. 'Just at the edge of your light there, I can see English – those are sections of the Old Testament.'

'What's going on, Tom?'

'I'm not sure. It's like someone has taken out an insurance policy and covered themselves with every form of overlapping religion.'

His foot knocks against something. 'Shine your light down here for a second.'

She flashes the beam his way.

'Down at my feet.'

'My God, what is it?'

He crouches. 'The bed – it's made from bibles.'

She steps closer and kneels beside him.

Tom pulls at part of the single bed. 'The frame is made four bibles high and by the looks of it, one . . . two . . . three deep. They've been used like bricks to build a small wall, with the openings facing outwards, so the inside fits tight against a single mattress.' He manages to force some pages open. 'Looks like masonry nails have been driven through them and into the floor to hold them together.'

Valentina moves her hand beneath the torchlight and over the bed. 'And the mattress and quilt are both lined with more bible pages.' She is the first back on her feet. 'Now tell me you don't find this creepy.'

Tom gets up as well. 'I don't. I've seen similar things.'

'You have?' she says incredulously.

'Some people are frightened of being attacked – of being

possessed – in their sleep. They're afraid that when their defences are down they become vulnerable. I guess this is similar. Your girl is scared that when she's asleep, some evil alter will take over her body.'

Outside, in the living room, there are voices and noises.

'Forensics and a search team,' she explains, seeing he's on edge. 'We'd better back away while they do their jobs.'

They return to the main room and Tom stands to one side while Valentina takes charge, issuing instructions to several different people.

Within minutes, portable lamps are being brought in and men in latex gloves are unlocking silver suitcases. All of them take a second or two to stare at Tom's strange pink shirt and baggy grey pants.

Someone shouts something in Italian from the bedroom where they've just been, and Valentina flies in there.

Tom rushes to the doorway.

Everyone's crowded around the tiny wardrobe.

Inside, curled up on the floor, is a young woman.

Covered in blood.

59

Louisa Verdetti is in a deep and peaceful sleep.

A much-craved and wonderfully healing rest that is slowly dissolving the traumas of one of the worst days of her life.

Losing her patient, getting punched in the face, arguing with her boss and being interviewed and scolded by the cops are all gradually being reduced to mere grains of sand on her beach of mental history.

Another few hours of dream time and they'll be filed and forgotten. She'll be fit to go again. Ready for whatever mysteries and machinations a fine new day has to throw at her.

But not yet.

Not now.

Right now she's good for nothing, and the last thing she wants on her mind is a ringing phone.

But there it is.

For a moment – a very long and sleepy moment – she pretends that it isn't real. The noise is part of a dream she's having. Perhaps a call from an ex-lover, pestering her to give him another chance.

But it isn't.

It's real.

And it's not going away.

Worse than that, the phone is ringing in the cold darkness on the other side of her super-soft and super-warm quilt.

She reaches out, pulls the receiver into her cosy world and manages to mutter her name. '*Si*. Verdetti.'

What Valentina Morassi says to her banishes any last vestiges of comfort.

Louisa sits bolt upright in shock.

She listens until the Carabinieri captain is done.

The now dead phone dangles in her hand while the news sinks in.

Yesterday's nightmare isn't over.

In fact, it just got worse.

The psychiatrist dresses without showering or even running a comb through her hair. She's in such a rush that she only takes time out to use the toilet and wash her hands before dashing to her car and driving to the hospital.

Suzanna – or Anna, or Cassandra, or whoever she

damned well is – is in the ICU at the Policlinico, fighting for her life.

Louisa is breathless when she arrives. She stumbles into the triage area almost as frantically as a panicking relative.

She introduces herself at reception, and a nurse leads her to a long-faced man in green scrubs called Ricardo Contessi. He's one of the luckless trauma surgeons working the graveyard shift. 'Your girl's okay – but only just.' He extends his left arm, tilts it so it's palm up and demonstrates. 'She cut herself, something like twenty times. Most of the incisions were superficial – made horizontally across and around the wrist – though she's damaged a tendon and we have had to stitch that. However, there was one more disturbing cut, made vertically, running a long way down the arm.'

Louisa flinches. Self-harmers know horizontal cuts are usually safe. Vertical cuts are different. They're genuinely suicidal. A good dig into any of the major arteries running down the forearm usually proves fatal.

Contessi slowly traces his index finger down his own pale and hairy forearm. 'Fortunately she started a few centimetres lower than the radial and ulnar intersection. Most of the damage around there was muscular. But she did nick one of the lower branches of the ulnar artery, and that means she lost a lot of blood.'

'She'll be okay?'

'I think so. The paramedics did a really good job on the way over here. She's already bandaged up and sedated.' He nods to a ward sign on a wall. 'She's on an open ward. Some Carabinieri officer, a woman, is at her bedside.'

Louisa realises it must be Valentina. She scratches her head and finds there's no longer hair up there, just a thick, muzzy nest that bats or birds have no doubt settled in.

The surgeon holds up a clipboard. 'There's some

216

confusion over the patient's name. Do you know what she's called?'

A small laugh escapes Louisa's exhausted body. 'Play it safe, call her Suzanna Anna Cassandra Fratelli.'

He raises an eyebrow as he writes on his notes. '*Grazie*. I'll look in on her before I knock off. *Ciao.*'

'*Ciao.*' Louisa takes a slow breath and walks the short distance to the ward.

Valentina is pacing and talking on her cell phone right next to a sign that says they shouldn't be used.

Tom is asleep in a low chair.

A young uniformed guard is standing by the curtains and a nurse is busy at a desk opposite – but not so busy that she can't occasionally catch the eye of the handsome soldier.

Anna is out for the count.

Louisa approaches the bed and is saddened to see how frail her patient looks.

Valentina finishes her call and turns to the clinician. 'We found her unconscious beneath a false floor at the bottom of a wardrobe in her apartment.'

Louisa can barely imagine how desperate the woman must have felt.

'And Anna Fratelli is her real name?'

'Seems so. There were no bills in the apartment. I guess you'll be able to pull her full medical records now?'

Louisa glances at her watch. 'Not at three a.m. But yes, in a few hours we should be able to get hold of them.'

Valentina looks towards the bed. 'Do you have any idea what's been going on in her mind? What's made her like this?'

The clinician bends over the bed and clears a strand of hair off Anna's forehead. 'I could ask you the same thing. I wouldn't be at all surprised to find out that whatever is troubling her is also at the root of the crimes that you're investigating.'

Tom stirs in the chair, then slides a little further down, his head resting on a cushion pressed against the wall.

Louisa watches Valentina watching Tom.

Valentina senses the psychiatrist's eyes on her.

Louisa smiles. 'As a professional observer of human behaviour, I'd say you two were more than just friends.'

Valentina doesn't answer.

'Okay, I'm sorry I spoke. I can take a hint: private is private.' Louisa coughs and moves on. 'So, work-wise, is there anything else I need to know about Anna? Anything you found at her house – drugs, that kind of thing?'

'No drugs. At least, nothing more than the usual – headache pills, allergy tablets and such like. You need to see her bedroom, though. I'll send over some photographs.'

'Why? Why do I need to see it?'

'To believe it. She's turned the room into a religious bolthole. The walls, floor and ceiling are completely covered in pages torn or copied from bibles. Hundreds of rosary beads are dangling from the ceiling. It's quite freaky.'

Louisa falls silent.

'What is it?'

'I was just casting my mind back. I don't think any of the other alters expressed any Catholic beliefs or traits.'

'Well, this is full-on Catholicism. She's even made her bed out of bibles, as though she's scared of sleeping without God being close to her.'

'What an awful way to live – frightened during the day and then even more frightened of going to sleep.' Louisa scratches at her nest of uncombed hair and looks down at her comatose patient. 'I feel so sorry for her. I wish I could just drop a rope into that subconscious pit and pull her out of there.'

For almost a minute, both women just stare at Anna.

She looks so weak.

Her pinched white face is accentuated by eyelids the

colour of raw meat. Her scarred arms are bandaged, and medical tubes tentacle their way off into hanging bags and monitoring machines.

Louisa breaks the sombre silence. 'Look, I'm sorry we took her out, back to Cosmedin. It was a stupid thing to do. If Valducci hadn't been tugging me along on a lead, I would have called you and asked you about it.'

'And maybe not given my guard the slip?'

'And not given your guard the slip. Is he in trouble?'

Valentina lightens up. 'He's not yet scrubbing toilets with a toothbrush, but he's not far from it.' She gestures to a water cooler just a metre away. '*Aqua?*'

'*Si. Grazie.*'

Valentina fills two plastic cups and hands one over. 'There's something else you should know. On my way over, I got a call saying more than a dozen exercise books have been discovered at Anna's place. All filled with drawings and writing.'

'Life logs.'

'*Scusi?*'

'DID sufferers are aware that the host is taken over by multiple personalities, so the alters write journals, daily diaries about what's happening to them. That way, when the host momentarily regains control of the body, it's possible to put some pieces of the puzzle together.'

'Wait a minute. Are you saying that all Anna would know about what has happened to her – what's been done with her body – is when she reads about it in a journal filled in by the alters?'

'That's about it.'

Valentina doesn't say it, but she thinks it.

This could be a breakthrough.

The logs might well explain the mystery of a severed hand in a church in Cosmedin and a dead eunuch on the banks of the Tiber.

60

It's almost four a.m by the time the Carabinieri arrest team process their newest prisoner.

Down in the shower block a shameful freak show is under way. Soldiers crowd around to see the guy with no balls and the smallest penis known to man.

'I should have sold fucking tickets. Get back to work!' barks custody officer Piero la Malfa.

Outside, at the admissions counter, Federico Assante is trying to shrug off a heavy night's drinking and go through the prisoner's clothes. He got home after what everyone would admit was a pretty emotional day and decided drink was the best short cut to a place where all the shit with Caesario and Morassi had never happened.

Then Valentina had called.

That damned woman was relentless. Even when he didn't answer the phone, she left haunting messages, the kind you can't ignore, the type that keep the pressure on and don't let you rest.

Federico pulls apart the stack of forensically bagged clothes in front of him. Black trainers, black socks, black jeans, black pants, black T-shirt, black hooded top and black gloves. That ball-less buffoon either has a black fetish or he dresses professionally for the night-time.

Federico is sure it's not a fashion choice.

Black doesn't only help burglars, robbers and rapists blend into the shadows; it completely screws eye-witness reports. Without distinctive clothing or something visually unique to tie to an offender, judges and juries are wary of any testimony that includes the phrase 'I think it was black.'

The young lieutenant is dispirited. There's nothing to give him a clue to the identity of the man, and so far the son-of-a-bitch hasn't said a word.

Maybe he's mute as well as ball-less.

Assante looks again at the prisoner's sum possessions: two hundred euros, a handful of Kleenex tissues and a spool of old fishing line. The line is significant: it's handy to tie people up or choke them with. Apart from that, there are car keys and an interesting piece of cheap jewellery.

It's a black pendant on a rope necklace.

He gets a shiver as he turns it over in its clear forensic bag.

It's exactly the same as the one the nurses at the hospital took from Anna.

'Anything come back on his prints yet?' Federico calls to la Malfa through the open door to the cell block.

'*Domani!*' comes the reply. 'Why the fuck don't you go upstairs to your own office and do the job yourself?'

'Come on, man. I told you how much I've had to drink. I can barely search for the toilet. Give me some help here.'

'*Vaffanculo stronzo!*'

'Hey! *Per favore.*'

La Malfa stomps off somewhere.

Lazy fucker, thinks Assante. He'd have helped out if the tables had been turned.

He pulls up a second chair, puts his feet up and closes his eyes. Twenty minutes' sleep is what he needs. A quick nap, then he'll do the job himself.

Somewhere off in the distance he hears raised voices.

Iron doors clanging shut. Keys rattling. Drunks swearing. Someone throwing up. More swearing. Cops laughing.

The chunky old radiator he's curled up next to coughs and hisses, and within a few minutes he's drifted off.

'You want this or not?'

Federico is still half-asleep, and the voice doesn't really register.

'I said, do you want this or not?'

La Malfa is standing over him, waving a piece of paper. 'I'm knocking off. With a little luck I'll be home before my wife wakes and starts bitching at me.'

Federico looks at his watch. Six-thirty a.m.

Unbelievable.

It feels like he shut his eyes ten seconds ago, not two hours back.

La Malfa slaps the paperwork on his chest. 'We hit the jackpot with your guy's prints. By the look of it, he's got more history than Julius fucking Caesar.'

61

The room is so filthy, Tom and Valentina have spent the last few hours scratching or sneezing.

Their arms are still wrapped around each other as morning creeps icily through the gaps in the ragged curtains and beneath the ill-fitting bedroom door.

They're huddled together, still dressed, on a stained mattress smelling of strangers long since gone.

They were both so tired when they got back from the hospital they just curled up tight and fell asleep.

Through the haze of waking, Valentina peers for her Mickey clock on the bedside cabinet, and realises it's not there. A grim reminder – not that she needs one – of the blaze that destroyed her apartment, robbed her of parts of her own past and almost cost her a precious part of her future too.

She kisses Tom until he wakes. 'Come on,' she says softly, 'let's make love in the shower, then get out of here and find some breakfast.'

He's still not ready to open his eyes. 'God, woman, you're insatiable. Is there not just time for me to wake first?'

She slides her body on top of his. 'Nope. I'll wake you in the shower.'

And she does.

She wakes him so well that neither of them complains about the barely warm drizzle that oozes painfully from a filthy shower caked in limescale.

A five-minute drive, just after eight a.m., finds them a bar that's already filled with locals bolting espresso like shots of vodka before rushing off to work.

Valentina plates up croissants, jam, cheese, fruit, water and coffee. She pays, and joins Tom at a table in the corner beneath an overhead heater that sounds like it's on its last legs. 'I'm starving,' she says, grabbing a croissant before she's even sat down.

Tom takes everything off the old brown tray and slides it on to a spare table so they have more room. 'I hope today isn't quite as eventful as yesterday.'

'I'll drink to that.' She takes a slug of coffee and then looks straight into his eyes. 'Before we talk work – all the nasty shit – I need to tell you something.'

'What?'

She leans forward so that she can whisper. 'I want to say that not only are you the best lover I've ever had, but I've never been happier in my life than I am right here, right now, with you.'

The sweetness catches Tom off guard.

He puts a hand to her beautiful face and kisses her a little longer than suitable for a public place.

What she said was a code for 'I love you' and he knows it. He just wishes he was more confident, more practised in expressing his own feelings, but he isn't. It's the price he has to pay for too many years as a priest.

A few ironic claps splatter across the tabletops around them.

'I'm very happy as well,' manages Tom.

Valentina blushes. 'I can tell from that kiss.'

They both laugh and reach for their coffees.

Tom drains the last of his espresso and changes the subject. 'What are your plans for today?'

'Well, providing you don't get us arrested, when we're finished here I'll call Federico and see what he got from the guy we arrested at the apartment last night. After that, I want to re-interview Suzanna.' She corrects herself. 'Sorry, Anna. And I'd like you to be there for that.'

'Me? Why?'

'Professional reasons.' She smiles. 'Or maybe I just don't want to leave you today. I want you on hand for my personal satisfaction.'

'And what if I don't want to satisfy you?' He picks up a croissant and a small pot of strawberry jam.

'Then you're dumped. History. Gone. I'll even throw you out of that palace we slept in last night.'

He scoops jam on to his plate and scrubs the end of the croissant in it. 'And that's supposed to be a threat?'

She laughs. 'No, seriously, this case obviously has some confusing religious dimensions. It would be good to have you around to make sense of them.'

'Glad to help in any way I can.'

Valentina hesitates for a moment. 'I'm not sure I'll be able to pay you – you know, like we did in Venice.' She struggles to explain. 'Given our relationship, I'm worried it might seem a little – corrupt.'

He sees her point. 'It's really not necessary. I'll settle for sleeping with the boss.'

'Deal.' She drinks some water. 'While we're seeing Anna, I'll have Federico run background checks on her – medical, criminal, social records, et cetera. We need to find out where she works, where she gets her money from, who she knows and who knows her.'

'And who's scaring her so much she has to rest in a bed of bibles.'

'Exactly.' Valentina forks a slice of cheese on to her plate. 'I really want to go through the diaries we found at her apartment. I told Louisa about them last night when you were sleeping. She says they're probably life logs – a sort of diary kept by each of the alters. I'll try to get her opinion on those too.'

'Have you thought about the fire – who might have done it?'

Valentina has. Long and hard. She plays down what she really thinks. 'Someone who had a grudge against whoever lived there before I did? Maybe they owed money or had crossed some *mafioso*. Or it could be lunatic teenagers; vandals these days are *pazzo*.'

'That's not who did it.'

'Or maybe the owner of the building, wanting to cash in on insurance.'

'That's not it either.'

She knows he's right.

Tom stretches his hand across the table and takes hers. 'Whoever started it wanted to kill you. They wanted you dead so you wouldn't uncover some nasty secret to do with this case.'

'That might not be true.' She squeezes his fingers.

'I think you know it is.'

She has no option but to put him right.

'What if it's not? What if it's *you* they were trying to kill, and not me?'

62

Federico is almost sober.

He spends twenty minutes steaming the booze out of his system in a shower at HQ.

For breakfast he grabs black coffee from the canteen and drinks it while chain-smoking two cigarettes on the steps of the station house. It's not healthy, but it's the closest he'll ever get to a low-calorie, zero-fat meal.

Back at his desk, he enters the new information he has on the male prisoner languishing downstairs in the cells and pulls up his record. On his computer monitor he stares at a slightly younger version of the guy they arrested.

The text below the mug shot tells him it's Guilio Brygus Angelis and he's thirty years old. He's unmarried and has no children.

No surprises there.

Federico scrolls down. Guilio was born in Athens and moved to Rome with his mother, Maya, when he was only three. It figures. Both the Christian and surnames are Greek, not Italian.

Maya worked in a city library and died a year later.

The report doesn't say how.

Federico reads on. There's no trace of the kid being fostered or adopted. He only appears on official records again in his early teens. It seems he was in trouble.

Serious trouble.

His juvenile record shows convictions for possession of drugs, assaults on two teachers and even an attack on a Catholic priest inside a young offenders' detention centre where he spent just over a year.

By his late teens, the librarian's child had added another volume of serious charges, including burglary and wounding. He spent his twenty-first birthday in jail for theft, assault and breach of previous bail orders.

Recently, though, there's no trace of any convictions and no outstanding warrants for his arrest.

On paper, Guilio almost looks as though he's turned over a new leaf.

Or at least he did, until he got caught red-handed in Anna's apartment and nearly beat Valentina to death.

Federico stops scrolling and sits back.

One thing puzzles him.

Why are there no listed associates? From what he's just read, it doesn't seem as though this guy ever hung around with gangs or teamed up with anyone to commit his crimes.

That's unusual.

He dives deeper into the files and digs around in the assessment notes from the governor at the detention centre.

Eventually he falls on a clue.

Guilio is described as 'painfully shy', 'explosively violent' and 'an out-and-out loner'. The centre's psychiatric report says that 'pre-puberty castration can be expected to have resulted not only in his anger and violence but also in his introversion'.

Federico logs off and catches the elevator to reception.

He steps outside for a final cigarette before starting his interview with Guilio, and watches people drift by the front of the Carabinieri building. The weather's turned wintry again. Everyone's wrapped tight in coats and scarves and gloves. It's his least favourite time of the year. Give him summer any day. Girls with long smiles and short skirts. That's how God intended things to be.

63

Administrator Sylvio Valducci has foreign guests arriving within the next hour. This means he's more than happy for Louisa Verdetti to meet the Carabinieri on her own. With a little luck they'll lock her up and throw away the key.

Even before her early-morning call to him, he'd already decided that from now on she could take all the risks with this so-called DID patient, and if things turned out all right then he'd take the credit.

His one brush with the law has given him plenty to talk about at lectures around the globe. If things go pear-shaped, then at least by distancing himself from the action, he's renewing the possibility of sacking Verdetti.

Louisa knows all this as surely as if Valducci had said it to her face and then mailed her a summary of his words.

He's a health-care politician. In the job purely for power and bonuses, not because it's a vocation.

It's only a five-minute walk from the psychiatric wing of the hospital to ICU, so Louisa arrives long before Tom and Valentina. The young Carabinieri guard who was there last night has been replaced by a surly-looking older one who goes to great lengths to check Louisa's credentials and have her sign a log book.

It seems the patient – the newly named Anna Fratelli – has had a good night. The stitching done by the trauma team has held firm and the spell of sedation has left her patient stable, conscious and calm. According to the ward sister, there's no reason why she shouldn't be transferred back to the psychiatric department after she's been checked by her doctor.

Louisa has just finished being updated when Tom and Valentina fill the doorway of the sister's office.

'*Buongiorno*. How is she?' asks the captain.

Louisa holds up a report in her hand. 'Good, by the sound of it.' She nods to the sister, who is watching from her desk, and adds, 'Let me update you outside, and then we can go and see her.'

Valentina's pleased to be getting on with things. She feared medical complications would mean putting a hold on the interview.

Tom says hello to Louisa as they walk from the sister's office, and then falls in line behind them.

'She's been moved to a room of her own,' announces the clinician, 'so we can talk to her in there, but I don't want her stressed. Best to chat for a little while, give her a break and then you can talk again if it's really necessary, okay?'

'That's fine,' confirms Valentina.

'Did you bring the photographs and diaries you spoke of last night?'

'No. But copies are on their way over to your office. You should have them within the next couple of hours.'

The doctor enters the room first, uncertain of who she's going to be talking to. Will it be Anna, or one of her many alters?

The patient is asleep in a bed set up at a thirty-degree angle. Her eyes are closed, but begin to flicker open as she

229

responds to the click of the door handle and sounds of people entering her room.

The psychiatrist rolls the dice. '*Buongiorno*, Anna. *Come lei è?*'

'*Bene*.' Her voice is weak and sleepy. She tries to gather her wits and politely sit up a little.

Louisa lifts a clipboard from the bottom rail of the bed. 'Do you remember what happened to you yesterday? How you came to be in here?'

Anna looks down at her bandaged arm. 'I was hiding in my apartment and I cut myself.' She glances up at the doctor. 'You know I do that kind of thing.'

There's shame in her eyes.

'It makes me feel safe. I just cut too deeply.' She looks at Valentina and Tom, then back to the doctor. 'Who are they?'

Louisa reassures her. 'They're friends. Valentina Morassi is a Carabinieri captain. You have met her before.'

'I don't think so.'

She doesn't press the issue. 'The man with her is her friend, Tom. He's a former priest.'

He steps forward so Anna can see him clearly. 'Hi, Anna, I'm pleased to meet you.'

She relaxes a little. 'A priest?'

'Yes. I was at a parish in Los Angeles for almost a decade.'

Anna looks as though she might cry. 'I'm very frightened, Father. Do you understand?'

Tom knows better than to correct her. He takes her trembling right hand gently in his big palms and sits on the edge of the bed, facing her. 'I think so. I saw your apartment last night and the bedroom where you were hiding.'

She grips Tom's fingers so hard that his skin turns white. 'Do you think she'll know I'm talking to you?' Anna glances nervously towards Valentina and Louisa. 'That I'm here with all of you?'

230

'Who, Anna? Who will know?'

Anna closes her eyes, dips her head and prays. '*En ego, o bone et dulcissime Iesu, ante conspectum tuum genibus me provolvo, ac maximo animi ardore te oro atque obtestor, ut meum in cor vividos fidei, spei et caritatis sensus, atque veram peccatorum meorum poenitentiam, eaque emendandi firmissimam voluntatem velis imprimere.*'

Valentina leans forward and whispers in Tom's ear. 'What's this prayer?'

He keeps focused on Anna's closed eyes and whispers back. 'I'll tell you later.'

Anna's voice gets louder, almost as though each sentence gives her more strength.

'*Dum magno animi affectu et dolore tua quinque vulnera mecum ipse considero ac mente contemplor, illud prae oculis habens, quod iam in ore ponebat tuo David propheta de te, o bono Iesu: Foderunt manus meas et pedes meos: dinumeraverunt omnia ossa mea. Amen.*'

She takes a long breath, then opens her eyes and smiles at Tom. 'Have you come to save me, to protect me?'

'We all have,' says Tom, 'but you must tell us who we have to protect you from.'

Anna looks surprised. 'Mother, of course. Our Holy Mother.'

Louisa calls time out. She fears the questioning will trigger the appearance of another alter. Reluctantly, Valentina agrees to adjourn to a staff room down the corridor.

She bites her tongue while the clinician has her say on how and when the interviewing can continue.

'So what do you suggest?' Valentina asks impatiently. 'We leave it another day? Because that's just not going to happen.'

'An hour. Or two. Let her feel comfortable and stable in her own state.'

'I have a major criminal inquiry running. I really can't

make progress if you keep interrupting just as she starts to tell us what or who she's frightened of.'

'I know. I understand your situation, but my duty is to protect her mental health.'

'And mine is to find the person or persons who dumped a body by a river, severed some woman's hand and is clearly scaring your patient to the point of madness.'

'I respect that. And while I'll work with you to help clear up your crimes, I won't do it at the risk of making a very disturbed patient even more traumatised.' Louisa turns to Tom. 'What was the prayer all about? What does it mean?'

'It's a plea for help, made straight to Christ.'

'Aren't all prayers?' queries the clinician.

'No, not at all. Some are to God the Father, some to angels, some to the Holy Ghost. There are different prayers, for different bodies and different purposes.'

'And this one?'

'It's an intense one. One said personally and directly to Jesus at desperate times. When perhaps life is in peril or a big problem is being faced. It's really a cry for faith to be fortified, and a declaration of repentance and devotion.' Tom repeats its words in his head, then translates the end of the prayer: 'With deep affection and grief, I reflect upon Thy five wounds, having before my eyes that which Thy prophet David spoke about Thee, O good Jesus: They have pierced my hands and feet, they have counted all my bones. Amen.'

The two women say nothing.

To Louisa, a proud atheist, the words are meaningless, while Valentina's police training inevitably directs her beyond the elements of devotion, supplication and sacrifice and instead focuses on the key words *pierced hands, five wounds* and *bones.*

'Strictly speaking,' continues Tom, thoughtfully, 'this should be said kneeling down in front of a crucifix. The prayer begins, "Behold, O good and most sweet Jesus, I fall upon my knees before Thee . . ." I guess if she hadn't been so weak after the sedation and surgery, she'd have got out of bed and knelt.'

Valentina shakes her head. 'It's not that. Remember her apartment? All the crucifixes were on the ceiling, not the walls.' She realises the full implication of her own thoughts and adds speculatively, 'I think this is something that she would recite over and over in bed. I can easily imagine her lying there every night in the dark in that freaky bible bed, looking up at the shadows of the hanging rosary beads and repeating this until she eventually falls asleep.'

Louisa's still playing catch-up. 'She was hoping this prayer would keep her safe throughout her sleep?'

'She was banking on it,' answers Tom. 'But safe from what? The Virgin Mary? That just doesn't make sense.'

'In my experience, DID patients often don't.'

'She didn't say Virgin Mary,' observes Valentina. 'She said Holy Mother. Is there a difference?'

Tom has to think. 'Theologically – and pedantically – maybe. Mary was a virgin before she was chosen by God to carry Jesus. At this point she would not have been a mother.'

Louisa interrupts them. 'I think you're chasing down the wrong alleyway, or should I say church aisle.'

They look to her to elaborate.

'I think she meant *holy* in a sarcastic way. As in her own mother – a mother so holy she's always right and never does any wrong.'

Valentina sees her point. 'Could be. You're thinking she's traumatised by parental abuse?'

'It would fit the pattern for dissociative identity disorder.'

'How?'

'Long story. Let me try to explain. Briefly, one day Anna gets abused by her mother.'

233

'Physically or sexually?' asks Valentina.

'Doesn't matter. Certainly not for the sake of this example. Anyway, she's shocked and hurt by the abuse. Mother starts to make the abuse routine; this stresses Anna, who develops a mechanism to cope with it. So next time Mother comes seeking her kicks, Anna dissociates.'

'What do you mean?'

'She imagines that she's somewhere else and that whatever horrible thing her mother is doing is not happening to her. It's happening to some other kid. Someone tough enough to take it.'

Distressing as it sounds, Valentina can see the logic. 'Go on.'

Louisa does. 'So, when Mother turns up to routinely abuse Anna, Anna routinely sends out her alter-Anna, a stronger and more detached side of her, to cope with the abuse. The longer this goes on, the more permanent the alter-Anna, probably Little Suzie Fratelli, as we've come to know her, becomes.'

'How do you explain the others?' asks Tom. 'Cassandra, the Roman victim; Suzanna Grecoraci, the mother of two children; and Claudia from the Sabines.'

'Sometimes a second or third abuser – or different levels of abuse – enters the dimension, and therefore a second or third alter is needed. As layers of trauma are added, more layers of alters – protection – are necessary.'

Tom hasn't bought totally into the theory. 'I know child abuse is one of the horrors of our modern-day world, but isn't it usually the father, not the mother, who's the offender? And isn't it highly unusual for a mother to sexually abuse her own daughter?'

Valentina interrupts. 'Yes, but not unheard of. And remember, it can be a stepmother as much as a mother. There's a famous case in Britain of a serial killer who abused her daughter sexually, physically and psychologically for years. She and the girl's father even killed her sister and buried her under a patio.' Louisa becomes practical. 'As I said earlier, now that we have her real name, we'll search all the local doctors' records for any history of physical, mental or sexual abuse.'

'We'll do the same,' counters Valentina. 'We'll trace her mother and father and search for criminal records, social reports, anything that suggests incest or sexual assault from neighbours or extended family.'

Tom says nothing. He's lost in his thoughts. Thoughts that suggest what's going on could be even more than child abuse.

64

Guilio Brygus Angelis is brought into the interview room with handcuffs around his wrists and chains around his ankles.

Federico Assante introduces himself, sets a voice recorder whirring, reads him his rights and sits back without saying anything.

He wants to take stock.

This is an unusual case, with unusual victims. Now he's face to face with an unusual suspect.

Angelis looks slender and harmless.

Certainly no giant.

At a guess, he weighs in at less than eleven stone. That said, he's not carrying any body fat, and his arms are rippling with sinewy muscles. He certainly keeps himself fit; no doubt with some form of fight training. Federico wonders if there's even a special martial art for eunuchs, like there is for Shaolin monks.

He studies the guy's face.

No eyebrows.

Amazing how one missing feature messes up your whole appearance.

No beard line either. It gives him a strange softness that male models have. Metrosexuality.

The goon has the skin of a ten-year-old boy. Federico runs fingers over his own stubbly beard. It would be great not to shave again.

But not at the price of having your nuts cut off.

Then there are his eyes.

Federico has seen eyes like that before.

Many times before.

Savage eyes.

Criminal eyes.

Eyes that don't blink when a fight's about to break out. Eyes that don't look away when there's blood spilling and knives flashing under the street lights.

Now Federico's got the measure of him.

He's ready to start the interview.

'So, Guilio, do you feel like talking to us today? Or do we just send your silent ass for trial on charges of breaking and entering, assault and maybe even the attempted murder of Anna Fratelli?'

Angelis is using his index finger to doodle in the dust on top of the interview table.

He finishes a line, lifts his eyes and lets a cold stare settle on the detective's face.

Smug bastard.

A hard-working cop, but not that bright.

The fool thinks he's much cleverer than he really is.

Thinks he knows what's going on, but he doesn't have a clue. He certainly has no idea about how wrong he's got it. Okay, he's smart enough and energetic enough to take some prints and use them to pull a rap sheet.

Big deal.

Sooner or later that was always going to happen.

And by now he's probably also traced his home address and got some other fools to pull the place apart.

No matter.

They won't find anything. Certainly nothing that will make any sense to them.

But they know about Anna.

And that's a shame.

Anna should be invisible.

She shouldn't be seen by jerks like the one sitting opposite him, or that woman detective and her big thug.

It would have been good to have spent more time with them.

To have dealt with them properly.

'What's it to be, Guilio? We talk, maybe try to work in some mitigation to the charges, or you go straight to court and look forward to an eternity of being ass-fucked in prison?'

Angelis lets a smug smile spread across his face. 'I'd like a lawyer. Get me a brief within the hour and maybe I'll be good to you when I file my own charges.'

Federico laughs. 'Of what?'

He leans back and crosses his arms. 'False arrest. Assault. Defamation of character.'

'That's funny. Ha ha. We caught you right in the middle of the apartment, Guilio. Hiding in the damned dark.'

His arms stay crossed and his eyes remain fixed on the lieutenant's face.

Federico gets a bad feeling.

'Have you asked Anna about me?' Angelis pauses and reads the detective's face. 'I thought not. When you do, you'll find out why I was there.'

'What do you mean?'

'She wanted me there. She asked me to be there.' He uncrosses his arms and leans across the table. 'I was protecting her, you idiot. Not attacking her.'

65

To everyone's relief, Anna is still Anna.

Louisa Verdetti passes out a tray of drinks. Cola Lite for Valentina and Anna, *espresso doppio* and water for Tom and herself.

Valentina's phone rings. She apologises and ducks outside the patient's room to take the call.

Louisa hopes she stays there.

Getting through the layers of alters and down to the host is something of a clinical breakthrough. The chance of an uncluttered discussion with a DID sufferer is precious, and she's scared to death that questions about crimes and investigations are going to send Anna plunging back behind the cover of one of the alternative personalities.

'Do you feel okay to continue with our chat?' she asks kindly.

'Of course.' Anna sounds as sprightly as if she were being asked directions on a warm summer Sunday. 'What is it you want to know?'

Valentina's sudden return interrupts them.

She smiles apologetically, clicks the door quietly behind her and despite seeing that Louisa is in mid-conversation, addresses Anna directly. 'Do you know a man called Guilio Angelis?'

'Yes. Guilio works with me.'

Valentina makes her way to a chair alongside Anna's. 'We discovered him in your apartment yesterday, before we found you. Did you invite him inside?'

Now Anna has to think. A lot has happened since yesterday. She remembers doctors leaning over her, masked faces, blood everywhere, *her* blood, and before that – only blackness.

Blackness in the wardrobe, where she was frightened.

Blackness in that safe place in her own mind where she goes when terrible things start to happen.

And before that?

Slowly she starts to remember.

'Guilio came from work to help me.'

Valentina lets out a deep sigh. 'You asked him into your home?'

'*Sì.*'

'How do you know this man, Anna?'

'Like I said, I work with him.'

'Where?'

'Rosati's, in the Piazza del Popolo.'

'How long have you worked there?'

'Three, four years. I started in the cafeteria and was there for – oh, maybe a year, perhaps a little more, then I've been in the *ristorante* part of it ever since.'

'And Guilio?'

Another pause. 'About the same time. I think we even started the same week. He is a very good waiter.'

Valentina has one more attempt to shake a story that she knows is going to result in the guy who assaulted her being released. 'Anna, this is really important. Are you absolutely sure that you invited Guilio Angelis into your apartment yesterday and that he had the right to be there? He didn't force himself in? He wasn't threatening you in any way?'

'No.' She looks offended. 'Guilio's my friend. He's always been my friend. Why would he want to hurt me?'

Valentina curses softly to herself and stares into Anna's eyes.

The woman's not going to change her story, that much is clear.

She glances towards Louisa. 'Give me a minute. I have to ring my colleague.'

'Sure.'

As Valentina leaves, Louisa hands out glasses for the drinks, pops the tab on Anna's cola and pours it. 'You don't have to carry on with this session, you know. If you're too tired, or you find talking to us distressing, we can put it off until another time.'

Anna squeezes out a smile. 'No, I'm fine.' She puts her hand on her bandaged arm. 'Apart from this.' She turns her head towards the door where Valentina exited. 'Have I said something wrong?'

'No, not at all.'

'Is Guilio in trouble?'

Louisa doesn't know how to answer. 'You'd best ask the *capitano* when she comes back.'

Several more minutes pass until Valentina reopens the door.

It's clear something unpleasant has happened.

Her cheeks are flushed and there's no trace of a smile.

Anna looks agitated. 'Why were you asking me about Guilio?'

Valentina settles back into a chair next to her. 'We had to check that his story was the same as yours. We had to make sure he didn't force his way into your apartment and try to harm you.'

Anna falls silent.

She seems to understand.

Valentina suspects she still hasn't got the whole story. 'Anna, have you always lived in that apartment?'

Tension ripples across her forehead. '*Si.*'

'It's unusual, isn't it?'

She stares down at her glass of cola. 'You mean my bedroom, don't you?'

Valentina nods.

'It's the only way I feel safe at night.' She looks to Tom. 'You understand, don't you?'

Tom doesn't, but he tries to give her the impression he does. 'Help us all to understand, Anna.' He smiles sympathetically. 'Tell us in your own words why you do that to your room.'

'God protects me. Jesus protects me. When I'm in the midst of his words, I believe in Him and I believe He will protect me.' She closes her eyes. '*Yea, though I walk through the valley of the shadow of death, I will fear no evil; for thou art with me.*' She opens them again. 'I truly believe that, Father.'

'I'm sure you do, Anna – and you are right to.' Tom tries to be gentle. 'But exactly what – or who – do you need His protection from?'

'I told you earlier. Mother.'

'Do you mean the *Holy* Mother, the Virgin Mary, or your own mother?'

Anna clenches her fists.

She crosses her wrists and holds them like a crucifix across her breasts. 'Don't you know? Don't you understand?'

Tom can see that whatever trust she had in him is evaporating as fast as a waft of frankincense at morning Mass. '*I* do know, Anna, but I need you to tell these other people.' He gestures to Louisa and Valentina. 'They won't believe me if *I* tell them; it has to come from you.'

Anna starts breathing deeply.

Very deeply.

Panting hard.

Louisa wonders if she's starting to hyperventilate.

Anna stretches her arms wide and pulls her shoulders back, like a swan opening its wings.

Valentina moves to the edge of her seat.

Something's going to happen, and this time she's going to be prepared. There'll be no surprise head-butting, and no bust lips.

'The Mother is all we *are*!' shouts Anna.

Only she's no longer Anna.

Tom stands and takes a step towards her.

'Mater, who is all, is within us.' She tears at the bandage on her cut arm.

Louisa jumps from her seat and tries to stop her.

'Mater, who is all, is with us every day.' She pushes Louisa away and claws at the stitches.

Valentina is now on her feet and has reached the bed.

'From Her we are – and to Her we go!'

She grabs Anna's wrists and restrains her.

'From Her we are – and to Her we go!' The nonsense is no longer being shouted, it's being screamed. 'From Her we are – and to Her we go!'

Only one person in the room understands what's happening.

Tom Shaman sits silently and listens.

It makes perfect sense to him.

66

The whole place stinks.

Federico wonders if he's going to get ill from just being here.

No way was he going to let that androgynous son-of-a-bitch loose on the streets until he'd personally been to where he lives and found out what's hiding.

It's filthier than the Black Hole of Calcutta.

But he can't find anything incriminating.

No drugs. No weapons. No stolen goods.

The search team has already tossed Guilio Angelis's squalid apartment in the Aventine more thoroughly than a Michelin-starred salad, but Federico's determined to shake it some more.

He holds a handkerchief to his nose as he joins an officer in a tiny bathroom with a postage-stamp window smeared in green mould.

The stench from the toilet makes him want to hurl.

It's never seen bleach.

Correction: by the look of it, it's never been flushed.

'Show me the cistern again,' instructs Federico. 'Let's make doubly sure there's nothing bagged and hidden in the water.'

The young officer drops the seat cover, steps up and lifts off the heavy white ceramic top of the water tank.

Federico climbs up on the adjacent sink and cracks his head on the ceiling. '*Madonna porca!*' He rubs it. Static crackles off his latex gloves and makes his hair rise. He inches forward and peers down into the brown water around the ballcock and flush lever. He grimaces as he plunges his hand into the murky soup and fishes around. 'Why is the water here so filthy?'

'Bad plumbing. Rusty pipes,' says the officer from below. 'You drink this stuff and you're either dead or immortal within the hour.'

'No kidding.'

Federico jumps down. 'Nothing.' He strips off his glove because water's seeped in and looks at the sink. 'Don't tell me, this dirty pig doesn't even have a bar of soap? I can't believe it.'

'We've got some sterile wash in a kit bag, sir.'

'Get it.' Federico shakes the water off his hand and then remembers his manners, '*Scusi, per favore.*'

While he's waiting, he wanders back to the small lounge.

No TV.

How can anyone live these days without a television?

No balls and no TV.

What the hell does this guy do for fun?

Federico looks around.

There are no books either.

He doesn't read, doesn't watch the tube, doesn't have sex, doesn't even jerk off.

He does nothing.

This guy is Mr Nothing.

Federico wanders into the next room.

The bedroom doesn't even have a bed. Only a mattress on the floor.

No sheets.

He pulls open a small built-in wardrobe.

The search team have already stripped it of clothes and shoes.

It's empty, except for some old sheets of newspaper lining the bottom.

He lifts some up.

They're not old papers.

They're pages from bibles.

Hundreds and hundreds of pages from dozens of different bibles.

'It's all going to be okay. I can help you. God will protect you.'

Tom moves his chair so that Anna can only see him and is not distracted by Louisa or Valentina. 'I know you believe in God, that you pray to Him and that you trust in Him.'

Anna holds his hand as tightly as she can, but it's a grip of fear rather than reassurance. She's on the brink of tears.

Stress is building rather than subsiding.

'Are you all right?' asks Tom gently.

'They're going to kill me.' The first tear rolls down her left cheek. 'Please don't let them kill me.'

Tom strokes the back of her hand. 'No one's going to hurt you.'

'They have to. They say they have to.'

'Who, Anna? *Who* has to?'

'The Galli and the Sisters.' She sniffs and reaches towards a box of tissues. 'I know they'll kill me.'

Tom stretches, picks up the box and hands over several of the soft white tissues. 'No one's going to harm you, I promise.'

Her mood changes.

She looks angry and speaks in a strange and hostile voice.

'Anna has wronged us. She is *sacer*! Mater says we must take those who are given to the gods and bury them alive around the sacred walls of our womb.'

Meekly Anna responds to the new alter. 'I've done nothing wrong.'

The angry voice counters, 'You are a threat to us, a threat to our existence here in the womb and to the discovery of the book.'

'I am no threat!' the quieter voice pleads. 'And it is no womb. The place you hold me in is an infernal cell, a cave in the depths of Hades!'

'Be careful, sister, or by morning you will find earth in your mouth. Now come with us.'

'No! I hate it there. Leave me alone.'

The two voices almost overlap now, the words fast and furious, a verbal stream of inner turmoil. There is no difference between them in tone. 'You will never be alone, we will always be with you, in your sight and in your spirit.'

'Let me be! I'm frightened of this darkness. Please let me out, let me go outside.'

'There is no outside for those who are not with us.'

'Enough!' shouts Louisa. She's out of her seat and pushing her way past Valentina and Tom.

Anna lashes out. 'Be gone! I will feed you to the dog with three heads.'

'There is no dog! You are making it all up to frighten us.'

'Great Cerberus can already taste your blood and bones.'

Louisa pulls an emergency cord dangling from the ceiling. She turns to Tom and Valentina. 'Please leave the room, and let me deal with this.'

They back slowly away, both uncertain whether Louisa can really handle the situation.

Anna's eyes are bulging, her face flushed with blood. The alters are battling for control of her.

'Mother is coming for you. Mother is mad at you.'

'She's not real. I don't believe in her.'

'She can hear you, Anna. She can hear you and she's going to punish you.'

Tom and Valentina are brushed aside as nurses and the duty doctor rush into the room. From outside the glass they watch Anna being pinned down and sedated.

Finally Louisa emerges.

She's scarlet with anger.

'You don't care, do you? You just don't care about anything or anyone other than yourselves and your stupid case.'

'Calm down.' Valentina takes a step back so the clinician is less in her face.

'Calm down?' Louisa can't believe her ears. 'I just had to

panic-call a doctor to sedate my patient. She's torn the stitches in the arm that we had to sew up after she almost killed herself, and you – *you* ask me to calm down!'

Valentina is unfazed. 'I'm not asking you, I'm *telling* you.'

Louisa steps into her space again. 'In here, *you* don't tell *me* anything. In here, care for the patient comes first, way before what you want and your blessed criminal investigation.'

She turns and storms off down the corridor.

Tom and Valentina are left standing next to the Carabinieri guard minding the room. Green curtains have now been pulled around the windows, but there's a gap big enough to see the medical team finishing the patch-up job on the strangest patient ever to occupy a bed in ICU.

'What now?' asks Tom.

Valentina shakes her head. 'Good question. What indeed?'

68

Only when they get out of the pressure-cooker heat of the hospital and stand in the cold fresh air does Valentina realise exactly what she and Tom have to do next.

'Shopping,' she announces, with a certain sense of fun. 'We've got to go shopping.'

She zaps open the Fiat and adds, 'You look ridiculous in those things that you're wearing, and I feel filthy in this stuff. I haven't worn the same clothes for two days running since I first slept over at a boyfriend's house.'

Tom opens the passenger door. 'And that was how long ago?'

She grins at him over the car roof. 'Ex-boyfriends are not the kind of thing a lady talks about.'

And that's the best Tom can get out of her.

The journey into the city doesn't take long, but Valentina spends a large part of it making calls.

Calls to fix a new place for them to sleep that night.

To her insurance company to inform them about the blaze at her apartment.

To Federico.

'You okay?' she asks Tom, as she finally hangs up. 'You look lost in thought, and not a particularly pleasant one.'

'It's not.'

He watches a scooter almost rip off the passenger-side wing mirror. 'We should think about some of the things Anna said.'

'In particular?'

He's not sure how much to speculate and how much to keep to himself. 'You know how you and Louisa have been discussing whether Anna was abused as a kid, maybe by her own mother?'

'It seems a way to explain her multiple personalities.'

'Well, she mentioned sisters today. Did you notice?'

'I did, but I couldn't work out whether she meant blood sisters or sisters in some kind of organisation or movement.'

'Neither could I,' admits Tom. 'Either way, she was indicating that whatever horror she's mixed up in, there are other women involved. Maybe they're at risk as well.'

'Only women,' notes Valentina.

Tom has to think back. 'No. Not true. She mentioned Galli.'

She's none the wiser. 'And Galli is who?' She slips the Fiat into a parking bay at Carabinieri HQ. 'I've never heard of him before.'

'Them, not he.' Tom unbuckles his seat belt and waits until they're both out of the Punto before he completes the explanation. 'They were priests. Eunuch priests who existed hundreds of years before Christ. By the way, where are we going?'

She takes his hand. 'Not far. Don't worry, we'll soon have you properly dressed. Eunuch priests? Did you know any?'

'I knew some who *should* have been eunuchs.' Before Tom can continue, a waft of wind fills his pink parachute of a shirt and puffs him up like the Michelin Man. It gives Valentina a fit of the giggles while she pats it flat. 'Let's hurry up; you must be freezing without a coat.'

'No, I'm fine; I'm a super-tough American, remember.'

'Of course you are. You keep on believing that.'

His clothes provide endless amusement as they walk along Via del Corso and duck into a discount designer store full of fervent fashion fans. Young women nudge their beautifully dressed boyfriends and point him out with whispered asides. Trendily dressed Italian men slalom around him, as though just touching such unfashionable clothes might be sartorially contagious.

'Do you see anything you like?' asks Valentina, unable to stop smiling.

'The exit. That's what I'd like most.'

'Understood!' She grabs two packs of Calvin Klein boxers from a basket.

He looks surprised. 'You know my size?'

Her eyes sparkle. 'To the centimetre.'

Tom fries with embarrassment. He picks up a plain blue shirt from sale stock. Valentina shakes her head at him and heads for a rail marked *New Arrivals*.

Ninety minutes and almost a thousand euros later, she has him fitted out with everything from socks to a Dolce and Gabbana scarf.

Valentina has the sales assistant drop his old clothes in a bin behind the check-out and Tom leaves dressed in a long-sleeved white polo jumper from Collezioni Armani, a pair of Hugo Boss jeans and a new overcoat.

The air outside is icy sharp after the heat of the shop.

He takes Valentina's hand, his other clutching a spray of shiny bags. 'I feel like I've just been in one of those before and after makeover shows.'

'Except the before was pretty good already.' She checks her watch. 'Now me.'

He looks shocked.

She points across the street to a snack bar. 'How about you grab a table in there and I'll meet you in half an hour?'

He knows he's got off lightly. 'You sure?'

'I just saw how bad you are at shopping for yourself. Watching me choose clothes would be Purgatory, no?'

He thinks about doing penance and going with her, but she's already on the move, so he lets her go and drifts towards the bar.

Valentina shops at lightning speed.

She resists the luxury of lingering over anything, and quickly collects a black wool trouser suit, white and black blouses, faded blue jeans and a monochrome cardigan.

Choosing underwear takes more thought and care than it's done for a very long time.

She finds herself agonising in the shoe area before grabbing practical flats rather than a pair of high slingbacks that she's sure were calling out her name.

Tom spends the time toying with a beer and thinking of Anna, her 'sisters' and the eunuch priests.

From what he remembers, the Galli were attached to a secret sect devoted to a prophetess who had followers spread throughout Greece, Rome, Anatolia, Crete and beyond.

He shuts his eyes and tries to recall everything he can about this strange pre-Christian era, when rituals and prophecies were the most powerful things on earth.

He's still crawling through the dust of societies long

crumbled when he notices Valentina standing over him. 'Planet Earth to Major Tom, can you hear me?'

He rouses himself. 'Sorry.' He touches the nearly empty beer glass. 'One drink and my sharpness has gone.'

She feels guilty about not letting him unwind. 'I'm afraid we have to go. I got a call from Federico while I was in the shops. He's back at the incident room and we need to start a briefing.'

'No problem.' Tom struggles to his feet, gathers his bags and traipses after her.

They walk briskly, a difficult thing to do in Rome. Not just because the pavements are crowded, but because they're so uneven and the slightest rain turns them into ankle-twisting water traps.

Back at the station, they stuff their shopping in Valentina's car, and steal a kiss before entering the grand old building. A slight hesitation and a glance over his shoulder tips Tom off to the fact that she's looked for CCTV cameras first and then decided she really doesn't care who sees them. A small act, but nevertheless one that sends a big jolt of warmth running through him.

Maybe this relationship is going to turn out to be even more than he'd hoped for.

69

Things have gone wrong.

Horribly wrong.

The meeting hasn't even started, but Valentina knows it

from the tense, grey look on Federico's face as he approaches her.

The briefing room is filling with people, ready for the case update. Tom sits quietly at the back, his eyes seldom leaving Valentina.

Federico beckons her to one side. He's keen to make sure they're not overheard as he breaks the bad news. 'Angelis is back on the street.'

'So quickly?'

'After Anna supported his story about inviting him into her apartment, we had no grounds to hold him on the charge of breaking and entering. He asked again for a brief while I was out, and the duty solicitor sprang him.'

'Caesario sanctioned this?'

He shrugs. 'In fairness, he couldn't stop it. Without the illegal entry charge there was no way we could justify the assault charge.'

Valentina feels her temper rise. 'I got thrown all over the apartment and almost killed, and the law doesn't call that assault?'

'Self-defence. He says he thought you were an intruder.'

'Bullshit. I banged on the door. I rang the bell and screamed out that I was Carabinieri. I made so much noise that people on the two floors above knew who I was.'

Federico shrugs again.

She slaps a hand on the wall.

He tries to placate her. 'It could be worse.'

She glares at him. 'And how?'

'He could have complained. Started an action for assault.'

The anger shows on her face.

'Ridiculous, I know, but it would still have caused problems.'

Valentina knows he's right. Caesario would have beaten her with a complaint as surely as if it were a riot baton.

She determines not to let the setback throw her. 'Okay, let's get over it and get this meeting started. Anything else?'

'I searched Angelis's apartment before we turned him loose. The place was a pigsty. He had a stack of bible pages in the bottom of his wardrobe. Looked similar to the stuff on Anna's bedroom wall.'

'It doesn't take us very far. He's admitted knowing her, being in her apartment.'

'It shows that maybe he shares the same fears as she does.'

'That's interesting. Still not enough to re-arrest him, though.'

'I know.'

She pats his shoulder. 'I appreciate you going the extra mile and searching his place.'

She walks to the front of the room and settles down at the main table, pleased that Federico put himself out. It's clear he's trying to build bridges.

She's about to silence the pre-meeting chatter when Caesario sticks his head around the door.

'Morassi!'

She can feel everyone's eyes on her as she gets up and follows him outside. She guesses Angelis has made that complaint after all.

Damn!

No doubt there's going to be a full internal inquiry, maybe even suspension while it's carried out.

'Sir?'

'I apologise for interrupting your briefing, Captain, but I'm afraid it's necessary.'

She notices him looking down at her hands, nervous that she might be recording him.

'An official complaint has been lodged against you.'

Valentina doesn't react. She'll hear him out. She simply defended herself, did nothing to be ashamed of, certainly nothing that she wouldn't do all over again if she had to.

Caesario continues, but he almost looks apologetic rather than triumphant. 'Sylvio Valducci, the administrator at the Policlinico, has obtained a court order protecting Anna Fratelli and restraining you – or us – from seeing her or contacting her in any way. That includes telephone calls or anything else you could dream up.'

Valentina is stunned. It's not Angelis after all.

'The hospital claims that you and Lieutenant Assante personally put the mental health of their patient at risk. They say you did this on several different occasions, and in spite of warnings and pleas from the head of their psychiatric unit.'

She knows what's coming next.

Suspension.

What a weasel. Caesario is even prepared to take down his lap dog Federico if that's what it takes to get at her.

'With respect, sir, all interviews with the prisoner have been carried out under medical supervision, and whenever we were asked to back off, we did. Straight away. No hesitation.'

'Do you have any evidence – forensic or circumstantial – that proves she is involved in any criminal activity?'

Valentina thinks twice about trying to explain rationally how Anna manifested dissociated personalities from centuries ago who seemingly had knowledge of current crime scenes. 'No, sir.'

'A lot of work, money and time, and you've really made no progress?'

'Sir . . .'

He halts her with his hand. 'Don't try to defend it, Captain. This woman patient is now out of bounds to you and your inquiry team. She's off limits, do you understand?'

'Yes, sir.'

He turns his head towards the briefing room, well aware that it's full of officers awaiting her return. 'Where are we on the rest of this case?'

She hesitates.

'Aside from this lunatic woman, are you close to giving me any clear explanation for why we have a dead, ball-less man under a bridge on the Tiber and a severed hand in a church in Cosmedin?'

The look on her face says she isn't. 'No, sir. It's extremely complicated.'

'Then let me simplify things. Have we identified the murder victim?'

Valentina looks pained. 'We lifted prints from the corpse, but they don't give us anything.'

'And the dismembered hand?'

'The same.'

'So nothing?'

'I wouldn't go as far—'

He cuts her off again. 'No identities on the dead or injured. No suspect to interrogate. No forensic evidence to land a charge on anyone, and as far as I can see, not even a hint of a motive. How much closer to nothing can you get than that?'

Valentina can't help but colour a little. 'We have leads and theories, sir. Given time, we—'

'May well get someone else killed?'

She bites her tongue.

Major and captain just stand and stare at each other.

He says nothing.

She says nothing.

The conversation's over. Now is the moment when he's going to suspend her.

Caesario smiles.

He's going to let her stew in her own juice. Marinate in her anticipation of his next action. 'Do you know what I'm going to say to you now, Captain?'

She swallows hard.

'I'm sure you do.' Another smile. 'As of this moment, you are suspended from duty. You will receive written confirmation of your suspension before you leave this building. This suspension implies no guilt or pre-judgement; it is merely necessary to remove you from the process that will now unfold. On receipt of the suspension notice, you will surrender your firearm, any Carabinieri equipment, identification and authorisation. You will not instigate, nor receive, any contact from colleagues, at either this workplace or any other within the force. You will be notified in due course of any charges brought against you. You are entitled to representation at any future hearing should one be convened. Do you understand what I've told you?'

She stays strong. 'Yes, sir.'

'Good. Do you have any questions about the process I've just outlined to you?'

'No, sir.'

'Then please go and wait outside my office while the appropriate documentation is prepared and where you will be formally relieved of your command.'

Valentina starts to turn away.

He puts a hand on her arm and whispers in her ear, 'You really should have taken up my offer, Morassi.'

70

Tom Shaman sits silently in the briefing room and watches.

Gossip about Valentina spreads like a virus.

A poisonous whisper here joins with speculation there.

Within minutes, everyone is infected by suggestions that she's being sacked, suspended or reprimanded. The cause seems to be anything from insubordination to fraud or even corruption.

At first Federico does nothing to stop the outbreak. Finally he steps in.

'Can I have some quiet, please?' He walks to the chair where Valentina sat and stands behind it. 'Captain Morassi is busy with the major, so let's make use of your precious time and begin the briefing in her absence. I want to run through house-to-house enquiries and medical, employment and social services searches on both Anna Fratelli and the prisoner we released this afternoon, Guilio Angelis. After that, I want a team chasing the forensic lab for progress on all their reports. I want an update on the translation analysis being done on the biblical text pasted on the walls of Anna's apartment . . .'

Federico stops.

His attention switches to the back of the hall.

Major Armando Caesario is standing there. 'Lieutenant, due to unseen and serious circumstances, you need to adjourn this meeting immediately.'

Chairs start to scrape back on the old wooden floor, but there's no accompanying chatter.

Tom fades into a corner behind a whiteboard as the room empties.

He hears the door shut.

'Lieutenant, I have just suspended Captain Morassi pending an investigation into a very serious matter.'

'Sir?'

'The administrator at the Policlinico has made allegations of serious misconduct against both you and her. As a consequence, he has obtained a protection order stopping us interviewing or interfering in any way with the treatment of their patient, Anna . . . Anna . . .' He wriggles his fingers as he fumbles for her name.

'Fratelli, sir.'

'Fratelli.' Caesario takes a beat, then asks his next question. 'How do you view Captain Morassi's actions in relation to Fratelli, Lieutenant?'

'In what way, sir?'

'In reference to how she conducted herself with the patient. Did she bully her? Was she aggressive with her? Physically violent?' Before Federico can answer, Caesario spots Tom by the whiteboard.

'Who are you? What are you doing here?'

Tom answers calmly, 'I'm waiting for Captain Morassi. I'm a friend.'

The penny drops. 'Oh, the *friend*. I understand. Well, friends should wait downstairs in reception, not in here.' Caesario steps aside and motions to the door.

'Sure.' Tom reluctantly leaves.

The major turns back to Assante. 'Why was *he* in this briefing room?'

'Captain Morassi thought he could help.'

'Dear God, what is the force coming to?' Caesario lets out a long sigh. 'I never thought I'd see the day when we had women captains, let alone a situation where one might think her ex-priest lover could be of use to an investigation.'

Federico finds himself compelled to defend her. 'He did find the body by the river, sir. And he did overpower the prisoner, Angelis, when he assaulted Captain Morassi. And being an ex-priest, he may have something to offer on interpreting some of the biblical links to the case.'

'Oh, really? Well then, maybe he'd make a better officer than her.' Caesario looks over to the door. 'Before we were rudely interrupted by the captain's *lover*, I was asking you about her behaviour towards Fratelli. You didn't answer me.'

'I'm sorry, what exactly was the question again, sir?'

'Was Morassi violent towards the prisoner? There was that

incident in the cell block; did she provoke it?'

'No, sir.'

Caesario's not getting the answers he wants.

'Think again, Lieutenant. Perhaps it wasn't quite as you and she wrote it up. Did Morassi provoke the prisoner the night she was arrested? Was the patient just defending herself?'

Federico sees what the major is driving at. 'It wasn't like that, sir.'

'Think harder, Assante. Because if it had been like that, it would also be consistent with the story told by this man we released, Angelis. Maybe Morassi didn't clearly identify herself as a police officer. Maybe she did make a wrongful entry into Fratelli's apartment and this man was just reacting like a protective friend.'

'I wasn't there at that incident, sir.'

Caesario gets himself up close to Federico. 'This is one of those moments when you have to make a decision. Decide whose side you are on. You need to work out whether you want to be a witness or a defendant.'

Federico tries to play dumb. 'How do you mean, sir?'

'Well, let's look at your own behaviour towards Anna Fratelli. Were you acting that way of your own volition, or were you simply following Morassi's orders?'

He hesitates.

'Were you following orders, Lieutenant, or were you disobeying them?'

'Following them, sir.'

'I thought so.'

Federico can't leave it there. 'But Major, neither of us did anything wrong. We respected every demand by the medics to back off as soon as the patient looked even remotely stressed.'

'Save it, Lieutenant! If that's your approach, then I can listen to the rest of what you have to say at your disciplinary hearing.'

Federico looks down at his shoes.

Caesario puts a fatherly hand on his officer's shoulder. 'What I imagine, Federico, is that you were put in a difficult – no, not difficult – an *impossible* position.' He pats his shoulder. 'You were given instructions by your captain, and because you respect rank, you followed them as best you could. However – and this is a very important *however* – I am also sure you voiced your concerns to the captain about her ethics in pursuing such actions.' He gives him a knowing look. 'I am equally sure that you may now be able to recall those concerns and list them in a witness statement that you could write out for use in a case against the captain.'

Federico doesn't respond.

'It would be greatly to your benefit – both immediately and subsequently – should you be blessed with full recall about Captain Morassi's unbefitting and unethical behaviour. If such a statement were made now, I would be able to allow you to continue as the lead officer in this case and promise that charges are not brought against you. After all, you will be a key witness for the prosecution in the court martial that is bound to follow.'

71

Tom doesn't have to wait long in reception.

Valentina soon appears. She looks drained of all colour. In her hands are two carrier bags. Her personal belongings, newly cleared from her desk.

'Come here.' He opens his arms and embraces her tightly. 'Everything will be fine.'

Valentina is more angry than tearful.

She didn't expect fairness. Certainly didn't expect favours. But she also didn't anticipate this.

She pulls away from him. 'Let's talk in the car, not here.'

He understands.

Valentina produces the veneer of a smile for the front desk staff as she leaves the building.

'Your major came into the briefing room after you left.'

'I guessed so.' Valentina zaps the car open and they slide inside. 'He gave me a letter suspending me, pending an internal inquiry and a possible court martial. Then he told me that he'd made you wait in reception.'

Tom nods. 'I heard him speaking to Federico. Sounded like he was warming him up to take over from you.'

'Big surprise.'

She starts the engine, clicks off the park brake and moves out of the yard.

'They were talking about the night you got injured, and I got the feeling Federico was being asked to say it was your fault.'

Valentina turns on the radio as the Fiat noses out into the traffic. 'I can't talk about it right now, Tom. I don't know whether I want to scream, get hideously drunk or find a gun and blow Caesario's head off.'

'Screaming is the best option out of the three.'

She does.

Very loudly.

Tom covers his ears.

When she's finished, they both laugh.

He dips the radio. 'As a matter of interest, where is home tonight?'

'Not that fleapit we stayed in. The insurance company is

going to cover a hotel until they've inspected the place and filed a report. I have somewhere in mind.'

He can't help but be impressed. Even when her world turns to garbage, she's still together enough to look after them both. Seems women the world over do that. Guys take a body blow and they go down. They wallow or drink themselves unconscious. Women take a knock and they just ride it, get on with the job of looking after themselves and those they love most.

Minutes later, Valentina parks at the front of a functional three-star on Via Mario de' Fiori.

'Let me book us in,' says Tom. 'If the press get a whiff of the suspension and come hunting, then you'll be harder to trace.'

She slaps a credit card down on the reception desk. 'I don't want to be hard to trace.' She stands tippy-toe and kisses him.

The front desk is busy and they have to wait.

Tom takes the place in.

It's cosy enough.

Off to his right is a lounge area with light wood-panelled walls, and some of those dark chesterfield leather settees that you see in old English homes. A large desk in the corner supports a computer and printer, and there's a long coffee table filled with magazines and leaflets about Rome. To his left, a thick red carpet flows down a marble staircase into the reception area. There are only two people working behind the high curved desk, hence the delay. Behind them, Tom sees the key slots and mail for a total of seventeen rooms. There are no frequent-visitor leaflets and nothing promoting other hotels across Italy or Europe. He guesses the place is probably family-owned and not part of a chain.

All pluses in his book.

Valentina dangles a brass key and a warm smile before him.

He follows her upstairs to a first-floor bedroom.

It's decorated in soft peach and gentle gold, with matching ceiling-to-floor curtains and a bed large enough to land an Airbus on.

Valentina kicks off her shoes and throws her coat on the quilt. 'Wine! I don't care what colour or temperature, just open some, please. I'm going to the bathroom.'

Tom finds the minibar.

He selects two small screw-top bottles of Frascati and empties them into glasses. Valentina reappears from the bathroom and all but downs the cold white before sitting on the bed alongside him. 'I was just thinking, now that work isn't in the way, we should do something touristy. You've not seen anything of Rome except police stations and bodies, so let's fix that.'

He touches her face. 'I've seen everything I want.'

'Aaah, you say all the right things.'

He puts an arm around her and kisses the side of her forehead. 'I'm happy just to grab dinner here and stay in the hotel if you prefer.'

She shakes her head. 'No, I'd like to get out. I don't want to sit and brood. I need to move around and be distracted.'

A muffled ring fights its way out from the pocket of the crumpled coat she's thrown on the bed.

Valentina ignores it.

She sips her wine and it rings again.

Tom unfolds the coat and offers her the noisy pocket. 'Maybe it's good news.'

She doubts it. She dips her hand in and takes out her phone.

Tom goes back to the minibar in search of more wine. By the time he's retrieved some from the back of the bottom shelf, she's finished the call.

Her face looks as empty as their glasses.

'It was Federico. He's been suspended as well.'

72

Guilio Brygus Angelis doesn't go back to the stinking hole he calls home.

He may never go back.

The cops didn't find anything there, he's sure of that, but he knows it's only a matter of time before they get lucky.

He learned that a long time ago.

You can take all the precautions in the world, but if you hang around in the same place too long, eventually the cops get lucky. They talk to neighbours, shopkeepers, local kids. They get a hold of you.

Well, he won't be staying around long enough for that to happen.

It's starting to rain – a shower, that's all – but he backs up into the doorway of a cheap souvenir shop.

Doorways are always good places to be.

And this is an excellent one.

It's the perfect place to watch the comings and goings at the Carabinieri command building right opposite him.

He's amazed by how many cops come out to smoke.

No sooner are they through the front doors than their big cop hands are jabbing filters in their snarky little mouths and they're lighting up.

Lieutenant Assante throws down a match as he lights up and walks out into the rain.

Guilio follows him to his car, a beat-up Lancia parked a block away.

Doesn't look as though the Carabinieri pay very well. There's a child seat in the back. No doubt his money goes on his kid, or kids. He looks like the type who'll have as many as his wife will make him.

Guilio notes the number and watches as the cop climbs in and drives off without even putting on his seat belt.

Reckless.

The guy is just asking for trouble.

73

Drinking and walking are universal answers to most problems.

When the minibar is dry, Valentina resorts to the latter.

Motion to cope with emotion.

Lots of emotion.

In fact, she's fired up and emotional enough to walk the length of the Appian Way, and then some.

She's proud of the career she's built herself. Rightly so. Proud of the crimes she's solved, the people she's helped and all the badasses she's locked up.

How dare a sexist dinosaur like Caesario try to take that away from her?

She walks Tom all the way out to the Piazza Navona, but to no avail. Bernini's ever-flowing Fontana dei Fiumi does nothing to lighten her mood.

From there she drags him east through the back streets,

across Corso del Rinascimento and Via della Rotonda to the awe-inspiring Pantheon.

Inside, neither of them manages more than marginal interest in the guide's stories of Agrippa, Hadrian, Constantine and the dozens of other historic figures who created, refurbished, worshipped or were buried beneath its famous dome.

The walking and the sights aren't working.

Valentina just can't clear her mind.

As the night starts to frost up and their feet begin to break down, they seek refuge in a touristy restaurant off Via della Fontanella di Borghese.

Tom chooses octopus cooked in a light tomato sauce with pecorino cheese, followed by mezze maniche pasta with bacon.

Valentina isn't that hungry, but gets tempted by a light tempura of *baccalà* and anchovies, followed by a small portion of tagliatelle with artichokes.

They pick out a reasonable bottle of Amarone della Valpolicella and try to talk about anything and everything except her suspension and the case she's been taken off.

Only when a second bottle has been opened does she feel ready to stop avoiding things. 'I suppose tomorrow I should find myself a solicitor.'

'Don't rush into it. Things could look different in the morning.'

'I won't, but I need representation.' She stares out of the window at the bright lights and the crowds of noisy strangers, and feels isolated and vulnerable. 'This isn't my city, Tom. Aside from you, I don't have friends here.'

He tries to reassure her. 'You probably have more people on your side than you think.'

'I doubt it.' She swills wine in her glass. 'When will you need to leave?'

The questions stings. 'Not until you tell me to.'

'*Grazie.*' His gesture of kindness makes her feel tearful. The only other person who would have been this understanding and supportive was her cousin, Antonio.

She curses herself for letting her guard down and thinking about him.

One moment of sadness, and memories of him flood in on her.

She blinks tears from her eyes. 'This damned disciplinary case could take weeks.'

'Then I'll stay weeks.'

'Or months.'

'Then I'll stay months.'

She doesn't laugh, but there's a suggestion of a smile. 'Years? Maybe a lifetime?'

'Now you're pushing it.'

Finally the laugh comes. She looks into his eyes and thinks that if he does stay, then she might just cope with all the madness that Caesario and his cronies are going to throw at her.

They ask for the bill while drinking the last of the Valpolicella.

Tom tips the waiter, and at the door helps Valentina into her coat.

Outside, the night is crisp, and they link arms snugly as they walk back towards the Spanish Steps.

Valentina is feeling mellow and more than just a little drunk. She gestures to the fountain at the foot of the steps. 'Rome is beautiful – but it doesn't stop your life turning to rat shit.'

'Your life's fine, Valentina. You are defined by who you are and who you love, not by your job and what your boss does to you.'

Even through the haze of too much alcohol, she knows he's right.

She holds him tighter and hopes she doesn't fall and make a fool of herself before they reach the hotel.

An almost full moon shines on them, and Tom briefly looks up at it. For the first time that night he isn't thinking of Valentina.

His thoughts are with another woman.

One lying in a psychiatric bed across the city. A woman terrified of the dark and the evil she's certain it will bring.

74

There are no windows in the room.

No natural light can spill in from the world outside the hospital and make the occupant feel part of normal life.

There's only the homogeneous, alien whiteness of the forever-buzzing fluorescent tubes.

But Anna Fratelli knows the day is over.

It is night-time.

She knows it as surely as if she was standing outside and watching the great Roman sky grow black around her.

She clutches a bible that one of the nurses has given her and rubs it over her body like a bar of soap.

No inch of skin is left unlathered.

The words of the Lord will protect her.

His are the only true words.

Mother is wrong.

What She says about Him is wrong.

Anna kisses the bible and stands it, cover facing her, on the cabinet beside her bed.

She kneels and prays.

'*En ego, o bone et dulcissime Iesu, ante conspectum tuum genibus me provolvo, ac maximo animi ardore te oro atque obtestor, ut meum in cor vividos fidei . . .*'

They will come now.

From out of their own darkness, from places beyond the womb, the others will come.

And one will take her.

'*. . . spei et caritatis sensus, atque veram peccatorum meorum poenitentiam, eaque emendandi firmissimam voluntatem velis imprimere . . .*'

The doctors have given her medicines. Pills. Liquid on spoons. Drips. They've put them in her mouth and in her veins and told her they'll make her better.

She doubts it.

Maybe it's the drugs that are making her sleepy.

Or – more likely – it's the others.

It's always tiring when they take her. They sap her energy and drain her.

She feels increasingly listless.

She looks across the room for the paper and crayons that the nurses let her have.

No pen. No pencil. You might hurt yourself.

She's too tired to reach them. Her eyes close for a second.

Cassandra is there.

She's dressed in a beautiful white *intusium* topped by a lavishly embroidered white and gold *stolla*. She looks as pale as moonlight as the soldiers trundle her past in a rough wooden chariot.

Cassandra's eyes see Anna. She calls to her. 'Have faith, sister. You and I are strong. I am coming to help you. I will be with you soon.'

Anna can feel Cassandra's voice penetrating her.

Touching her soul.

In the wall mirror in the hospital room she sees her lips moving, but it is Cassandra's calm and dignified voice she hears.

She walks to the mirror. Stands before it and sees Cassandra talking directly to her.

'Mother cannot hurt you. Whatever She does to you, sweet Anna, She cannot harm you.'

Behind Cassandra, crowds are jeering and throwing things at her. Stones. Rotten fruit. Broken pottery.

Anna covers her face for fear of being hurt. She turns from the mirror. She slowly rotates three hundred and sixty degrees.

Cassandra is there again.

Her hand has been cut off.

Blood drips in pools of jelly from the stump.

Her eyes roll back in their sockets.

Anna turns back to the mirror.

Behind the bible, blood pours from her stitched arm while she mouths the words that Mother says most . . .

You mustn't tell, Anna.

Mustn't tell

Mustn't tell.

75

For a fleeting second, Valentina has forgotten about yesterday.

Her eyelids blink, her brain tells her body she's awake, and her first thoughts of the day are about Tom.

But they're quickly chased off.

Someone has let the bad thoughts out as well.

Suspension, Caesario and court martial.

They're all there again, banging on her window and pulling faces at her.

Tom's out for the count, breathing as peacefully as a baby. She slides from his warmth and goes to the bathroom.

The face peering back at her from the harsh light of the mirror above the sink looks scared and drained and old.

It's not her.

Valentina determines that she's not going to be that face.

Not for much longer.

It's not even five a.m., but she gets dressed and lets herself silently out of the room. There's something in the boot of the car that she wants.

Her feet make slapping noises and echoes in the deserted car park.

It's cold enough to see her breath in front of her.

She beeps open the central locking of the Fiat and grabs the carrier bags of personal belongings she collected from her desk when Caesario suspended her.

It hurts to even touch them.

As she walks back to the room, she realises she feels something more today than just anger and frustration.

Shame.

Its icy fingers are digging into her shoulder and won't let go.

How will she tell her parents that she's been suspended? How will she break it to friends back in Venice and to her old boss, Vito Carvalho?

Vito might actually understand. She confided in him about her brush with Caesario, so he might not think badly of her.

She lets herself back into the bedroom, trying to be as quiet as possible.

But Tom hears her.

He turns the bedside light on and screws up his eyes. 'Where have you been?'

She holds up her bags. 'The car. I wanted to get these.'

He glances at the digital clock near the lamp. 'So early? It's not even five.'

'I know. I'm sorry.' She climbs on the bed, kisses him and turns the light out. 'You try to get some more sleep.'

She smells of fresh air and the start of a new day. Her hair and skin are cold and sensual.

'Not yet. Kiss me awake some more.'

Too tired and drunk to make love last night, Valentina now desperately needs sex. She needs it to renew herself.

Tom drags her clothes off.

He cups her breasts while she straddles him.

Her long hair falls around his face as she bends and covers his mouth and neck in kisses.

It's an eternity before they're spent.

They lie together in blissful post-coital slumber. Shafts of sharp winter sunshine arrow through gaps in the curtains and lodge in the wooden floor.

They wake at almost exactly the same second.

Valentina kisses him lightly.

'Will you order some breakfast while I shower?' She steps naked from the tangled quilt and escapes to the bathroom.

'Sure.' Tom watches her every step. 'Anything special?'

'Carbohydrates!' she calls from the bathroom. 'Lots and lots of carbs.' She sets the shower going. 'And juice. And coffee.' Her voice becomes more distant. 'Oh, and maybe some fruit. Berries if they have any.'

He dials room service and orders croissants, pastries, muffins, a fruit platter, granola, some low-fat yoghurt, cranberry juice and a pot of black coffee.

Valentina emerges from the bathroom dressed in a thick white robe, her hair wrapped in a towel.

Tom kisses her as he squeezes past and heads for the shower. 'Food should be here in a minute.'

He takes a fraction of the time she did, and is already towelling himself dry when he hears the door open. For a second his heart jumps.

She's in danger.

He rushes naked into the room.

An astonished young man in a white jacket and perfectly pressed black trousers all but drops the heavy silver breakfast tray he's carried from the lift without spilling anything.

Even Valentina looks shocked

Tom pulls up, only a pace away from throwing a wall-breaking punch.

'Sorry.'

The word is hugely inadequate, but it's the best he can manage. He turns as nonchalantly as is possible when you're naked, and creeps back in agonising embarrassment to the bathroom.

'He's very jealous,' says Valentina as she signs for the breakfasts and adds a generous tip.

It's enough to restore normality. The waiter smiles and heads off to the kitchen.

'What was that all about?' She grins at Tom as he reappears, a towel now around his waist.

'Sorry. I thought for a moment that you were in danger.'

She moves plates and cups off the tray. 'I wasn't. And by the way, don't you think I know to use a safety chain?'

He glances over to the door and sees the brass slider.

She rubs his arm as he stands close. 'But it's nice that you care. You want coffee?'

'Just juice for the minute.' He lifts the carrier bags off the bed. 'What's so important in here that you had to raid the car at the break of dawn?'

'Give me the one in your left hand. I'll show you.'

Tom passes it over.

Valentina empties it on the bed.

Three thick volumes of photocopies flop out.

'They're copies of Anna Fratelli's journals. Her life – or should I say, *lives* – in her own tortured words.'

76

Louisa Verdetti sits in Sylvio Valducci's office biting a thumb-nail and waiting for her boss to finish a call.

Finally he clunks the phone down on its cradle.

'Both the police officers you complained of have been suspended.' He smiles triumphantly.

Louisa doesn't say anything.

He gives her another second.

Surely she appreciates his power? What he's done for her? What he *could* do for her if she was nicer to him?

It's a while since any woman's been nice.

A good session of nice with the not unattractive Signora Verdetti and he could see her as something entirely different from the pain-in-the-ass clinician always nagging for more funds.

But there's not even a hint of the gratitude he's hoping for.

'What, no thank you?' He jerks his arms. 'You don't think I had to pull strings to get these police officers kicked out of your way?'

She concentrates harder on the hangnail.

'Well, let me make something clear to you. There's no room for excuses now. I expect to see results, Louisa, and I expect to see them soon.'

'I didn't want them suspended!' She's so angry she can't

look at him. 'I asked you to make a call to someone senior to see if there was any way to get them to back off and give me some space and time alone with Anna.' She feels sorry for Valentina. Being appreciated as a woman in the medical world is tough, but in the Carabinieri it must be close to impossible. 'What will happen to them?'

He lets out a small laugh. 'You care?'

'Yes!' Louisa looks down at her hands. Her thumb's bleeding where she's chewed the nail. 'They were only doing their jobs.'

Now he's angry. 'Oh, please! No bleeding hearts. Be a bit more professional.'

He loves the fact that she's feeling guilty, feeling *so* bad about things that she can't help but let off steam.

'What's done is done. You've got your personal victory and beaten the bad lady captain and her army, so enjoy it. Then forget it and get your job done.'

In a sense, Louisa has already forgotten it.

Her mind is back on her patient. 'She damaged herself again last night.'

'What?'

'Anna. She tore at the stitches again.' She makes a motion towards her forearm. 'Drove the corner of a bible into her wounds until she'd opened them all up.'

77

Tom and Valentina finish the mountain of breakfast.

They stack used crockery on the tray and slide it outside their hotel room before attacking Anna's journals.

Tom spreads photocopies on a largish desk in the corner near the TV.

Valentina sprawls across the gold-quilted bed with the two other sets of documents. It doesn't take long for her to see the big picture. 'These diaries stretch back at least fifteen years. It looks like even pre-puberty, Anna was troubled by multiple personalities.'

'And the stories and history are all jumbled up,' says Tom.

'What do you mean?'

'Look.' He shows her the first page, marked *The Ancient Diary of Cassandra*. 'Here she calls herself Cassandra; that's a Greek name. She refers to the Greek god Zeus, but the Etruscan goddess Minerva.'

'So what?'

'Then she says that she's a descendant of the house of Savyna; that was Renaissance period.' Tom traces a finger over the appropriate text. 'Next she describes "the people of Cosmedin" – I think that's from the medieval period, but her husband is called Lucius, and that's an old Roman name.' He turns the page. 'And this story about the Bocca, the Mouth of Truth, it's *completely* anachronistic: church and legend are from totally different time periods.'

Valentina smiles at him. 'Boy logic. Why is it men are obsessed with seeing things in a set order? You're looking at the writings of a highly disturbed woman suffering from multiple personalities, not a graduate entering a history paper. What are you reading into it?'

'I'm not sure. I just noticed that all the timelines crossed.' He tries to better articulate what's really troubling him. 'It's as though her suffering stretches back through time, through the entire history of Rome.'

'You're reading too much into it. These are fantasies, to mentally protect herself from whatever abuse she's endured. She's grabbing at visual fragments of every legendary story she's ever heard.' Valentina fans out some of the papers she's been reading. 'Come and see this. In here, she pretends to be normal. She adopts totally different alters with common names like Maria, Melissa or Francesca. Thankfully, nothing awful appears to have happened to them.'

Tom leans over the bed to look. 'What are they?'

Valentina's mood goes melancholic. 'They're almost what every teenage girl thinks about. More daydreams than anything. She writes about seeing a nice boy in a park, kissing him by some fountains, spending time in the sunshine at her grandmother's house, picking flowers from the garden.'

Tom touches Valentina's hair. 'Maybe she had some good times after all.'

'I hope so.'

They drift back to their separate piles and read in silence, only speaking to call out the name of any new alters they discover.

After an hour, they've counted more than a hundred.

'I'm out of my depth here,' confesses Tom, laying down the papers and rubbing his tired eyes. 'I understand demonic possession, but not this dissociative identity disorder business. It's like Anna has an out-of-control personality machine inside her that can't stop manufacturing new identities.'

Valentina gives it some thought. 'That might not be a bad comparison.'

'What?'

'Anna's brain being like a broken machine. I mean, we all adjust our personality to cope with whatever life throws at us, right?'

'Right.'

'So maybe life threw too much at Anna and her personality machine broke down trying to cope.'

'You still believe it was something in her childhood?'

'Has to be. After everything she said yesterday about her

sisters and her mother, I would put all my money on Louisa's childhood abuse theory.' Valentina shuffles through some of the photocopies of the diary in front of her. 'I think the answer lies in the original alters, Cassandra in particular.'

'I've got a lot of stuff from her.' Tom holds up a stack of sheets. 'Listen to this; this is after Cassandra's death in Cosmedin. *They gather my bones and ashes. Loyal fingers seek out every part of me – what I was, what I am, what I will be . . . They poke among the embers of a pyre that was soaked in cups of oil and bouquets of perfume. My husband is not among the grubbers. He is long gone. Vanished after the feasting . . . No doubt he is now in our matrimonial bed, slaking his thirst for wine and boys.'*

Tom lowers the paper. 'Don't you think it's weird that this alter – the Cassandra alter – continues to exist after she's been killed?'

Valentina isn't as shocked. 'Why not? I guess if you're a DID sufferer, it's up to you to decide whether you want to let your alter live on after it's died.'

Tom reads another section. '*Arria is here, of course. Sweetest Arria. She will be among the first to remember me at Parentalia. Was not Dies Parentales made for women with faces as sad as Arria's?*'

Valentina is puzzled. 'What on earth are Parentalia and Dies Parentales?'

'They're one and the same. Basically, a remembrance celebration for the dead. It ran from the thirteenth to the twenty-first of February.'

She searches her pile of papers. 'Is there a date on her diary entry?'

'No date, but I found this between several other entries that were in the personalities of fourteen- and fifteen-year-old girls.'

'So Anna was probably a young teenager when she was already dissociating, or whatever the medical term is.'

278

'Probably.' Tom is keen to finish the passage. *'The urn they have fashioned for me is a cheap one. From its lack of elegance I know already that they will not carry me to my husband's tomb. I am pleased . . . I shall not wait for him beyond the three canine heads of Cerberus.'*

'What's Cerberus?' Valentina asks. 'Didn't Anna mention that yesterday when she became agitated and started arguing in several voices?'

'Yes, she did. Cerberus is a Latinised version of the Greek Kerberos, and according to mythology, it's a three-headed hellhound owned by Hades that guards the gates of the underworld.'

'I guess that makes sense,' Valentina says flippantly. 'A multi-headed dog to kill off multiple personalities.'

Tom explains a little more. 'Cerberus had one head to watch over the past, one to guard the present and the third to look into the future.'

'Quite a pooch.'

'And a hungry one. All of the jaws hungered solely for live human meat. Cerberus was the perfect monster to ensure that no living soul entered the afterlife. It was also said to have a mane and tail made out of serpents, much like Medusa's hair.'

'Not exactly Fluffy.'

'Fluffy?'

'The three-headed dog in Harry Potter. One of the advantages of having a young niece who needs taking to the movies.'

Tom puts the paper down. 'Mythology is everywhere these days. McDonald's will be selling Zeus burgers soon.'

'Are you willing to bet their Greek franchises don't already do them?'

'No. Joking aside, the mythology might also be some kind of clue.'

'How so?'

'Well, when Anna first started talking about Mother, I thought she meant the Holy Mother.'

Valentina nods. 'Me too. So?'

'Well, yesterday she also used the term Mater.'

'That means Mother.'

'Yes, I know that. But she said something odd, like: "Mater, who is all, is within us", and that made me realise we weren't in the realms of Roman Catholicism any more.'

'We weren't?'

'No.' He picks up Anna's diary again. 'And *this* confirms it. In here she talks about other women. She says: '*Before me I see my sisters. The others of the spirit world. Those who have for ever been and will for ever be. They are the keepers of the secret. The prophetesses.*'

Tom looks pleased with himself.

Valentina still doesn't get it. '*Sisters?* Some feminist movement? Nuns?'

He shakes his head. 'No, not nuns. I didn't want to speculate until I'd thought it through.'

'What, Tom?' She presses him. 'Come on, you need to give me something.'

He waggles the papers in his hand. 'Cybele.'

The name means nothing to Valentina.

'*Cybele!*' he repeats with extra stress. 'I should have got it much earlier. I had coffee a few days ago with Alfie, and we found the name Cybele linked to the Field of Mars and to several temples in Rome.'

'Tom, I really don't follow. Cybele who?'

He blows out a sigh. Explaining this could be difficult. 'She's as old as time itself. Known to the Greeks as Meter, to the Phrygians as Matar Kubileya and to the Romans as Magna Mater – the Great Mother.'

'We're talking about Mother Nature?'

'Not quite. Not as simply and benignly and abstractly as we refer to Mother Nature these days. It's more complex than that. People began worshipping Cybele centuries before Christ. She was the ultimate matriarchal icon, and some even say she was responsible for the birth of feminism.'

'And all this is bad how?' Valentina jokes.

'Bad for men. She had a lover called Attis. He was unfaithful to her, and in revenge she drove him insane and made him castrate himself. Male followers in the sect of Attis were eunuchs, just as they were in the sect of Cybele.'

Valentina starts to see connections to her case. 'We're back to those . . . what were they called . . . galleys?'

'Galli.' He makes a scissor action with his fingers. 'Only after they'd experienced the snip were they allowed to become priests. These were the only males permitted to be close to any of the sect's priestesses.'

She climbs off the bed and moves to the desk. 'Let me look at that section.'

He passes it to her.

She scans it a little, then reads aloud: '. . . *the mortals take my burned remains to their dank resting place in the Columbarium. Here among the shelved peasantry is my place in the potted history of poorest Rome. My niche in society.*'

She looks up from the photocopy. 'Columbarium? As in Columbia?'

'No. A *columbarium* is a public resting place for the ashes of the dead; it's where poor people stored their loved ones when they couldn't afford tombs. Urns were kept on numbered shelves, so relatives could come and find them and pay their respects.'

'During Parentalia?'

'Exactly.'

She carries on reading. '*No ornately engraved plaque marks my spot. No statue or portrait. Nor any message of love. Just a number. My sisters and I wonder if beyond the grave they can hear us laughing. The number is X.'*

She hands the paper back to Tom. 'Why would the number ten be amusing for Cassandra and her sisters?'

Now it's Tom's turn to look lost. 'The number ten means nothing significant to me. You'll find myths and legends that talk not only about Cybele, but also about various sibyls.' He spells it out for her. 'These are often the same prophetess, but I can't recall the number playing any symbolic part.'

'Maybe we shouldn't get too excited about all this. It's probably just some crazy nonsense that went off in Anna's head when she was imagining being dead Cassandra and living beyond the grave.'

She puts her arms around his neck. She's had enough of the case for now. Enough of ancient Greeks and Roman myths. Enough of her suspension and her uncertain future. In fact, enough of everything except Tom. 'Thanks for staying. For being with me throughout this madness. *All* this madness.'

He puts his hand on hers. 'Think nothing of it; there's nowhere I'd rather be. Besides, Paris was far too cold for an LA boy. I had to go somewhere.'

She gives him a friendly slap on the side of his head.

'Hey!'

Mischief flickers in her eyes. 'Hey what?'

She dances away from him like a boxer, hands up in pretend fists. 'What are you going to do about it, eh?' She feigns a slap with her left and then clips him with an open-handed right. 'Woo-hoo! Come on, Mr Beeg Man, let's see you fight for your place in the Roman sun.'

'Right.' Tom springs up with a smile as broad as Canada. 'You are now *so* going to get it.'

Valentina jumps up on to the bed and bounces some more. 'I hope so. I *really* hope so.'

78

Anna Fratelli can't move her arms or legs.

As well as the chemical straitjacket of sedatives they've imposed upon her, she's also pinned down with bed restraints.

Valducci is taking no chances. He's reduced her to a state where she couldn't even harm a proverbial fly if it settled on the tip of her nose, let alone injure herself again.

The Velcro fastenings on her wrists and ankles mean that her every waking moment is spent staring at the ceiling of the new high-security room they've moved her to.

Her only distraction is spotting the occasional movement of an overhead camera that records her 24/7.

Louisa Verdetti watches the camera feed with sadness.

She understands the need for the chemical restraints but thinks Valducci has overstepped the mark with the bonds.

So typical of him.

He selfishly jumps at any chance to show he's in control and can dominate and intimidate.

She can see Anna's lips moving but she can't hear anything.

She fiddles with the audio control on the monitor, but all she gets is loud hiss.

Maybe Anna is silently mouthing the words to some prayer.

She turns the volume up to the max.

Nothing.

A deafening voice erupts through the speakers as the technical fault fixes itself.

By the time Louisa has turned it down and her eardrums

have stopped banging, she's missed the start of whatever is being said.

But it's clear that it's not Anna who's talking.

It's another alter.

The mean and powerful one that appeared when the cops were interviewing her.

'Stupid girl! You disgrace us. Look at you lying there on your back, spread out like a cheap peasant whore about to pleasure the dimmest of farmers. You are not fit to be Cybeline.'

A weaker voice answers, 'I'm sorry. Please, forgive me. It is not my fault that I am like this.'

Louisa feels like her heart is going to break. She was hoping Anna had put the trauma of simultaneous manifestations behind her.

Clearly not.

'*Sorry?*' The dominant alter stresses the word poisonously. 'You do not have the right to even think about apologising to me. You are past that, child. You are lost to me.'

Louisa realises she's wrong.

This is not just any alter. By the sound of it, this is the ultimate and most powerful one of them all. The Mother.

'Lost, child! Do you hear me?'

'No, please!' Anna begs. 'I have tried my best. I have done almost everything that you have asked of me.'

Louisa quickly pulls a small notepad from her white doctor's coat and scribbles.

This moment could be key to unlocking the mysterious traumas that have messed with Anna's mind.

'Almost is not enough!' The words are shouted out. 'You have failed me. Failed all of us. Now I ask only that you show me the loyalty your sisters have.'

'Mater!' Anna is close to tears.

'Stop sniffling!' Her face wrinkles with contempt. 'Your

weakness disgusts me. Weakness leads to treachery. Have I not taught you to be stronger?'

Anna is too upset to speak.

Louisa finds herself torn between note-taking and intervention. If she ends it now, the Mater personality may submerge beneath the others and she could lose valuable insight into how to treat Anna.

'Answer me!' shouts Mater, viciously. 'Have I not taught you to be stronger?'

Anna answers with a whimper. 'Yes.'

'Then you must know what I have come to do.'

There's panic now in Anna's voice. 'Forgive me, I beg you. I had to run away.' She struggles for breath. 'I could not hurt my own sister.'

'Your sister was treacherous. I had to make sure she would not betray us. As I have to make sure you will not.'

Anna thrashes against the bed restraints. 'No! No! You're hurting me, Mater!' Her body thumps against the mattress, creating a sound like thunder. 'Stop! Stop! You're hurting me!'

Louisa has seen enough.

She rushes from the monitors to the room.

'Please let me go!'

One of the wrist restraints breaks loose.

'I cast you from the sanctity of the womb, I damn your soul to eternal exile beyond the boundary of the sisterhood.'

'No, please, Mater! *Please* don't.'

'The jagged stone teeth of the Tarpeian Rock are too good for you. Strangulation on the Gemonian Stairs too honourable. I cast you down from a place above the clouds so that your organs and your bones will be obliterated like an ant crushed beneath a giant's heel.'

Louisa opens the door of the electronically locked room just as the other wrist restraint breaks.

Anna falls from the bed. She is left dangling by her tethered feet, screaming in wild panic.

'Anna, Anna, it's okay!'

Louisa tries to lift her back on to the bed, but can't.

'Let me help you. You're okay.'

She quickly releases the ankle restraints and lowers her to the ground.

Face down on the cold floor, Anna mouths three words: 'The Tenth Book.'

Louisa kneels alongside her.

'Shush. Be quiet now. Everything's okay.' She puts two fingers to the pulse point in the patient's neck.

Anna's body spasms.

Her eyes widen and she grabs Louisa's arm. 'Find . . . the . . . Tenth . . . Book.'

She spasms again. Then lies lifeless.

Louisa can't detect a pulse.

Anna isn't moving.

Her heart has stopped.

79

Federico Assante's wife Mia has gone out for the day with their young daughter.

He has no idea what they're doing or when they'll be back.

Right now he has no idea about anything.

Mia left straight after breakfast, and he's sure she knows something is wrong.

She always knows.

Federico can't bring himself to tell her that he's been suspended and sent home.

He's too ashamed.

To Mia and her family, his job is everything. She's always talking about how proud she is that he's a policeman. A photograph of him in full ceremonial uniform stands on a cabinet in every one of her relatives' homes.

He'll never be able to tell her.

For the moment he's told her he's off sick. An injured back. Backs are always a safe bet. Not even doctors can prove you don't have some form of back pain.

But he knows he can't bluff for ever.

The curtains of their apartment are closed. He sits in the white vest he's worn for two days, chain-smoking over a low coffee table filled with magazines that he's not reading.

From somewhere in the pocket of his badly creased black trousers his cell phone sends out a tinny imitation of the iconic *24* ring tone.

Not even Jack Bauer could save this day.

'*Pronto.*'

'Hey, Federico!'

It's Enrico Ferrari. Unbearably upbeat and almost the last person he wants to talk to.

Federico pictures him, doughnut in hand, sugar on lips, his diary spread open in front of him as he calls around to find drinking chums.

Well, Federico doesn't want to go out.

Not now. Not ever again.

'Enrico, I'm sorry, this is a bad time, I—'

'No it's not!' he insists cheerily. 'This is actually a good time – a *very* good time.'

'Enrico, I'm not really in the mood for—'

'But Skywalker, your waiting is over.'

'Enrico!'

His friend isn't deterred. 'No, no, listen, this *really* is a good-news call. I just read the full mitochondrial DNA test results on both Anna Fratelli and the severed hand recovered from the Bocca in Cosmedin.'

'You lost me, Enrico.'

'They're sisters.'

'Sisters?'

'See, the news is so good you have to repeat it. Your handless victim is Anna Fratelli's *sister*.'

Federico can't get his head around it.

Anna never mentioned she had a sister.

One of the alters was referred to as Little Suzie, but from what he can remember, she wasn't a sister to any of the others.

Come to think of it, the medical records they'd pulled didn't mention any sister either.

'Hello, are you still there?'

'I'm just trying to work things out. You're saying that Anna's sister had her hand cut off?'

'Oh boy! How did you ever make detective? Yes, that's pretty much what I said. Though if you want to quote me verbatim, I actually said that your handless victim is Anna's sister.'

'How are you so sure?'

'You really want to know?'

'I do, but keep it simple. Cop simple.'

'Okay. Look, we have forty-six chromosomes; twenty-three we get from our mother and twenty-three from our father. We also get some mitochondrial DNA from our mother only. Using the mitochondrial DNA for sibling identification is quite accurate, because all children born of a certain female should share this DNA.'

'And the father?'

'Different. Totally different fathers. Sorry, I shouldn't say "totally different" because of course they can't be *slightly* different fathers. I mean, they're either different or the same, aren't they? You see what I mean? It's like being a little bit pregnant; you can't be − you're either pregnant or you're not.'

'Enrico, you made that as clear as mud. Just swear to me that you're sure of this.'

'Of course I'm sure. It's my job to be sure. I can categorically tell you that Anna has a different father to her sister.'

Federico thinks things over. Not only about what Enrico has told him, but also about what *he's* not told Enrico. Time to come out with it. 'I should have stopped you telling me this. Enrico, I got suspended yesterday.'

'I know.'

'What?'

'I know about your suspension and about how I'm not supposed to call you and all that crap. News travels fast, bad news travels fastest.'

'Do you know *why* they suspended me?'

'No. And I don't want to. Whatever you did or didn't do, I know you had your reasons. And besides, even if you fucked up, so what? We all fuck up some time, and at times of the biggest fuck-ups you need your biggest friends, right?'

'*Grazie.*'

'*Prego.* So you want that we go out and get juiced tonight? Maybe help your biggest friend get his big fat leg over some drunken signora?'

Federico manages his first smile for twenty-four hours. 'For sure. I'd like that very much.'

80

Louisa hits the panic button and starts CPR on Anna.

In a film or TV show, everything would be okay, but Louisa knows better. Statistically, her chance of saving her is only about fifty-fifty.

She starts with mouth-to-mouth and is already working chest compressions when the crash team and their portable defibrillator arrive.

Louisa steps back. 'She seemed to have some kind of fit. When I came in, she'd blacked out and wasn't breathing.'

'Probably asystolic,' says a young male doctor. 'We'll see what we can do for her.' He turns to two nurses. 'Hook up the machine; get me Vasopressin as well.'

Louisa drifts to the rear of the room as they lift Anna back on to the bed and start the fight to save her life.

'She's flatlined!' shouts a nurse.

Anna's gown is pulled open. Electrodes are stuck above the right and below the left breast. Controlled electric shocks juice into her.

'Nothing so far.'

Louisa looks down and sees her hands are shaking, something they've not done since she was in med school.

She'd give anything right now for a good slug of brandy and a long draw on a cigarette, or maybe something even stronger.

'Again!' someone shouts.

Louisa takes a deep breath. It's an old machine, manually run, not like the AEDs in the main wards.

Defib seldom works first time.

They have to get the shock level right, so they often go in with too low a charge.

The second or third go should do it.

'Again!'

Bodies scuffle around the bed.

Hands seem to be all over Anna, eyes stuck to monitors recording vital signs.

'Again!' They all step back once more and watch in frozen hope.

Then they're on her again. Devouring information. Checking her heartbeat, her pulse, her eyes.

More CPR.

A long silence.

'Call it.'

Louisa can't believe what she's just heard.

Two words. Said in a depressingly calm tone.

'Call it.'

A male wrist juts out from the scrum of green scrubs. 'Time of death: 11.55.35.'

The room starts to sway.

Louisa has to sit before she falls.

She watches the crash team swirl around the bed until they become just a tilting haze.

Anna is dead.

81

Valducci surprises her.

He turns out to be a perfect boss and gentleman.

No lecture, no bawling out, no horrible speculation about what happens next.

Just a glass of brandy. An offer of tissues. And the insistence that Louisa goes home.

She doesn't have to be told twice.

She walks from the psychiatric block to her car and pauses to take in as much fresh air as possible.

Anna's dead.

She tries to block it out.

Unless she's mistaken, it's a little warmer than yesterday. She looks at the bare branches of the silver birch trees around her. No buds. No sign of spring. But it really can't be that far off.

Anna's dead.

The thought keeps slamming into her. Demanding she dwell on it. She still can't believe it. She hoped that maybe with the cops out of the way, there was going to be a chance to concentrate on her treatment. Get her well again. Not watch her die.

Tears well up in her eyes. She has to be strong. Fight her way through the loss. It's not her fault. She's told herself that a dozen times.

The stress of living with those multiple personalities must just have proved too much for Anna to bear. All that fear of night-time and the imagined evil must have piled up and broken her.

Louisa unlocks her Alfa and slips inside.

The radio shouts at top volume as she turns the ignition key and it makes her heart jump. She's edgy. Tense. Stressed.

Anna's dead.

She jabs the off button to silence some jock moron with no sense of respect. She doesn't want to hear anyone or anything right now. But there's no escaping her own thoughts.

What more should she have done?

What *less* could she have done? Was she guilty of pushing things too far, of digging up layers of trauma that would have been best left untouched?

She dials Valentina's cell phone. The captain has a right to know. Even if she's suspended, she should still be told, and Louisa is in no doubt that it's her duty to tell her.

'*Pronto*, Morassi.'

Louisa hesitates.

The policewoman sounds annoyed. Just from the way she answered she sounds angry.

It's no wonder that a call from the woman who got her suspended isn't welcome.

Louisa thinks about hanging up, but decides to be tough and plough on. 'Capitano, it's Louisa Verdetti.' She doesn't pause now, doesn't risk any interruption. 'Anna Fratelli died about an hour ago. I thought you should know.'

Valentina's not sure she heard her correctly. 'Anna what?'

'She's dead. She died of a heart attack in her bed at the hospital. I thought you'd want to know.'

Louisa can't talk any more. She flips the clamshell phone shut. Normally she wouldn't be so rude, but today she can't even say goodbye, let alone answer another question.

She slips the Alfa into gear, drives through the hospital gates and heads home.

In her bathroom cabinet is a box of Valium that she keeps for times like this. Times when all her training and the wisdom of three decades of living just aren't enough. She's going to pour a glass of brandy much bigger than the one Valducci gave her, go to bed and drug herself into a long, deep sleep.

The road slips beneath the car tyres and the world smears itself across the vehicle's windows.

The traffic approaching Via Margutta is horrendous.

It always is.

Louisa's apartment is in a gated courtyard off to the right, a little past where Picasso lived and just before the apartment where they filmed *Roman Holiday*.

The electronic gates buzz open and the red and white

security barrier behind jerks up like a railway crossing. Her Alfa crunches over the gravel and she parks up in her own space, just below her ivy-covered balcony.

Being home makes her feel better. Safe from the horrors of the day. Absolved from the guilt of Anna's death.

She opens the door to the apartment block, holds it for a young couple behind her and picks up mail from her drop box.

Bills. Bills and more bills.

Thank God she earns a decent wage. She has no idea how normal people manage in a city as expensive as Rome. Half her block is already full of rich foreigners, because locals can't afford the rents.

She jams the bills in her teeth while she juggles her hand-bag and opens her apartment door. The place still smells of the remains of some fish she forgot to throw out.

She vows to do it now. Empty the stinking bin before she crawls into her bed and floats off into a comforting blackness.

She puts her hand on the light switch.

But never manages to turn it on.

Years in a hospital tell her that the sweet-smelling cloth pressed to her mouth is soaked in a trihalomethane.

Chloroform.

As unconsciousness creeps through her, she realises the man holding the cloth is half of the young couple she just let in.

82

'They'll make us scapegoats.'

Federico's words hang in the air, snagged like a knot

somewhere down the phone line between him and Valentina.

'How so?' she finally asks.

He blows cigarette smoke as he paces. 'We get suspended for intimidating a mentally ill patient and she ends up dying of a heart attack. This is a heavy stone they are going to drop on our toes. It's good for the hospital – it clears them of blame – and good for that bastard Caesario.'

Valentina's surprised to hear him talk so venomously about the major. 'We should meet. Do you know somewhere?'

Federico thinks for a second. 'Galleria Borghese. It's not far from the centre.'

'I know it.'

'I have a friend who runs the private dining rooms inside the villa. You don't get many Carabinieri taking time off for cultural tours.'

'Within the hour?'

'Within the hour.'

They hang up.

The villa and adjoining museums are set in lavishly landscaped gardens on the Pincian Hill, north of the Spanish Steps. Works by Old Masters adorn its multitudinous rooms and have been viewed by millions.

The former vineyard is only walking distance for Tom and Valentina, so they are already there, admiring more than a hundred acres of parkland, when Federico arrives in his clapped-out Lancia.

He grinds a cigarette butt into the gravel and calls his friend.

Minutes later, they're met on the entrance steps by a dark-suited young man with big brown eyes.

After much cheek-kissing and back-slapping, they're shown to a small room and left alone with beautiful china espresso cups and crystal water glasses.

Sitting opposite each other for the first time since their suspension, Valentina can't help but get several things off her chest. 'I never expected Caesario to suspend you; I thought you and he were very close.'

'You mistake closeness for obedience. When my major tells me to report directly to him rather than the new girl, I report to him. That doesn't mean I will fabricate evidence for him, or support him if he has an agenda that I don't think is ethical.'

'*Grazie.*'

'*Prego.*' He takes a contemplative sip of his espresso. 'Any ideas how we can get out of this?'

She lets out a huff of exasperated air and sits back in her chair. 'We need to talk to Louisa Verdetti and see how strongly set against us she is. Louisa's key to it all. I suspect the official complaint was more of her boss's doing than hers.'

'If she testifies that we acted properly, then the case collapses.'

'That's about it. But she'll need some talking to, especially now that Anna is dead.'

Federico finishes his coffee, 'How exactly did she die?'

'Not sure. Louisa said it was a heart attack. That's all I got from her.'

'Did she ring to blame you? Could you tell anything from the tone of her voice?'

Valentina has to think. 'No. It was a really short call. But I don't think she was ringing to rage at me. There was no pent-up anger in her voice. It was more like she just thought I should know.'

'That doesn't make sense.'

'Why not?'

'Well, presumably she already knew you had been suspended, so if she was calling you despite that, then it indicates some kind of closeness. I think maybe she rang because she was upset and thought that you'd be more understanding than her boss.'

Valentina sees his point. 'Could be.'

'That gives us room for hope.'

She's not so sure. 'Strictly speaking we shouldn't go near her. She'll be a witness at a court martial.'

He flinches. 'Don't say those words.'

Tom speaks for the first time in several minutes. 'I could talk to her, though.' He sounds distant, because he's studying a leaflet he's found on a window ledge. It details paintings and sculptures at the villa by luminaries such as Bernini, Canova, Raphael and Caravaggio. 'I have her address from when we were at the Ponte Fabricio and I got her a taxi home.' He holds up the leaflet. 'Does this remind you of anyone?'

Both Federico and Valentina squint to see.

It's a portrait of a woman. A goddess with dark eyes and a distinctly dimpled chin.

A goddess who looks identical to Anna Fratelli.

83

The blanket is warm.

Warm, but rough and unfamiliar.

The bed she's lying on is not her own.

Louisa Verdetti is on the slow and painful road to consciousness.

Her head aches, and for a moment her chloroformed

mind plays tricks on her. She's a student again, helping out in a field hospital in a Third World country. She's dozed off at the end of a hard day's work and is sleeping in one of the supply tents; the headache is a hangover courtesy of a bottle or two of rough red shared with a hunky aid worker from Sweden.

If only that were the case.

Slowly Louisa starts to focus.

Everywhere is brown.

Dark – *depressingly* dark – brown.

Her fuddled brain tries to snatch information. The smell of damp. The hardness of the surface she's lying on. The near pitch darkness.

She's underground.

Buried.

Her heart skips a beat.

Buried alive.

Louisa sits up.

Childhood claustrophobia sucks the air from her throat.

She tells herself not to panic. She's no longer a young girl accidentally locked in her grandmother's gardening shed.

Panic is the worst thing she can do.

Relax. Breathe slowly. Nothing bad is going to happen to her.

But it already has.

The rough knitted blanket slips from her shoulders as she puts out a hand.

A wall.

Lumpy. Not plastered. Damp. Crumbling.

Like the wall of a cave.

She feels an aching in her chest.

Breathe. Force yourself to take long, slow, deep breaths. Let it out slowly.

All her panic training comes back to her.

In through your nose. Out through your mouth.

You're fine.

You're okay.

Everything's going to be all right.

Memories choke her now. The chloroform. The man and woman she let into her apartment block.

They did this.

They drugged her and have taken her somewhere.

But where?

And why?

A flash of yellowy-orange suddenly blinds her. She guesses from the accompanying sound and smell that the light is coming from rags soaked in oil or paraffin and bound to a heavy stick.

She backs up.

The torchlight shows her where she is.

Underground.

Behind bars.

In a cell carved out of solid rock.

84

'No answer.'

Valentina puts her cell phone down on the shiny mahogany table inside the private meeting room at Galleria Borghese. 'I've tried Louisa's work and private cell numbers. Nothing.'

'Then I'll go and see if she's at home,' says Tom. 'Given

Anna's death, it's likely she's taken some private time.' He's still distracted by the likeness of Anna in the painting in the leaflet.

'This picture's purely coincidence,' says Valentina, taking it off him. 'Half of the girls in Rome look like that.' She gives it a second glance. 'In fact, I think Anna's actually much prettier than whoever she is.'

'I'll drive you,' volunteers Federico. 'When we're finished here.'

'We could go now,' says Valentina, dropping the leaflet on a shelf over a radiator. 'We're about done, aren't we?'

'Not quite,' says Federico. 'My fat scientist friend, the one who has the hots for you, has come up with some interesting biological information.'

'Hopefully not about himself,' says Valentina.

'Thankfully not. The handless victim at the Bocca della Verità and Anna Fratelli were related. Sisters.'

Valentina frowns. 'I thought your friend said they were different blood groups.'

'Same mother, different fathers.'

'There seem to be lots of family references going on,' observes Tom. 'Anna and her alter personalities frequently talked about Mother or Mater, and now we have a direct physical link to a sibling.'

Valentina looks to Federico. 'What did Anna's social and medical records turn up?'

'Now there's a story.' Federico takes out a small black Moleskine notebook from his jacket. 'Anna's birth certificate, school and medical records show that she was the daughter of Armando and Ginerva Fratelli from Gerusalemme.'

'Let me guess. Her parents are dead?'

'No, far from it. They're both sprightly sixty-year-olds. They did have a daughter called Anna, but she died when she was barely three days old.'

Valentina shakes her head. 'Someone stole their dead daughter's identity and brought up a child under a false name?'

'Worse. The Fratellis had *twin* daughters. Anna's sister, Cloelia, died at the Policlinico the same day. They both had fatal lung defects.'

Valentina is intrigued by the awful coincidence. 'The same place our Anna died.'

Tom crosses himself. 'Sounds like systematic paedophilia. There was a case in California where a paedophile ring scoured the death columns in local newspapers for child fatalities. They'd immediately apply for birth certificates for the dead kids because they knew that records systems seldom work properly and almost never proactively cross-check with each other.'

'In Italy it is even worse,' adds Valentina. 'Try moving cities and you quickly discover what a mess the authorities are in.'

Federico doesn't quite understand. 'What do these kind of gangs want the children's documentation for?'

Valentina explains. 'They abduct babies and very young children with the idea of abusing them throughout their childhood and teenage years. They keep them imprisoned and hidden until they are completely brainwashed into accepting that they're part of the abuser's so-called family.'

'It would explain Anna's multiple personalities,' adds Tom. 'Louisa said that her multiple alters are most likely a response to years of abuse.'

'Christ!' Federico can't help but think about his own young daughter. 'They're not just stealing their identities, they're stealing their lives.'

85

The man Louisa remembers from her apartment block is standing outside her cell, holding a flaming torch between his face and hers.

Through the glare she can see that he's no longer dressed in the mundane blue jeans, jumper and short wool coat she last saw him in.

He's clad from head to toe in a long, heavy cloak of purple, like the off-the-shoulder *himation* the ancient Greeks used to wear.

Louisa hopes this is all some crazy dream, an odd brain trip that will finish any second and then she'll wake up, shower and promise herself never to eat cheese again late at night.

The man tilts his head and studies her eyes. 'How do you feel?'

She's not quite sure how to answer.

Angry? Frightened? Furious?

They're all perfectly good ways to sum up her feelings, but she guesses he's not really concerned with her emotions. 'Sore. My throat hurts. My head aches.'

He smiles sympathetically. 'That's the chloroform. The effects will pass quickly – as I'm sure you know.' He looks over his shoulder to someone out of view. 'Get her water and some white willow bark to take away the pain.'

Louisa hears the muffled noise of retreating footsteps. She can't see, but it sounds like the floor is made of dirt and grit and isn't paved in any kind of way. Her senses are returning, and beyond the smell of the torch she detects the iron tang of dampness and the chatter of other voices.

'Why are you doing this to me?'

The man in the cloak frowns a little. 'The patient you refer to as Anna – Anna Fratelli – we need you to secure her release from incarceration in your hospital.'

'Anna is—' Louisa bites her tongue. She realises there's no advantage to telling them what has happened – on the contrary, if they know she's dead, it will merely demonstrate her own lack of value to them and put her life in danger. 'Anna is very sick,' she adds. 'She's both physically and mentally ill. Moving her from expert medical care isn't advisable.'

'I didn't ask for a diagnosis,' says the man. 'Her release is all we want.'

Louisa tries to establish more of a rapport with him. 'I don't remember seeing you at the hospital. You didn't visit. At least not as far as I can remember. Are you a friend?'

'I *am* a friend, a very close one, but visiting is not what I do.'

Louisa thinks better of asking him to explain exactly what it is that he does do.

On the wall to his left, a skeletal shadow grows long, then crawls up the ceiling of her cell as a woman appears in the flickering torchlight.

Her face has been made a ghostly white by some strange thick make-up, but Louisa still recognises her from the apartment block. Like the man she was with, she's now dressed differently. She's wearing a flowing green cloak that is similar to his but is split on the right side and fastened over both shoulders rather than just one.

She passes a metal goblet of water and a handful of dry, powdery tablets through the bars to Louisa. 'Take two of the willow bark now and two a little later if your head still aches.'

Louisa has never had time for alternative medicine, but swallows the pills anyway. The fact that they're looking after her is a good sign.

At least for now.

'Why do you want to get Anna out of hospital? What are you going to do with her?'

'She is a prophetess,' says the woman. 'One of our sisters—'

The man silences her with a look that could blister skin. He turns back to Louisa. 'It is not your concern. Trouble yourself only with how to extricate Anna from the fortress and falsehood in which she is held.'

Louisa takes another sip of the water. 'I need to think. You can't simply walk into one of the world's biggest hospitals and steal a patient.'

'Then think. And do it quickly. Your life depends upon it.'

86

Federico parks his rust-bucket car in Via Dell Babuino.

While he and Valentina sit and talk in the warmth of the car, Tom bangs shut the back door and braves a soft shower as he walks to Louisa Verdetti's home.

He turns up the collar of his new coat and cuts through Via Dell'Orto di Napoli into Via Margutta. His gaze bounces off elite lines of art galleries and restaurants, and he makes a mental note to return with Valentina.

He finds Louisa's address behind a large iron security gate, which, not surprisingly in Italy, has been propped open solely for convenience.

The courtyard is breathtaking.

A long and deeply gravelled drive opens up to reveal a quadrangle of ancient, ivy-clad houses that are amongst the most expensive in the city. Some have been turned into select offices for high-earning local professionals and the rest are rented out to cash-rich foreigners.

Tom walks past terracotta fountains and abundant flower beds before he finds Louisa's block.

Behind a clear-windowed oak door he sees a red-faced, middle-aged man bawling out two maids.

Tom raps on the door pane.

The man breaks from his thundery attack, puts on a sunny smile and opens up for him.

'*Si?*'

Tom is hit by a backdraught of alcohol fumes. 'I'm looking for Louisa Verdetti.' He steps in from the rain without being asked.

'And you are?'

'Tom. I'm her friend from America.'

'Wait.' The man points to the two maids. 'You wait too. I haven't finished with you.' He picks up a phone and hits some numbers.

Tom smiles sympathetically at the two women, who are now talking to each other in what he thinks is either Polish or Russian.

The man puts the receiver down. 'She is not there. You want to leave a message?'

Tom searches for a pen in his pocket and picks up a yellow Post-it pad off the small desk. 'Sure. Do you have any idea where she is?'

'*Ospedale.*'

'No, she's not at work.' Tom writes down his name and cell number.

'Not working, being treated. She has some problem with her ankle, I think.'

'I don't understand.'

'Some neighbours just called by to see if she was all right. They saw her earlier being helped into a car by a man and a woman.'

Alarm bells ring with Tom. 'Why?'

The man seems puzzled. 'Because she couldn't walk properly. They were concerned and went out to help. The driver waved them off and said everything was okay and not to worry. It seems she had twisted her ankle and fainted and they were taking her straight to the hospital.'

Tom doesn't buy it. 'What time was this?'

He shrugs. 'Not long ago. About an hour or two.' He points to the waiting maids. 'I was inspecting the rooms. They would be cleaner if I did them myself.'

'Can you tell me the name and address of these neighbours you mentioned?'

The man looks at him suspiciously. 'I'll come with you.' He turns to the maids. 'You two do not move. That should be easy for you.'

87

Federico is leaning in a shop doorway, smoking and watching the rain fall, as Tom puddle-splashes his way back to the car. 'No luck?' the lieutenant calls as he steps from his shelter and flicks the last of the cigarette into the potholed road.

Tom shakes his head and slips into the back seat, behind Valentina. 'Damned weather! I look like a drowned cat.'

She turns and weighs him up with a smile on her face.

'Oh, I don't know. I quite like the wet look. It reminds me of when you've just showered.'

Federico grumpily grunts his way behind the wheel, ending all possibility of further flirtation. 'So what's the story?'

Tom struggles out of his wet coat as he answers. 'Louisa was at home just a short while ago. Some neighbours saw her being driven off by a man and woman they've never seen before.'

'Did you speak to them?' asks Valentina.

'Only the man; his wife was out. He said he came out of his apartment after hearing a lot of noise on the gravel. At first he thought Louisa was drunk, because she was held up between the couple.'

'Drugged?' asks Federico rhetorically.

'The neighbour says they were virtually carrying her. The man waved him away. Gave him some story about her passing out after she twisted her ankle and fell on the stairs. He said they were taking her to hospital.'

Valentina turns to Federico. 'Is there anyone you trust at work who can do a check at the clinics, see if she was admitted somewhere?'

'*Sì*. I know such people. I can get it checked, but I don't think we'll find anything. If someone's fainted, you sit them down, give them air and maybe some water. She would have been well enough to have talked to her neighbours.'

Valentina knows he's right. 'Anything else?'

Tom wipes drips of water from his face. 'No. The door guy at her apartment is a jerk. Probably overworked and drunk most of the time. He said he hadn't seen anything suspicious.'

Federico runs the palm of his hand back and forth across the top of a steering wheel that's grown shiny from years of hard Italian driving. 'I'm trying to think why anyone would want to drug and abduct a psychiatric clinician.'

'The usual reasons are sexual, financial or emotional,' observes Valentina. 'Some sleazy creep has been stalking her?'

Federico asks the obvious. 'Sure, but what's the link to Anna?'

Valentina's trying to figure it out. 'Maybe she's been taken by someone who blames her for Anna's death?'

Federico's nicotined fingers drum a heavy bass on the wheel. 'I hope not. I really hope not.'

Valentina explains to Tom: 'If it's a revenge kidnap, then we've got no chance of getting her back. They're going to kill her.'

88

They've left a dented steel bucket in the corner of the cell for her to use as a toilet.

But Louisa can't.

Her body is desperate for relief, but her brain is screaming no.

She stands and stretches.

Paces.

Leans against the cold and rusty iron bars, then shakes them until the noise echoes down distant tunnels.

But nothing takes her mind off the bucket and her bladder.

Thank God she's only drunk a little water, and not the vast amounts of coffee she usually does.

She stares at the bucket.

They've not even left a bowl of water or any soap to wash her hands with.

Suddenly the severity of her situation crushes her.

An unexpected cry leaps from her mouth. Once out, it seems to drag several uncontrollable sobs behind it.

She's shaken by her surprising outbreak of emotion.

She tells herself she's a strong woman, a professional, used to fighting her way through things. She hasn't cried for years and shouldn't be sobbing her heart out now.

She palms away the tears and studies the streaks they've made on her dusty hands.

She has to pull herself together.

Make the best of the situation she's in.

Mustn't let anyone see that she's frightened to death.

She doesn't so much walk to the bucket as charge at it.

It's not going to beat her.

They're not going to beat her.

She grinds it into the dust, unbuckles her belt, slips down her two-hundred-euro trousers, squats and pees.

Job done.

She re-dresses, moves to the front of the cell and shakes the bars again. 'Hey! Hey! In here! Someone! Hey!'

She carries on shouting and shaking until the purple-cloaked man reappears.

She reads his face.

He looks irritated that he's been summoned by the noise she made. He's human, that's all. Nothing special. Beatable.

'I've finished thinking,' she says.

'Good.'

'I need a phone.'

His eyes say *not a chance*.

'I need a phone so I can call work. I usually check in with my boss and my team when I'm not there. I confirm appointments and discuss cases. It already looks strange that I've not called for so long.'

He gives it some thought. 'It makes sense. Wait and I will come back to you.'

Louisa watches him turn and walk away. She can't believe he just told her to wait. Like she has a choice. *Wait* is not a word she's ever liked, but in her current circumstance it's been elevated to the top of the things she most hates and fears.

But wait she does.

Half an hour later, he reappears. With him are two more men, but their cloaks are scarlet.

Louisa steps away from the bars as Purple Cloak unlocks them. The others enter and Louisa has to do a double-take. Their faces are startlingly feminine, but their hands and feet are distinctly man-sized. Without talking, they grab her wrists and click on a pair of steel handcuffs.

'Ow!' Louisa looks down at the metal gnawing her wrist bones. 'They're hurting.'

'You'll get used to it,' says Purple Cloak.

One of his henchmen – or hench*women*; Louisa's now not sure – disappears behind her. She's about to turn around when the other one jerks her by the wrists.

The stab of pain distracts her.

A black hood is pulled over her head.

A stretch of thin rope is looped around her neck and pulled tight.

Purple Cloak speaks. 'Don't scream. Don't panic. You'll only make things worse for yourself.'

Louisa struggles.

He holds her shoulders. 'Listen! Nothing bad is going to happen. We can't get any reception down here, so we're taking you to a place where you can make your call.'

The reassurance doesn't work.

Louisa is panicking. Panicking like she's never panicked before.

The shock of the hood has triggered her claustrophobia.

She feels like giant balls of cotton wool are being stuffed down her throat.

She tells herself to stay calm, breathe through her nose.

Her chest aches.

Her heart is racing.

Thin streams of air trickle into her heaving lungs.

Her shoulder bumps against something.

They're moving her.

'Come on,' says someone. 'Let's get her out of the womb.'

Womb?

She must have misheard. They must have said *room*.

Hands grip her elbows and tow her along.

She feels sick and dizzy.

There are other voices now. Women shouting to her, or maybe it's children.

Louisa starts to hyperventilate. She needs to stop. Stand still. See light and space. Calm down.

But they won't let her.

Her knees buckle.

She gasps for air.

Blackness is just a breath away.

89

Tom and Valentina eat at their hotel.

Federico stays with them for a glass of wine, but gets a call from his wife and says he has to leave.

Left alone, they leisurely pick their way through a platter of Tuscan prosciutto, before seeing off two small but delicious plates of mushroom risotto. A particularly fine and fragrant bottle of Vermentino di Gallura runs out during their main course of fresh lobster, pasta and salad.

'More?' asks Tom, holding the bottle aloft.

She pulls a face. 'Would you hate it if we didn't?'

'Of course not.'

They both know what it means. The meal is heading to a close. Work is rearing its ugly head.

Tom mops a little of the lobster sauce with a piece of torn bread. 'Are you starting to think about Anna?'

'A little.' She pins some pasta down and starts to twirl it on her fork. 'Though I'm trying not to.'

'And Louisa?'

'Also.' Her appetite's gone now. Killed by hearing the names Anna and Louisa. 'When I try to make sense of everything that's happened – the murder, or murders, Anna's death, and this latest development with Louisa – my head feels like it's exploding.'

Tom understands. 'I don't know how you cope with such horrors as part of a daily job. I came upon death quite a lot as a priest, but nowhere near on the scale that you do, and there was seldom the same amount of violence involved.'

She untwists the speared pasta and uses her knife to scrape her fork clean. 'You know, murder is usually straightforward. Wife kills cheating husband. Cheated-on husband kills cheating wife. Jealous jilted lover kills reunited husband and wife, that sort of thing.'

'Plus the drug killings.'

'Plus the drug killings. Then there's not much more on the spectrum until you reach serial killers.' She pushes her plate away from her. 'Where do you think sociopathic cults or paedophile gangs fit in?'

'Somewhere between the mentally ill and the spree killers? You want coffee or anything?'

'*Non, grazie.*' She picks up her glass and swirls the last of her wine.

Tom tries to beckon a waiter to pay the bill, but has no luck. 'You remember the number ten came up when we first talked about Cybele and the cults and the myths of the other sibyls, the prophetesses?'

Valentina has to force herself to remember. 'Something to do with the number on the shelf at the depository where the poor left their cremated loved ones.'

'The Columbarium, that's right. Well, it's been driving me crazy. I realised afterwards that while ten doesn't mean anything to me, nine does.'

Valentina sits back. She fears a long and difficult story is about to keep her from the soft comforts of her bed. 'Treat my brain gently. I've had a few glasses of wine, I'm stressed to the limit. And I'm getting very tired.'

'Okay, I'll make it simple.' Tom blots his mouth with a white napkin before he begins. 'According to Roman mythology, a sibyl offered nine books of prophecies and wisdom to Tarquinius Superbus, the last king of Rome, in return for a vast fortune.'

She grimaces. History – Roman or otherwise – was never her strong subject. 'For how much?'

'No idea. I don't think anyone ever knew. Legend just says it was a fortune. Anyway, Tarquinius says no deal, and so the sibyl burns three of the books and then says she wants the same amount of money for the remaining six. Tarquinius still says no deal, so she torches another three.'

'Plucky girl.' Valentina drains the dregs of her glass in appreciation. 'She'd be my choice to beat the *Deal or No Deal* banker every time.'

'So, we're down to three books, for which the sibyl demands exactly the same amount of money she did for the original nine. This time Tarquinius cracks and hands over the cash.'

'Why? What made these books so valuable?'

'Good questions. Sibyls were prophetesses. As well as foresight, apparently these texts gave great advice on what to do as and when disasters fell upon the empire.'

'A sort of *Dummy's Guide to Pestilence and Plague*?'

Tom can't help but laugh. 'Yes, if you like. Joking aside, the three sibylline books that remained were so treasured that they were kept in a guarded vault in the Temple of Jupiter on the Capitoline Hill. They were only brought out and consulted during times of crisis.'

'Such as?'

'Pretty much what you said: famine, pestilence in the agricultural areas, meteor showers, slave rebellions, invading armies, those kinds of things.'

'I've never heard of these books. Are you thinking that they somehow have a connection with Anna and all her alters?'

'We know there's a connection to Cybele; it's pretty likely that that extends to associated cults and the sibylline books or teachings.'

'I suppose these books are in Latin or Greek or something horribly hard?'

'Worse. They're gone.' Tom catches the eye of a passing waiter. '*Il conto, per favore.*'

The young man nods and takes a split second to check out Valentina before waltzing away to get the bill. 'The temple they were kept in was burned down and the books destroyed along with it.'

'If only they'd backed it all up on hard disk,' jokes Valentina.

'Actually, they tried to do what I suppose is almost the ancient equivalent of that. They had scribes write down verbal accounts given by everyone and anyone who'd ever read or heard anything from the books. They called the new volumes the Sibylline Oracles.'

It makes her laugh. 'God, could you imagine asking everyone who'd read the Bible to give their own account of various passages and lessons? It would be hysterical!'

Tom sees the funny side. 'Or maybe a best-seller. Uncharacteristically, the Church seems to have missed a trick there.'

The waiter arrives with a small bill on a big silver plate.

Tom counts out cash and adds a handsome tip, despite the fact that the young man can't stop staring at Valentina.

'I guess you get that a lot?' he jokes as the waiter glides away.

'Never happened before,' she says innocently. 'You ready for bed?'

Tom puts down his napkin and courteously steps behind her chair to hold it as she rises. 'I've been ready since we got rid of Federico almost two hours ago.'

90

'She's waking up.'

Louisa hears them talking before she sees anyone. People are moving all around her.

Her fluttering eyes finally focus.

She's staring up at a ceiling.

A real ceiling.

Not the rough roof of a cell.

The picture before her slowly becomes clear.

She's in a strange room that smells of dust and wet plaster.

It doesn't matter.

At least she's not underground. She's not in a cell. Not in an enclosed space.

She hunches up on to her elbows.

A blurred shape enters her eyeline.

'You passed out.' It's the man in the purple cloak. 'You panicked and collapsed when we were moving you.'

Louisa looks around. His scarlet-robed henchmen are hovering in the background, along with a woman in a shimmering pale cloak who turns and walks away as soon as she notices Louisa looking at her.

The woman in her apartment block? Purple Cloak's accomplice?

No, Louisa doesn't think so.

She looked older. Somehow more important.

Purple Cloak leans over her again. 'Let's get you some water. You haven't drunk anything for about twelve hours.'

Twelve hours!

The words crash around in her mind like a frightened bird stuck up a chimney.

'What?'

'It's a little after eight a.m. You've slept through the night. Probably a combination of shock and stress.' He remembers the circumstances of her abduction. 'And perhaps a little after-effect of the chloroform.'

Louisa takes a plastic cup of water from him. She notices he's right-handed and wearing a heavy gold ring bearing the image of a woman astride some ugly wild animal. '*Grazie.*'

She drinks it in two gulps.

He smiles. 'I'll get you some more.'

Louisa can see the room better now.

It's weird.

She can't quite think what it reminds her of.

Then she gets it.

It's like a half-decorated room in a new house. The walls

316

are dark peach, the colour of fresh plaster. There are ladders lying on the floor, dust sheets piled in a corner, and a strong smell of gloss paint.

She sits up a little more.

No windows.

It panics her slightly.

There are workmen's portable lights off to her left, cables snaking away to some hidden power source or generator.

She's certainly in some newly built or newly refurbished building – somewhere that is going to be seen by the public, otherwise what's the point of decorating it?

'Here.' Purple Cloak pushes the topped–up water cup into her hand. 'Don't even think about wondering if you can run away. Even if I took you outside, you'd have no idea where you are, and our people are guarding all the tunnels and exit routes.'

Tunnels.

Was that a slip?

Louisa sips the water.

The more she thinks about it, the more she realises that the word tells her nothing. Rome is like a rat run.

The whole subsoil of the city is riddled with secret tunnels, caves, dungeons and ruins.

She could be anywhere.

She passes back the empty cup.

'Good. Now, how about you make that call to your office and explain to us how we can recover Anna?'

'I need my phone,' she says wearily.

He clicks his fingers and someone goes off to fetch it. 'I know. We brought you here so you can get a signal. It would have been impossible in the cells.'

Cells.

Plural.

Cells.

And tunnels.

Louisa pushes her luck. 'I'll need to go back home and change. I can't go into work wearing yesterday's clothes; it'll look suspicious.'

He seems amused. 'If necessary, we can give you fresh clothes, but you won't be going home until all this is over. And if you don't achieve what we want, then you won't be going home at all.'

One of the henchmen returns and hands his boss Louisa's phone.

Purple Cloak flashes a thin smile. 'We've even charged it for you.' He gives Louisa a long and considered look. 'Now, who are you planning to call? What are you going to say? And how exactly do you intend to help us get Anna back?'

Louisa has thought this through. A hundred times. She clears her throat with a rusty cough. 'We've taken her out of the hospital before. We took her to Cosmedin, near to where she was arrested, to see if we could unlock any memories that would help us with her therapy.'

Purple Cloak stays poker-faced. 'Go on.'

'I'm going to call my assistant and tell her to get Anna ready to go out again. I'll say I've been reading through the case notes and want to take her on another cognitive trip.'

'You can authorise that?'

'Of course. That's why you brought me here, isn't it?'

He accepts her point. 'Where would you say you were taking her? How will she get there?'

Louisa knows she has him hooked. 'Wherever you like. You tell me.'

He thinks for a moment, then looks pleased with himself. 'Piazza di Santa Cecilia. Do you know it?'

Louisa does.

It sends a shudder rippling through her.

'Yes. I can go into work, collect Anna and bring her there with my assistant.'

He holds up the phone. 'No. You'll get your assistant to bring her. You only go free as and when we see Anna.'

That's not the way Louisa was hoping to play things. 'I'll have to be there to sign her out,' she lies. 'It can't be done.'

'It can. Find a way. And remember, if you try to trick us, we *will* kill you.' He passes the phone over. 'Show me on the display who you are going to call before you press any buttons.'

Louisa takes her cell and thumbs her way through the electronic directory.

Her hands are shaking. She can feel her breathing quickening.

Another panic attack is on its way.

Finally she holds up the name and number for him to see.

He peers closely at the display. 'Okay. Make the call.'

91

Valentina's been lying awake for ten minutes.

She's naked in bed, facing Tom and doing nothing but watch him breathing gently. Just being beside him makes her feel calm and safe. She can't remember looking at a man in this way before. Just staring at him, studying him, trying to understand more about him.

She lifts her left hand from beneath the warmth of the quilt and puts it gently on the side of his face.

He shifts a little.

Right now he seems more like a baby than a man, and she has to stifle a laugh.

She scrutinises his face.

Her old boss Vito always said a man's face was a map to his life. A thin white scar runs just below the hairline on the left side of Tom's head.

A fall as a child?

A tumble off his first bike?

This little white snake looks old enough to be either.

She touches his hair. It's thick and dark, but not completely black. It's somewhere north of chestnut brown. She looks closer. She spots a few grey hairs in the part that joins his almost military-short sideburns. It suits him. Makes him look distinguished. He may be one of those rare beasts who gets even more handsome with the passing years.

Valentina's cell phone rings. Her eyes dart in the direction of the noise.

It's on the dressing table and out of reach.

Tom stirs.

She was hoping to keep him asleep a little longer.

She slips from the covers and quickly grabs the phone.

She intends just hitting the dismiss button, but recognises the caller.

Louisa.

'*Pronto*,' she says, somewhat apprehensively.

'Valentina, it's Doctor Verdetti.' Louisa leaves no pause for a usual response. 'I don't have much time, so please don't chatter like you normally do; just listen carefully for once.'

Valentina is instantly on edge.

Louisa has never called herself doctor, and the off-hand reference to chattering is peculiar, to say the least.

'Tell me first,' Louisa continues, almost brusquely, 'what

kind of night did Anna have? She looked awful when I last saw her. I'm hoping she's much better this morning.'

Valentina quickly picks up on the verbal clues. Whoever Louisa is with, whoever has been scaring Anna so much she felt it necessary to sleep in a bed of bibles, doesn't know she is dead – *mustn't* know she's dead – and is probably listening in right this second.

Valentina plays her part. 'Anna is all right. A little weak. I think you need to see her for yourself. When will you be coming in?'

'Good, that's exactly what I wanted to hear. Actually, I won't be coming in. Just the opposite. I've been looking through Anna's notes and have decided that therapeutically she needs another trip out. It will give us a chance to learn more about how she reacts to certain surroundings. Could you get her wrapped up nice and warm and bring her out to the Piazza di Santa Cecilia? I'll meet you there.' Louisa looks to the man in the purple cloak leaning close to her and whispers, 'What time?'

He holds up his watch and jabs the dial with a stubby index finger.

'Can you get her there by eleven o'clock?' she asks.

Valentina guesses she has no choice in the matter. 'I'll do my best.' She reaches for a hotel pen and notepad. 'Is there anywhere in particular in the piazza you want to meet? Anything special you want me to bring?'

Louisa whispers again to the man at her side: 'Where exactly do you want her brought?'

He hesitates. 'The fountain outside the church. That will do for now.'

'The fountain outside Santa Cecilia. No need to bring anything other than your normal baggage and Anna.'

Valentina understands the 'baggage' to be back-up police. 'Okay. We'll see you at eleven.'

The line goes dead.

Valentina glances at her watch. She has two hours to get a plan together.

92

Father Alfredo Giordano is in an unusual and awkward position when his cell phone rings.

He's bare-chested, in only his pyjama bottoms and has just come out of a Downward Facing Dog.

Right now, he's balanced on his hands counting a five breath in The Crow.

Alfie has never held The Crow pose for a full five before. He usually crashes sideways at the start, slips backwards on reaching two or bangs his forehead on a very shaky-handed three count.

Right now, his palms are well spread and he's rock solid on a four, so no way is he going to answer that phone until he's made the full five.

'*Cinque!* Yee-haaaw!' He rolls out of the yoga pose and pads across the polished wooden floor of his tiny room. He pulls his cell phone from the charger cable stuck in a wall socket and answers with gusto: '*Pronto, Giordano – il padrone di yoga fantastico!*'

His old friend daren't ask what he's up to. 'Alfie, it's Tom. I need your help.'

'You have it, my friend.' He takes a deep yogic breath. '*Il padrone* can fold you into a Bird of Paradise or twist you into a One-Legged King Pigeon. Which would you prefer?'

322

'Alfie, this is serious. What do you know about St Cecilia's?'

He drops the comedy routine. 'St Cecilia's in Trastevere?'

Tom switches on the speakerphone function so Valentina can hear, then glances at notes on a pad. 'The one in Piazza di Santa Cecilia; that's Trastevere, right?'

'Yes, yes, it is. What's wrong, Tom?'

'I'll fill you in later. Please, Alfie, just tell me what you know.'

'Okay. The church is very famous. Let me think . . . it was built in something like the third century. It has an amazing Romanesque campanile . . . lots of rebuilds over the ages, notably the ninth and I think eighteenth centuries.'

Tom scribbles furiously. Valentina watches over his shoulder.

Alfie continues with his list. 'Oh, one of the weirdest things, there's a convent adjacent to the church, and the sisters there shear the lambs from Sant'Agnese fueri le Mura and use the wool to make sacred vestments. Inside the church there are paintings depicting the beheading of St Cecilia. You remember the story of her?'

Tom has to jog his memory. 'Lived her life wearing sackcloth, married but stayed a virgin out of devotion to the Lord?'

'Haven't we all,' interrupts Alfie with a tang of irony.

Tom continues to download the rest of what he knows about St Cecilia. 'Patron saint of musicians, feast day in October – no, sorry, November. And her killers had great trouble putting her to death.'

'Seven out of ten, or B plus, whichever you prefer.'

Valentina flaps her hands in frustration. Fascinating as this is, it isn't helping rescue Louisa.

Tom ignores her. 'I'm not finished. Didn't she suffer some Rasputin-like death? Her persecutors tried to kill her two or three times and failed?'

'I'll up you to an A minus. They attempted to suffocate her in the bath at her house. When that failed, they decided to behead her. That didn't go well either. The executioner tried three times to decapitate her, and then, seeing that she was still alive, fled in fear.'

'And she didn't die until three days later, after she'd received Holy Communion.'

'Another thing,' adds Alfie. 'The original church is widely believed to have been built on the place of her home and martyrdom.'

Tom writes down *ruins of old home beneath church* and underlines it as Valentina reads over his shoulder. 'So are there a lot of tunnels and open areas beneath the ground at Santa Cecilia?'

'A lot?' Alfie sounds almost incredulous. 'Tom, there's a whole city beneath Rome. The place is built over this soft volcanic rock and there are miles and miles of catacombs. Have a look at the crypt at Santa Cecilia and you'll understand what I mean.'

93

The blindfold is a big improvement on the hood.

Louisa is hugely relieved not to have her head covered and a rope tied around her neck.

It's the kind of observation she never dreamt she'd make, but it's true.

'Relax. It's okay,' says a man holding her right elbow and helping her walk.

But it's not okay.

Louisa still feels claustrophobic. Hidden claws are scratching at her lungs. She knows it's only a matter of time before she has another fit if they don't get this damned thing off her.

They make her climb several steps.

Steps that are steep and turn sharply in on themselves.

It's a spiral staircase.

A never-ending one.

Her heart rate is alarmingly elevated, and it's increasing all the stress she's feeling.

'You're doing fine, it's nearly over,' says the voice at her side.

Louisa steps up, but there's no step there. She stumbles. Unseen hands catch her. 'You're at the top. It's okay.'

A door opens and she feels a rush of cold, wintry air.

Paradise.

The sensation of being outside stops her feeling panicky.

They make her walk for about ten seconds.

A car door clunks open.

'Watch your head,' says her new minder. 'We're putting you in a vehicle; you're going to have to slide in.'

He grabs her by the back of her hair and manhandles her into the rear of the car.

Louisa can smell leather.

Leather and sweat.

She puts one down to the car's upholstery and the other to the bulky body pressed against her.

Even without seeing him she knows he's huge.

She knows it because her back-seat buddy has biceps like boulders and one keeps cracking the side of her head every time he shifts in his seat.

After several minutes of driving, a voice booms out from the front of the car. 'You can take the blindfold off her now.'

The guy in the back seat squashes her as he fumbles around her head and unfastens it.

'*Grazie.*' Louisa keeps her eyes closed to begin with. Even through her lids, the daylight is bright, and the tight binding has made her pupils and skin sore.

The first thing she sees is the back of the front passenger seat, then the windows on her side of the vehicle. They're heavily tinted, the kind that are so dark that from the outside you can't see in. She's in some expensive four-by-four, but she can't see any badging and can't work out the model or make.

She turns to the man alongside her and tries to give him a friendly look. Year One psychology taught her that if kidnappers see their captives as human, they have more difficulty hurting them.

She's not so sure it has any effect.

The guy's every bit as big as she imagined, but surprisingly he's rake thin and has arms like the hind legs of a bull. She realises that her inner prejudices equated the unwashed smell with someone fat.

'Thanks for taking that off,' she says, gradually widening her eyes to get them used to the light. 'I thought I was going to pass out.'

'Shut up!' shouts the driver, without turning round. 'Just sit there and shut the fuck up!'

Louisa takes the hint.

In the silence that follows, she works out that the short-tempered driver is Purple Cloak and the other two men in the car with her are the two Scarlet Cloaks she saw when they were holding her underground.

As they crawl over the cobbled and congested back streets, she takes strange comfort in the familiarity of seeing traffic jammed up all around her.

Are the doors centrally locked?

She thinks they probably are. It would be stupid if they weren't.

And even if they weren't, could she flip the handle and make a run for it without being grabbed by the half-bull, half-man creature sitting next to her?

She reckons not.

The most sobering thought is that if she tries and fails, she knows she won't get another chance. They'll watch her even more closely. Distrust her even more.

She has to be patient.

The chance will come.

She distracts herself with more traffic-watching. The road around her is now completely jammed. Car horns blare every other second. Drivers mouth madly at each other from their little vehicular goldfish bowls.

The traffic starts to move.

It's like someone flicked a switch.

The car she's in glides past a huge furniture van that's now shoehorned down a side street and is no longer blocking the traffic.

They turn the corner and she instantly recognises where she is.

They're approaching the Tiber.

Just minutes from the rendezvous site.

94

Santa Cecilia stands on the west side of the river, almost equidistant between the Ponte Palatino and the Ponte Portese.

Valentina sees it for what it is.

Architectural mesmerism.

It's one of those buildings that draws the eye to everything that's not really important.

For a start, there's the distraction of a walled and gated courtyard so well designed that even in the depths of winter you can imagine the riot of colour set to explode in spring. Then there's a vast fountain, dominated by a giant ancient cantharus – a water vessel second to none.

But none of what's on show is what's really important about Santa Cecilia.

As Alfie told them, the fascinating stuff is inside, below ground, and in all the stories and legends that hover around the place.

Valentina weighs it up from the car, almost a hundred metres away. 'It's useless. Those damned archways, gates and pillars at the entrance to the courtyard block out so much of the church. Without a full surveillance team, I feel like a Japanese tourist trying to cover a moon landing with a point and shoot.'

Federico Assante is sitting low in the back. 'Did you see Tom go inside?'

'About a minute ago.' She wonders if she's doing the right thing. If she'd called Caesario, he'd have had to take her seriously and put a proper team out here. On the other hand, she'd have lost a golden opportunity to ensure that Louisa would drop her testimony against herself and Federico. She glances at her watch. Three minutes to eleven. 'We'd better get in position.'

Federico ties on a headscarf Valentina bought en route and wraps up tight in blankets that she brought from the hotel. The only thing that could give the game away from a distance is his feet. They bought a pair of low-heeled black women's shoes, but Federico has taken to them like a drunk to ice.

Valentina gets out of the car and goes round the back.

Now she's out on the street, she presumes her every move is being watched.

She opens the rear door and begins to act in character. 'Take it easy now, you're very weak. Let me help you out of there.'

The lieutenant tries to keep his head down and his back bent as he clambers out of the car.

Valentina puts a protective arm around him, just as she would a frail old grandmother. 'We're going to walk you over to the fountain, where we'll meet Dr Verdetti.'

Federico shuffles along, acutely aware that nothing about his walk is feminine. The best he can do is move slowly so it looks like he's weak and in pain.

The wind across the street blows up into his face and threatens to dislodge his headscarf. He grabs it and inches it further down his forehead .

It takes them almost a year to make the hundred metres to the fountain.

Or at least it feels like that.

The wind kicks up again, and with it comes the first spit of a light shower. Valentina uses it as an excuse to hold Federico close to her, his face all but buried between her breasts.

Not that he minds.

She glances at her watch. Almost five past. There's no sign of Louisa.

She swivels her head and looks around, as would anyone innocently trying to find their boss at a public meeting point. Nothing.

All stake-outs and stings get the adrenalin rushing, and this one is no different. Both Valentina and Federico are fully tanked, and they have to use all their professionalism not to do anything rash.

A group of pensioners emerges from the church, chattering enthusiastically.

Valentina takes some comfort from the fact that Tom is inside somewhere.

If she needs him, she knows he'll come through for her.

The shower starts to become more of a downpour. The rain driving into her face gives her an idea. 'Come on, let's get you back to the car before you get soaking wet.' She turns a bewildered Federico round and all but frogmarches him towards her Fiat.

'Hey!' he whispers anxiously, head pressed to her arm as they walk. 'What are you doing?'

Valentina ignores him.

Her instincts tell her they've already been spotted.

She's pretty certain the kidnappers will recognise her motive as just being protective of a sickly patient.

But it's a gamble. A big one.

She pulls open the passenger's door and gently manoeuvres the swathed Federico inside. She leans into the car and whispers, 'Keep your head down. Wait until I'm all the way back inside the courtyard, and then drive off and park up a few streets away.'

Valentina doesn't wait for an answer.

She shuts the door, turns around and takes out her cell phone.

In the distance she sees movement near the fountain.

Not Louisa.

A tall, wiry man.

Staring at her.

She looks down and pulls up Louisa's cell number on her phone.

She dials and looks up again.

The man is walking towards her.

Louisa's phone is ringing out.

Valentina takes a long, slow breath to calm the thumping in her chest and starts to walk towards the staring man.

95

Louisa's phone is ringing.

Purple Cloak is sitting behind the wheel of the four-by-four in a side street adjacent to Santa Cecilia. He takes Louisa's ringing phone out of his jacket pocket and reads the display. 'Valentina?'

'My assistant.'

He hands it over the back of his seat. 'Put it on speaker-phone and watch what you say.'

Louisa presses the accept button, fearful that she might miss the call, then switches to speaker function. 'Valentina, *ciao*. Where are you?'

'*Ciao.*' She tries to sound unstressed and normal. 'I'm just walking to the fountain. I had to take Anna back to the car because it's raining hard and she's really not too well. I thought she might pick up an infection. Where are you?'

Louisa looks to her captor.

He mouths back, 'In the church.'

'I'm inside Santa Cecilia. Wait for me by the fountain, I'll be out in a second.'

Purple Cloak nods his approval.

She switches off the phone and hands it back to him.

Or at least that's what he thinks she's done.

He slips it back into his jacket, unaware that Louisa never

331

ended the call. The line is still open and will stay open providing Valentina doesn't hang up.

'What now?' asks Louisa.

'My brothers and sisters will look after things. You sit tight. When we have Anna, I will let you go.'

Louisa suddenly realises she's made a mistake.

A big one.

She assumed that only Purple Cloak and his two henchmen had come to the church with her.

Now she knows she's wrong.

He mentioned sisters. No women travelled with them.

Louisa looks through the rear window.

Parked tight to their bumper is an old Land Rover, with a man behind the wheel.

She drops her head into her hands. He must have been driving several members of the gang to the scene.

She realises she's put Valentina in grave danger.

And herself.

96

Valentina knows the line is still open.

The voice that followed Louisa's is too muffled for her to understand, but she can make out that it's a man.

There's also no trace of echo.

That means that it's more likely that Louisa is in a car, rather than in the church as she said.

Valentina glances ahead. Rain is falling hard again and the man in her sights near the fountain has paused and is getting soaked as he answers a call on his own phone. Normally, someone would just let it ring and call back when they got somewhere dry, so he's pretty much blown his cover. She listens to Louisa's open line, and it's now obvious that whoever is with her is talking to the guy standing by the fountain.

Valentina starts to piece the puzzle together.

If Louisa is in a car and not in the church, then she can't be far away. Logically, if the vehicle is close by, it's most likely to be in one of the official bays in Via di San Michele, off to one side of the piazza. Kidnap gangs never park illegally; they don't want to risk drawing any kind of attention to themselves.

Valentina pauses under the main gated archway and reception block at the entrance to the courtyard.

She has to act fast.

Lightning fast.

The man by the fountain finishes his call and looks towards her.

She stops and kills the open line to Louisa.

Casually she calls Tom. 'Louisa's in a car. Probably in a bay by the right-hand side of the courtyard when you come out. I'm almost with the targets.'

She rings off and walks towards the fountain.

Despite the rain, the courtyard is still busy with people coming and going. Multicoloured umbrellas sprout up around the flower beds like fast-growing exotic blooms.

Valentina's nerves jangle as Tom comes within ten metres of her.

He doesn't even glance her way.

As far as she can tell, there's no panic in his movement. He's walking briskly, but not so fast that the rainfall doesn't easily explains his haste.

She allows herself a small smile.

He'd make a good cop.

The tall, wiry man in the courtyard is now barely three metres away.

He's in her peripheral vision but she's avoiding eye contact.

To her surprise, he walks straight past her.

Then he stops and turns.

Only now does Valentina realise he's not alone.

97

Tom finds it hard not to stay in the courtyard and protect Valentina. He knows she's a professional soldier, trained to deal with situations like this, but his instinct is to hang around and make sure she's okay.

Once he's passed under the arch of the entrance block and emerged into the piazza, he picks up his pace.

He turns sharp right and then goes around the corner into Via di San Michele.

Immediately he's confronted by dozens of parked cars.

All their windows are obscured by the falling rain.

People moving around with umbrellas make his view even more difficult.

Opportunistically, a guy with Rasta dreadlocks is standing near a wall, selling cheap brollies.

Tom pays ten euros for the first one he can grab.

He doesn't give a damn about the price or about getting wet; he wants it to hide beneath as he moves from car to car studying the occupants.

Three quarters of the way along the bays, one of the park-ups stands out.

A green Land Rover.

It's noticeable not because it's an exceptional vehicle, but because the windows have all misted up and the driver's used a hand to wipe off the condensation to see through.

Thing is, it's not the kind of street where there's anything much to see.

Tom collapses his umbrella and moves to the driver's side.

He knocks on the window.

It glides down about a third of the way.

He bends down and speaks English to a stern-looking man in his late twenties.

'Excuse me, I've just locked myself out of my car.' He gestures to the heavens. 'Dumb, eh? Do you have a phone I can use to call my wife to come and bring some spare keys?'

The man frowns at him. 'No.'

Behind him, in the darkness of the back seat, Tom can just make out another man. He's sitting upright but struggling with something he's holding down on his lap.

The window glides shut.

Tom bangs on it. 'Hey! Come on, man, I need some help. I'm getting soaked.'

The glass glides back down.

The barrel of a gun pokes out of the blackness. 'I said *no*! Now fuck off.'

98

The thin man in a long black trench coat smiles at Valentina. 'Are you waiting for someone?'

335

He's as charming as dozens of other deluded guys who've tried to chat her up over the years.

'Yes, my boss.' She shrugs at the rain. 'I hope she hurries up.'

Trench Coat comes up close and from inside his pocket presses a gun against her left hip. 'Don't move and don't scream.' He's lost his charm now. 'If you do, then this church will have another martyr.' He looks into her eyes, and when he sees the fear and compliance he's looking for, he adds, 'Where's Anna?'

Valentina feigns panic. 'Oh God, don't hurt me, please don't hurt me.'

'I don't want to.' He jabs the gun deeper into her side. 'Where's Anna? You're supposed to have her with you.'

Valentina lifts her hand shakily and points through the archway at the end of the courtyard. 'I took her back to the car because of the rain. She's sick. Where's Doctor Verdetti?'

Trench Coat ignores her and glances around.

'*Please* don't hurt me, I've done nothing wrong.'

The gun stays pressed into her left hip. 'Keep your voice down! What kind of car is it and where did you park?'

Valentina stares at the ground as though she's too frightened to look at him. 'Fiat. It's a blue Punto. It's not far . . . er . . . just outside in the piazza, right opposite here.' She keeps her eyes fixed on the floor. Two sets of male feet stop just off to the right of her.

'Go get her,' says Trench Coat. 'Be quick!'

The feet disappear.

Valentina feels another push in her side.

'We're going inside the church to wait for a little while.' He slides his body across hers so he's face to face with her. 'I'd hate you to get all cold and wet.'

She feels his hand move inside her jacket, slide beneath her jumper and grab her by the waist.

His touch revolts her.

She has to fight an impulse to drive her right knee so far into his testicles they'll come out of his mouth.

Being closer allows him to pull the gun out of his right pocket and hold it flat against Valentina's abdomen, barrel digging into her diaphragm.

He puts his face close to hers. From a distance they could be mistaken for lovers about to kiss. 'My little friend here is itching to get inside you,' he whispers in her ear as he moves the cold tip of the barrel against her warm skin. 'I don't blame him. It must be really nice inside you.'

Valentina takes a deep breath.

He mistakes it for fear. 'Don't be scared. If you do exactly as I tell you, then in less than twenty minutes all this will just be an awful memory.'

99

It's not the first time Tom Shaman has looked down the barrel of a gun.

A gangbanger once pulled an Uzi in his church in LA and robbed the entire congregation. The kid was high on crystal meth and ended up getting shot on the church steps by a gang senior who'd come to pick his mother up from the service and found her screaming and terrified.

Tom learned two basic things from all those badasses back in Compton. Firstly, there are frequent shooters, guys who only draw guns when they're going to fire them. Secondly, there are bluffers, posers who pull a weapon but have never let off a shot in their sorry little lives.

Tom figures the man behind the metal being pointed at him is not a frequent shooter. He's a bluffer.

But of course, that's only a guess.

A dangerous guess.

'Whoa, mister!' He throws up his hands. 'I don't want any trouble. I just needed some help.' The big American backs away, hands high in the air. 'Man, no one told me Rome was like this.' He doesn't leave the way he came, but heads down the vehicle towards the back.

He knows the guy's watching in his wing mirror but figures that doesn't matter. He'd have to be a contortionist to shoot over his left shoulder with the gun in his right hand.

Tom's about to make his move and he knows he has to be fast.

He is.

He jerks the door open with his left hand, steps forward half a pace and cracks his elbow into the driver's face. He reaches across him, grabs his gun hand and crashes it repeatedly into the steering wheel.

The screams tell him he's broken the guy's wrist.

The man in the back of the car makes his move.

He lurches forward and tries to swing a punch.

Tom grabs the fallen pistol off the driver's lap and fires a shot into the roof of the car.

Gunfire has a special way of spooking people. Especially in closed spaces.

Louisa flings open a rear door and bolts for freedom.

Her minder slips out of the car and levels a pistol at Tom.

The two men stare down their guns at each other.

Off in the distance, Tom sees Louisa running for her life.

100

Valentina is under no illusion that being inside a church means she's safe.

If her last case in Venice taught her anything, it's that churches aren't at all sacred when it comes to criminals and killers.

The guy in the black trench coat forces her into a pew and sits tight alongside her. 'Kneel and pray. Don't do anything stupid.'

Valentina does as she's told.

She intertwines her fingers, bows her head and looks as reflective as any of the devout visitors around her.

Her mind is certainly on different things, though.

By now, it's going to be obvious that there's no Punto parked near the piazza and no Anna sitting patiently in it. And Tom will have discovered whether or not Louisa and her captors are in a car just around the corner.

For a second Valentina does what everyone else around her is doing: she prays. Prays that Tom is all right and that Louisa is still alive.

It's the first time she's been on her knees in church since her cousin died.

The phone in Trench Coat's pocket rings.

He catches it quickly.

Valentina knows that in doing so, he's taken his hand off the gun.

It's her cue to stop trusting in the good Lord and do what she's been trained to do.

She cups her hand behind Trench Coat's head and smashes his face into the edge of the wooden pew.

All eyes are now on Valentina.

She glances at the body slumped at her feet, shuffles forward and puts her foot across his neck. If he moves she'll feel it.

'I'm a police officer,' she shouts down the aisle. 'Please leave the church, immediately.'

No one moves.

Valentina stoops, fishes in the guy's coat pocket and recovers his gun. It's an old Glock with a Crimson Trace laser grip.

She holds it up high. 'I said, I am a police officer. Now get out of here before someone gets shot!'

The church empties in a deafening rush for the doors.

Valentina ignores the last of the stragglers.

There's blood all over the back of the pew, and for the first time she's wondering whether the guy on the floor is just unconscious, or dead.

101

A woman passing by screams hysterically.

The man who's just levelled a gun at Tom's head glances to his left.

It's all the American needs.

He plants a drop kick deep into the guy's guts and follows with a hard right-hander into his mouth.

Amazingly, the guy's still upright. And still holding the weapon.

Tom throws a left, then twin punches with his right.

Now he goes down.

Hits the floor like a TV dropped from the top of a tower block. The gun clatters from his open hand.

The four-by-four's engine roars into life.

Seems the driver's got his act together.

Tom spins round.

That's his first mistake.

He clutches at the now closed driver's door, but it won't open. The central locking's on.

He pulls again at the handle as the Land Rover lurches up on to the pavement.

That's his second mistake.

He hasn't noticed a man climb out of a similar vehicle parked a few metres away.

An agonising pain erupts in Tom's right shoulder.

It's followed by another behind his left knee. The combination of blows sends him sprawling into the road.

Instinctively, he rolls.

He learned at school that if you stay still in a street fight, then you're as good as asking for a beating.

Now he sees the cause of the pain.

A baseball bat slaps into the brown water beside his head.

Tom grabs the club but feels a terrible burning in his right shoulder. Something's busted.

He can't hold on.

The wood slips from his fingers.

The guy takes a swing and slaps Tom on the side of his ribs.

Tom tries to roll again.

The bat man takes a stride to his left, raises the club and starts a swing that he's sure will pop Tom's head like a watermelon.

Only he never makes it.

Instead, he freezes midway during the draw-back.

A sharp pain erupts inside his chest. It feels like someone has stuck a knife in his heart.

And that's because someone has.

The throwing hand of Guilio Brygus Angelis is still extended, his fingers pointing at exactly the spot at which the ancient dagger was aimed.

102

Rapid response units from the Carabinieri and the Polizia Municipale arrive within seconds of each other.

Both forces got panic calls from the public after Tom had fired the gun in the car. Both also had reports of a woman in the church brandishing a gun and claiming to be a cop.

Guilio is on his knees alongside Tom. 'I've got to get out of here. Can you move?'

It takes Tom a second glance to realise that his Good Samaritan is the stranger he fought with inside Anna Fratelli's apartment.

He's got a dozen questions in his head and no time to ask any of them.

'Help me up.' He stretches out his left hand.

Guilio needs both his hands to pull Tom up. He glances at the body with the blade in it. If he pulls it out, he knows the guy will die, but if he leaves it, he will lose a dagger that's two thousand years old and a set of his own fingerprints as well.

He leaves it.

He turns to Tom. 'Follow me, or they'll make you part of this.'

Tom lurches after the quick, slim figure disappearing down Via di San Michele.

Police sirens and whistles fill the air as he follows him into the shadows of a tributary of thin alleys trickling away from the church.

Pain is now starting to devour Tom's shoulder, leg and ribs. He can barely pull himself upright as he runs.

He has no chance of keeping up with Guilio as he weaves a route through a labyrinth of back streets and passages that few locals even know of.

'Down here!'

Tom has no idea where 'here' is. He stops for breath beside some low railings.

'Here!'

The shout is from below him.

He swings his right leg over the small metal fence that's supposed to keep the public out of what looks like one of Rome's many excavation sites.

There's a long drop down the other side.

He knows he doesn't have time to look for a safer route.

He jumps.

His left leg buckles on impact and he falls heavily on to his damaged right shoulder.

Guilio shows no concern. He's busy.

His hands are pushing hard against the black stone wall located directly beneath the barrier.

As hard as he possibly can.

He groans and strains again with all of his weight and might.

Nothing happens.

He turns and puts his back against the wall. Once more he pushes for all he's worth.

His feet slip in the grit and soil.

Tom watches in amazement.

A thin section of the wall slowly starts to swing open.

103

Valentina keeps her gun trained on the body at her feet.

Whoever this jerk is, he holds the key to why Anna was so screwed up, and what's behind all the killings.

She can't wait for Trench Coat to come round.

The *chiesa* is silent.

Disturbingly silent.

Empty churches have spooked her since she was a kid, and this one is certainly a major kid-scarer.

She glances over her shoulder.

Two people are there.

A man and a woman.

They're moving towards her and the man has a gun aimed at her head.

Valentina stays cool.

He's slightly built and looks older than the woman – much older, maybe even in his sixties.

'Lift your hands and move into the aisle.' He waggles the gun towards where he wants her to go.

'Not going to happen.' She looks challengingly into his pale blue eyes.

'Lift them!'

She places her bet. 'I really don't think so.' She looks away from him and keeps the Glock pointed at Trench Coat. 'You'll have to shoot me before I give this creep up.'

The old guy's gun kicks in his hand.

There's a muzzle flash and a barking boom.

Valentina's heart all but explodes.

She's made the wrong call.

She doesn't feel any pain, but then again, she's been told that at first you don't.

Still nothing.

Now she's sure it was just a warning shot.

A warning duly observed.

If he's prepared to let off a gun in a church, he's desperate. Desperate men – even those who don't intend to kill – often end up doing so.

Over in the pews near the entrance she spots two more figures.

Men, she thinks.

Younger than Shooter, maybe the same age as Trench Coat.

'Drop it – drop the gun.' He waves his pistol and speeds up his walk towards her. 'Now!'

Valentina gives it up.

The clunk of the pistol on the floor is the cue for them to rush her. Not just Shooter and his female sidekick, but the watchers by the door.

A hand with a vice-like grip clamps around her neck. It forces her face first over the pew.

She feels the hard metal of a gun barrel against her temple.

Behind her, the young woman speaks for the first time. Her voice is shaky and nervous. 'Is he okay, is he breathing?'

There's a lot of movement. Valentina guesses they're trying to resuscitate Trench Coat.

'Attis, can you hear us?' Someone slaps his face. 'Attis, wake up!'

Valentina notes the name. She's sure she remembers Tom mentioning it. Slowly it comes back to her. Attis was the unfaithful lover of the goddess Cybele, who was driven so crazy he castrated himself. Given the chance, she'd do the same to him, then stick the guy's balls in Shooter's mouth.

But for now, all she can do is listen and try to make sense of the voices.

'He's okay. He's coming round. Get him to his feet.' This is Shooter.

'Come on, let's get you up.' This is a woman, an older, more authoritative one. 'Let's get moving.'

'Which way?' Another woman.

'No choice.' It's the older one again. 'We'll have to go through the crypt.'

'What about *her*?' It's the gentler woman speaking.

There's silence.

'She comes with us. We'll deal with her later.'

104

Carabinieri snipers with Mauser SP66s crawl into position on rooftops in and around the courtyard of Santa Cecilia.

Soldiers speedily bundle visiting tourists and rubbernecking locals out of the church grounds and beyond the piazza.

Overhead, an Augusta-Bell helicopter hovers menacingly. The 412 CRESCO is fitted with high-powered video cameras, infrared lenses, ground and surveillance radar and advanced heat-seeking thermal devices. Its eagle-eyed ops team is all primed and ready to track any sudden runners.

The crew watch paramedics stretcher an injured man into the back of an ambulance and then disappear with their sirens blazing.

Across the Trastevere back streets, troops spill from soft-topped Land Rover Defenders and start to stake out a dragnet.

No one is going to escape.

Public stabbings and gunfire in churches don't go down well in Rome, as some jokers are about to find out.

From his command vehicle, Major Lorenzo Silvestri, the head of GIS – the Gruppo di Intervento Speciale – processes in information from his men, then calmly gives word for the operation to begin.

His team is the cream of the Carabinieri. Special-ops troops, specifically trained in hostage release, hijack situations and counter-terrorism.

Right now, they're moving faster than the blink of an eye.

They enter in a cloud of tear gas, bursting through three main windows above the church and along two specific ground-floor routes.

Lorenzo's soldiers move with startling synchronism. They sweep the sacred aisles with a deadly mix of Heckler and Koch MP5s and Berettas.

In less than two minutes they establish that the vast church floor and its side rooms and upper galleries are clear.

Lorenzo scratches his stubbly silver-grey hair and watches feeds from helmet cameras as his team enters the crypt. If anyone is still hiding, this is the place they'll be.

The church lights are cut.

Soldiers slip on night-sight goggles and slide unseen into what they call the black zone.

Lorenzo knows the crypt well; it's a riot of rich colours from ceiling to floor, with spectacular statues and innumerable marble pillars that create an amazing array of painted arches.

But none of this shows on his infra-red camera feeds.

Just the odd glowing movement of soldiers and blurred backgrounds.

He crosses himself and prays that a gun battle doesn't break out down there. The crossfire would be horrendous.

The ROS veteran glances at his watch. Three more minutes have passed.

His radio feed crackles. 'Clear!' shouts one of his men.

'Clear!' confirms another.

'Clear!' The final confirmation rolls into Lorenzo's earpiece.

They've all drawn blanks.

Every nook, niche, corner and confessional has been searched and they've found no one.

Lorenzo sits back from the monitors and stretches his long legs.

Where the hell did the bad guys go?

He has to see for himself.

He steps from the warmth of his ops vehicle and walks through the wind and rain of the piazza.

He enters the church courtyard, questioning whether the operation was necessary.

Maybe it was a bad case of crowd hysteria.

Perhaps the congregation heard a nearby delivery truck backfire and panicked.

Then he dismisses the notion.

It wouldn't explain the stabbing, nor the eye-witness accounts of hearing shooting in the church and a woman identifying herself as a police officer.

But he's still not satisfied.

Neither the Carabinieri nor the Polizia have been able to confirm that they had any officers in the church or even on duty anywhere near the building.

Was the woman one of the criminals?

Lorenzo doesn't rule it out.

Crooks have long known that pretending to be a police officer is a good way of emptying a building. The public see a gun and they're relieved to learn it's being held by an officer of the law so they do whatever they're told.

The major makes the sign of the cross as he enters the centre aisle and bows his head.

He has worshipped in this church.

He's sat and knelt in here with his wife and children and he's furious that he's been forced to return in full combat gear with a gun dangling from his hip.

On the left-hand side of the church, a third of the way from the main entrance, he notices the pews have been disturbed.

Two of them are splayed open into a big V.

Between them is a pool of blood.

The furthermost pew is stained red.

He's seen people faint in church – it isn't that uncommon – but light-headed fallers get away with a bruise and a bump. They don't bleed like a haemophiliac in a razor-blade factory.

Lorenzo's radio crackles again.

He answers it, looking apologetically towards the altar. 'Silvestri.'

His lieutenant comes online and has to shout over loud crowd noise and honking car horns behind him. 'Major, we have a man outside who seems to have an explanation for all the trouble.'

Lorenzo looks to the giant crucifix over the altar. 'Thank you, Lord, I was beginning to believe you had deserted me.'

105

They cover Valentina's eyes.

Not in any sophisticated way. They don't use a hood or a

blindfold. They just throw a coat over her head and tie a belt around her neck to keep it there.

For a professional like Valentina, it's the kind of action that gives away a lot of clues.

For a start, they seem more bothered about her not seeing where they're going than the fact that she's already had a good look at all their faces and can identify them.

She's not sure if this is a good thing or not.

It's good if they're as disorganised as she hopes they are. If they're simply coping with things as they blunder their way along.

But it's bad – *very* bad – if they're not so amateur. If they're thinking that once they've questioned her about where Anna is, they're going to kill her rather than let her go.

A sobering thought.

Only one thing brings Valentina some comfort. For now they want her alive.

She has time on her side.

Not much. But time enough.

Time to think. Time to bluff. Time to escape.

The coat over her head is doing a good job of stopping her seeing, but all her other senses are working overtime.

They've walked her downstairs, into the crypt, then walked her some more. Made her stand still. Turned her sideways on and then pushed her through a doorway.

Valentina's memorised it all.

She can retrace her steps, follow her senses, if she has to. If she gets the chance to.

Now the air is colder.

It smells different too. Not of candle wax and church polish; of something earthier, something much baser.

Damp.

It has the metallic smell of damp and animal droppings, probably from mice or rats.

Someone grabs her shoulders, turns her round and holds her as she walks forward.

She's guided down three or four wide steps.

They turn her left for a few steps and then right again before straightening her up.

They let go of her shoulders and allow her to walk along the flat again.

The twisting and turning has made her a little unsteady. She puts her hand out to avoid falling over.

It touches stone.

She's sure it's stone.

It's rough, hard and lumpy. Totally unlike the plaster or marble of a church.

She rubs her thumb across her two fingers.

Wet and slimy.

The walls are damp.

She guesses she's in some kind of underground passage-way. Perhaps an ancient bolt-hole for priests or nuns at the nearby convent, a place they would hide from persecutors.

Or perhaps it's something else.

Tom's comments spring to mind. Pre-Christian cults, castrated followers of Cybele and Attis, ceremonies and rituals involving human sacrifices.

Is she in the midst of all that?

She remembers too the writing on the walls of the Sacro Cuore del Suffragio – DOMINA. DOMINUS. TEMPLUM. LIBERA NOS A MALO. Mistress. Master. Temple. Deliver us from evil.

Is that where she's being taken? To the temple?

Valentina realises that she's not gagged.

She wishes she was.

It's not a good sign that they're not afraid of her scream-ing or shouting for help.

Maybe it's because the gun is still on her. Occasionally jabbing into her flesh and often accompanied by a command

351

for her to hurry up. Or is it because they're now so far underground that she could scream herself hoarse and no one would hear her?

She thinks it's the latter.

She knows they're already a very long way below and beyond Santa Cecilia, where her fellow soldiers are now no doubt swarming all over the church.

But that's where her knowledge stops.

And that's what frightens her most.

106

Lorenzo Silvestri lights Federico's cigarette for him.

He has to.

The lieutenant's hand is shaking too much for him to be able to do it himself.

Federico hasn't been scared by the gunfire, the stabbing, the sudden influx of Carabinieri troops or even the fact that he now has to explain what he and Valentina were doing at the church.

He's frightened that Valentina is dead.

He's scared stiff that he misunderstood what she'd asked him to do and as a result she's been killed.

'So tell me,' says Lorenzo, fresh from learning over his earpiece that Federico and his captain are suspended and shouldn't be doing anything except staying at home and getting fat on cupboard snacks, 'what were you and Morassi doing at Santa Cecilia?'

Federico tries to explain. 'We'd both been working a case

352

involving a psychiatric patient called Anna Fratelli. She'd been arrested in connection with a violent incident in Cosmedin. Subsequent enquiries based on what she said to us also resulted in a mutilated male body being found on the banks of the Tiber.'

Lorenzo senses this is going to get complicated. 'Hang on!' He pulls a small notebook and pen from a button-down pocket on the leg of his combat pants. 'Right, continue.'

'Anna Fratelli died in hospital last night. The doctor in charge of her, Louisa Verdetti, phoned Captain Morassi. It was a strange call. Valentina worked out that Verdetti was being held hostage by someone who wanted to break Anna out of the psych unit.'

The major's mind is reeling. 'I'm full of questions here. Who, what and why being at the front of that queue. But first, tell me, are we talking about someone who wanted to take Anna Fratelli's dead body, or someone who wanted to kidnap her because they thought she was still alive?'

'The latter.'

'Okay. But why did this doctor . . .' he glances down at his notes, 'Verdetti, call your captain? Were they friends?'

Federico shakes his head. 'No. Far from it. Verdetti was the one who got us suspended. She complained to our top brass that we'd pushed Anna too far during interviews and had made her sickness worse.'

'And did you push her too far?'

Federico hesitates. 'No, sir. I really don't think we did.'

'Explain something to me, Lieutenant. When my men checked with our control room, there was no record that you and Morassi were attempting this recovery operation. Had neither of you called it in?'

'No, sir.'

'Why not?'

'Sir, even before we were suspended there was bad blood between Captain Morassi and our commanding officer, Major Caesario.'

Lorenzo begins to see the picture. 'Bad blood or not, you still should have called it in. I know what Caesario is like but you should have gone by the book.'

Federico looks penitent. 'Yes, sir.'

Lorenzo stops him with the palm of his hand. It's clear he's taking a radio message in his earpiece. '*Grazie,*' he says to whoever is on the other end. He looks back to Federico. 'One of my units has just found Doctor Verdetti. She's fine. Panicky as hell, but she's unhurt.'

107

Guilio puts his hand on Tom's arm. 'Keep a hold of me. We have a little way to go before I can put a light on.'

Tom grabs a clump of jacket and allows himself to be dragged into the darkness.

'We're going down two steps. Watch that leg of yours.'

'Thanks.' Tom can't see his own hands, let alone watch his leg, but he appreciates the concern.

Within a dozen steps, Guilio brings them to a halt. 'Just stay still while I find something.'

From out of the pitch blackness comes the rough scraping sound of a match being struck. It takes several attempts before there's a burst of orange flame.

In the tiny halo of light, Tom sees a paraffin lamp and Guilio concentrating on winding up a wick.

As the flickering flame gradually grows in the dusty glass chamber, the room becomes visible.

It's fashioned out of ancient stone.

There's no furniture.

Nothing hangs on the bare walls.

The floor is no more than an endless slab of compressed dirt and grit.

Tom can't see the ceiling, but he's sure it's unsafe and given his luck will collapse any minute.

Guilio seems to read his mind. 'Don't worry, it's not going to fall down. This place has existed for more than two thousand years, so it'll be safe for another twenty minutes.'

'Where are we?'

Guilio squats beside the lamp and holds his hand near the glass to catch a little heat. 'It's an old house. There are two rooms, one to cook and eat in, another for sleeping and breeding.'

'So it should be part of the excavation out there?'

'It will be soon enough. The archaeologists are so focused on identifying artefacts that they've already recovered they have no current desire to open the dig further.'

Tom gets the feeling that he's only brushing the surface of Guilio's knowledge. 'Do you know lots of places like this – secret hideaways beneath the city?'

Guilio laughs. 'Most Roman kids do. If you're brought up here, it's like living on top of a thousand old building sites covered with boards and sand. Dig a bit and you just find one den after another.'

Tom lowers himself to the floor and rests against the stone wall. His left knee is throbbing. The kick he took has aggravated an old injury.

Guilio watches him feeling the leg. 'What have you done to it?'

'It's been dodgy for years. Every now and again it locks up

when I take a knock or a fall. I saw a doc in Paris and he thinks it's full of gunge, bits of cartilage and gristle.'

Guilio pulls a sympathetic face. 'You need one of those keyhole ops.'

'No thanks.' Tom stretches out his right arm and grimaces. 'Shoulder might be worse than the knee. I think that guy with the bat has bust something.'

'Let me feel.' Guilio kneels in front of him. 'Say when it hurts.' He uses his fingers to feel his way from the shoulder to the neck.

Tom flinches. 'Whoa! You got it.'

Guilio keeps one hand in place and slips the other beneath Tom's shirt. 'I can feel a huge bruise. That's before I even get to the bone.'

'Then don't get there,' urges Tom.

Guilio ignores him. 'You've got a cracked clavicle. There doesn't seem to be nerve damage, at least not from the way you reacted. When we get out of here, I'll give you something for the pain and we'll make a sling. All you can do is rest it. There's no miracle cure for fixing collar bones.'

'Impressive diagnosis. You a doctor?'

Guilio smiles. 'Let's just say I was taught a lot about the human body.'

Tom stretches out flat.

It feels good to lie down and straighten his spine and shoulders.

He mentally checks off all the aches and pains and realises it's going to take days for his body to recover from the beating. 'I need you to tell me something,' he says into the flickering shadows.

'What's that?'

'Everything. I need you to tell me it all. Let's start with your relationship with Anna and finish with how come you were at Santa Cecilia at exactly the same time we were.'

108

A black rat runs into the underground cavern and stops.

It's been drawn by the light, the warmth and the smell of the paraffin lamp.

It takes a beady look at Tom and Guilio, then turns and scrambles away.

Neither of them comments.

More important matters are being discussed

'It's difficult to know where to begin,' says Guilio. 'Do you or that policewoman friend of yours have any idea what's going on?'

'Let's pretend we don't – that way I have more chance of understanding.'

Guilio sits cross-legged on the opposite side of the lamp. 'Anna and I were brought up together, and I don't mean in the traditional sense.' He lets out an ironic laugh. 'I guess you've heard about the children in Romania being raised in the Piata Victoriei subways?'

'I have.'

'And the slumdog orphans in Mumbai and the homeless street kids in Rio?'

'Unfortunately, yes.'

'Well, Italy has its own secret child scandal. Anna and myself, along with a number of other kids, were brought up here in conditions like this.' He gestures to the four walls of the room. 'We were bred and raised underground in the cat-acombs and ruins of Rome.' He picks up the lamp and twists up more of the wick. 'Only we weren't free from adult inter-vention. Just the opposite. They were the reason we were below ground. Only when we were judged to be fully compliant with the demands of the sect were we allowed to live out in the daylight.'

Tom's not sure he fully understands. 'You said sect; what are you talking about?'

'It's a branch of the cult of Cybele. It has its roots in a pagan movement going back thousands of years.'

'Phrygian, then Greek and Roman, based around a prophetic goddess and her belief in female powers and male subordination.'

'You know of Cybele?'

'Only a little. I never imagined that any of her prophet sects still existed.'

'That's how they want it – the less people know about them, the more they get away with.'

'Does the number ten, or the Roman numeral X, mean anything specific to you?'

Guilio drops his head. 'It refers to a secret text they call the Tenth Book.'

'What's in this tenth book?'

'I've no idea. It is heavily protected. Few people have ever seen it, and I suspect no men. The sect is *very* female-focused, so I probably only know a part of what goes on.' He tries to make a joke of it. 'Boys are of no particular value. They don't even want us for our sperm, just for their rituals. It is the girls that the Mater values. They are the ones thought to have the power of prophecy and the ability to learn and protect the secrets of the cult.'

'Mater?' Tom remembers Anna's fearful references.

'That's the name given to the female leader of the sect. I've never seen her without her mask and robes, but from what Anna says, she's a wrinkly old witch in her late sixties or seventies. She and her trusted circle of crones run every-thing.' He picks up a stone and throws it into the darkness, where the rat can be heard squeaking and fighting with something. 'They believe they're direct descendants, blessed followers of the goddess Cybele.'

'I still can't take all of this in. How and why did the kids end up down here?'

Guilio throws another stone. 'Every time the sect looks like it may become extinct, new children, often babies, are brought underground into the womb and raised there. The children become adults and the cycle of complicity and abuse is perpetuated.'

'The womb?' Tom spits out the word in disbelief.

'That's what Mater calls the underground complex where she nurtures the children.' He uses his finger to draw in the dirt in front of him. 'Once you go below ground, there is basically a long tunnel with a series of passageways running off it. You drop level by level until it opens up into a large temple. Then there's another tunnel that runs out from the other side into more passageways and rooms. But there's only the one main entrance tunnel.'

Tom fights back a building anger. You can dress child abuse up in all the quasi-religious finery you like, but it's still child abuse and it still makes his blood boil. In his time as a priest, he heard the confessions of several paedophiles and found most of them to be disturbingly smart people who used their intelligence to manipulate youngsters for their own gratification. Sex wasn't the only thing it was about, either.

Power.

Power was the common factor.

Power and absolute control over another human being's life. It made the offenders feel like gods.

Or in this case, goddesses.

Guilio rubs out his drawing in the dirt. 'Mater was always tough on Anna. She'd get beaten more than the rest. Beaten and abused on a regular basis.'

'Sexually abused?'

The finger drawing has gone, but Guilio carries on rubbing hard with the palm of his hand, as though he's trying to wipe away the memories. 'People think sexual abuse is always old men and young girls, but it's not.' He looks up, and even in the half-light the distress in his eyes is clear to see. 'Anna had to sleep with these old hags. She was made to do things with them that would make you sick, and if she didn't please them properly then they'd beat her and starve her. And for the boys there was just aloneness. No contact of any kind. No closeness was allowed. Not with each other, not with the girls or even the adults. You were taught just to stand and watch, always be on hand to serve. I was fortunate enough to be slaved to Anna, and when the pain became too much for her, we decided to escape.'

Tom's heart goes out to him. It's a miracle the guy's not as mentally screwed up as Anna was.

Guilio wipes grit out of the palm of his hand and throws a stone in the general direction of the rat. 'Anna and I escaped from the womb some years ago, maybe four or five now, I can't remember. I tried to protect her as best I could, but she always lived in fear of Mater and the others finding her and dragging her back.'

'That's why you were in her apartment the night Valentina and I came round?'

'That's right. I'm the only one she trusts. The only one who knows what she went through. If the others get their hands on her, they'll kill her.'

Tom knows he should tell Guilio that Anna is dead.

He should tell him right now.

It's the decent thing to do.

But he can't.

'Can you explain how Anna came to be covered in blood when she was found near the Church of Santa Maria in Cosmedin?'

Guilio rubs at the ground again. 'Some of the sisters and the Galli caught her returning from the shops. She wanted to buy me a present and made me go in the *supermercato* while she went for a card and some kind of surprise. By the time I came out, they were bundling her into one of the four-by-fours.'

'And you knew where they'd take her?'

'I thought they'd either head back to the womb or to the Bocca. They know Anna has a strange fear of it. In some of her states she gets frightened and imagines she's being killed there. I gambled and went to Cosmedin.' He rubs furiously in the dirt again. 'If I'd been quicker getting there, or not so stupid to have let her shop on her own, then she'd still be safe.'

'You can't blame yourself.'

'I can.' He picks dirt from the angry grazes on his palm. 'When I got there, I saw that they'd draped workmen's covers over the portico of the church so no one could see from the street. It was clear something awful was going to happen. By the time I got inside, they had Anna in a robe. They were holding her down and trying to force her hand into that big marble mouth.'

'So you scared them off?'

'Not quite.' He sucks dirt from his bleeding skin. 'There was quite a fight. I can't remember everything, but I know I grabbed this sword that they were threatening to use on Anna. I swung it to frighten them and it hit one of the women.' He looks up at Tom. 'It cut her hand off.' He sucks again at the palm of his own hand. 'I hadn't meant to harm her, just frighten her. But it seemed like it was God's will that it should have happened. There and then, that's exactly what I thought. This is God's will. So I picked the hand up and I shook it at them and said, "This is the work of Christ, my saviour and my Lord," and it scared them. They backed off and ran for their lives. Or at least the women did. Two of the Galli rushed at me; a third dropped his weapon, an ancient sword that is used by the Korybantes to beat on ceremonial shields. Anna grabbed it and tried to defend me, but I told her to go. She stayed at first, but then I screamed at her and she ran off.'

Tom starts to fit bits of the jigsaw together. He understands now why Anna was at the Bocca and how she came to be wandering the streets, but there are gaps, very big gaps in Guilio's story. 'So you swung the sword and cut this woman's hand off, and that's how Anna got blood on the gown we found her in?'

'That's right.'

Tom doesn't believe him. 'So where's the victim? Where did she get treated?'

Guilio shrugs. 'The sisters would try to heal her themselves. They would have used Mater's medicines, natural herbs, pagan practices.'

'They don't sound like adequate treatments for a severed hand.'

'No, probably not. If she'd died, they would have buried her in the womb. They bury all the corpses around the outer walls; it's supposed to evoke supernatural forces to protect the sect.'

'A spiritual force field.'

'If you like.'

Tom looks around the lamp. 'Some of what you're telling me doesn't add up.'

Guilio does his best to appear offended. 'I don't understand.'

'Then I'll make it clear. You're lying to me. The blood on Anna's gown didn't come from whoever had her hand cut off. Forensic tests prove that it came from someone else.' Tom leans into the light, 'The question is, who? Who else got injured in that church, and what else are you not telling me?'

109

Valentina Morassi is pleased with herself.

She thinks she's staying remarkably calm, given that she's been abducted by gun-wielding maniacs who have a coat over her head.

Pressed down in the back of a vehicle, she has no knowledge of what route they took across the city, no idea now whether she's north or south, but she does know one thing as they bundle her out of the back of the four-by-four.

She's in the countryside.

There are no petrol fumes, and even though it's winter, she can smell cattle, mud and grass.

Wherever this little patch of farmyard is, it isn't that far away from the centre of Rome and the underground passageway they took out of Santa Cecilia.

She also notes the uneven surface beneath her feet. Gravel. Not the smooth, washed kind that you find on rich people's drives. This is chunky gravel, like the rough stuff a farmer would want laid to run a tractor over.

'Get her inside, quickly.'

That's Shooter's voice. She's heard it enough to recognise it. He's no longer holding her; she can tell from the touch on her arms that duty has been delegated to the women.

Valentina thinks about making a break for it.

She can handle two women.

No problem.

But the coat isn't just thrown over her head, it's tied there. She can feel that the belt has been tightened around her neck.

If she wants to fight, then she's going to have to do it

blind, and given that someone has a gun, that's just too risky.

'Lift your feet, we're going up a step.'

The warning comes from a woman to her left. A young voice. Almost considerate.

The air around her changes.

No longer fresh and country-like.

More homely.

She can smell food. Maybe she's in a house.

The floor beneath her feet is flat and even. She listens to their footsteps as they walk. She's on wood, wood flooring.

'Are you taking her straight through?' The other woman is talking, the one on her right. 'Or do you want to keep her here for a bit?'

'Let me find out.'

Feet clop off.

Someone pulls out a chair; its legs scrape horribly on the floor.

'Sit down.' Shooter's voice. Hands on her shoulders, guiding her, shifting position, pushing her down.

Valentina sits.

The chair is hard. Also wooden, from the feel of it on the back of her thighs. She slowly lifts a knee. It touches a table.

She's in a kitchen, sitting at a country-style table.

She mentally retraces her steps. The door is behind her and over to her left. The house must be secluded, set back, or they'd be worried about passers-by seeing her with a coat over her head.

Maybe there are no windows.

'Okay.' Shooter's voice again. 'We can take her down now.'

Hands under her armpits. 'Come on, stand!' A woman's voice, harsh, a hint of roughness and authority.

Valentina gets up and backs away from the table.

364

They turn her left, and then left again.

She's in another room. It smells of decorators. Fresh paint. Wet plaster.

There's the click of a latch.

A cold draught.

'You're going down some stairs; be careful or you'll fall.' It's the kind woman again.

Valentina stretches out her foot like a ballet dancer starting a movement.

It's steeper than she anticipated.

A hand steadies her from the front.

At least one of them is ahead of her. The others must be following behind.

Is this the point at which she should strike out? A heavy kick would drop whoever is in front of her down the stairs. A sharp turn and rush up the stairs would flatten whoever is directly behind her.

But what if there are two or more people behind her?

Valentina knows she's only going to get one chance.

And it's not yet come.

She concentrates on what's happening. Her feet are touching stone. She reaches out a hand and the wall feels like stone too. She's sure she's descending some old steps into a cellar or basement.

They even out.

She hears the door above her close.

She's trapped.

The atmosphere down here is different. There are many people in this room. They smell of smoke.

Smell of men.

'Take her through.' Shooter again.

Something buzzes. A short, sharp noise. Electronic.

There's a clunk of metal.

A squeak, like the oil-thirsty hinges of a heavy gate.

Unseen hands push her forward.

Someone grabs a clump of clothing around her shoulder and takes a tight grip.

'More stairs,' warns Shooter.

There's a hint of laughter in his voice.

'*Lots* more stairs.'

110

The paraffin lamp has almost burned out by the time Guilio finishes his story.

Now Tom has the full and unmitigated account of Anna Fratelli's fateful night in Cosmedin.

The truth is even more difficult to stomach than the lies Guilio was trying to fob him off with.

The eunuch looks through the yellow light into the face of the ex-priest. There's one more thing he has to admit to – and he's uncertain how he'll take it. 'The fire. The one at the policewoman's apartment. I started it.'

Tom tries not to show his shock and anger. 'Why? Why did you do it?'

Guilio fiddles nervously with his hands. 'I didn't mean to hurt her. Or you. I didn't even know you were there until I saw you coming out and being treated by the ambulance people.'

'You could have killed both of us.'

'No. Not true,' he protests strongly. 'I'd seen her leave. I thought the place was empty. I just wanted to scare her away from Anna, frighten her off the case.'

Tom's not letting him off that lightly. 'What about neighbours? They could have died.'

Guilio plays with the lamp to hide his awkwardness. 'It was a small fire. I'd rung the emergency services before I'd even started it.' He looks up at Tom. 'Believe me, if I'd wanted to kill either of you, I could have done. I'm sorry, really sorry.'

'I believe you are,' says Tom. 'I can't speak for Valentina, but I forgive you, and I'm sure God forgives you. Your desperation is understandable.'

'*Grazie.*' Guilio leans into the light. 'I need you to help me get to Anna. I have to see her, make sure she is all right.' He looks close to tears. 'Anna means everything in the world to me.'

Tom knows she does.

Guilio's love for her is probably all that's kept him sane. Without that, and his role as her protector, he'd have gone mad long ago. 'I have to be outside,' says Tom. 'I need to get a signal to call Valentina. And I have to speak to Louisa, Anna's doctor. They'll be able to tell you about Anna.'

Guilio squints through the patchy light at his watch. 'We've been down here more than an hour. It'll be safe to go now, but not the way we came in.'

Tom looks surprised. 'There are other ways?'

'Of course.' Guilio points towards where the black rat ran off. 'There's a thin passage through there. It will bring us out about half a kilometre away.' He picks up the lantern and inspects it as he starts to walk. 'We've probably got just about enough paraffin to get us there.'

Tom trudges along after him. 'I still need to know why you were at Santa Cecilia, and why did you help me?'

'I've been following you. Ever since I was released. I watched you with that priest having coffee near St Peter's and I watched that other policeman, the one who questioned me.'

'Federico.'

'*Si*, the lieutenant.'

'Why?'

'Simple. You didn't want to hurt Anna, you wanted to protect her, and I was trying to think of a way to reach out to you.'

Guilio swings the lamp low to shine it on a nest of black rats. 'Unusual. You don't normally get this many black ones underground. The excavations must have disturbed them.'

The rodents don't bother Tom; his church in LA was infested with them.

They turn a corner and they're both pleased to see daylight filtering through a sloping tunnel straight ahead.

As they get closer, it's clear that the light is being diced through an old gateway.

All around there is rubble and broken rock.

Guilio extinguishes the lamp and hides it away before opening the gate.

The sky is dull, but it still makes them squint.

They've emerged at the bottom of a hillside near a quiet road north of Santa Cecilia, but Tom has no real idea where he is as he phones Valentina's number.

Please God, let her be all right.

It trips to her voicemail message. 'This is Valentina Morassi, I can't take your call at the moment . . .'

He cuts it off.

She's probably busy calling him. Maybe she's already left messages for him. He checks his own voicemail.

Nothing.

That seems strange.

He's sure she would have rung him. Especially in light of the fact that she sent him after Louisa and hasn't heard from him since.

The silence gives him a bad feeling.

He dials again, lets the answerphone play through, and then leaves a message. 'Valentina, it's Tom . . .' He checks his watch. 'It's almost one o'clock. Please call me when you get this.' He clicks off and looks at Guilio sitting on the kerb lighting the stub of a cigarette that he's found in the gutter.

The guy looks as grey as the pavement, almost as though he's a chameleon blending in with his new surroundings.

Tom scrolls through his phone's memory and finds Valentina's office number. He knows she's not there but figures it's the only way he's going to get Federico's cell phone number.

He just hopes his Italian is good enough to charm someone into giving it to him.

111

Lorenzo Silvestri sits in his office, staring at Federico Assante and Louisa Verdetti.

His chair creaks under his two hundred pounds of battle-trained muscle, as he rocks on the back two legs and sizes the pair of them up.

They don't seem hysterical and they don't seem jerk-offs. But the story they've been telling is incredible.

His number two, Captain Pasquale Conti, has a reputation for double-checking everything, and so he's far from done with them. 'Doctor Verdetti, please tell me again, are you sure that the place these people held you was further below ground than just a basement or old wine cellar?'

Louisa's hands are still trembling, but that doesn't stop her being annoyed. 'They scared me, not turned me stupid. I know where they held me. I took as much notice as I could, and it was *way* below ground level. They had some kind of cells there.'

'And they did this because they wanted to kidnap this patient of yours, Anna?'

'Anna Fratelli.'

'And Anna's now dead, but they don't know it?'

Her temper is close to snapping. 'Correct.'

'And you have no rough idea of the location of the place where they held you?'

Louisa knows this is the biggest clue she can give them, but she has nothing. 'I'm afraid not. I was drugged going into my apartment and the next thing I remember was waking up in the cell they kept me in. It was small and made me panic, I have some claustrophobia problems from my childhood.'

Lorenzo can see she's distressed. 'Are you okay, Doctor? Would you like to take a short break?'

Louisa shakes her head. 'No. I want to get on with it.' She just wishes this nightmare was over and she could start trying to make her life normal again.

She shuts her eyes and pictures the dark hole they held her in. 'The place had iron bars, like you'd expect a police cell to have, but they were very old and rusty. There were no windows. No daylight. In fact, no light at all.' She feels her heart start to race. 'Everything was pitch black until they came along with their torches. Not the battery kind; rag torches like you see in those old cave-man movies.'

'Primitive torches?' queries Lorenzo.

Louisa sees them clearly. 'Yes. I could smell the stuff, flaming rags soaked in oil or paraffin.'

Lorenzo takes it all in. These days it's so easy to run miles of electric cable to almost anywhere you want, so there has to be a more sinister reason behind the use of old-fashioned torches.

Then there's the location.

Either someone has made use of some old and now disused jail facility, or else they've gone to great lengths to create one because they regularly hold people against their will.

Pasquale resumes his questioning. 'Doctor, do you think you were the only one who had been held there?'

Louisa hasn't thought about that. 'I don't know. At one point I thought I heard voices, maybe a young woman, but I never saw her or anyone else.' She looks flustered and is struggling to breathe normally. 'I'm sorry, just talking about it is making me edgy. I really don't know. It all seems like one big unbelievable nightmare to me.'

'It's fine. Don't stress yourself.' The major gives the nod to his number two to carry on with the questioning.

Pasquale continues as carefully as he can. 'Doctor, when they moved you, you said the place you woke up in looked like it had just been decorated. Can you explain what you mean?'

Louisa takes a deep breath and slowly exhales. 'It was more like it was in the process of being decorated. The walls had only just been plastered and smelled wet. There were dust sheets on the floor, cans of paint, and I think some kind of small machine in the middle of the room.'

Pasquale turns to Lorenzo. 'Maybe a generator or a heater to dry out the plaster?'

'Could be. Have someone check tool-hire shops.'

The captain presses on. 'That's good, that's helpful. Did you see anything else?'

'No. They covered my eyes and walked me out of there to a car park.'

'How far? How far from the newly plastered place to the car?'

Louisa's hands start to shake again. 'Not far. They took me up a staircase, a spiral one, I think. I seemed to be doubling back on myself and I was dizzy when it levelled out. Then they walked me a few paces . . . to the left.' She swallows her fear and tries hard to get the sequence right in her head. 'I remember that as we came out into the cold, someone pulled me over to one side. We were standing on a gravel surface, or something like gravel. We didn't go far, maybe eight, ten steps, and then they pushed me into a car.' She corrects herself. 'No, not a car, one of those big things. A Land Rover. I saw it when I jumped out near the church.'

Lorenzo's impressed. 'You've got good recall. A good memory.'

She smiles for the first time for a long while. '*Grazie*. It's the medical training. If you forget little details, you end up killing someone.'

Lorenzo has to stop himself from adding that it's the same in his job. He looks towards his colleague. 'Get the analysts to identify all possible sites in Rome with private drive-in areas that have applied for major building permits. Have the list cross-checked with recent tool-hire sales, deliveries of plasterboard and rental of other building equipment. Check particularly to see if any of them are linked to excavation sites, old ruins, converted churches, any structures that may be attached to public buildings.'

Pasquale finishes jotting down his exhaustive list and leaves.

Lorenzo turns back to Louisa. 'We're going to need to ask you some more questions, but not for a while. I'll arrange for a protection team to take you home and watch your apartment while you get changed and get some rest.'

Louisa looks drained. '*Grazie*. I'd also like to call some people, if that's okay?'

'Of course it is, but you mustn't talk about what's happened to you. This is an active operation, and our best chance of catching your kidnappers is in the next twenty-four hours. They'll be panicking right now, covering their tracks and making mistakes, but they'll get over that within a day or so and go back to being professional, so we have to take our chance. Do you understand?'

Louisa nods.

As she gets up to go, she catches herself looking at his hand for a wedding ring.

There's a thick gold band around his finger.

Why is it the best ones are always taken?

112

Valentina twists her ankle for the second time and curses the never-ending stairs.

If there wasn't a gun at her head, she'd have a tantrum that no one would ever forget.

She tries to ignore the pain and calculate how far below ground she is.

It's harder than it sounds.

After every twenty steps, the stairs level out for a couple of paces.

Then they begin again.

The first two descents were extraordinarily steep and straight, the next five more spiral, but the steps were still stone and not metal, the kind of tight circular steps, thin in the middle and wide on the outside, that you find in an ancient bell tower.

Valentina does some maths.

So far, she's come down more than a hundred steps.

That's useful information.

As a cop, she's walked the floors of many hotels during surveillance operations, and a hundred and fifty regular steps equals about five floors of the average hotel.

That's deep.

And they're still descending.

She just hopes there's a big bed, flat-screen TV and heavily stocked minibar at the end of it all.

Fat chance.

Twenty steps later, the journey ends.

She can hear people around her sighing in relief.

'Can I take that thing off her head now?' asks the kind one. 'She must be dying from the heat.'

Someone must okay it, because Valentina feels hands working on the coat belt pulled around her neck.

It's off.

Valentina feels good. She inhales the cool air and does her best not to look frightened or flustered. If *she* appears relaxed, then it will make *them* relax, and relaxed criminals often make mistakes.

By the look of it, they're in some kind of wine cellar.

A large open space with little gated alcoves.

Valentina realises her first impression is wrong.

Very wrong.

The place is lit by old-fashioned torches, burning in special metal holders on the walls, and the gated alcoves aren't gated alcoves at all.

They're cells.

Off to her left, she spots a child in what looks like a white nightdress, curled up on the floor near the bars of one of the cells.

For the first time, she starts to panic.

There's no way that they're going to let her see this and then allow her to go free.

No way on earth.

113

Once Louisa is out of his office, Lorenzo Silvestri speaks more openly to Federico. 'We've issued alerts for your captain, but so far there's no trace of her. Are you sure she went into the church after she left you at the car?'

'Pretty certain. I waited as she asked me to, and I watched her go through the courtyard and head to the fountain. I couldn't see beyond there.'

'Then you drove off?'

'Yes. That's what she wanted me to do. I guess she thought the rain would be a good excuse for me to be in the car and not at the fountain. She probably figured that would buy her and Tom time to get to Louisa.'

'From all accounts it seems this Tom put on a good show,' observes Lorenzo. 'You said he is her partner?'

Federico feels awkward. 'Yes, sir, they go back to when Captain Morassi was based in Venice. I think they've been friends for a long time.'

The major is more interested in the logistics of what happened than in their social lives. 'Just a shame they didn't stay together outside Santa Cecilia instead of Morassi compromising herself by going into the church alone.'

Federico feels guilty that he was stranded in the car as the decoy while all hell was breaking loose. 'Sir, if they're still holding her, do you think it's likely to be in the same place they kept Louisa?'

'That's logical. Let's hope they only have one underground playpen, or else we're in trouble. Rome is a big city.'

Federico can't help but ask the question: 'Do you think she's still alive?'

'There's a good chance. She was no doubt taken because they think she can help them get to Anna, but we have to be realistic. Once they realise they've been tricked, your captain becomes a real problem. A problem they will have to get rid of.'

Federico's phone rings.

'Take it,' says Lorenzo.

He fishes his cell out of his pocket. '*Pronto.*'

'Federico, this is Tom, Tom Shaman.'

'Tom, hang on, let me put you on speakerphone.' He fiddles with the function and holds the phone between himself and Lorenzo. 'This is Valentina's partner.' He places the phone in the middle of the major's desk. 'Tom, I'm in a room with Major Silvestri from the Carabinieri's special operations unit. They were called in to take control of the operation at Santa Cecilia.'

Tom's a little thrown that Federico is not on his own. 'Okay.'

'Have you heard from Valentina?' asks Federico.

His spirits fall. 'That's what I was calling you about. Is she not with you?'

'No.'

'Tom, this is Lorenzo Silvestri. We're searching for her. Where are you at the moment? Can you come and talk to us?'

Tom is reluctant to do that. The Carabinieri suspended Valentina, so he's not entirely sure he can trust them. There's also the fact that the man next to him left his knife sticking in the heart of one of Louisa's kidnappers. 'I'm across town; I'm not quite sure where, to be honest.'

'That's not a problem. We're on Via di Ponte Salario, a little north of Villa Borghese. We'd like you to come over here as quickly as possible to help us find Valentina.'

Tom covers the mouthpiece so his answer is muffled. 'I'm sorry, Major, I'm having trouble hearing you. I'll call back.'

The line goes dead.

Lorenzo leans across the table and flicks the phone towards Federico. 'Call him back straight away.'

Federico picks it up, searches the call log for the last received number and dials it.

'Straight to voicemail,' he says.

Lorenzo looks annoyed. 'We have to talk to this guy, urgently.' He shoots Federico a stern look. 'We've got a dead body on the ground near the church. Could he have done that?'

'I'm not sure. He's a big guy and he's handy enough, but he doesn't strike me as the violent type.'

Lorenzo's not so sure. 'Paramedics pulled a knife out of the dead guy's heart. Did you ever see Tom carry a weapon?'

Federico shakes his head. 'I'm sure he didn't. Listen, I really don't think you can look at Tom for that. It's just not his style. Valentina told me he used to be a priest.'

'Some priest.'

Federico doesn't see any point arguing, They're searching for suspects and he'd be saying the same things if he was on the other side of the table. For now, though, he has a question of his own. 'Major, are you going to inform the serious crime unit about this? I mean, isn't this something that Major Caesario and his team have to be appraised of and involved in?'

Lorenzo gives him a relaxed smile. 'Is that what you want, Lieutenant? ROS has the authority to run this as a contained operation; do you really want me to wake Caesario from his slumber in the officers' club and have him slow things down? Or would you prefer to help me clean up his shit and then us take the credit with the Commandante Generale?'

114

Tom stares at the phone he's just turned off.

If Valentina is missing and not traceable by the Carabinieri, then she's either dead or she's been abducted by the same people who took Louisa.

She's smart and tough.

If she's alive, she'll buy time for herself, but not much. Guilio is the only one who knows anything about the sect and has any chance of leading him to Valentina, but he's not going to want to cooperate with the cops, and he's certainly not going to be helpful if he learns that Anna is dead.

The young eunuch is staring at Tom and gets bored of waiting. 'What is it? Is Anna all right?'

'No, no, she's not. I'm afraid I can't take you to her.'

Guilio looks shaken. 'What?'

'That was Federico Assante, the lieutenant who interviewed you. He's sitting with members of the Carabinieri's special operations group and he wants me to go over there and help them find the place you mentioned. The place where Anna and Louisa were held and where they now think Valentina, Captain Morassi, is also being held.'

'They've got her as well? I don't understand.'

Tom can see he's confused. Good. He needs him to stay that way for a while. 'As you know, everything went wrong back there at the church. What matters now is that we tell the Carabinieri how to get inside the place you called "the womb" so they can clean up and save lives.'

Guilio falls silent. His anguish is visible as he tries to work out the consequences. 'I can't. If I go anywhere near them, the Carabinieri will arrest me again. My prints are all over that knife.' He pauses. 'Whoever it was attacking you, I'm sure I killed him.'

Tom can see that the thought distresses him. 'They'll understand. It was self-defence. You were doing what you thought was right and saving me from being killed.'

Guilio paces nervously. 'I can't. I can't go to the cops. I have a long record; they'll throw the book at me and lock me up for ever. You don't know what they're like.'

'What's the alternative?' asks Tom. 'We can't just sit here doing nothing. This thing has to end, and we have to end it.'

'We can do that. I know how we can end things, but you'll have to help me and you'll have to promise not to call the cops in. No cops, absolutely no cops. Right?'

Tom nods.

'*Va bene.*' He bites anxiously at his thumbnail and becomes lost in a fresh worry. 'What we're going to have to do is dangerous. You may have to kill to get Valentina back. Kill or be killed. Are you prepared to do that? Because if you're not, if this woman doesn't matter that much to you, then you'd best tell me now.'

Tom's mind flashes back to his life in Compton. To the time he stepped into a late-night street fight and took the lives of two gangbangers who were raping a young woman. Their deaths still haunt him.

He sees the men's faces in his sleep and often imagines

whether they might have straightened out their lives if only he'd used a little less force and managed to get them jailed instead of buried.

'Yes,' he says reluctantly. 'If it's really necessary, then I'm prepared to take the life of a bad person in order to save that of a good one.'

115

'I know what you're thinking.' Shooter has a cocky smile on his face. 'And you're right.' He gestures towards the other cells. 'We can't let you go after you've seen this.'

He's a few paces away from Valentina, almost at the back of the three women who've come down with them.

As he walks towards her, she wonders what's happened to Trench Coat, the man someone called Attis. He must have stayed above ground for medical treatment.

'Life down here is not so bad.' Shooter is now so close to Valentina that all she can see of him is his piercing blue eyes. 'Let's put it this way, it's much better than death down here.'

Behind her, Valentina hears the sound of someone unlocking one of the cells.

Her cell.

'How we treat you is entirely dependent upon you.' He takes her arm and pushes her towards the dark opening.

She resists a little. Digs in her heels. But it's more instinct than serious resistance.

Shooter pushes her hard and she's not strong enough to

stand firm. Not unless she fights him, and now's not the time for that.

'We'll let you cool down for a while, then you really do have a lot of explaining to do.'

She stares defiantly at him.

No sign of weakness.

No hint of fear.

Shooter is plainly one of the top dogs. What he says goes. The others take their lead from him and ask his permission before acting, but Valentina isn't going to give him an inch of ground. Every second that she stands up to him increases the chance of Verdetti, Federico or even Tom bringing help.

Shooter goes through the pockets of her coat, pulling them inside out and leaving them dangling, like he's playing some childish game. 'So who exactly are you? And more importantly, where is Anna?'

Valentina knows her cover as Verdetti's assistant is blown. It was exposed the moment she picked the gun up from the floor of Santa Cecilia and it evaporated completely when she shouted out that she was a police officer.

'I'm a Carabinieri *capitano*,' she says with pride and defiance.

Shooter doesn't look impressed.

She smiles confidently. 'You know that by now there will be troops all over Rome looking for me.'

He steps away and closes the cell door. 'You're right. They'll be up and down the streets, asking questions in the shops and bars, in the houses of known criminals. They'll be assembling roadblocks on the autoroutes and maybe even stopping people at the train stations and airports.' He smiles back at her as he turns a big old key in a big old lock. 'But they won't be coming down here. This is the one place you can be sure they won't come looking.'

116

Tom finally recognises where he is.

He's west of the river.

Off to his left is Isola Tiberina, and the place where he found the body of the dead man. And while the murder is still a mystery to the police, it no longer is to him.

Guilio has told him everything.

They cross the Tiber at the Ponte Palatino and turn sharp right on to the Lungotevere dei Pierleoni.

The distinctive campanile of the Chiesa Santa Maria in Cosmedin, the home of the Mouth of Truth, comes into view and Tom realises for the first time how close the various crime scenes are. Being driven around by Valentina, they appeared to be much further apart.

It's clear from his agitation that Guilio doesn't like being out in the open, and he makes little allowance for his companion's injured shoulder and leg. 'Come on, we have to hurry. We can't hang around out here like tourists.'

Tom's body is cramped up because of his injuries. He struggles for breath as Guilio sets a blistering pace down Via dei Cerchi and along the edge of the open banked fields of Circus Maximus, where chariots once raced and crowds of almost a quarter of a million people watched.

It takes them more than half an hour to make it to the Piazza di Porta Capena. Guilio spots a pharmacy. 'Wait here, I'll get some things to help with the pain and make you more comfortable.'

Tom's now sweating hard and feeling weak.

He rests against the brick wall of a shutdown clothing shop, another victim of Europe's savage economic downturn.

A police siren breaks the heavy hum of passing traffic.

He slides into the darkness of a doorway as Carabinieri patrol cars screech around the corner and head south.

Guilio comes out of the shop with a handful of white bags, his eyes fixed on the direction where the cop cars are headed. 'I've got *fasciature* – bandages – to make a sling, and something a little special for you.' He looks mischievous. 'Let's get out of sight so I can strap you up.'

They head around a corner and down a shadowy alleyway.

The first drops of a shower fall as Tom strips to his waist so Giulio can make a sling and arrange the arm in a position that takes some pressure off his right shoulder.

'Feels as awkward as hell,' he complains. 'I dread to think how I'm going to cope when I need the toilet.'

Guilio's worrying about more important things, like how useful the guy is going to be.

Maybe taking the walking wounded into battle isn't a good idea after all.

He pulls a small white box out of his jacket pocket and shakes it. 'We struck lucky. Some old lady was collecting her prescription of oxycodone and I picked it out of her basket. It's going to help you a lot more than a few Advil.' He unscrews the bottle and passes it over. 'No point measuring it. Take a swig now, and if you're still hurting badly, take another.'

Tom slugs some back and feels even guiltier. The pensioner was probably given the opioid because she was in a lot of pain, and now she's going to be without relief because of him.

'Okay, let's move again.' Guilio takes the bottle back and pockets it. 'We've not got much further to go.'

He's lying.

After another fifteen minutes of hard walking, Tom feels less pain but is dizzy and drained.

He gets a brief rest while Guilio ducks into a hardware-cum-convenience store and returns with two carrier bags bulging with new purchases and a rucksack. He opens the sack and empties the bags into it. 'There's a sandwich shop three doors down.' He ties the rucksack up and swings it over his shoulder. 'Let's get some food and see if we can build your strength up.'

Ten minutes later they're sitting on stools, wolfing down ciabattas with prosciutto, mozzarella and tomatoes, along with several litres of cool water and enough espressos to fuel them to the moon and back.

Guilio settles the bill.

Back outside, the showers of the last hour have turned into heavy rain. The black skies do their worst and the two men are soaked to the skin as they approach San Sebastian Gate and the start of the Via Appia Antica.

'Do you know where you are?' asks Guilio.

Tom does.

He looks up at the huge block of marble that forms the base of the gate, and its magnificent crenellated towers. 'This is the start of the Appian Way.'

'That's right. Italy's Route 66. The most famous road in our country.' He points to the archway. 'This is the bit of ancient highway that gave birth to the famous saying "All roads lead to Rome". It was started three hundred years before Christ and ran for more than three hundred miles, finishing at Brindisi on the Adriatic. From there, ships left for Egypt, Greece and North Africa. This road we're walking on carried Rome's armies to some of their greatest victories.'

'Let's hope it does the same for us.'

Guilio laughs. 'It wasn't all good. It was also the place

where more than two thousand members of Spartacus's beaten slave army were crucified.'

They trudge on in silence.

Set back on their left is the Chiesa del Domine Quo Vadis, the Church of Santa Maria in Palmis.

Tom doesn't need any history lesson on this landmark. It's home to a slab of marble said to bear the imprints of Christ's feet. The spot where St Peter had a vision as he was escaping from Nero's soldiers. Christ is reported to have been walking past him back into Rome, when Peter turned and shouted: '*Domine, quo vadis?*' – 'Where are you going, Lord?' Christ answered: '*Eo Romam iterum crucifigi*' – 'I am going to Rome again to be crucified.' Peter took this as his cue to turn around and head back into the city and accept his own death and martyrdom.

Guilio shouts, 'Through here.'

By the time Tom looks up, his guide has disappeared again.

The only place he can have gone is through an implausibly narrow gap in a large ancient wall.

Tom breathes in and painfully crushes his damaged shoulder through the gap.

Guilio is waiting for him. He's crouched down, pointing at something on the horizon. 'You see in the distance the Catacombe di San Callisto?'

Tom can't. 'No, not really.' He puts his hand tenderly on the reawakened pain in his shoulder.

'Trust me, it is there, the famous Catacomb of Callixtus.' He points beyond a line of cypress trees. 'And over there are the Catacombs of Saint Sebastian.' He stands up. 'We are now between the two.' He floats his hand in a one-hundred-and-eighty-degree arc. 'Beneath our feet are a hundred acres of hidden catacombs, tunnels and galleries, some up to twelve miles long. There are more than half a million tombs and tens of millions of secrets buried right underneath us.'

'And Valentina is being held down there?'

Guilio looks at him distrustfully. 'Valentina *and* Anna.'

Tom knows this is the moment.

He can't put it off any longer.

The time has come to tell Guilio that Anna is dead.

117

Guilio can tell that something bad is about to be said.

He's right.

Tom gives him the truth. 'Anna's dead.'

The words drop like stones down a deep well.

It takes several seconds for them to make an impact.

'What?'

'I'm sorry. She died in hospital.' Tom moves closer, extends his hand to Guilio's arm.

Guilio smashes it away. 'Dead? She's dead and you didn't tell me?' Blood flushes to his face. His hands ball up into fists.

'I couldn't. Louisa's life was in danger and now Valentina's is.'

'Aaaw!' Guilio vents a deep scream and with both hands punches his own head. 'No! No! No!' He sinks to his knees on the wet ground and doubles up.

Tom stands over him.

He puts a calming hand to the back of Guilio's head. 'I'm very, very sorry. She died of a heart attack. I don't know all the details, but I know everyone was shocked. They really were all trying to help her.'

Guilio doesn't look up.

He can hear Tom but his words are muffled clouds blown around by a hurricane of emotion.

Already he's starting to blame himself.

He promised Anna he would look after her, wouldn't let anything happen to her. He told her not to be afraid, that he would always be there for her.

But he hadn't been.

He'd failed her.

No two ways about it. When she needed him most, he'd been somewhere else.

He let her down and now she's dead.

Tom moves away a few paces. Guilio has literally been struck down with grief and he understands that he needs space.

He has to come to terms with the initial shock.

Tom has stood many times with the loved ones of those who have just died, and he knows that acceptance of their death comes in waves. Slow waves. Only today, there's no time for slow. Every second that Guilio spends crying and grieving brings Valentina closer to death.

Yet he has to be patient.

If Guilio shuts down, he's lost.

He has no idea where the opening to the so-called womb is, or where to go even if he manages to get inside.

And he has no weapons.

Until now, he hasn't even thought about such a thing.

He touches his pocket and feels the cell phone. The Carabinieri will have traced it by now; they'll have a lock on it, he's sure of that.

But will they arrive in time?

Too early would be disastrous.

Too late could be fatal.

Guilio stands up.

He turns.

His face is heavy with despair and loss.

Tom can tell he's close to losing him. 'Anna believed in God. I know she did, and you certainly know she did.' He walks slowly forward and tries to bridge the chasm rapidly opening between them. 'She is at peace now. She's no longer frightened and can no longer be hurt by these people.'

'She's dead.' Guilio's face contorts. 'Dead! You can't get more hurt than that.'

'I know. And these people must be held accountable for that. *You* can help make them accountable.'

Guilio stares blankly across the fields.

Tom hasn't reached him. The gap is too big. He puts his hand on Guilio's arm and is relieved that this time it's not brushed away. 'You can't save Anna, but you can save someone who cared for her. Someone who wanted her to be looked after and who risked her life not just to help her but to catch the people who had hurt her.'

Guilio understands what Tom is saying.

He also knows he's being manipulated.

But he can't simply walk away, even though that's what he wants to do. He can't run to the loneliest spot on the earth and cry his lungs out like he needs to do.

Something won't let him.

He tried to protect Anna because it was the right thing. And he knows that walking away from Tom and the woman he loves would be wrong.

'I'll help you.' He nods several times, more as though he's confirming things to himself than to Tom. 'I'll help you, even if it's the last thing I do.'

118

A shaft of honey–coloured sunlight forces its way through a crack in the dark, thunderous sky.

Guilio walks towards a lightning-blasted apple tree and swings on a thick dead branch until it splinters away.

Once he's broken it off, he rubs the splintered end on the field wall until it sharpens into a spike.

He walks back to Tom and throws the stake into the ground just in front of him. He slips off his newly bought rucksack, puts his hands around the back of his neck and unclasps a rope necklace from beneath his shirt.

Tom recognises the black triangular stone dangling from it.

It's identical to the one Anna had.

The same as the shape drawn on the confessional wall at the Sacro Cuore del Suffragio.

Guilio digs into his pocket and produces a spool of what seems to be fishing line. He ties it to the clasp on the necklace and then moves to the right-hand corner of the field.

Tom follows him, bemused and fascinated.

'You can help,' Guilio announces as he squats. 'Hold this for a moment.'

Tom takes the spool.

Guilio places the longest edge of the scalene pendant on the ground, with the shortest edge to his left.

'Give me the spool for a second.'

'Sure.' Tom hands it down.

Guilio makes sure the rope and the line attached run as precisely as possible along the upward slope of the triangle.

He stretches out a third of a metre of line and then stands up and presses it into the ground.

He checks the angle again, adjusts it a fraction and then turns to Tom. 'Take this end and walk in a straight line until I shout stop.'

Tom wants to ask a dozen questions, starting with *why*, but he doesn't.

As he walks, Guilio shouts for him to move a little to the left or a little to the right.

'Okay! Stop!' Guilio slowly moves towards him, checking the lie of the line as he goes.

'This isn't the middle of the field,' says Tom. 'I'm no expert but I can tell it's not the centre.'

'That's fine. I don't want it perfectly in the centre. That's the whole point.'

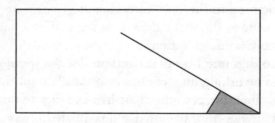

As Tom takes up his position, Guilio retrieves his pendant and fishing line and swings the new rucksack over his shoulder again.

Next, he traipses to the left-hand corner of the field and repeats the entire process, with the shortest side of the triangle now on his right.

He ties it down and walks slowly. Makes sure the line is meticulously straight until he reaches a point just past where Tom is standing.

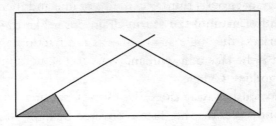

'Here!' he says triumphantly as the lines cross.

'Really,' says Tom with more than a touch of sarcasm. 'And what exactly is *here*?'

'Be patient.'

Guilio drops to the ground. He puts his ear to the turf and systematically slaps all around the spot.

He pauses, undoes the pull-cord on the neck of the rucksack, searches inside and pulls out a gleaming garden trowel.

Tom watches as he digs, but still can't see evidence of anything except scuffed-up grass and soil.

Guilio's working up a sweat.

He digs and scrapes one way, turns and digs the other.

Soil stacks up around him like he's a human mole.

He stands and scrapes the trowel in a circle, stopping every now and again to shift stubborn stones and thick lumps of clay.

He gets down on his knees again and dips his hand into the thin circular trench, which is less than a metre in diameter.

He starts pulling up huge chunks of turf.

Tom's not sure what he expected to see, but it certainly wasn't this.

In the cleared circle something flat, cream-coloured and round becomes visible.

It's a giant marble disc.

A kind of manhole or storm-drain cover like the Bocca della Verità.

On it is the face of a woman.

The goddess Cybele.

Guilio brushes away the soil.

Tom now sees that her face is covered by lines – the lines of a pentagram.

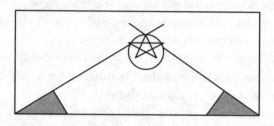

119

The cell stinks.

Valentina tracks the stench to an unemptied slop bucket by the far wall.

She almost heaves.

Was this used by Louisa?

The thought gives her some strange comfort. They were careless with Louisa. They let her have a phone; they let her trick them into taking her out of here.

There's still hope.

Still hope.

She picks up a rough blanket from the back of the cell. It smells of a woman's perfume. Louisa's, she's sure of it.

Through the bars she sees the other cells. Three of them, she thinks.

A child is moving in one of them.

She only catches a glimpse of the girl, but she looks very young. Pre-teen? Most likely.

What kind of monsters would keep children underground?

Valentina knows the answer.

'Hello!' she calls tentatively.

Her voice echoes thinly in the stagnant air.

'Hello! Is there anyone there?' She waits several seconds. 'I'm a police officer, who's out there?'

Nothing.

Valentina is sure the kid's still there. She's certain she'd have noticed them bringing her down here.

'Listen, I know you're there. I want to help you.'

Nothing.

And then a mumble.

An answer. Too meek to be understood, but still an answer.

'My name's Valentina. What's yours? What are you called?'

Wall torches suddenly flicker.

A door's been opened. A draught has blown them.

She hears footsteps off to her right. No matter how hard she presses her face against the iron, she can't see anything.

'Move back!'

The voice is loud and surprisingly close.

Valentina's as frightened as she's ever been.

But she doesn't move.

Shooter grins through the bars as he puts a key in the lock. 'I told you to move back. Looks like I'm going to have to teach you a lesson in obedience.'

120

All five corners of the pentagram are marked by what look like small slits filled with earth.

But they're more than that.

They're locks.

Only by working anticlockwise and putting alternate angles of the triangular pendant into the slits is Guilio able to flip off the fastenings that are holding the cover down.

He stands up, breathless. 'This is one of the secret entrances, an emergency way into the womb. Once inside, you will need to follow me and do exactly as I tell you.' He looks at the American to check he has no problems with what he's just said.

Tom uncaps the bottle of oxycodone. 'I understand. I'm on your coat tails.' He takes several swigs of the medicine. He knows he's going to need all the painkiller he can get for what's about to happen.

'Good. I'm not going to lie to you. It's going to be dangerous in there. There are several tunnels that will take us through to where the sisterhood lives. Not all of them are safe.'

Tom screws the cap back on the bottle and slips off his coat. 'Subsidence, you mean?'

'That's a risk, but it's not what I meant. Some are deliberately unsafe. They have been designed to protect those in the womb and kill intruders.'

'But you know your way, right?'

'I think so.'

'You *think* so?'

Guilio manages a grim smile. 'Just as there was a

sequence to follow to unlock that hatch, there are sequences when we get inside. If I get one of those wrong, then we're in trouble.'

Tom unbuttons his shirt and struggles with the sling.

'What are you doing?'

'I have to get out of this. I'm no good to you or myself with only one hand free.'

Guilio knows he has a point. Better to hurt a cracked shoulder bone than to die trying to protect it.

He helps with the bandage. 'How does it feel?'

Tom stretches his fingers. 'Pins and needles from having it elevated, but I'll be fine.'

Guilio doubts it. One whack on the cracked bone and the guy is in a world of pain. He crouches and dips into the rucksack. 'Torches.' He passes over a black rubber flashlight and jams one in his own belt. 'And weapons.' He smiles as he holds out a fistful of household tools.

Tom examines them one by one. A ball-peen hammer, a pointed seed dibber and a razor-sharp carpet fitter's knife. He feels sick. Using any of these things will be an awful experience. To be effective, he'll have to maim or kill an opponent.

Guilio reads his face. 'Second thoughts?'

'No, but I hope I don't have to use any of these.'

'You will.' He leaves the bag for a second and stands up to face the big American. 'You have to be ready to use *all* of them. Once we're in there, they'll be on us like rats on cheese. Hesitate, and they'll kill you.'

He doesn't wait for Tom's reaction; he returns to the rucksack and pulls out his final purchases. 'These two are on hire. I hope we live to return them.'

He hands over a strange orange contraption. 'It's a nail gun, fully charged, with a spare battery and a magazine of long ring shank nails.' He points it at Tom's head. 'It's no pistol. You'll need to get up close, but if you do, it'll be every bit as deadly as a bullet.'

Tom checks for the on–off switch and fires it up. Indicator lights flash and it trembles for a second in his hand.

'The man in the shop said it'll spit out three nails a second.'

Tom squeezes the trigger. It jolts in his hand, but nothing seems to happen.

An inch from his right foot, he sees the glistening top of a galvanised steel nail, sunk deep into the turf.

It raises a smile from Guilio. 'Impressive, eh?'

Tom turns it off to save the battery. There's no smile on his face. Just focus. The kind he used to reserve for the worship of God.

He turns the nail gun over in his hands.

He's aware now of what it does and what he'll have to do with it.

'Let's go,' he says flatly. 'I'll never be more ready than I am right now.'

121

Major Lorenzo Silvestri stares at the clock on his office wall.

He wishes he had the power to stop it.

He'd give anything to be able to halt those hands and gain himself an extra twelve hours.

As one of the most experienced members of GIS, he knows he has to strike quickly. Unfortunately, speed and careful planning are not easy bedfellows.

If he rushes things, then whoever has Morassi will certainly kill her, and maybe other hostages as well.

But if he takes too long planning the search and rescue operation, then the kidnappers will cover their tracks and he may never find them.

'Anything on Shaman's phone?' he asks Pasquale Conti.

The captain's face answers before he does. 'We had tech problems. We got a GPS lock and then lost it.'

'What?'

'I know. I could kill them too. They're working on it.'

'You got one location, right?'

'Right. The phone company is playing ball and we managed to get a fix on where he called us from.'

'Which was?'

'He was near Parco di Porta, heading towards Via Appia Antica.'

Lorenzo drums his fingers on the desk. 'How do you know he was heading that way?'

'He turned his phone back on and we got a second brief fix on that, then it went dead again.'

'Interesting. Who did he call after us?'

'Morassi. The call lasted less than ten seconds.'

'Sounds like she didn't pick up.'

Lorenzo slides a sheet of paper across the desk. 'The captain's profile, from our intel unit. She's a hotshot. A real high-flyer. Golden girl in Venice. That's where she met this Shaman guy; they worked a murder case together.'

Pasquale taps Valentina's photo. 'You're right about the hot bit. Man, she's very, very hot!'

'Enough!' Lorenzo grins and slides over the brief on Tom. 'Check out the boyfriend. The pic is from his visits to HQ.'

'Not my type.'

'Be serious. I called an old friend in Venice, Vito Carvalho. He used to be Morassi's boss and briefly worked with

Shaman. Turns out the guy used to be a priest in LA, until he stepped into a gang fight one night.'

'What happened?'

'Three on one.' Lorenzo takes a beat. 'The hoods were raping a young girl and had knives. Shaman beat the living daylights out of them. Left two dead and I think the third is still running.'

'The original Good Samaritan.'

'That's not quite what Vito christened him.'

Pasquale's intrigued. 'Which was?'

'Arcangelo Uriel.'

Pasquale is none the wiser. 'Uriel?'

'Heathen.' Lorenzo shakes his head in mock disbelief and crosses himself. 'If you were a good Catholic, you would know that Uriel means "Fire of God". When the Almighty wants the dirty stuff doing, Uriel is the halo he hollers for. From slaying demons to burying Adam in Paradise, Uriel has always been the guy for tough jobs.'

Pasquale looks again at Tom's ID picture. 'And now he's here in Rome, playing angels and demons. Lucky us.'

122

The drop from the field to the first level of the underground tunnel is enough to remind Tom that his knee is still swollen and unstable.

To make matters worse, it's so cramped down there that he has to crawl along on a stony surface.

'Wait!' he shouts, virtually into Guilio's backside, just a couple of feet away from him.

'Shush!' comes back a whispered shout.

Tom waits patiently behind the huddled form. He hears the thin noise of stone scraping on stone, and guesses the scalene pendant is at work again.

Guilio squeezes to one side and hands back his flashlight. 'Shine it over there; I can't seem to move this last lock with only one hand.'

Tom takes the light and twists its head so the beam floods more strongly.

Guilio works away in the cramped space.

Several minutes pass.

'Got it!'

He ties the scalene pendant back on to the strap of his rucksack and manoeuvres his body round.

Tom sees that he's pulling up another disc, pretty much the same as the one they entered through.

It breaks and collapses inwards.

Guilio falls forward and almost tumbles head first down after it.

The broken cover makes loud but dull thumping sounds as pieces hit the earth two metres below.

A muffled sound, like distant rolling thunder, echoes through unseen tunnels.

'That was close!' Guilio looks into the hole. 'We have to drop down through several more portals like this one before we reach the gallery that will lead us to where I believe your friend is being held.'

Tom nods. There's nothing in his mind now but the job in hand. He's ready to deal with anything and anyone that he comes across.

Guilio twists his body round so his feet dangle into the darkness.

He drops out of sight.

Tom follows.

This time he's doubly careful to make sure his good leg takes most of the impact and that his damaged shoulder stays clear of the stone tunnel walls.

Within a dozen paces, the tunnel doglegs right and then opens into a larger area.

Tom's relieved to be able to stand.

He pulls out his flashlight and sweeps the beam in front of him.

The walls have been cut out of sandstone. Four layers of deep shelves stretch from a dark earth floor to a high earth ceiling.

He knows where he is.

Long before he sees the first bones and the empty eye sockets of the stacked skulls, he knows he's in an ancient cemetery.

A necropolis.

It could be Christian, or maybe even Etruscan.

He remembers Guilio saying they were journeying between – and beneath – the catacombs of Callixtus and Sebastian. Somewhere off in the hardened soil around him are the now well-trodden tombs and crypts of martyrs.

Brave people who died fighting for what they loved most.

123

Shooter grabs Valentina by the throat.

He's a couple of inches taller than she is, and despite his age, he's muscular enough to force her up on to her tip-toes.

'Lesson number one, you only speak when I tell you to.'

His hand tightens. She can feel her airway closing off.

Shooter's smirk widens as he walks her backwards to the rear of the cell. He crashes her into the rough stone wall and lets go.

Valentina opens her mouth and gasps for air.

She never sees his punch.

It catches her full in the lips and teeth.

She wobbles and starts to fall backwards.

Her feet almost cross and she falls.

But not flat out, just into an undignified sitting position.

Shooter smiles and holds up his grazed fist. 'Teacher says you've still got some learning to do.'

Valentina puts her hands submissively to her face.

Blood trickles over her fingers. Her lip is split wide open, almost exactly in the same place where Anna caught her back in the Carabinieri cell block.

Shooter drops to his knees and grabs her by the throat again.

It's exciting to hold her like this. To look into her eyes and see the fear rising.

It's what he likes most.

He slips a hand between her legs and claws savagely at her trousers.

He sees the fear turn to panic.

'Not so feisty now, are you?'

She's terrified, he can see it. She recognises his power; knows he can do to her whatever he wants.

Valentina doesn't struggle.

She reminds herself that what happens next is not about pride, it's about survival.

124

The walls of the new tunnel are covered in ornate plaster paintings on white backgrounds, the lavish and intricate kind found on some sarcophagi.

Tiny human figures are crowded into horizontal and vertical storylines and from afar make no sense at all.

Tom tries to decipher the dozens of cryptic scenes.

There are people mourning: women and children kneeling and crying, men carrying bodies, funeral pyres being built.

There are battle scenes too: soldiers fighting on foot and on horseback, swords half raised, shields fully lifted in desperate defence of the cruel slashing blades.

Towards the end of the gallery, a particular stretch of sarcophagi catches his eye.

A number of women are clambering out of a chariot.

They're being chased by soldiers.

Some get caught.

They're pulled to the ground by the men.

It is the Rape of the Sabines.

One woman has escaped.

She is running towards a bridge, a crossing guarded by a fierce she-wolf. A handful of soldiers are pursuing her.

Tom has to rub soil away to see more clearly.

The soldiers are crossing the bridge, tracked by the wolf. The woman is hiding underneath. She's shown alongside a wide stretch of river.

He has to clear more dirt away to see the continuation.

Beneath the bridge is what looks like a crucifix.

It isn't.

On closer inspection it's a soldier, lying on his back, a sword stuck in his stomach.

The woman has vanished from the scene.

Guilio appears at Tom's side. 'What are you doing?'

He points to the wall and the start of the sarcophagi. 'This story – it's the one Anna told us.'

Guilio doesn't understand.

He looks at the wall, and as it begins to make sense, he feels a sharp and unexpected stab of grief.

He puts his fingers to the clay and lovingly traces the outline of the female figure.

Anna.

The strange connection makes an even greater sadness well up inside him. His eyes fill with tears.

Tom's attention has already drifted on to a new scene.

A woman in fine long robes is in the centre of what looks like a market square. Again she is surrounded by soldiers.

He directs his flashlight and looks closer.

It's the same woman.

Cassandra.

She looks identical to Anna. Identical to Cybele.

Tom leans closer.

Perhaps his eyes are playing tricks. Maybe these evocative surroundings are influencing him.

For a moment he dismisses it.

If you reduce any woman's facial features to those the size of a fingernail, then they all probably look the same.

But Tom knows that's not true.

All around him is evidence of craftsmanship so supreme that he's sure the perpetrators could fashion any different feature they wished.

The woman *is* Anna. Anna in the image of Cassandra and Cybele.

Tom looks at the crowd massed around her. They're

angry, waving their fists, stretching out their fingers to grab at her noble robes.

There's a man on high ground holding a scroll. He's reading to the mob and the woman is now being dragged towards him by the soldiers.

Tom turns away briefly to check on Guilio.

The eunuch is on his knees. Eyes blood-red from crying. Fingers still fondly touching the tiny sculptures of Anna.

Such grief threatens to undermine any attempt to free Valentina. Tom has to get him to snap out of it.

He puts his hands on Guilio's shoulders and tries to comfort him. 'You'll always have good memories of Anna. Your thoughts of her and your love for her are precious and will stay with you until the end of time.' In a deliberate and almost priestly gesture, he puts the palm of his right hand to Guilio's forehead. 'I pray that your suffering will pass quickly. In return, I beg you now to ignore your grief. Put it aside for the moment and have the strength to help me to finish what we came down here for. Please help me save the life of the woman I love.'

Guilio gets to his feet and looks lost.

Tom takes him into his arms and holds him tight.

'What's been done and is being done down here is evil. Pure evil. We can't let these people get away with it. You must be strong now.'

Guilio pulls away.

He wipes his eyes with the back of his hand and lets out a small, embarrassed laugh. 'I haven't cried since I was a child.'

He turns and leads the way into the darkness again.

As Tom follows, he looks to his side.

On the wall is the final scene in the market square.

Anna's hand isn't placed inside the Bocca della Verità.

It's on a sword that has been plunged into the guts of one of the guards.

125

Shooter looks down on Valentina.

The cop bitch doesn't look so smart and arrogant now.

Flat on her back, face bloodied up, smart white blouse and black trousers full of filthy marks.

Now she looks different.

Now she looks like she knows who's boss.

Shooter is.

Mater wouldn't approve. She doesn't like violence. Well, not unless it's violence that she's ordered, then of course it's fine. Justified. Necessary. But Shooter's violence is much more than those things.

It's pleasurable.

And as Battakes, chief of the Galli, he's entitled to indulge himself once in a while.

He pulls the cell door shut and enjoys its terrifying clunk.

He stares at Valentina through the bars. Despite the battering he's given her, there are still no tears.

She has guts, he'll give her that.

And she's pretty, too.

No, more than pretty – she's really quite beautiful.

Shame he doesn't have the equipment to rape her, because he'd like to.

That's what Mater doesn't understand.

He still has the urge.

A *raging* urge.

Sex is in the mind, not just in your balls, the old woman should know that.

He looks again at Valentina. She's sitting up now, trying to get her shit together. Very nice. Those long legs stretched out like that are a fine sight. Shooter would like to see her undressed. Maybe jam things in her. Ram her full of sticks and dirt until the rage dies down.

He turns from the bars. Walks away while he still can.

She's lucky.

Lucky that he remembered his place. His sacred place in Mater's universe.

There's a noise behind him.

A clank.

And now his back feels wet.

He turns and can't believe what he sees.

She's thrown her bucket of cell piss over him.

He's soaked in urine.

And she's laughing at him. Grinning through the bars.

'You ball-less fucking faggot!' She flaps her arms with anger. 'Is that the best you can fucking do?'

She bangs the bucket crazily on the bars. Metal on metal. Loud echoes bounce all over the place. 'Is it? Is that really your best shot?'

She keeps cracking the bucket, venting all her anger in a wild, frenzied outburst.

It amuses Shooter.

Amuses and arouses him.

She's like a lioness.

Maybe it's his job to tame her.

'Testa di cazzo!' She throws the bucket at the bars and turns her back on him.

'Big mistake,' says Shooter, slipping his key into the lock. 'You just made the biggest mistake of your life.'

126

Tom and Guilio quickly descend two more levels.

It seems odd that the further beneath ground they go, the bigger the space around them gets.

They turn a corner.

Ahead is a giant statue of Cybele, flanked by two stone lions.

'Wait,' instructs Guilio, with raised hand. 'There's something I need to tell you.'

Tom comes to a halt.

Ahead he can see that instead of crude sandstone, there's a lavish array of spectacular wall paintings, devotional graffiti and decorated amphorae.

The face of Cybele is everywhere.

'This is one of the main veins,' explains Guilio. 'That's what the sisterhood call the approaches to the womb. The exits are known as arteries.'

'So we're close?'

'Very.' Guilio looks tense. 'And that means we'll soon encounter traps.' He points ahead. 'Maybe even along here.'

Tom feels his heart hammering. 'What kind?'

'I only know of a few.' Guilio gestures at the painted ceiling. 'Some veins are rigged to bleed. There are pipes hidden in the ceiling that can shower us in acid.'

Tom looks up.

'You won't be able to see them. They're well concealed. And they're pressure-activated. One step on a trigger plate and our flesh will be melting.'

Tom feels his skin crawl.

'Mater, or chosen ones like the chief priest of her Galli, sometimes deactivate them so that searches can take place. We may get lucky.'

Tom doesn't feel lucky. 'Is that it? That's the end of the Indiana Jones stuff?'

Guilio smiles. 'No. We might have a chance to get past if that was all there was to worry about.' He points at the ground. 'There are gravitational floors in some of the veins.'

'What do you mean – the floors tilt?'

'Exactly. Sections are supported only in the centre. Walk on one side and they'll tip. If that happens, we'll just drop into a pit below and be left to die.'

'And all these horrors have been here for how long?'

Guilio shrugs. 'Hundreds, maybe thousands of years. They're effective, though.'

'Being a former Galli, you know all these traps; you know where to walk, right?'

Guilio's face says that that's not the case. 'The Chief Priest is the only man who knows that.' He looks apologetically at Tom. 'I've never been here before.'

Tom's in shock. 'What?'

'I've only ever been through the main entrance.' He reads the expression on Tom's face. 'There is no possibility we could have gone that way. It is too well guarded.' He sees he needs to explain. 'Across the fields, off the Appian Way, there is a farmhouse and some outbuildings. There are barns stacked with straw and the sisterhood tend a small dairy herd. Everything appears normal. The main stone house is large and looks like it is being modernised and extended. In fact, it's like a fortress inside. Off the kitchen is a door to the cellar. The cellar itself is a huge antechamber in which the guards live and sleep. At the far end is the easiest entrance to the womb. Every gateway – and there are many – is controlled by fingerprint sensors. So if your prints are not registered with the guards,' he waggles his right hand at Tom, 'and believe me, it's a long time since mine were, then you don't get access to the stairways and you can't get to the sacks – that's what they call the cells where your friend is being held.'

'So that triangular key that you're using, that's more symbolism and tradition than anything?'

Guilio touches it as he talks. 'It is important as both. The angles of the triangle physically locate the positions of the secret ways. Throughout the centuries it has been both a symbol and a key, and as symbolism is based on maintaining traditions, Mater has ensured that the old veins are kept healthy and functional.'

Tom can't help but feel sickened by the whole thing. He sees similarities to the Josef Fritzl case – the Austrian monster who imprisoned and abused his own daughter underground for more than twenty years, forcing her to bear seven of his children.

'We have to get moving,' says Guilio, his body half turned towards the treacherous tunnel that lies ahead. 'Now you need to follow several metres behind me and walk as close to the centre as possible. The paintings and art are designed to draw you over to them. Give in to their allure and you may well end up giving away your life.'

127

Shooter grabs Valentina by the shoulder and spins her round.

He slaps her so hard with the flat of his right hand that the left side of her face feels like it's been set on fire.

She cannons into the cell wall.

She recovers her balance, sticks her bloodied chin out and spits in his face.

Plucky bitch.

Shooter smiles at her. He's enjoying this.

Really enjoying it.

He unleashes a vicious backhand slap to the right side of her jaw.

Valentina totters and then falls.

She shuffles back in the dirt. Tries to squash herself into the corner of the cell.

'You stupid bitch! Did you think you could disrespect me and I'd just walk away?'

He steps forward and tries to grab her feet.

Valentina kicks out at him.

He stamps hard on her thigh.

The dead leg stops her kicking.

Now he grabs her feet. Grabs them and pulls them until she's in the centre of the cell.

Valentina can't help but scream.

Shooter leans over and punches her in the face.

The blow shuts her up.

He rips open her blouse.

Her stomach is irresistible. He claws a five-finger scratch mark down to her waistline.

The rage is growing.

Boiling up inside him.

He grabs at the top of her trousers and tears open the button.

Shooter glances up to see her face. To catch the fear about to flicker in her eyes.

But he's a fraction too late.

Valentina slams her right hand against his stomach.

It feels like nothing.

A girlie slap that doesn't even knock the wind out of him.

But it's more than it seems.

He knows that from the expectant look in her eyes.

Valentina places her left hand on top of her right, and keeps pressing.

Now he gets it.

He knows exactly what she's done.

She's stabbed him.

He sees it now. She's broken the thin wire handle off the bucket and stuck him with it.

Skewered him like a pig, and won't let go.

Shooter grabs her hands, but Valentina uses the shock to shift her weight and push him back.

He tries to fight her off. The more he strains forward, the more he pushes the rusty metal further into his gut.

Shooter topples backwards.

Valentina follows. Driving the metal deep into the abdominal wound.

Her soldier's instinct and training have kicked in.

No let-up. No mercy. No rest.

Not until he's dead.

128

The dusty wooden boards creak and groan like a dying man.

Tom and Guilio stop in their tracks.

Both glance to their left.

The noise is coming from the wall.

Tom glances to his right.

The floor is rising on that side. 'Stay still!' he shouts.

He takes half a stride to his right and hopes he's corrected the balance.

The ground steadies again.

Both men take a deep breath and try to work out what has happened.

They're standing on a section of false flooring.

Centuries of dirt have shifted under their weight and are now spilling like the sand of an egg-timer over the edges of the trap.

Tom guesses that once it's been dislodged, the floor will become increasingly unstable.

Guilio needs to walk at least another metre to get off it, Tom another five, unless he turns and goes back a metre.

They're both now standing slightly off-centre. Guilio a little too much to the left. Tom too much to the right.

They look at each other.

They know their lives now depend entirely upon mutual trust.

If Guilio makes a run for it, Tom is dead.

And vice versa.

'On three,' Guilio suggests. 'We both step to the middle, okay?'

'Okay.'

'One . . . two . . .'

They take a final glance at each other.

'Three!'

They move.

The floor creaks.

Then slowly corrects itself.

They smile at each other.

So far, so good.

'Let's try again,' says Guilio. 'Nice and slowly.' He extends his arms and stretches a foot out in the manner of walking a tightrope. 'Just take really careful, slow steps.'

There's a creak over towards the left-hand wall. Tom ignores it and copies Guilio.

The creak grows louder.

Much louder.

Tom looks left.

A whole section of painted wall cracks and crumbles.

Pieces of it fall on to the tilting floor.

Heavy pieces.

Tom takes another step.

Guilio is just one stride from safety.

A huge piece of plaster falls from the ceiling.

'Run!' shouts Tom.

Guilio glances over his shoulder and sees the falling debris.

He jumps to safety.

Tons of rubble crash down.

The floor tips violently.

Tom is only two metres from the edge.

He moves quickly.

The rubble is still falling. The angle of the tip worsens.

One metre from safety.

Tom loses his footing.

He seems to fall in slo-mo.

His right leg slides as the floor rises.

He spins. Skids. Tumbles.

Guilio stretches out a hand.

It's no use.

He's too far away.

Their fingertips brush each other.

Tom disappears into the blackness.

129

Valentina's hands are glistening with viscera and blood.

She wipes them on Shooter's corpse and doesn't even flinch.

There's a gun tucked into his belt. The idiot thought he didn't need it.

Valentina takes it.

And his cell keys as well.

She searches his body for anything else of value. There's a special radio, like the ones used by subway staff, a cell phone, a small Maglite, some matches, cigarettes and money.

That's all.

She searches his shirt pockets, flips him over and checks the back pockets of his pants.

A spare magazine for the Glock.

She looks again at the old cell keys. They may well open the cages just down from her, but she knows they won't open the security gates on the levels above. She heard electronic buzzing. That means he must have a swipe card of some kind.

She searches him again.

Nothing.

Valentina feels a jolt of panic. Her plan is in ruins. Without a card of some kind, there's no way out.

Still, she has the gun.

She checks it.

It's the one he fired in the church. The magazine's been refilled since then. She slides it back in and flips off the safety catch. If she can't get out, then at least she'll kill a lot of people trying.

Slowly she emerges from the cell, and makes her way towards the torches and the staircase.

As she feared, the gate there is a modern one, with an electromagnetic catch.

She shines the tiny Maglite across the lock and over a pillar next to the gate.

Her heart sinks.

There's a fingerprint sensor.

Valentina looks across to the dead man in the cell.

Maybe she could carry him this far. That's possible.

She sprints back to the cell and jams the torch in her trousers.

Just lifting Shooter is a Herculean task.

His limbs are floppy. His flesh slippery with blood.

She sits him up. Grabs him under the armpits and lifts him. He's heavier than she thought. She has to press her body against his and force him against the wall to stop him collapsing like a rag doll.

Within seconds, she needs a breather.

It means standing face to face with the corpse, his head on her shoulder, his dead cheek pressed against her skin.

Valentina takes a deep breath, squats and executes an almost perfect fireman's lift.

With Shooter draped over her shoulders, she makes her way across the uneven floor to the security gate.

Once there, there's a new problem.

She can't reach his hand and lift it to the sensor.

She drops the corpse and there's a sickening squish of loose organs and spilling body fluids.

She manoeuvres him so he's facing the gate.

His hand still won't reach the sensor pad.

'Damn!'

Once more she grabs him under the arms and heaves him into an upright position.

She doesn't have enough hands.

She needs to shift one hand from under his armpit to grab

his right hand, select a finger – presumably his index one – and swipe it across the sensor.

If she tries that, then the body will fall.

She drops him again and looks across to the cells.

The girl she saw in the nearby cell is watching her.

Valentina moves towards her.

The poor kid looks frightened to death.

Valentina remembers that she's soaked in Shooter's blood. It must be all over her face, her hands and her blouse. 'It's all right, don't be afraid.' She holds up the keys she took from Shooter. 'I'm a policewoman. I'm coming to get you out.'

The kid backs away, eyes wide with fear.

Valentina wipes blood from her face.

She finds the lock, and slips the key in.

A splash of light shows that the girl is covered in bruises.

There are cuts all over her hands, legs and arms.

She can't be more than ten.

Maybe even younger.

She has big brown eyes that no doubt once shone with fun, and an oval face with an impossibly cute, dimply chin.

Valentina pushes open the cell door.

She stares more closely at the girl.

The kid looks just like Anna.

130

Tom is either unconscious or dead.

Guilio's not sure which.

The tilting floor is jammed open, caught by the rubble

that has piled up. He kneels on the edge of the safe part and stares into the abyss. 'Are you all right? Can you hear me?'

He knows he can't afford to wait here. Such a loud noise may well have been heard in the other chambers. Galli guards could already be on their way.

Maybe he should just leave him.

But he knows he can't.

He shuffles closer to the collapsed wall and shines his torch down into the blackness.

About a metre beneath him he sees what he thinks is Tom's body.

He moves the light around. Tom appears to be collapsed on some kind of ledge.

It's not a ledge.

Guilio can see more clearly now. The fallen debris has all slid into a heap, like slurry from the back of a tipper lorry, and Tom is face-down on top of it all.

Hardly a soft landing, but no doubt better than falling all the way to the bottom – wherever the bottom eventually is.

Guilio slips the rucksack off his back and dangles his legs over the edge.

It's trickier to get down than he first thought.

It seems the only safe place to jump is actually on top of Tom. If he does that, then apart from hurting him even more, there's a risk he will dislodge the pile of rubble and send them both crashing into the depths of the hole.

He sits and tries to work out what to do.

The pit beneath him stinks worse than a sewer.

Tom lets out a weak groan.

He's coming round.

Tom moves his left arm. His fingers feel rock. He tries to get a grip to turn himself over.

'Careful!' shouts Guilio. 'You've fallen into a hole. Don't turn to your right or you'll drop even further.'

He's not sure if Tom's heard him.

There's another groan.

No, not a groan.

And it's not coming from Tom.

Guilio suddenly recognises the awful smell.

Animal dung.

There's something down there.

Some kind of animal is making its way across the floor of the pit.

'Tom! Move yourself! There's something coming for you!'

131

Valentina swings open the heavy iron door and slowly steps into the child's cell. 'I'm not going to hurt you. You can trust me. I'm going to take you out of here.'

It's a gamble the child's ready to take.

She runs to the policewoman, grabs her waist and presses herself tightly against her.

It breaks Valentina's heart to see such desperation.

She strokes the youngster's hair and lets her cling for a moment.

From the grip around her, it's clearly been a long time since the kid felt safe in someone's arms.

She stoops a little and puts her hands either side of the child's dirty and bruised face. 'My name is Valentina. I'm in the Carabinieri and I'm going to look after you.' She strokes her cheek tenderly. 'What's your name?'

Tears well up in the youngster's big brown eyes. She shakes her head.

'It's okay, you can tell me. What are you called, sweetheart?'

The child opens her mouth, but no words come out.

Valentina is about to ask again when the girl shows her teeth and jabs a finger pointedly to the back of her throat.

'Oh my God!' Valentina grabs her and hugs her tight. 'You poor baby.'

Someone has cut out the child's tongue.

Valentina tears up.

How could anyone do such a thing?

There's a noise from the stairwell.

Footsteps coming their way.

The kid bolts from Valentina's arms and disappears into the shadows.

She thinks about running after her, but instead rushes to where Shooter is laid out. She quickly grabs him under the arms and pulls him back and out of sight behind the stairwell.

The gate buzzes and clicks open.

Valentina listens intently.

The door clicks closed.

No voices.

One set of footsteps.

She draws the Glock from her waistband.

It's a man.

Valentina recognises his hunched shoulders and thin outline.

Trench Coat.

Shooter's radio unexpectedly crackles.

Trench Coat turns.

Valentina has no choice.

Her first shot hits him in the face.

The second blows a hole in the centre of his rib cage.

He hits the ground with a thump and Valentina sees something shimmer as it spills from him.

She runs to the body.

Handcuffs.

Her mind is working at warp speed.

She digs for the key in his pocket and runs to the gate at the foot of the stairs.

The cuffs won't help her bypass the fingerprint scanner, but they will stop Shooter's friends getting down. She clicks one of them to the gate and the other to the bars of the pillar, near the sensor.

Now she sets off after the kid.

But she's not in her cell.

She must have run off during the shooting.

Valentina walks past the other cages.

Ahead in the darkness, off to the right, she sees a pool of light. A staircase, leading down.

There are no locked gates, no guards.

The stone steps lead to an open area of marble.

There's a centrepiece made up of three identical waist-high statues of Cybele. They are arranged with their backs to each other to form a triangle.

Beyond the statues are two huge oak doors. Sitting beside them is the child from the cell, her head buried in her hands.

She looks up as she hears Valentina.

Instead of being comforted, she looks terrified.

Valentina realises she's still holding the Glock.

She slides the gun into the back of her waistband. 'Please, sweetheart, let me help you; let me look after you. If you do what I say and stay with me, everything will be all right.'

The kid stares intently into the policewoman's eyes. She's

learned the hard way – the only way that abused children understand – that lies show in the eyes of adults long before they leave their mouths.

Valentina stretches out her hand and takes hold of the tiny fingers.

They're icy cold.

She gives them a gentle squeeze, then covers them with both her own hands. 'I'm going to call you Sweetheart until I learn your name.' She lifts the chilly hand, kisses it and clasps it between her own palms. 'We need to get you warmed up. When we get out of here, I promise you the biggest, creamiest hot chocolate drink that's ever been made.'

The little girl smiles.

Valentina helps her stand.

They walk together to the giant doors and push one open.

The kid clings tight and becomes even more anxious.

Beyond the doors is a vast space.

Uneven in dimensions.

Scalene in proportions.

A temple.

The walls are decorated with rich and intricate woodland scenes from Phrygia, Crete, Turkey, Greece and Italy. All depict Cybele and her prophetesses.

The ceiling is as beautifully painted as that of the Sistine Chapel. The floor is covered in minuscule mosaics.

The whole place is lit by dozens of torches burning in triangular cones fixed on the walls.

Against the longest wall is a huge elevated altar covered in hundreds of multicoloured flower petals. Opposite, three metres off the ground, is what looks like a marble ledge. Valentina presumes it's a pulpit for priests or priestesses.

In the middle of the temple floor there is a large triangular grid. Valentina doesn't walk across it, but she peers down

421

and can see that it's a big drop. She knows enough about ancient religions to guess that this is a sacrificial pit.

A loud, dull thud makes her turn.

The heavy oak door they came through has swung shut.

There's another sound.

Dull and repetitive.

Muffled.

Valentina thinks it's coming from beneath her feet rather than outside the temple.

She struggles to place it.

It's an even, almost rhythmical knocking noise, now so loud she really should be able to see what's causing it.

But she can't.

It stops as unexpectedly as it started.

But the peace lasts barely a second.

An even stranger noise starts.

A high-pitched buzz.

Not electronic. Something more natural.

The sound grows quickly.

More bass than treble.

The kind of noise you feel more than hear.

The kind of tone that makes your heart shake.

A black fountain erupts from the triangular pit.

It springs up as though someone has struck oil.

Valentina pulls Sweetheart close to her.

The spray spins high in the air, swirls like a typhoon and slowly starts to lose its shape.

It's not oil.

It's a dense cloud of frenzied flies.

Sarcophagidae.

Flesh flies.

Gruesome insects that feed on the dead. Mannerless little monsters that lay their eggs in corpses.

Valentina's seen them many times.

But only under a microscope. Only dead and clamped between the metal teeth of a pathologist's tweezers.

Never like this.

Never loose and wild and in their millions.

132

Tom's fall isn't as bad as it looks.

He's had the wind knocked out of him and his cracked clavicle is screaming like a werewolf.

But he's sure nothing else is busted.

The main problem is, he can feel the rubble moving beneath him.

Sliding.

Shifting slowly, like brown sugar.

His left hand grips loose rock.

Despite the pain, he manages to work his right elbow between hard chunks of stone.

Up above, Guilio is shouting, but he can't work out what he's saying.

He gets some leverage and manages to roll on to his back.

He can see Guilio now, panic on his face, mouthing something.

The rubble pile beneath him drops. It's like a plane hitting an air pocket. He falls half a metre and almost slips off.

Tom digs his heels in.

Pushes himself back up.

Edges towards the wall.

Glancing down, he sees something strange.

Two shining dots.

Eyes.

They're moving towards him.

The head of an emaciated lion appears in the half-light.

Its mane is thick with dust and grime.

Its jaws are wide open.

Tom scrabbles for a rock, and instantly realises that because of his shoulder injury, he can't throw right-handed.

Nor can he lift one-handed the size of boulder necessary to bludgeon to death a hungry lion.

He throws a medium-sized stone.

It whacks the beast on the shoulder but does nothing to stop it.

The animal roars and becomes wary.

It can feel the rubble shifting as it climbs towards its surprise meal.

Tom hurls a chunk of plaster.

It catches the beast on the nose.

Another growl.

Tom's ears have cleared of the buzzing. He can hear again. Hardly a bonus, given the circumstance.

He pulls his legs up.

The rubble slips some more.

So does the lion.

It slides back and scrambles and scratches to keep its footing.

The bright eyes twinkle.

A blood-curdling roar rolls from its greedy yellow mouth.

It starts to charge.

Tom throws another rock.

It misses.

The lion is inches away.

He draws his knee back and slams the sole of his foot into its face.

It's a good connection, enough to put a man flat on his back.

But not enough to stop a wild animal.

It rolls its head and comes again.

Tom can't get enough of an angle to kick out.

The lion is on him.

Growling and biting.

He shifts his leg and the giant jaw crunches into stone.

There's a loud thump next to him.

Guilio is in the pit.

The animal reacts quicker than Tom.

But not quicker than Guilio.

The nozzle of his nail gun finds the fur of the beast. He pumps a five-inch nail into its head.

The lion is dead before it even starts to roll away.

But Guilio is trapped beneath it. The pile of rubble shifts again.

Tom reaches out for him.

The pile collapses.

Guilio and the lion disappear into the darkness.

There's a crash of rock and a cloud of dust.

Tom clings to a section of still crumbling rubble.

He looks up.

The edge of the floor is within touching distance.

If the pile he's standing on slips any more, he won't make it.

But if he jumps, Guilio will be stranded.

The dust blows away.

The beast's body is wedged between boulders halfway down the pile.

There's no sign of Guilio.

Tom cups a hand around his mouth. 'Are you okay – can you hear me down there?'

The answer is faint. 'I'm stuck. My leg's jammed.'

'Hang on.'

Tom can't see further than the dead animal.

The pile starts to shift again.

He looks up at the edge of the floor above.

He jumps.

There's no point them both being stranded.

If he can get out, he can get help.

Tom dangles by his fingers.

His right shoulder is a ball of pain. He knows he has to ignore it.

If he doesn't, he won't survive.

Nor will Guilio.

He fumbles for a better grip, and manages to pull himself up a little.

His left leg bangs against the wall.

He explores it with his foot.

It's worn and jagged.

Uneven enough for him to get a toehold.

The precious leverage enables him to get up on to his elbows.

He can hear shouting below as he swings his right leg up and rolls to safety.

There's shouting – and something else.

Growling.

Across the ground, he notices again the statue of Cybele.

The goddess is flanked by two lions, not one.

He peers back into the pit.

The growls come from way beyond the body of the dead lion.

Guilio's agonising screams rise from the bottom of the black hole.

There's nothing Tom can do.

Except listen to him being eaten alive.

133

The flesh flies are everywhere.

They swarm around Valentina and Sweetheart, settling on their skin and crawling into their ears.

Valentina remembers her mortuary lessons.

And wishes she hadn't.

Sarcophaga nodosa is more than just an unpleasant-looking insect with revolting feeding habits.

It's also a carrier of leprosy.

A fatally loaded disease bomb.

A fly hits Sweetheart in the eye and makes her do a panic jig.

Valentina holds her and tries to comfort her. The insects are crawling into her long hair and down her shabby night-dress. Valentina beats them off but they're instantly replaced by hundreds more.

They have to keep moving.

They must get out of here.

She pulls Sweetheart's hand up to shield as much of her face as possible. 'Keep your mouth covered; don't let these horrid bugs get in there or up your nose.' The youngster looks terrified as she leads her towards the doors.

The sooner they get out of here, the better.

They reach the doors and Valentina flips the handle.

Locked.

She tries again to see if she's mistaken.

Maybe it's just sticking.

Definitely locked.

She lets go of Sweetheart's hand and takes a hefty kick at the weak point where the doors meet.

They don't budge.

She looks up and sees ten feet of solid oak.

The flies will have picked her bones clean by the time she's forced them open.

'Stand back!' She moves Sweetheart away. 'Stay over here and don't move.'

She pulls the gun and takes aim at the heavy brass lock, careful to make sure that she's at an angle, so if there's any freak rebound she doesn't catch shrapnel.

The Glock kicks in her palm.

It's not a clean shot.

She's nicked the lock, but the oak is so thick, the bullet hasn't even gone all the way through.

Valentina lets off three more rounds.

The brass mangles up but the edge of the door shows no sign of splintering as she hoped.

Her temper flares.

She steps close to the door and fires off five shots in a circle around the lock.

She may as well have saved the ammunition.

She jams the Glock back in her waistband.

She has an idea.

A crazy, desperate idea, but it might just work.

Valentina runs through the thick cloud of flies to the flower-covered altar and climbs it.

She's after one of the flaming torches.

The flies are so thick, it's like working beneath a blanket.

It takes several minutes, but Valentina finally frees a torch from the wall.

She jumps from the altar and looks across to the opposite wall.

High on the pulpit ledge, behind a wall of glass, she sees an old woman in a long red robe is staring at her.

She looks like Cybele.

Alongside her are other old women, their faces all turned down towards the temple floor.

Valentina's eyes flash hatred as she carries the torch away.

Flies sizzle in the wafting orange flames.

She pulls Sweetheart even further away from the giant doors, then kneels down with the torch and holds it to the oak.

She's going to burn a way out.

Then she's going to find those cruel old crones and make them wish they'd died decades ago.

134

Guilio's final screams are already haunting Tom as he picks up the rucksack and walks away from the pit.

He knows there's nothing he could have done.

There was no way he could have stopped the second lion.

But he still feels awful.

If Guilio hadn't jumped in the pit, Tom would be dead.

It seems wrong that he lost his life in such a way.

Tom shines his torch into the darkness and walks slowly towards the end of the gallery, staying as close to the centre as he can.

He hopes there are no more traps.

After fifty metres the tunnel comes to a dead end, just as the others have done.

Only there's a difference.

A big difference.

There's no hatch on the floor. No marble disc through which to pass to another level.

Instead, there's a huge felled tree.

It's either set into the wall or the wall has been built around it.

Tom touches it.

It's a big old chunk of a thing, its bark riddled with ridges, gnarls and knots where branches have been lopped off.

The tree is a sign.

A sign of nature.

It must have symbolic connections to Cybele and Mother Nature.

He remembers that the last time he was around trees was when he was in the field above the catacombs, where Guilio painstakingly used the scalene pendant to locate the position of the entrance to the Cybelene chambers.

He grabs the rucksack and searches inside for the pendant.

Only when he's emptied everything does he see it tied to one of the straps.

Now he can't remember exactly how Guilio used it.

Did the eunuch start with the shortest side in the right-hand corner of the field, or with one of the longer sides?

Tom digs out the spool of fishing twine and decides to start with the shortest, so that the pendant leans in towards the centre of the wood.

Suddenly he's all fingers and thumbs. He needs something to mark the lines with. Something to hold the other end.

And he needs something to cut the twine with.

He doesn't have any of those things.

He looks again in the rucksack.

He daren't use the nail gun on the wood. The impact could trigger some kind of trap.

But maybe, if he's careful, he could use the nails and tap them in gently.

He frees several from the magazine and grabs the carpet knife to cut the twine and score lines.

He pictures Guilio in the field and gambles that he started bottom right with the scalene pendant long edge down and shortest edge up.

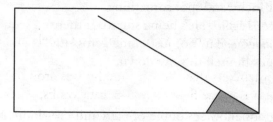

He replicates the actions on both ends of the wood and sees where the lines meet.

Bingo.

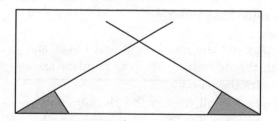

He runs his fingers along the bark where the line is and finds a sliver of silver set in the wood. A silver-lined groove big enough to take the shortest edge of the pendant.

He pauses.

What if there's more than one?

What if he puts the pendant in, turns it and discovers it's part of a sequence that has a time limit?

But what sequence?

What on earth could it be?

Tom stares at the huge chunk of tree and starts to drive himself mad. He has to come up with something.

And quick.

He searches the wood with his fingers. There's a chance he'll get lucky and spot something.

He stops again. He's being stupid. If there's a sequence, he has to *understand* it, not just come across it.

He tells himself to slow down.

Stay calm.

Think logically.

He grabs another couple of nails and cuts more twine.

After several false starts, he turns his thinking upside down.

Literally.

He holds the pendant upside down in the furthest top left-hand corner of the wood. He runs a line from here all the way down until it crosses the plotted lines made from the bottom right-hand point.

Bullseye.

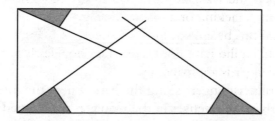

He finds another silver-lined slot. It's below and to the left of the first one.

He tries not to get excited.

432

He moves the pendant to the top right and inwards and runs another line down to the centre.

Perfect.

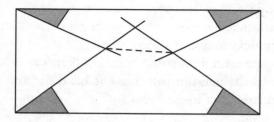

He stands back and admires his ingenuity.

The three silver-lined slots mark the point of their own scalene triangle.

More importantly, there's a sequence, and it involves all three slots, but what is it?

Does it run clockwise, starting from the highest – the first slot he discovered?

Alternatively – because the second one he found is sited to the left of the first – does it run anticlockwise?

He can't decide.

Beyond the wall, he hears a bang. A short noise, like a loud whip cracking or a car backfiring.

Could this be an exit into the street?

Could Guilio have got his bearings hopelessly wrong and a new danger is approaching?

Decision time.

Tom slips the tightest-angled corner of the pendant into the first lock. It takes a heavy push to get it in, and he's frightened it will break.

But it doesn't.

It makes a satisfying click.

Tom turns it.

It clicks again.

But what next?

He looks at the second slot.

To the left – or to the right?

Beyond the wall, he hears another bang.

Then another.

It's gunfire.

Tom goes with his instinct.

He jams the pendant into the left-hand slot and turns it anticlockwise.

135

The huge temple doors are turning black.

But they're not burning.

Valentina can't believe it.

Why doesn't the wood catch fire?

She guesses it's to do with the age and strength of the oak. The fact that the flames from the torch are just not powerful enough to set it ablaze.

Maybe she's being impatient.

She places the torch on the floor, where the two doors meet.

It has no effect.

Snapping point.

She pulls out the Glock and heads towards the pulpit.

If she can't burn their way out, perhaps she can blast them out.

The old woman is still there.

Hands on the glass, scowling down at Valentina.

Well, screw her.

Valentina swings the pistol up and lets off a shot.

The glass doesn't even splinter.

It's like throwing pebbles at the windscreen of a truck.

She lets off another two shots, grouping them near the first.

The crone smiles.

It would take a SAM missile to blow the glass, and both women know it.

But Valentina's not giving up.

She gathers more torches from the walls and stacks them by the door.

At least the flies don't like the smoke, or the flames.

She hugs the child close to her and reassures her again. 'We'll get out, Sweetheart, don't worry. I promised you. Any minute now, we'll be out of here.' She kisses her cheek and hugs her again.

At the far end of the temple, a hidden door slides open.

Five of Mater's most trusted guards enter.

Sweetheart sees them and silently screams.

Only when she points at the armed men wearing scarlet hoods and robes does Valentina realise the full extent of the trouble they're in.

136

The second lock pops as sweetly as the third.

Tom's heart is all but in his mouth as he completes the

sequence by plunging the pendant into the third and final slot.

He twists it and hears a satisfying click.

He gives the front of the big tree a shove.

It doesn't move.

He can't believe it!

He's sure he got everything right.

He pushes again.

This time a large section falls away. There's an almighty crash. A cloud of dust billows up on the other side of the passageway.

Tom squeezes through the gap.

The unmistakable crack of gunfire echoes towards him.

Twenty metres away there are flames.

More shots ring out.

Through the smoke, Tom sees walls and doors.

The gunfire is coming from where the fire is.

It has to be Valentina.

He runs towards the flames and takes a kick at the doors.

They bounce but don't break open.

He takes another run.

A harder jump.

They still don't move.

Tom's eyes fall on the three statues of Cybele forming a centrepiece a little further from him.

He dislodges one and picks it up in a bear hug.

It's as heavy as a truck, and the weight is killing his damaged shoulder.

He grits his teeth and ignores the pain. He hoists the heavy statue so he can hold it like a Scotsman tossing a caber.

He charges the flaming doors.

Cybele's stone head breaks off on impact.

Tom shifts all his weight behind the base.

The doors burst open.

137

Valentina pushes Sweetheart behind her and drops the first of the Galli with a body shot.

Two other guards are coming up fast behind him and another two are spreading wide to outflank her.

The front two open fire.

A marble pillar soaks up their shots.

Valentina fires around it. Two rounds to the right, three to the left.

One of the bullets wings a guard in his leg. He falls clutching his upper thigh and screams like a trapped pig.

Valentina sees Sweetheart standing open-mouthed behind her.

She pulls her tight behind the pillar, while blindly pumping off an arc of covering shots.

More gunfire rips into the marble by her face.

She sinks to the floor – sniper level – and scans the smoke and swirling flies for the remaining three gunmen.

The doors crash open behind her.

She wheels around and is about to let off a volley of shots when Tom sprawls on to the temple floor.

She spins back round, knowing that his intrusion will also have distracted her attackers.

Two of them are rushing her.

Blunderers.

Her trained soldier's hand pumps out four shots, two apiece.

They drop like flies.

Something for the flesh-eaters to snack on later.

Three down – two still to go.

But she can't see them.

Tom grabs Sweetheart and carries her out of the room, her feet wriggling in the air.

Outside the burning door he pulls up quickly.

He's face to face with Mater.

A gleaming ancient sword is raised in her right hand.

It slashes downwards.

Tom swings Sweetheart out of the way.

The sword nicks the top of his right hip.

He turns to face the blade.

When she makes the next swipe, he'll move back a pace and disarm her.

He never gets his chance.

A burst of automatic gunfire rakes Mater's legs.

Tom turns.

Three black-uniformed soldiers are rushing towards him, sub-machine guns still spilling smoke. He guesses they've overwhelmed the Galli guards at farm level and worked their way down.

He lifts Sweetheart into his arms and covers her eyes. Just the sight of the troops in combat gear is enough to terrify her.

Lorenzo Silvestri recognises Tom from the intel he's been given. 'Where's Valentina?'

'In there.' Tom holds Sweetheart tight to his chest and points to the temple.

Lorenzo and one of his team don't break stride as they rush the room.

The third soldier peels away to attend to Mater. He glances at her, then shouts into his radio for paramedics.

The bullets have shattered her kneecaps.

Within seconds, more troops appear.

From inside the temple comes the ripping sound of rapid gunfire.

Tom kneels, and tries to reassure Sweetheart that she's

going to be safe. 'Don't be frightened. These soldiers are good men. Whatever horrible things have happened to you, it's all over now. All over.'

And it is.

Lorenzo Silvestri walks back through the charred and splintered double doors, smoke swirling behind him, his sub-machine gun slung low.

He smiles at Tom and steps aside.

Valentina is a pace behind.

Her face is covered in blood. Her hair is messier than it's ever been. But to Tom she looks wonderful.

By the time she sees him, he is already next to her and holding her.

They kiss and cling to each other as though the world has just begun. And in a way, it has.

They hold on tight and become aware of a strange feeling, one not at all linked to their emotions.

Tiny hands are wrapped around both their legs.

Hands that are holding them every bit as tightly as they're holding each other.

138

Paramedics patch up the wounded.

Valentina's face looks worse than it feels. Her lips are split and bloated. There's a cut on her cheek that thankfully doesn't need stitches and some jaw ache that she knows will disappear once she's had a bath and opened her second bottle of red wine.

Tom's in slightly worse condition.

Now that the action's died down, his shoulder is a mass of pain, and he's enormously grateful for the big syringe of morphine a paramedic is squeezing into him.

Mater is being stretchered away with a tourniquet around one of her legs, while another paramedic works frantically on her shattered kneecaps.

Valentina diverts Sweetheart's attention while soldiers pass by carrying a body bag out of the temple.

There are more to come.

Valentina killed four of them. Lorenzo's men finished off the fifth.

She sits on the floor with her back to the temple wall, puts her arms around Sweetheart and pulls her up on her knee. 'It's all over, baby. This is the last time you'll ever see this stinking place.' She strokes her hair and the child rests her head on Valentina's blood-soaked chest.

Tom buttons up his shirt as he walks over to Lorenzo. 'There's a man trapped further down the tunnel.' He points to the hole in the wall that he came through. 'I think he's dead. There's some kind of pit back there with a lion in it.'

Lorenzo looks sceptical. '*Un leone?*'

'It's a long story.' Tom tucks his shirt into his trousers, which one-handed is harder than he's ever imagined. 'There were two of them. We only managed to kill one.'

Lorenzo nods to the darkness ahead. 'Show us.'

Tom leads the way. 'This is the route we came in by. I was told there might be some kind of booby traps, and the floor seems to be one of them.'

They climb through the hole in the gallery wall. 'Best stay close to the middle. The section of floor that I was on just flipped. It's on some sort of rocker mechanism.'

Lorenzo and his team reach the edge of the pit and peer in.

440

A guttural growl rumbles up from the fetid hole.

Seemingly without any instructions, the team springs into action.

One soldier produces a coil of zip-wire and attaches it to his colleague's belt. The second man slides a light on to his machine gun and drops into the pit.

Within seconds there's a burst of gunfire.

Tom guesses the animal's dead.

The zip-line hangs slack around the belt of the soldier standing beside Tom. From below there are the sounds of rocks being moved.

A full minute elapses before the shout comes up: '*È morto. L'uomo è morto.*'

Tom knows what it means.

He was right.

Guilio is dead.

He crosses himself and remembers the young man's bravery, an act of courage that saved his own life.

He turns to Lorenzo. 'I'd like to go down. Is that okay?'

The major looks at him questioningly. 'With that shoulder?'

'Your medics have given me so much stuff, I won't feel pain until the start of the third millennium.'

Lorenzo sizes him up. The Major is tall, but Tom's even taller and broader. He motions to one of his men. 'Give me another zip.'

It hits his hands quicker than Tom's seen pitchers throw a baseball.

Lorenzo clips it to his own belt and turns back to Tom. 'Take this line holder and wrap it around your waist, then we'll lower you down this tilted floor; that way there's no big sudden drop to jar you.' He throws the line over to Tom and shouts into the hole: 'The civilian's coming down; give him some light and help him through the last part of the drop.'

Tom moves into position and Lorenzo instructs another soldier to help him take the weight.

'Okay! Let's ease him down.'

It seems strange to Tom to be sliding down the same section of ground that almost cost him his life.

The soldier's light nearly blinds him as he looks down. He glances away and sees the lion that Guilio killed.

The soldier's hands guide Tom's feet past piles of rubble and on to the bottom of the pit. 'Okay!' the officer shouts up to Lorenzo.

Tom sees what's left of Guilio's corpse.

His head has been chewed off. His arms and legs bitten away.

Tom feels like being sick.

He forces himself to kneel beside the mutilated torso. A man who in his mind is a martyr in the truest sense of the word.

He places his hand over Guilio's heart and recites an adaptation of the twenty-third psalm: 'The Lord is your Shepherd and now you shall not want. He led you down the paths of righteousness for His name's sake, and though you walked through the valley of the shadow of death you feared no evil. Now our sweet Jesus will prepare a table for you in the presence of your enemies. He will anoint your head with oil and ensure your cup is eternally full. He will perpetually be at your side and will restore your soul. He will grant you the right to dwell in his house for ever. Amen.'

The soldier with Tom makes the sign of the cross and then helps the American to his feet.

'*Grazie.*' As Tom thanks him, he spots a shrine to Cybele set in the wall.

The sculpture of her is the same as the one he saw in the catalogue at Galleria Borghese. She is holding an open book.

The Tenth Book?

'Can you shine your light over there?'

The soldier points his MP5 at the marble.

Tom has a hunch.

More than a hunch.

He takes Guilio's scalene pendant from his pocket and tilts his head so that he considers the rectangle of the book as though it was horizontal rather vertical.

He remembers how he moved the slab of tree that blocked the end of the gallery.

There was a hidden triangle of key slots sunk in the middle of the bark.

He runs his fingers over the two marble pages.

Each line of the book is carved deeply, and there is lavish Latin writing engraved all over them.

He looks again.

It isn't Latin, or even Greek.

He doesn't recognise it.

It could be Etruscan. Maybe Phrygian.

The soldier steps closer and focuses the light for Tom. 'What are you doing?'

'Just trying something.' He shows him the black stone pendant. 'This is a key. If I can find the right locks, we may discover something behind here.'

'As long as it's not lions, I don't mind.'

He smiles and points his light down and off to the left. It illuminates an open steel gate about a metre high and half a metre wide. 'They came through there. The place is full of animal shit and bowls of dried food. There aren't any more, I already checked.'

Tom is relieved. 'Can I have the light back, please?'

The soldier obliges.

The book is small enough for Tom to scan it quickly. He notices for the first time that the left-hand page is scored with diagonal lines that cross in the centre. He explores it for hidden slots.

There aren't any.

Then it occurs to him that the crossed lines create a giant X.

X for ten.

He's sure he's found a connection to the Tenth Book.

But what is it?

He shifts his focus to the right-hand page. There are no obvious clues. It looks almost identical to the left-hand one except that there are no diagonal lines. Tom knows the clue is staring him in the face, but he can't see it.

He suddenly remembers the optical puzzles where you stare at a pattern and when your focus slips, another, far more intricate one becomes visible.

He concentrates hard.

Too hard.

He blinks. Relaxes. Tries again.

He's conscious of the soldier next to him, and it's distracting.

He lets his focus go and clears his mind almost as though he were preparing for prayer.

From the marble page appears an image he's more than familiar with.

A pentagram.

An inverted one.

He daren't blink. Mustn't move an inch. Can't let it vanish.

He stretches out his hand and tries the pendant in the first point.

It fits.

He presses it in and feels a latch click.

Slowly and carefully, he works his way anticlockwise

along all the other points of the pentagram. Each contains a hidden lock.

The fifth and final lock gives off a satisfying click.

But nothing happens.

Nothing opens.

He must have to pull, push, slide or lift something.

But what?

The soldier looks at him quizzically.

The book doesn't move. The statue doesn't move. Nor does the wall in front of them.

They push and pull some more.

Nothing moves.

The soldier lifts the light to Tom's face. 'What did you expect to happen?'

'Good question. I'm not sure. Something to open, I guess.'

The soldier gives him a sympathetic look. 'Okay, come on, we should get out of here.'

They turn around and head towards the exit.

On the far wall, over to the left, the soldier's light picks out something.

A passageway.

Tom grabs his arm and points the flashlight at the opening. 'Was that there before?'

The soldier shakes his head. 'No. I checked the whole place and I didn't see it.'

Tom heads towards it.

'Wait!' The soldier gives him a stern look and nods at the gun in his hands.

Tom sees his point.

He follows a couple of metres behind the officer.

Partway through the opening, he knows what kind of place they've entered.

It's a graveyard.

A *columbarium.*

Identical to the one Anna described in her crazed writings as Cassandra.

The place is vast.

High walls are filled with what look like dovecotes, personal spaces for ancient cremation urns.

Tom examines the edges of the shelves. They're marked with Roman numerals. The one he's looking at says DXX and the one next to it DXIX. He knows he's standing at 520 and 519. He follows the numbers down and back towards the entrance. On the bottom shelf, he finds what he's looking for.

X.

The amphora is painted with the face of Cybele.

A face that to Tom still looks disturbingly similar to Anna.

He wonders what he's found.

Just a pot of old ashes?

Or the remains of the oldest and most famous prophet goddess the world has ever known?

He's no archaeologist, but he already senses something strange about this find.

The Cybele pot and those immediately around it aren't as dusty as the others. Come to think of it, the entire shelf is relatively dust-free.

Tom carefully moves all the pots off the bottom shelf.

He pulls it.

It takes a good tug, but it comes free.

He stares down into a narrow trench.

A trench filled with books.

Books full of secrets.

Secrets people hoped to take to the grave with them.

139

The outside of the unassuming farm has been turned into a military compound.

In the centre is a four-wheel-drive Mercedes Unimog, the size of a small barn. It's stacked with equipment and stands ready to tow vehicles away, bulldoze down walls and perform all manner of muscular tasks.

Several Iveco armoured vans have already been loaded with prisoners. A soldier slaps the side of one and it heads off down the dirt road, flanked by BMW R85 motorcyclists, blue lights flashing.

Up above, an Augusta-Bell helicopter keeps constant watch as the prisoners are taken down the Appian Way and back towards Rome.

Tom sits on a stone trough and draws breath.

He watches Valentina's heart breaking as she says goodbye to Sweetheart. The child is being taken away by social workers, and the parting seems to be hurting her every bit as much as it's hurting the kid.

She joins him at the trough, puts her left hand on his thigh and her head on his shoulder.

He takes her hand. 'Is she all right?'

'I don't think so. I don't think she's even in the same postal code as all right.'

He squeezes her fingers. 'There's no more you can do. You have to leave her to the experts now.'

She looks up at him. There are no tears in her eyes; just disbelief and disgust. 'Silvestri says they freed almost a dozen kids. Some are even younger than that little girl.'

'How many of the cult have they arrested?'

'A dozen men. All guards, by the look of it.' She glances towards the front of the farm. Mater is being lifted on a gurney into an ambulance. 'Along with the old witch, they've taken four women of about her age and another two or three who seem to be in their forties.'

Tom wipes rain from his forehead. 'The tip of the iceberg.'

Valentina knows what he means. 'Under interview, some of the old birds will start singing. They won't want to spend the rest of their lives in prison and should give up a good number of the other members.'

Tom turns further towards her. 'Down in the place where the lion killed Anna's friend, we discovered a secret chamber, a *columbarium.*'

'One of those old Roman resting places for the poor?'

He nods. 'We found a stack of books in there, all marked with the number X. They're being lifted out by your forensics people.'

She's intrigued. 'Do you know what they are?'

He thinks he does. 'The one on top was the most recent one. It was like a cross between an address book and a diary. On the left were telephone numbers and email addresses. No names. On the right were descriptions of the rituals they'd performed with children and names and descriptions of the children. I saw several pages talking about new arrivals and the initiation ceremonies they had to endure.'

Valentina drops her head and feels sick.

Tom puts his hand on her shoulder and rubs it. 'The books go back years, maybe even centuries. The Tenth Book has nothing to do with wisdom or prophecies; it's a never-ending paedophile directory and diary, that's all.'

Valentina looks up and her face is hardened by anger. 'You're wrong, Tom. Wrong because it contains the greatest knowledge of all: information on how to find these sick animals, and probably enough evidence to get convictions and send them to their own damned cells.'

EPILOGUE

Three days later

Valentina and Tom are shown through to Lorenzo Silvestri's office.

Neither of them is sure why they are there.

Lorenzo called and said they were to come. Valentina hardly questioned it. She's learned the painful way that it's best not to disobey the orders of a Carabinieri major.

The time of the meeting is seven p.m., and that gives her a clue. That and the fact that Lorenzo said they should both look smart. She thinks he's a good guy, and is guessing that she and Tom are being invited along to share a glass of wine with the troops, get a slap on the back and hopefully an update on the case.

Lorenzo greets them both with a smile as broad as the Tiber. 'Capitano Morassi.' He spreads his arms wide. 'You look even more magnificent than in *Vanity Fair.*'

She almost blushes. 'You saw those shots?'

'Valentina, *everyone* saw those shots.' He embraces her warmly. 'And Signor Shaman.' He pretends to stand back and admire him. 'Take away that sling and you look the perfect companion for our *capitano.*' He extends his hand and shakes Tom's firmly before pulling him close and kissing both cheeks. 'Sit down, please sit down.' He gestures to two black plastic chairs on the other side of his unassuming glass desk.

Lorenzo sits and folds his arms contentedly. 'So – I have much to tell you. Where should I begin?'

Valentina helps him out. 'How's the little girl we found in the cells?'

He nods. 'She's very well. She's called Cristiana, is eleven years old and has written a letter for you.' He searches the top of his desk. 'I'm sorry; I thought I had it here.' He reads the disappointment in Valentina's eyes. 'I'll find it later, don't worry.'

He picks a manila file off a stack of three trays. 'First, let's tidy up some loose ends.'

Both Tom and Valentina note his change of tone. Perhaps this isn't going to be any kind of celebration after all.

Lorenzo pulls out a black and white photograph and spins it round for them to see. 'Not pleasant, I'm afraid.'

And it isn't.

The picture shows the corpse of a woman in a shallow grave.

Her hand is missing.

Valentina picks it up. Her mind races back to Cosmedin and the time she stood in the bloodstained portico with Federico. This was the start of it all. She looks towards Lorenzo for an explanation.

'We found the corpse inside the underground complex. The pathologist thinks she was buried alive.'

'Dear God.' Valentina returns the photograph to the major. 'Scientists at the RaCIS told us that the blood from the severed hand came from Anna's sister, Cloelia. Is that correct? Is this body that of her sister?'

'It is.' He waits for the news to sink in. 'Forensics also found DNA that links the killing to one of the men we arrested. Blood from Anna's sister was on this man's robes, and his DNA was found on her, so we have a strong evidential chain.' He puts the photograph back in the file. Sombrely he produces another picture and puts it down for them to see. 'This one you know. Anna Fratelli.'

They both look at it and feel a pang of sadness.

She could have been so much more.

Lorenzo rubs his chin thoughtfully. He dips into the file again, produces two more photographs and puts them either side of Anna's.

The first is a picture of the amphora that Tom discovered in the *columbarium*; the second is a mug shot of a woman in her sixties. The woman Valentina fired shots at in the underground temple.

Lorenzo taps Anna's picture. 'This is her genealogical table.'

'I don't understand,' says Valentina, although a part of her actually does, and she simply doesn't want to accept what she's hearing.

The major touches the mug shot. 'This is the woman they all call Mater. Her real name is Sibilia Cassandra Savina Andreotti.' He looks towards Tom. 'She claims to be a divine descendant of the goddess Cybele. I don't believe in goddesses.' He glances at Valentina. 'At least not that kind. But what I can substantiate is that she is Anna Fratelli's mother, and they both share the DNA of whoever was cremated and put in this pot centuries ago.'

The air seems to have been sucked out of the room.

Tom and Valentina are speechless.

Tom clears his throat and sits forward in his chair.

Lorenzo looks towards him expectantly.

'There's something I should say.'

Valentina looks surprised. She and Tom have barely spoken about the case in the last few days. They've been trying to forget it.

'The man who took me into the tunnels.'

Lorenzo names him. 'Guilio Brygus Angelis.'

'Guilio . . .' Tom says it almost reverently. 'He told me what had happened at Chiesa Santa Maria in Cosmedin. The sect members had recaptured Anna and taken her to the Bocca to frighten her and to find out if she'd told anyone about the temple and the rituals. They cut off her sister's hand and said they would kill her and then do the same to Anna if she didn't tell them the truth.' Tom takes a breath to make sure he recounts things accurately. 'Guilio appeared as Anna was screaming, and fought with the guards. During the fight, Anna picked up one of the ceremonial swords and killed the man who'd injured her sister.'

Valentina interrupts. 'That's why the blood on her robe was AB and didn't match that of the handless victim, which we now know was Rhesus negative and belonged to her sister.'

Tom is unsure of the biological evidence. 'I guess so; I'll take your word for it. There's more though that I need to tell you.'

Lorenzo motions for him to continue.

'In the panic, Anna ran off. The Galli took Mater and the injured sister away. Guilio was left with the dead guard. He put the body into a workman's sheet that had been draped over the portico so that people couldn't see inside. He carried the corpse to the boot of his car, then drove down to the Tiber and buried it beneath some rocks.'

'What about the mutilation?' asks Valentina. 'Did Anna do that?'

'No. Guilio did. At first he tried to make the death look like an accident. He laid the body down by the river, chopped out much of the stomach and threw it in the water. He then piled rocks on the corpse, probably causing the skull injuries, and fled.'

'We'll need you to make a statement.' Lorenzo gathers the photographs and returns them to their file.

Valentina wishes she was somewhere else. Anywhere other than back in the midst of already painful memories. She sits forward and tries to stay polite. 'Are we free to go now?'

'Not quite. There is still the note the child wrote for you. *Uno momento.*'

He picks up the phone and dials his secretary.

She doesn't seem to be there.

He hangs up and looks slightly annoyed. 'Sorry. I am having no luck today.'

Valentina gives him a resigned nod.

'Still. I must not let you leave without the good news.'

She looks bored. 'Which is?'

'The disciplinary charges against you and Federico have been dropped. I have spoken with our chief of staff and he has spoken to the Commandante Generale. You and Assante will both be reinstated tomorrow.'

Valentina is relieved and shows it. '*Grazie.* What about Louisa Verdetti's complaints against us?'

'Withdrawn.'

She raises an eyebrow. 'And how is she?'

'Getting better. The whole affair has shaken her up, as you would expect. Before you disappear, tell me, how do you feel about going back to work with Major Caesario?'

Until now, Valentina hasn't thought about it. She takes some seconds to answer and tries not to sound disrespectful. 'I'm proud of the job I do and proud of how I do it. I will be pleased to be back at work.'

'After a little holiday?' suggests Tom.

She smiles at him. 'After a big holiday, I promise.'

Lorenzo smiles at them both. They make a good couple. 'Only, if you don't want to work with Caesario, I'd be honoured to have you on my team in the GIS.'

455

She looks surprised.

'Don't answer now. Vito Carvalho tells me I'd be lucky if you worked with us, and I believe him.' Lorenzo checks his watch and gets up from his chair. 'I'm afraid I must ask you to go now. I have some pressing matters.'

Tom and Valentina scrape their chairs back and head towards the door.

'*Grazie,*' says Valentina. 'I'm grateful for your help with my personal problem.'

'You're very welcome.' He opens the door. 'Let me walk you out.'

Lorenzo walks alongside Valentina and makes small talk until they reach the end of the corridor.

'This could be your office,' he teases, pointing at a closed door with an empty nameplate.

She treats him to a warm smile.

He can see she's interested in the job. 'I'm serious. Go on, take a look inside.'

She feels foolish. 'Let me think about it, *molto grazie.*'

Lorenzo won't take no for an answer. He turns the brass knob and pushes the door open.

The room is full.

'*Sorpreso!*' choruses a crowd of familiar faces.

Party poppers and streamers explode and fill the air.

Valentina almost cries as she spots her parents – and Vito Carvalho – clapping her. Alongside them is Louisa Verdetti.

Finally she recognises half of the team from her own office at Carabinieri headquarters.

The day couldn't get better.

Except it could.

From out of the forest of legs, a small girl appears.

Sweetheart is wearing a new bright blue dress and a smile that melts every heart in the room.

Valentina picks her up and kisses her.

Tom Shaman stands back a pace.

He's never loved anyone as much as he loves Valentina.

He just hopes she understands why, when their holiday's over, he is going to have to move on.

ACKNOWLEDGMENTS

Big thanks to Luigi Bonomi for all his advice, tireless support and encouragement – there's good reason why he's regarded as the best in the business.

I'm hugely indebted to Guy Rutty, Professor of Forensic Pathology, East Midlands Forensic Pathology Unit, University of Leicester and Dr Tom Rasmussen, Senior Lecturer and Head of Art History at the University of Manchester. Both gentlemen strived to keep me on the roads of realism and accuracy, any short cuts and inaccuracy are down to me and the pursuit of a good story rather than them.

I'm grateful to all the wonderful team at Little, Brown but especially to Daniel Mallory and Thalia Proctor – I'd have been lost without their professionalism, smart observations and generous contributions. Thanks also to Jane Selley for the copy editing.

Last but not least, immense thanks to my wife Donna who gives so unreservedly and bountifully of her time, patience, love and inspiration. I'd still be on page one without her.